PROTOCOL 15

Nathan Goodman

This book is a work of fiction. Names, places, incidents, characters, and all contents are products of the author's imagination or are used in a fictitious manner. Any relation or resemblance to any actual persons, living or dead, events, businesses, agencies, government entities, or locales is purely coincidental.

THOUGHT REACH PRESS, a publishing division of Thought Reach, LLC. United States of America.

Copyright © 2016 Nathan A. Goodman
Cover art copyright © 2016 Nathan A. Goodman

ISBN: 978-1514266731

First Thought Reach Press printing April, 2016

For information regarding special discounts for bulk purchases, or permission to reproduce any content other than mentioned above, contact the publisher at support@thoughtreach.com.

Printed in the USA except where otherwise noted.

To my kids. May you grow up in a world safer than the one in my imagination. And to the men and women of our intelligence services, federal agencies, the US Navy's submarine service, and other branches of the military. Your duty and sacrifice do not go unnoticed.

Get a free copy of Book 1 of this series, *The Fourteenth Protocol* by visiting

NathanAGoodman.com/fourteen/

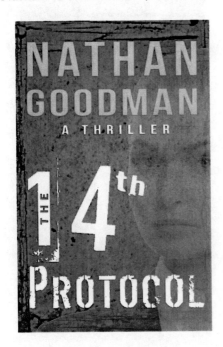

I'd like to thank the following people, without which this book would not have been possible. My heartfelt gratitude to each of you for your tireless contributions. J. Russell Martin, a 20-year veteran of the submarine services of the US Navy. Your attention to detail in evaluating the submarine scenes was invaluable. Eliza Racine, thank you for your work with the nuances of language translations. To my editor, Keith Morrill, thank you for taking such a detailed look at the manuscript and polishing it into something of much greater value. And to the many of you who acted as beta readers. The list is too long, but you know who you are. Thank you for pointing out what I was too close to see.

"Death smiles at us all, all a man can do is smile back."
- Marcus Aurelius, Meditations

Section One

An Arab Summer

1

I AM BECOME DEATH

Somewhere in Pakistan. June 3.

The coal-black of Waseem Jarrah's hair was distinguishable only by a chiseled patch of white that tore through one side. Jarrah, the most wanted terrorist in the world, put his hands on the trembling nineteen-year-old's shoulders.

"Khalid Kunde, your time is near," he said. "You are a soldier of Allah, and Allah's rewards will be grand. Remember, what you go to do now is but the first step."

A tear welled in the young man's eye, yet did not fall.

"I will not fail you," the apprentice replied.

"You are the younger brother of Shakey Kunde. His name is legend. His efforts to detonate a nuclear device on American soil were valiant, his sacrifice noble. But he failed in his ultimate mission. Nevertheless, he sits at the right hand of Allah, as will you. Do you know the words?"

The young man knew Jarrah wanted him to quote the words of Robert Oppenheimer, the original inventor of the atomic bomb.

Khaild nodded his head in affirmation, stared at the floor, then choked out, "The words are, *I am become death*."

Jarrah's eyes widened as he basked in the glow of his new apprentice. He replied, "*The destroyer of worlds*."

2

A SLEEPING ISLAND

NATO Listening Post, Kosrae Island, Micronesia. The Solomon Sea, 1,379 nautical miles north-northeast of Papua New Guinea. June 19, 11:33 p.m. local time (8:33 a.m. EST).

"You hear the chatter last night about the spy plane, that Air Force RC-135?"

"The Cobra Ball? Yeah. I think they were just flying around monitoring a Russki thing though."

"Which Russian thing?"

"Same old thing. Naval maneuvers. A pretty boring night, as usual."

"The Cobra Ball flying that same figure-eight pattern they normally do?"

"From what we could tell by watching on radar, yeah. But, they were way the hell out there, on the edge of our radar cup. We were only able to . . ." His attention diverted to a computer monitor in front of him. "Wait, did you see that? What the hell?"

A radar alarm blared on speakers mounted overhead and the two men scrambled to place headphones over their ears.

"Holy shit, that's a missile launch!" one said.

The other keyed his headset then spoke into the mic. "NATO COMSAT, NATO COMSAT, this is Listening Post Kosrae one niner two. We've just detected a missile launch. Currently tracking an inbound hostile from North Korean airspace. Can you confirm?"

A crackle from his headset replied. "LP Kosrae one niner two, this is COMSAT. Roger that, Kosrae. We see the launch, but we've got no track. You are our eyes."

"Understood, COMSAT. We see the inbound from central North Korean airspace, pushing through six thousand feet. Banking, banking now, turning due east. The heat signature of the missile registers as a Taepodong or Taepodong-2 class ICBM. This is the real thing. Repeat, this is not a drill. Given attitude, altitude, and direction, this could be a North Korean attack on Japan, sir. The hostile is headed right for them."

"Roger that, Kosrae. All stations have just been issued the alert command."

"The bird is increasing in altitude. The computer is recalculating the flight path. Hold on . . . I don't think its target is Japan, sir. At that altitude, the hostile will fly right over."

"What else is directly along that trajectory?" the other man said. "I don't care how far away it is. We've got to know what they're shooting at."

The operator traced his finger across the map on the computer monitor. "Let's see, there's the Midway Islands, but there's nothing there. After that . . . oh shit." The two operators looked at each other. "Hawaii."

The computer recalculated and spit out new coordinates for the projected trajectory of the hostile missile, and its most likely destination:

Latitude: 22-01'10" N — Longitude: 160-06'02" W
Lehua, Kauai, HI

"Oh my God, you're right. The computer confirms. It's Hawaii. Find out what's on the island of Lehua. Not that it'll matter if that ICBM showers the entire island chain with multiple independent warheads. The entire Hawaiian population will be incinerated." He keyed his headset again. "COMSAT, this is LP Kosrae. We've got confirmation." He read off the coordinates. "It's Hawaii, sir. Lehua, Kauai, Hawaii."

There was no reply from the other side. Only static.

"Sir?"

"Ah, roger that, Kosrae. Estimated time till impact?"

"Based on the calculated distance of 4,485 miles from the original source to target, and the fact that the hostile is now suborbital, traveling at an estimated 13,200 miles per hour, the computer estimates time till impact at three and one half minutes. That would make it exactly 3:32 a.m. Hawaii local time."

3

TO NEW BEGINNINGS

Headquarters of the National Security Agency, aka, "The Box."
Ft. Meade, Maryland. June 19.

In the NSA command center, the months had passed. First one, then another, and Cade wondered where they went. The passage of time knows no enemies. It has no friends. It holds no grudges. It's only solace is that it never changes, except when there is a hole in your life that you cannot fill.

Cade stared across the room at Knuckles. Ever since he had met the kid, he wondered how old he was. For all Knuckle's intelligence experience as an analyst at the National Security Agency, the chin on the kid's face could barely produce peach fuzz. He looked sixteen, maybe younger. Regardless, Cade knew the kid had brainpower that rivaled even "Uncle" Bill Tarleton, the NSA section chief, and the most brilliant code breaker in NSA's history.

Knuckles looked at Cade, who was still staring at him. "You look like you're trying to conjure the next winning numbers in the Pennsylvania state lottery," Knuckles laughed. "I know you're dying to find out how old I am. I'm twelve years old."

"No you're not," Cade said. "You're older than that. Come on, how old are you?"

"Not in this lifetime, pal."

"Oh come on. We work at the NSA. We're supposed to be able

to find out anything about anyone. You know I can find out."

"Personnel records are sealed, bright guy," Knuckles said. "Although . . ."

"Although what?"

"We could work a trade."

"What kind of a trade?"

"You teach me how to talk to girls, I'll tell you my real age."

Cade stared back, grinned, and then started to laugh until people turned to see what was going on.

"You want *me* to teach you how to talk to girls? I couldn't talk my way out of a paper bag where girls are concerned. Now, my friend, Kyle, he's who you want. He could convince a girl . . ."

"Well," Knuckles said, "from what Uncle Bill tells me, you and that hot FBI agent seemed pretty tight."

The prior year, during what was known as *the Thoughtstorm case*, Cade had become the FBI's only insider in the sweeping terrorism investigation. At the time, he worked as a hardware systems administrator for Thoughtstorm, Inc. When it turned out Thoughtstorm was involved with terrorists, he found himself in the middle of the biggest terrorism investigation since 9/11. It had been the beautiful female federal agent that had convinced him to be a material witness in the first place, and now he was in love with her.

Cade looked down. "Yeah, I know. She's the most beautiful girl I've ever been around. We worked so closely during the Thoughtstorm case. Things were so intense. I don't know, I guess we just spent so much time together that we kind of became a couple there for a while."

As the case ended, Uncle Bill had offered Cade an analyst role. Working at NSA had never occurred to Cade. But, with his old job as a systems administrator at Thoughtstorm gone, the idea of being more involved in espionage work appealed to him.

"But what about now? You're not together?"

"Doesn't seem that way, no. I wonder about it all the time. Whether coming to work here was worth it. Sometimes I feel like I stepped into a really cool new career for myself, but I lost Jana in the process. She spent so much time at Bethesda Medical Center recovering from the shooting. I spent a long time watching over her, first in the intensive care unit, then all that time in physical therapy. To tell you the truth, she shouldn't have survived it. But, the good thing is, she's been back at Quantico for a few weeks, trying to get in shape to requalify for active duty."

The hardest part in Cade's decision to work at the NSA had been separating from Jana. He may have been in love with her, but he had never known if she felt the same way. And, he had always known she was way out of his league to begin with. Both Jana and Agent Kyle MacKerron were now back at the FBI Academy at Quantico, regaining their strength, healing from physical injuries, and requalifying as federal agents. For Cade, who now lived in Maryland near the headquarters of the NSA, having the two of them nearby at Quantico was both heavenly and torturous at the same time. They were close, but he rarely saw them.

"I go over there whenever she lets me," Cade said. "We're both just so busy, you know? I get the feeling she's pulling away from me, almost as if she knows she's only going to be at the academy for a short time, then she'll get assigned to a duty station far away from here."

"Where's she going to be stationed?"

"From what FBI Director Latent tells me, due to her heroism during the Thoughtstorm case, she can choose to be stationed wherever the hell she wants."

4

WEAPONS GRADE POSTURING

Outside the United Nations Headquarters building, New York. June 19.

"Okay, Mike," the cameraman said, "they're cutting to us live in three, two . . ."

"This is Mike Slayden, WBS News, reporting live from UN headquarters in New York. More info coming in on yesterday's statements made by supreme leader of the Democratic People's Republic of North Korea, Jeong Suk-to. As you know, the country of North Korea has become a thorn in the side of the United States, as well as other nations. Supreme leader Jeong Suk-to's consistent rhetoric and threats have alarmed world leaders. This morning, United Nations Secretary-General Ashanti Birungi made a statement in front of the UN General Assembly. Mr. Birungi stated, and I quote, 'The North Korean government has made past claims as having achieved the manufacture of fissile nuclear material. Although these claims are as yet unsubstantiated, the United Nations has issued an edict to Supreme Leader Jeong Suk-to urging him to immediately withdraw his quest to obtain a nuclear weapon. North Korea now also claims to be nearing launch capability. If weapons-grade fissile material is combined with a long-range missile, the threat to human life is great. The time is near and the United Nations must act.'

"Tension between North Korea and Western allies has grown considerably in past months as the North Korean leader continues in a tirade of posturing.

"To further complicate an already escalating situation, in an unrelated issue, the Russian delegation to the UN is pressing the North Korean government as to the whereabouts of one of their delegates, who went missing one month ago on a diplomatic mission to the North Korean capital of Pyongyang. North Korean leaders in Pyongyang are refusing comment, fueling further speculation and distrust between Russia and North Korea. We'll keep you abreast of developments as they unfold. For now, I'm Mike Slayden. Watch your twenty-four-hour news leader, WBS, for news, weather, and traffic on the fives."

5

THE OVAL OFFICE

The White House, Washington, DC. June 19, 9:35 a.m. EST.

"Mr. President."

"Goddammit, General, what is it? I'm in the middle of a call with François Hollande!"

"Sir, we're tracking an *inbound*. Taepodong-class ICBM from North Korean airspace. Launched just minutes ago."

The president stared at the man, then blurted into the phone, "Président Hollande, mes excuses. Une situation plus urgente. Urgent matters of state."

He hung up the phone then looked at the General, whose face looked like the blood had drained from it.

"Where is it headed?" the president said. "Can we intercept?"

"Hawaii, and no."

"Hawaii? But there's over a million people in Hawaii! We can't . . . we can't shoot down the missile?"

"Population 1.4 million. No sir, we tried. Patriot anti-missile defense systems out at Pearl missed, twice. She slipped through, sir. I'm sorry."

The president buried his face in his hands.

"Time till impact?"

"Any moment."

"You can't mean that!"

"A SATCOM device is being moved in here now, sir. We've got two communication uplinks. One to Navy Hawaii Command and the other to a NATO listening post at Kosrae, Micronesia.

The listening post is tracking the missile."

Two young Air Force officers burst into the Oval Office, flanked by the national security advisor and two members of the Joint Chiefs of Staff.

The captain spoke into the SATCOM's mic. "Go ahead, Kosrae. The president is listening. Repeat what you just said."

"Roger that, captain. This is NATO listening post Kosrae, Micronesia. The hostile missile is in full descent. Time till impact on the island of Lehua, Kauai, Hawaii, sixty-five seconds."

"What's the population of that particular island?" the president said.

"Zero, sir," the major replied. "Lehua is an uninhabited outlying island of the Hawaiian chain, about twenty miles off Kauai. But I don't think that matters. If the North Korean government has finally combined long-range-missile launch capabilities with a nuclear tip, we could be looking at a total loss of the Hawaiian Islands."

"Forty seconds."

The volume of the president's voice exploded. "But we've had security briefings for months on the topic of whether or not the North Koreans had the technology to combine a long-range rocket with a nuclear tip. Dammit! CIA was so sure that they hadn't achieved it yet," the president said as he slammed his fist into the desk. "Why did I listen to them? Shit, we knew they had launch capability, but not the nuclear tip. My God, if I'd only known. If I'd only known. I could have done something . . . but I had no idea that that lunatic leader would actually take a first strike at us. A madman. A madman."

"Thirty seconds to impact."

The president paced the room. "How come we're not hearing from Hawaii Command right now?" he screamed. "Where are they?"

"It's three thirty in the morning there, sir," the major said.

"General, bring our military to DEFCON 2," the president said.

"Fifteen seconds to impact."

"Ah, sir?" cracked a young voice across the SATCOM radio device. "Ah, this is Seaman Jimmy Timms, Hawaii Command. Third watch, post number four, sir."

"Seaman Timms, this is Major Walter R. Robbins, United States Air Force. Son, just stay on the line with us."

"Yes, sir," the young seaman mumbled.

"Ten seconds to impact. Nine, eight, seven . . ."

"Ah, sir, what impact?" Seaman Timms said with all the timidity of a mouse.

"Three, two, one," the operator at LP Kosrae said. "Hostile missile is down. Hostile is down."

The president's hands dug into his hairline and he leapt toward the SATCOM device. "Seaman Timms, are you still with us? Son? Are you there? Dear God, where is he?"

"Yes, sir. I'm here, sir. I just, I don't understand what's happening. What was that countdown? I don't know who I'm on the line with, sir."

The men in the Oval Office looked at one another. The general whispered, "I don't know. Maybe it didn't detonate?"

"Don't you worry about that right now," the Major said. "You just talk to us, son. Tell us where you are stationed and what your duties are." He released the mic and said, "General, this seaman would be stationed on Kauai, correct? Kauai is just twenty miles due east of the missile impact zone. If a nuclear blast just occurred, he'd be able to see it. Hell, he should be dead right now."

"That's correct, Major."

Seaman Timms droned on in the background about his duty station, what his duties were, where he was raised, his mother's favorite recipe for chocolate chip cookies, which he was currently enjoying. The major interrupted him. "Seaman Timms, can you pinpoint which direction is west of you right now?"

"West? Well sure, sir. The sun sets just past the flag pole right out the window over there . . ."

"Son, stand up and look to the west. Tell us what you see."

"Yes, sir. Ah, sir, I don't see anything really. Just darkness. It's the middle of the night here. I mean, I can see the flagpole, of course, but after that, the hillside slopes off and drops down to the beach. But off in the distance, if that's what you mean, I can't see anything. No lights or anything like that, sir."

"All right, Timms, just keep looking out in that direction and report anything unusual. Someone will stay on the line with you. Thank you, son."

"Listening post, Kosrae," the Major said into the SATCOM. "Can you confirm a detonation?"

"Negative, sir. We see no detonation signature."

The president was the first to speak. "What the hell happened? The missile didn't detonate? Was it a dud?"

The general answered. "That's what we'll want to discuss with the Joint Chiefs. But if you ask me, it was no dud. My bet is that the psychotic leader of North Korea is playing with us. He's taunting us. He wants us to know he can get us whenever he wants. He's crazy enough to do it, and he's this close to putting a nuclear tip on one."

"A madman. An absolute madman," the president said as he straightened his hair. He cast a gaze on National Security Advisor James Foreman.

Foreman registered the president's piercing gaze and a cold shiver rode his spine.

"General," continued the president, "cancel that order to take us to DEFCON 2. Let's find out if the public knows about this missile launch. If not, keep it quiet, very quiet. I don't want a panic on our hands."

The president stared out the window in the Oval Office. "Something is going to have to be done about North Korea."

6

QUANTICO

FBI Academy, Marine Corps Base Quantico, Quantico, Virginia. About twenty-seven miles south of Washington, DC. June 19.

Jana pushed upwards, but the hill was daunting. Not only was she out of shape after spending four months at the hospital and physical rehabilitation center, but hot pain radiated from her spine. On that day at the bluegrass festival in Kentucky, one of the bullets fired by Shakey Kunde had pierced her Kevlar vest, clipped the seventh thoracic vertebrae, and come within a fraction of a millimeter of piercing her spinal cord. Had that happened, she'd have been strapped into a wheel chair for the rest of her life.

The physical pain wasn't so bad when she was sitting or holding still. And sometimes walking wasn't so bad. But running the obstacle course at the FBI training ground on the Marine base at Quantico resulted in a thrash of pain that pounded with each step. She began to hate her running shoes, although she knew they had nothing to do with it. And at one hundred and seventy-five dollars a pair, they'd better not.

Surrounded by a new class of FBI trainees traversing the running trail at Quantico, she struggled to keep pace. All but a few were faster than she was, and weakness lay on her mind like a cold weight. Pain or no pain, Jana wasn't giving up, and she damn well wasn't going to tell anyone about it. The FBI and its male-dominated leadership would just have to accept the fact that she was as tough as they were. She had proven that once already by jumping into the line of fire and facing down a terrorist.

Physical pain was one thing, but it was the mental demons that Jana found most disturbing. The bullets not only tore holes in her body, they tore a vicious gash up the middle of her psyche as well. And the damage to her psyche carried a much deeper component to it than she let on.

She first noticed it on the firing range after detecting a slight tremble in her right hand. The tremble came and went, but became most pronounced when she was on the firing line with her finger on the trigger of her SIG Sauer. Then, things got worse. Just the sound of gunfire began to unnerve her. Waiting her turn on the firing line began to rattle her to the core.

Worst were the nights when she'd wake from one of two recurring nightmares. In the first, Jana found herself dangling from the stairwell on the twelfth floor of the Thoughtstorm building. Gunfire permeated the space, and the air was filled with white smoke that felt like acid in her lungs. Her friend, Agent Kyle MacKerron, leaned over the stairs and put a vice grip on her arm. He was yelling to her, *you go, we go!* But then an eruption of gunfire tore through Kyle, killing him, and Jana fell down, down, down, into a screaming oblivion.

In the second, she'd relive the horrifying scene at the bluegrass festival. In the dream, she ran full speed toward the white van; its sides brightly decorated with a bouquet of balloons. She fired three rounds into the lock of the back door, ripped it open, and found herself face to face with Kunde. Then her gun would jam. The horrifying face of the terrorist roared, and he fired repeated rounds into her chest. He laughed a monstrous laugh, then plunged his hand into the steel canister and detonated the nuclear device. The white-hot flash was blinding. And afterward, Jana would face the horrors of the dead. They walked the earth all around her, most of their flesh burned off from the nuclear radiation.

In both dreams, Jana would awaken, screaming. Since she was not technically a member of this new class of FBI recruits, Jana had been assigned a dorm room all to herself. That was a good thing because not a single time had someone heard her scream in the night. If they had, they would have been duty-bound to report the dangerous post-traumatic stress that embroiled much of her sleeping and waking hours. Jana could tell no one. She was alone, alone with her fears.

And the truth was, she missed being around Kyle now that his retraining period at Quantico was over, and he had been reassigned. But mostly, she missed Cade, although she would never admit it.

7

THE FIFTEENTH PROTOCOL

The White House. The next day, June 20, 6:17 a.m. EST.

"It's confirmed then?" the president said.

"Yes, sir," replied his national security advisor, James Foreman.

"No doubt?"

"None."

The president faced away, his silhouette etched into brilliant morning light pouring from the window in the Oval Office. "I want it done. And no one can know. I want the full plan. Everything we discussed." He turned back around, yet, in the stark morning light, none of his facial features were discernible. "I want it done, I said."

"But, sir . . ." trembled Foreman's reply. His voice was hoarse, with a touch of gravel.

"I'm not asking. And I'm not going over it again," the president said. "The decision is made. We'd already planned for this contingency. Now, I'm adjusting our timetable and moving it forward. Look at me, Foreman. There can be no mistakes. It has to look like someone else did it. You make damn sure of that." The president handed the man a single sheet of paper— presidential authorization for the operation to take place. "If I ever see this paper again, it'll be your ass."

As the national security advisor took the paper, he looked like a man receiving a jury's unpleasant verdict. At the top of the document, just below the presidential seal, it read:

Classified: 15.8. E.O.
Access level C12 eyes only.

James Foreman did not have to read the rest. He knew what it said. His stomach churned—an ominous sign—and acid began to rise in his esophagus.

"Fifteen point eight," Foreman whispered. "President Palmer. My God, sir. The fifteenth . . ." his voice skipped and his hands began to feel clammy, "the fifteenth protocol."

The president sat at his desk and immersed himself in his work. Foreman knew it was too late for talk. He stood to leave, but his legs were shaking so badly he flopped back down. He exhaled, then stood once more and traversed the room, allowing the door to close behind him. He stopped just outside at the desk of the president's personal assistant to steady himself, then walked past two Secret Service agents before darting into the nearest restroom. It was a one-man'er that sat just twenty-five feet down the side hallway. No sooner had the door swung closed behind him did he begin to vomit. He didn't stop retching until there was nothing but bile. He was too late—too late to stop the operation from going forward.

8

THE CALM OF THE AEGEAN

French research vessel Marion Dufresne II, the Aegean Sea. Three nautical miles north-northwest of the Isle of Kia. August 29th.

"Come right bearing two two five, Mr. Cameron."

"Oui, capitaine."

"The seas are finally calm enough," the captain said from his leather seat inside the bridge. He propped his feet up. "It's about time. Any more weather delays and we'd all have been about out of a job again."

"Was it that bad, Captain?" Jean-Paul Cameron, the steersman, said.

"Was it that bad? You should hear the ship's owners complaining. Do you know what it costs to run a ship this size?"

"No, sir. Sir? Aren't we just about on top of the coordinates of the resting place of the HMHS *Britannic*? The one that hit a mine back in the First World War and sank?"

"Yes, Jean-Paul, yes. We are very close now."

"Is that where we are going, sir? Are we going to deploy the deep submergence vehicle, the DSV mini-submarine, to the ocean bottom to study the wreckage?"

"No, my young sailor, no. The university has no such appetites. No, this time our ship is filled to the brim with scientists. Oceanographers and geologists. They are interested in studying the minor geologic fault lines that run in between Kea and the Greek mainland. They say our mini-sub will submerge from our decks, then attempt to locate and map them."

"Sir? Each vessel at sea has a name, no? What is the name of our little sub?

"The DSV *Nautile*." The captain smiled. "So many questions."

"We have a full boat then, sir?"

"Yes, Jean-Paul, a full boat indeed. Full of people smarter than you or me."

"Hmm. I wonder what our chef, Rémi, will cook for us tonight. He studied at the Sorbonne, you know—"

A booming rumble that sounded like a muffled explosion rattled through the bridge. An emergency water-sensor alarm pulsed overhead, indicating that the hull had been breached.

"Merde," the captain said as he launched from his chair and grabbed a microphone. "All hands, all hands. This is the capitaine. Situation report. All stations, report in."

Four more explosive rumbles shuddered through the ship's superstructure at perfect one-second intervals. New alarms sounded on the control panel, indicating flooding in all four water-tight compartments.

"Capitaine! What's happening?" Jean-Paul stammered. "Did we hit something?"

"No, those were explosions of some kind. Besides, there's nothing out here to hit. It's a crystal-clear day. We must have had a catastrophic mechanical failure. The control panel indicates flooding below decks. How do we have flooding? Where are my status reports?" He punched three numbers into the phone keypad. "Engine room? Engine room?" he was yelling. "Pierre? Bastien? Is that you? I can barely hear you. What happened?" The captain concentrated on the screaming man's reply. "A what? Sabotaged? What do you mean we've been sabotaged? Can you—"

A final explosive rumble, this one clearly audible in the phone, shook the bridge. The phone line went dead.

"My God," the captain mumbled. He looked at Jean-Paul. "Everyone in the engine room was yelling. I couldn't understand, but they were saying something about a bomb, that we've been sabotaged. I don't understand. We are a research vessel. Why would anyone bomb a research vessel?"

"Sir!" stammered Jean-Paul. "What do we do?"

"The whole engine room is flooding. I think they're all dead. Send out an SOS. Do it now, son. Hurry. We're sinking and we've got to get everyone off." He punched more numbers into the keypad activating the overhead speaker system throughout all compartments of the ship. "This is the captain speaking. Abandon ship. Abandon ship. This is not a drill. All passengers and crew, abandon ship. This is not a drill. Move to the nearest life-boat station as calmly and quickly as possible. Abandon ship. All crew, all crew, man the life boats . . ."

9

SHE'S READY

*FBI Academy, leadership reaction and obstacle course.
September 1.*

"Come on, Baker! Make that hill one more time!" the instructor yelled.

Jana's lungs burned and her spine screamed in pain, but her face looked like gritty steel. If there was one thing she resolved of herself, it was to never let them see her pain. And certainly, never let them see the demons that now prowled inside her, lurking in the deep recesses of her mind. The demons only came in the quiet times, and Jana did whatever she had to do to keep them at bay.

Through the dirt-trodden trails, woven between pine trees, the hilly "leadership reaction and obstacle course" snaked through the woods of the Marine Corps base like an angry child who was never satisfied. It formed a loop with no start and no end. And, like a spoiled child, it demanded and demanded. The trail knew no mercy and felt nothing of the agony it extracted as pounding feet coursed through its veins. It lived and breathed and demanded food in the form of sweat and toil. And when it didn't get what it wanted, it threw a lashing tantrum and would not stop until it had blood.

Jana chugged further and further up the last daunting hill, the one Quantico trainees had nicknamed *the widow-maker*. The hill was one hell of a piece of work. But the hill wasn't the problem. The problem was that FBI trainers liked to *end* their training runs with the widow-maker. The instructors pushed each trainee to his or her breaking point across the unforgiving woodland trails. Then, when the trainee was about to crack, the group would round the last bend toward the widow-maker. In every training class, more than one trainee would succumb to the hill's sheer size and power. To them, it represented a monster that exposed their true fear. But to Jana, the hill was just another challenge, one that the male instructors thought the females couldn't conquer. It represented one more mocking sneer in a male-dominated culture, and she was determined to be viewed as an equal.

The worst part for the newest trainees was how the instructors would charge them up the hill at the highest speed possible, burning out every last ounce of breath, fortitude, and pain. Then, the trainees learned the truth—once they reached the top, the run was not over. It was just their assumption. In true FBI fashion, instructors would point them down the hill, then back up, and repeat. If ever there was a place that could push a recruit past their breaking point, this was it.

Jana hated it and loved it at the same time. It represented another ass for her to kick, another challenge she would eat for breakfast, another notch in her belt. Her silent motto had been *yes, I'm a girl—try to keep up.*

She looked down from atop the hill at the rabble of male trainees still slogging upwards. Some looked like they were running while standing still, and one was on all fours, crawling upward in a never-ending fight to reach the top. Back when Jana herself had been a new FBI trainee, she thought it pathetic to see another trainee literally crawling up the widow-maker. But now, watching this man, something changed in her thinking. Instead of feeling disgust, Jana felt a jolt of inspiration. The trainee was in an epic struggle against himself, and he wouldn't give up. He was well past his physical limits, yet he fought on. It catapulted her back to her time in the intensive care unit when she had overheard her physician say, *she's a fighter and it's the fighters that survive.*

Jana ran down the hill toward the man. She'd seen him before.

He was the typical age for a new trainee, around twenty-eight, and was a little out of shape. But he had a fight in him that came from somewhere deep down. *He's got guts, and guts is enough,* she thought. She dropped onto all fours next to him and began yelling, "Come on! Don't let this hill beat you! You're better than this! One hand in front of the other. One at a time, you can do this, that's it!" Other trainees already at the top turned around, then went down to join Jana to cheer on their classmate. Soon, everyone joined in. It was a glimpse into the spirit of the word "teamwork," and into a brotherhood few people ever see.

At the top of the hill, two instructors wearing embroidered golf shirts and navy-colored FBI ball caps nodded to one another. One said, "She's almost ready."

The other replied, "Thank God. Call the director."

"Call the director? What are you talking about?"

"He's been calling to ask about her progress every damn day for the last three weeks."

Section Two

An October Storm

10

THE SCENE OF THE CRIME

Submarine USS Colorado, *near the mouth of the Persian Gulf.*
October 16, 1:01 a.m. local time (Oct. 15, 4:01 p.m. EST).

The intercom in the control room of the submarine cracked to
life as the sonar operator, Petty Officer Third Class Thomas,
stationed in an adjoining compartment, called to the captain in
the control room. "Conn, Sonar. New sonar contact bearing 025.
Designate contact, Sierra One."

"Sonar, conn, aye," the captain replied. He then asked, "Is it
surface traffic?"

"No, sir. This contact is submerged. It's a long way out. About
twelve thousand yards off the starboard bow. Can't identify. The
computer's chewing on it now, sir."

"Sonar, conn, aye." The captain turned to the executive
officer. "XO, slow to ahead two-thirds. Station the section-
tracking party. We expecting any company?"

"Aye, sir. Helm, all ahead two-thirds."

"All ahead two-thirds, Helm, aye," another sailor said.

The executive officer picked up a mic. "Station the section-
tracking party." He then turned to the captain. "No, sir. Latest
intelligence shows nothing on the boards. Sure as hell wouldn't
expect to find another sub out here."

"Conn, sonar," sonar operator Thomas called, "I've got a
possible ID on that contact, sir, but you're not going to like it."

"Whad'ya got, Thomas? The computer can't identify it
definitively? I've got to know if this is a hostile, son."

"At this distance, the computer is only offering up a guess." Thomas winced as he delivered the news that this was an older-class ballistic missile submarine. "But, it's designated the contact as a Delta IV."

"A Delta IV? A Russian boomer? You've got to be kidding me. And, anyway, every sub the Russians ever built is in that computer's database. How could it not know for sure?" the captain said.

"I don't know, sir. But I've refocused the sonar at the contact's bearing to see if I can get a better reading. And there's something strange. I can hear the turning of the screws." Thomas tried to imagine a sub, its propellers turning while it sat dead in the water. "But it's like the Russian sub's not in motion, sir." Something about the thought chilled him.

"What do you mean the sub isn't in motion? You just said the screws are turning."

"Yes, sir. From what I can hear, I'd say the sub is not in motion. The computer agrees. It's weird, the screws are turning but the contact isn't advancing forward. And, I'm hearing . . ."

"Hearing what?"

"Grinding, sir. I hear a grinding sound."

Lieutenant Commander Omansky, executive officer of the USS *Colorado*, leaned toward the captain. "Sir, what if the Russian is grounded? It would make sense, right? The screws are making revolutions but the boat's on the bottom, causing the grinding sound."

"If it hit the floor, why the hell would it still have its screws making revolutions?"

"Conn, sonar," sonar operator Thomas called, "I can hear . . . its, shit, it's cavitating. I'm definitely picking up the heavy sounds of bubble formation and their subsequent popping. But, I don't get it. We normally only hear that when a propeller suddenly increases in speed."

"So?"

"The sound isn't coming from the screws, sir."

"Christ, if it's not coming from the screws, what's causing the cavitation sounds then? What the hell is going on?"

"At this distance, the sounds are very faint, but it's definitely cavitating. I can hear a huge plume of bubbles. It's like they're escaping from the hull. It's just that I can't—I can't make it out, sir." He paused, listening to the diminutive sounds. "Ow, shit!"

The sonar operator yanked the headset off, wincing against a sudden loud noise.

"Sonar, conn, what's going on?"

"Sir, I think the contact's hull just breached!"

"What?"

"There was a huge, metallic cracking sound. Sounded like the hull just cracked wide open. I could hear water rushing in. That submarine is flooding with water, sir."

Spinning around, the captain called out. "XO, man battle stations. Come right, heading 025. All ahead two-thirds."

11

THE TURNING OF THE SCREWS

Submarine USS Colorado, October 16, 1:02 a.m. local time. The Persian Gulf (Oct. 15, 4:02 p.m. EST).

"Aye, sir." The chief of the watch ripped a microphone from above his head and issued the command. "Battle stations. This is not a drill."

In every compartment of the boat, warning lights illuminated, indicating the heightened state of alert. Men scrambled through hatches to their stations both fore and aft.

In the adjoining compartment, the sonar supervisor said to the sonar operator, Petty Officer Third Class Thomas, "Concentrate, Thomas. This is the real thing. Just like I showed you."

The sonar operator placed the headphones back over his ears, but held them just off his head, fearing another loud cracking sound. The captain rushed into the tight space and leaned over his shoulder.

"Tell him what you heard," the sonar supervisor said.

"Sir," Thomas said, wiping a bead of sweat from his brow, "what I heard sounded more like a sub sitting on the bottom with its screws turning. Then the sub cracked apart and water rushed in."

"Before it cracked up, was there a high-speed screw? Did it sound like a torpedo hit the Russian?"

"No, sir. No torpedo in the water."

"You've got to be kidding me. No explosion? Well, it didn't hit a mine. All right, widen your sonar listening zone. We can't go tunnel vision and focus on just this one thing. We've got to know if there's anything else out there. If someone attacked that submarine before we came into the area, we have to know who."

"Aye, sir," Thomas said.

"What's the range to the downed sub?" the captain asked.

"We've closed to about six thousand yards, sir," replied the sonar operator. He pushed his hand against his headset in order to listen closer. "Wait, sir, I think I've got a new contact. That's affirmative. Designate the contact Sierra Two, bearing 029. It's submerged also . . . it's a high-speed screw! Wait, what the hell? Hold on, it's a high-speed screw all right, but it's definitely not a torpedo. I'd say it's at about ten thousand yards."

"Another submerged contact? Can you identify?"

"Not yet, sir. It's definitely another sub, but it doesn't sound very large, though. The revolution of the screw . . . Jesus Christ. It's very high pitched. What the hell is that?"

The captain turned toward the executive officer and said, "I don't know what's going on, but we're not taking any chances. XO, flood torpedo tubes one and four."

"Aye, Captain. Fire control, flood tubes one and four."

"It's . . . it's tiny," the sonar operator said, still listening with intent to the high-speed sounds of a submerged propeller. "Ah . . . computer's coming back now, sir. Computer identifies Sierra Two as the *Nautile*, a deep submergence vehicle. It's French. DSVs are used for research, aren't they, sir?"

Tension vacated the captain's brow.

"A DSV? Hell, there can't be more than ten DSVs in active service in the entire world. What is a French DSV doing out here in the Persian Gulf? What's her length, son?"

The sonar operator focused on the details displayed on the computer monitor. "DSV *Nautile* is only twenty-five feet long, sir. No wonder it sounded so tiny on sonar. It says she's equipped with the usual research gear, cameras, lighting equipment, two robotic arms, maximum depth of . . ."

"All right," the captain said, "that's a civilian mini-sub. It's no threat. You scared the shit out of me. Any other traffic on sonar,

Thomas? I doubt that DSV is out here on its own. It would have to be with a larger research ship nearby."

"Yes, sir. I've got surface traffic. Nothing hostile though. I've got a Russian fishing trawler about ten thousand yards off the port quarter, and a Chinese oil tanker about three thousand yards closer. She sounds low in the water; probably topped off with crude. And . . . a ship the computer identifies as the *Padma*, a research ship; one of those with the split stern. She's Pakistani flagged. Maybe that explains the DSV in the area?"

"Roger that. Deep submergence vehicles are lowered from the deck of a research vessel into the water by a crane. Or, they use a split-stern vessel like this ship has to deploy from."

"The computer's now got more data about the first submarine, our downed Russian, sir," Thomas said. "Since we're closer now, the sounds detected by sonar are clearer, and the computer's been able to definitively identify it. It's a Delta IV-class all right. It's a sub called the *Simbirsk*. It says she's a Russian boomer . . . but, wait, I don't get it. Sir? The computer says the *Simbirsk* was decommissioned in 1996 and *scrapped* in 2008. This sub isn't supposed to be in service anymore."

The captain shook his head then walked back to the control room, studying the computer printout. "Great. I've got a computer telling me a Russian ballistic missile submarine has magically come back to life out of the scrapyard and has cracked apart four thousand yards in front of me. That's quite a magic trick. The damn thing's so old that my dad probably chased it around in his submarine days during the Cold War. All right, people, let's work up closer to this thing. We need to find out what happened to it, and fast. Sonar?" the captain called into the open mic.

"Conn, sonar, aye."

"You hear a sound, anything strange, I mean anything, you call it out, son. I don't care what it is."

"Aye, sir," the sonar operator said.

"Is that little DSV mini-sub still pushing away from us along the same course?" the captain asked.

"Aye, sir," said STS3 Thomas, still pressing his hand against his headset. "Sir?"

"What is it, Thomas"

"Well, speaking of the DSV, I know it's just a civilian craft, but you said to point out anything that I hear."

"And?"

"It doesn't sound right, sir."

"How so?"

"Remember how at first I said it was a high-speed screw, and thought it was a torpedo?"

"How could I forget?"

"Well sir, there's something strange about the pitch of the screw. The pitch is too high. Based on the DSV mini-sub's listed aspect ratio, displacement, and the current revolution velocity of its screw, the little sub should be moving a lot faster than it is. It sounds heavy in the water, sir. I'm picking up a fair bit of cavitation from the single screw. Under normal operation, that shouldn't be there. I don't know if any of this is important, sir. It's just strange. It almost sounds . . . like she's weighted down."

"Conn, aye," the captain said.

The executive officer leaned toward the captain. "Captain, back to the downed Russian boat, what the hell is going on? We've got a ghost Russian sub that was supposedly scrapped several years ago. It obviously *wasn't* scrapped, and now seems to be sunk on the ocean floor *with its screws still turning*. What do you make of it?"

"Damned if I know, Charlie. Maybe it got attacked before we came on scene, or maybe they had an accident on board. Whatever caused it to sink and crack apart might have damaged their propulsion controls. We're going to have to find out what happened to it, and if they need assistance, fast. There could still be people alive on that thing. But, I agree with Thomas, there's no way that civilian DSV mini-sub limping off in the distance has anything to do with our downed boat."

"I agree. What's the play, sir?"

"We'll work right up to the downed sub as quickly as possible and find out if there's any signs of life. If there is, then God help those sailors. We'll have to notify Fifth Fleet and see what type of rescue assets are in the region. Wait a minute. We've got all that hydrographic ultrasound mapping equipment on board, right? Call that civilian geologist up here. Wake him up if you have to. I know that equipment was designed to map the ocean floor, but maybe we can use it to get a view of the Russian sub."

"Conn, sonar," cracked the voice of the sonar operator.

"Sonar, conn," the captain said. "Christ, son. What the hell is it now?" The captain rubbed his eyes. "I'm sorry, son. Speak freely."

"I've just been reading historical information about the mini-sub, the DSV *Nautile*, from the computer, sir."

"And?"

There was a long pause.

"Sir, the computer says the DSV *Nautile* was previously attached to a French research ship, the *Marion Dufresne*."

"So? What's the problem?"

"The *Marion Dufresne* was reported lost at sea. Three months ago, in the Aegean. She was sabotaged. Some of the crew were rescued. But everything, including the DSV *Nautile*, were assumed a total loss."

The captain's shoulders slumped and he looked at the executive officer. "No one's ever going to believe us. You just can't make this stuff up."

12

BEFORE SOMEONE ELSE TAKES A SHOT AT US

Submarine USS Colorado. *The Persian Gulf. October 16, 1:24 a.m. local time (Oct. 15, 4:24 p.m. EST).*

A clean-cut man dressed in civilian clothes rubbed his eyes, ducked his head as he passed through an open hatch into the control room, then said, "You asked to see me, sir?"

"You're the geologist, right?"

"Yes, sir. Carl Branson."

"Yes, thank you for reporting, Mr. Branson. Look, we've got a situation here and I need your help."

"Yeah, when the boat went to battle stations, I kind of figured something was up. Some kind of a drill?"

"Tell me more about the ultrasound equipment you've got on board. I know the admiral has us mapping the ocean floor throughout the Persian Gulf region, but what I need to know is, how accurate are the images the equipment can produce? What kind of resolution can you get?"

"The equipment is state of the art, Captain. Its topside equivalent would be a camera that could capture a thousand megapixels of detail. If you can get me close enough, I can see a shrimp on the ocean floor and tell you what it had for dinner."

"Lovely. How quickly can you have the equipment ready?"

"Ready for what, sir? It's ready now."

"We've just picked up some disturbing sounds on sonar," the captain said.

"I imagine that's what the battle-stations drill is all about?"

"This isn't Hollywood, Mr. Branson. It's no drill. There could be lives on the line here. I want your full attention. We think a Russian submarine might have just cracked up in front of us. She's about a thousand yards off our bow at the moment, sitting on the bottom. I'm going to work up close to her and I need you to use your ultrasound equipment to take a look at the bottom. We've got to see if we can tell what happened to her, and if they need assistance."

"Holy shit. It's not exactly what a geologist is used to doing, is it? The equipment can be ready whenever you are."

"Get to your duty station. And get on the comm. The executive officer here will go with you. I want as much detail as you can give me about that downed sub, and any damage it might have sustained."

13

FROM SILENCE TO RUBBLE

Abbattabad, Pakistan. About 316 miles north of Islamabad. Population 916,000.

On a two-lane neighborhood road in Abbattabad, Pakistan, a man sat in a car. Scorching sunlight radiated through the windshield, cooking the dashboard. The car was a nondescript, white four-door with a dent in the left rear quarter panel and a crack in the windshield that ran up the right side. The dinge of a year's worth of road grime clung to the aging paint the way a shawl might drape a grandmother bracing against the wind.

A woman in a house across the way had taken notice of the car an hour earlier. After checking her front window for a third time and finding the car still there, she removed a broom from her closet, wrapped a hijab over her head, and stepped onto the porch. The car driver was preoccupied and took little notice. He sat staring in the opposite direction, across the street at an abandoned building that had stood shrouded by fourteen-foot walls and secrecy for several years. He didn't avert his eyes from the structure, he just kept staring.

To the woman, he looked like he was lost in thought and couldn't break free. She thought this quite odd.

The large compound was vacant, yet had been occupied in the not-so-recent past. During those years, no one in the neighborhood had known who actually lived there. But the secret had finally been revealed. Now that it was completely deserted, she wondered what all the fascination was about.

The compound had a checkered past. During the days of its use, it had many occupants, yet only one owner. At that time, there was no way any of the neighbors could have known who owned the building. The man was never seen, ever. Sometimes other men would come and go from the compound, or women would make their way to market, only to return and disappear behind the heavy steel gates. The cement walls that surrounded the compound were thick and smooth, with no footholds, and towered just higher than the ground floor of the structure. Now, however, the drab-colored walls sported more than just sand-colored paint. The top of one side showed signs from the damage caused that terrifying night of May 1, 2011.

The night seemed so long ago. But in reality, the shock of those events played tricks with the woman's mind.

The weather had been even hotter than normal, and at about four in the morning she had awoken from a dream in which she had been in a car accident. The sound of shredding metal in the dream had been horrendous. Yet it was actually the sound of something happening at the compound across the street, etching itself into the nightmare. When the woman rose and peered out the front window, what she saw across the street made no sense. Hanging over the top of the smooth cement wall was what appeared to be the tail section of a helicopter. Not shaped like the ones she'd seen coming and going from the Pakistani Military Academy that sat just a mile away, but awkward in shape—it looked more enclosed. It was as though the rotor of the helicopter was built into the tail itself, instead of being mounted on the outside of it. When she saw a second helicopter of the same description fly close overhead, she knew something dreadful was happening.

As bizarre as the sights were, what struck her most was that she had not heard the sounds of either helicopter. No roaring engine, no thumping of rotors thrashing through the night air. It was as though they were silenced. And why would a helicopter try to land inside the walls of that compound in the first place? Did it crash? Was it some kind of new helicopter from the military academy and something went wrong?

It wasn't until a few moments later that she heard loud popping sounds. They would stay etched in her memory forever, scratched into the fibers of her brain. The first sound was a boom that shook the glass windows. It was almost loud enough to pierce her eardrums. The other sounds were quieter, like firecrackers muffled to a whisper. Whatever was happening across the street had her wide-eyed and gripping the curtains.

The last sight she saw across the road before bolting into her five-year-old's bedroom was a flash of light and several strange red dots, like those made by laser pointers, dancing their way across the outside of one of the compounds' upper-floor windows. She grabbed her child in her arms, flipped his bed on its side, and huddled on the ground behind it, her body in between the child and what she only described as "something evil happening across the street." When the night of terror was over, she silently thanked Allah that they were still alive.

As she refocused on the man in the parked car, she noticed a singular patch of white in his otherwise dark hair. He turned and looked straight at her, his eyes squinting in the bright sunlight. To her, the eyes carried the very essence of the word vengeance. A chill touched her spine near the base of her neck and rode across her shoulders on a shiver. There was something cold about the eyes; something dead.

He looked ahead, started his car, and drove away.

Had she known the driver was the most wanted terrorist in the world, Waseem Jarrah, she would have never made eye contact with him. She later described the stranger as having soulless eyes that seemed to revel in their own pain. Yet in them was painted a deep sense of satisfaction, as someone who had just found what he was looking for, and now knew exactly what to do.

As the car disappeared over the hill, it occurred to the woman that the compound, once the property of Osama bin Laden, was slated for demolition the very next day.

Jarrah looked in his rearview mirror at the woman staring at him as he drove away. A new chapter in his quest for retribution was in motion; retribution for the murder of his mentor.

14

SOUND COLLISION

Submarine USS Colorado. *October 16, 1:51 a.m. local time. The Persian Gulf (Oct. 15, 4:51 p.m. EST).*

The geologist, Branson, and the executive officer wove their way through the internals of the sub, toward the lowermost deck.

In the control room, the captain said, "Quartermaster, what's the current sounding?"

"Ocean floor is at seven hundred and seventeen feet, Captain."

"Roger that." He turned toward the dive control officer. "Dive control, make your depth six hundred feet. Five degree down bubble. All ahead one-third. Let's slow the old girl down. Chief of the Boat?"

"Aye, sir," chirped a reply from the COB, the senior-most enlisted man.

"Radio, conn. Deploy the Deep Siren communications buoy to the surface. We're going to be sending a coded transmission back to Fifth Fleet."

"Conn, radio, aye. Prepare for an encoded transmission to Fifth Fleet."

A young ensign on his first deployment asked the chief, "COB, what's a Deep Siren?"

"It's a special buoy made by Raytheon. At the moment, we don't want to leave our current depth and go close enough to the surface to raise our antenna to radio back to Fleet. And since we can't send radio transmissions when we're at this depth, we release a buoy which floats up to the surface. It's a satellite communications device. We'll use it to communicate to the Fifth Fleet."

"How do we retrieve the buoy when we're done?"

"We don't." The chief looked at the captain. "Captain? What's the message we want to transmit, sir?"

"Just handed it to the radio operator. He's keying it into the system now. That buoy is rated to float upwards at a rate of about a hundred and fifty feet per minute. Let's see, if we're at six hundred feet of depth, that'll take four minutes to rise to the surface before we can talk with Fifth Fleet. The admiral is never going to believe this. Good Christ, we could be looking at anything from an accident to a deliberate act of war. At any rate, if anyone is alive on that downed boat, a rescue effort has to be launched, and right-the-hell now."

"Aye, sir," the COB said. "Sir? Something has been bothering me."

"Just one thing? What is it COB?"

"It's just, sir, it feels like we're smack dab in the middle of someone else's dogfight. I'd hate to get caught at the scene of the crime, sir."

The captain stared back at him. "I hear you, COB. That's part of the reason we need to get this message back to command. I don't want to get caught down here and have it look like we're the ones who sank this Russian boat either." The captain's banging on the keyboard sounded like an old ticker tape machine gone haywire. He prepared the message describing what they had found, their plans to try to get a look at the sub using the advanced ultrasound mapping equipment, and the list of all other contacts currently on sonar.

"Sonar, conn. Any new contacts, Thomas?"

"Conn, sonar. No, sir. No new contacts."

"What is the target solution on that DSV mini-sub?" the captain said.

"Conn, sonar. Sierra Two, the DSV mini-sub is proceeding on its original course sir, bearing 029. She's lugging slowly east, toward Pakistan. She'll be out of range in about seven minutes, sir."

"Sonar, Conn, aye. Any sounds of life coming from Sierra One?"

"Conn, sonar. Just the turning of the screws and the same grinding sound. Sounds like metal grinding against sand. Some sounds of air escaping. But, no sir, no sounds that indicate signs of life."

"Shit." The captain plucked a sound-powered telephone from above his head to call the executive officer.

LCDR Omansky picked up the phone from the geology workstation in the sub's lowermost compartment. "XO."

"XO, get me an update on the ultrasound equipment. Are we ready to deploy the cable? We're about four hundred yards out from the downed boat."

"Aye, sir" the XO replied. "The geologist, Mr. Branson, is ready, sir. Permission to start streaming the ultrasound cable?"

"Permission granted. And XO, be sure Mr. Branson records everything, and be sure he understand the gravity of the situation. He's a civilian, and as much as I love civilians, I'd hate to have to flush him out one of the torpedo tubes if he screws this up."

"I heard that," Branson said.

"Aye, sir," the executive officer said.

"Captain?" the chief of the boat said. "The buoy is away, sir."

As the Deep Siren communications buoy floated toward the ocean's surface with its encrypted message in tow, the captain tried to think through all possible scenarios. If the downed submarine was intact, then it was possible that sailors were trapped inside. And in the submarine community, the unwritten code among sailors is that if submariners are trapped, no matter who they are, you do anything you can to help them. Aside from coordinating a rescue effort, the *Colorado* itself had no means of directly connecting to the downed boat to pull sailors out.

The other conundrum revolved around the fact that this boat was the *Simbirsk*, a Russian-made ballistic-missile submarine that had reportedly been scrapped years earlier. The captain was disturbed at the very thought of it. If the Russians reported to

NATO that they had scrapped the *Simbirsk*, yet had illegally sold her, what else had they sold, and to whom? *There's no way they'd sell her with warheads aboard*, thought the captain, *there's no way*.

"Chief of the Boat," the captain said, "give me a rundown of all systems."

"Aye, sir," the chief replied. "We're at battle stations, torpedo tubes one and four are loaded, tubes are flooded, and outer doors are closed. Depth, six hundred feet. Speed, ahead one-third. The Deep Siren communications buoy is deployed to the surface and still within tactical range. Awaiting further orders from Fifth Fleet. Ultrasound equipment is deployed and is scanning the ocean floor below. The cable is extended to seventy-five yards. Sonar operator listening for any signs of life aboard Sierra One. Sonar also just reported a single surface contact, Sierra Three, an Iranian fishing trawler."

A young communications officer spoke out. "Sir, incoming message traffic from Fifth Fleet. Received by the buoy, sir."

A paper printout pushed from a digital printer next to the communications officer. The captain tore it off and read.

"All right, no surprise there. We are to investigate the wreckage with all due priority. No shit." The captain pulled a phone from the overhead. "XO, how much more time does Mr. Branson need to finish the ultrasound survey? I'm getting nervous hovering over a downed nuclear submarine. Somebody might get the wrong idea. Know what I mean?"

"Aye, sir," the XO said. "Mr. Branson says his scan will be done within thirty minutes. We'll be back in the control room after that and can pull up the scans from there. For all his joking around down here, he actually knows what the hell he's doing."

"Thirty minutes, huh? Just in time to hit the mess deck," the captain said.

"Aye, sir. Apparently geologists just love chicken-fried steak and canned oranges. Sir, it will take a good thirty minutes after the ultrasound is completed for the computer to finish crunching the data it gathers. After that, we can look at the high-res images."

"Conn, aye," the captain said. "Tell Mr. Branson no steak for him until he's done."

The level of tension in the control room was palpable. Most of the sailors had never been under a real battle-stations alert. Sailors on other parts of the USS *Colorado* began to hear the scuttlebutt that a downed Russian-made submarine was on the ocean floor just below them. It was a sobering thought. Each sailor knew the dangers of their assignments, but none of them actually thought they'd be in a situation like this. The Russian-made sub had sunk, and sunk for a reason. It could have been hit by a torpedo, depth charge, mine, or had some type of internal catastrophe. But with no sounds of life coming from the hull, the full complement of submariners were likely dead.

The executive officer and the geologist walked into the control room. "Captain?" LCDR Omansky said. "The ultrasound scan is completed."

"We'll be able to see the first images in the next twenty-five minutes," Mr. Branson said.

"Thank God. I want to get to the bottom of this, no pun intended, and relay what we find back to fleet. In the meantime, we'll hold our position until we see what's down—"

"Conn! Sonar! New contact, designate Sierra Four, bearing 041. It sounds like it's submerging. I'd say we've got a fast-attack boat headed right for us, sir!"

"Range?" the captain yelled.

"About twenty thousand yards. She's increasing speed. Now that she's submerged, I'd say she's doing at least twenty knots."

"Goddammit. Helm, all ahead standard. Bring us up to speed slowly, son. He may not know we're here. I want to keep it quiet. Fire control, make torpedo tubes one and four ready in all respects. Sonar, conn. Got an ID on that fast mover?"

"Conn, sonar. Computer's making its ID now, sir . . . computer IDs Sierra Four as the PNS *Hamza*. An Agosta-class, Pakistani navy attack submarine."

Standing in between the sonar station and the control room, Branson leaned toward the XO. "Omansky," he said in a low voice, "what the hell's going on?" Lines carved into his forehead.

The executive officer replied, "Well, Mr. Branson, the downed sub on the bottom is Russian-made, but if it turns out that she's now Pakistani flagged, and this new Pakistani sub finds us near it, he's going to be pissed. Captain's trying to evade quietly before the new Pakistani sub finds us."

"Is the Pakistani a real threat?" Branson said, wringing his hands.

"Oh hell yes she is. Pakistani navy subs are French-built. Small, quiet, fast as hell, and they carry the Black Shark torpedo. We don't want to get into a scrap with her if we can help it."

From the sonar room, the operator called. "Conn, sonar. Sounds like she's going deep, sir."

"Sonar, conn, where's the thermocline? Still hovering at around one hundred and eighty feet?"

"Conn, sonar, yes, sir."

Branson whispered to the executive officer, "Omansky, what's a thermocline?"

"It marks the depth where the water temperature changes. See, when a large layer of warmer water exists on the surface, and colder water is below, the two different temperatures touch each other and form a kind of sound barrier. It's hard for subs to hear through a thermocline using their sonar. Right now, the water temperature is warmer above the depth of a hundred and eighty feet, and much colder right below it. The hostile Pakistani submarine is above and we're below."

"Conn, sonar. Sierra Four, the Pakistani attack sub, appears to be diving hard, sir. She's already at about one hundred feet of depth. Making no effort to stay quiet either, her screw is turning full bore."

"Son of a bitch, we've got a real hothead on our hands," the captain said. "XO, slow to ahead one-third. Rig ship for ultraquiet. We might slip right under this asshole without him hearing us."

The executive officer belted out the captain's orders. The geologist, Mr. Branson, pressed himself further against the bulkhead in between the control room and the sonar compartment. He wanted to stay in the control room to hear what was happening and thought that if he could melt into the wall, perhaps no one would notice him.

Having a civilian on a sub during such a high-tension scenario was something the US Navy wanted to avoid. But risks like endangering a civilian had to be taken in order to accomplish certain naval goals.

No one had ever done a full-scale mapping of the ocean floor in the Persian Gulf region. But with the number of wars that had gone on in the area, America and her allies needed details. What if a full-scale war erupted at some point in the future? High-resolution mapping of the ocean floor might mean the difference between success and failure.

Branson studied the faces of the officers and crew. With the exception of the captain, the executive officer, and the chief of the boat, they were a pretty young group. Most looked like they were still in high school, but in reality they were older. When he'd stepped aboard, Branson had met some of the young sailors, but now, they looked different. In a span of just hours, they had aged. The tension painted their expressions and protruded through jaw muscles that seemed to endlessly flex. They left port as kids and were now facing a level of fear most adults could not comprehend.

Branson struggled to keep his emotions in check. Being a geologist was almost never dangerous. And yet now he found himself thinking that surely, this wasn't happening. At some point, the captain would grab the mic from the overhead and announce that this had all been a drill. It was so surreal.

The decision to come on board a US Navy submarine and map an uncharted section of ocean floor sounded like such a good idea at the time. Now in the realities of life and death, Branson was astounded at his own naiveté. The chief of the boat walked over and stood beside him.

"Conn, sonar," sonar operator Thomas said. "Pakistani contact, Sierra Four, now penetrating through the thermocline. She's at about two hundred feet of depth, still moving under full propulsion."

"Sonar, conn. Range to the Pakistani?"

"About four thousand yards, Captain. She's still diving hard but . . . hold on, hold on. That sounds like . . . conn, sonar! Torpedo in the water, bearing zero six eight!" The sonar operator yelled loud enough into the comm that his voice could easily be heard in the control room without it.

"Is the torpedo actively pinging?" the captain said.

"No, sir!" STS3 Thomas said.

The captain spun toward the executive officer. "That means the torpedo is on a wire. Goddammit, they must know right where we are. Helm, all ahead flank, cavitate! Dive control, make your depth one hundred fifty feet."

As the diving officer responded, Branson put a vise-grip on the chief's shoulder.

"Chief, what the hell is going on? What does that mean? They fired a real torpedo at us? It's on a wire?"

"Torpedoes either acquire and hone in on their targets through active sonar pinging, or they are attached to a wire that leads all the way back to their boat. The Pakistani sub is manually controlling the direction of this torpedo through the wire."

"Hang on, everybody," the captain said. "This might hurt just a little bit." The sarcasm was only amusing to the captain.

The boat's bow pitched upwards in one long, violent motion as an enormous amount of air blasted into the main ballast tanks, pushing seawater out. The effect was like blowing up a balloon underwater and then watching it rocket toward the surface.

"Sonar, conn. Give me an update on that torpedo, son."

"Torpedo is turning upwards, sir. She's following us. Making turns for about fifty knots. Computer confirms, it's a Black Shark torpedo. Max speed, fifty knots, max range thirty miles. Range, fifteen hundred yards and closing. She can chase us all day and outrun us in a matter of seconds, sir."

"Goddamn Italian-made torpedoes," the captain said.

Branson watched as the captain clicked the button on an old-school digital stopwatch, leaned against the periscope assembly, and closed his eyes in focused concentration.

As the boat thrust upwards toward the surface, it leaned back at a thirty-degree angle. Any gear not strapped down slid off shelves and bounced across linoleum floors.

"Passing three hundred feet," the diving officer said. "Passing two hundred seventy-five feet."

The sonar operator and diving officer chirped out a cadence of echoing updates every few seconds, indicating their depth and the distance from the torpedo.

"Range to torpedo, six hundred yards."

"Depth two hundred fifty feet."

"Torpedo closing to four hundred yards."

"Depth two hundred feet."

"Torpedo picking up speed! Range two hundred and fifty yards."

Through shut eyes, the captain yelled, "Range and speed of the Pakistani sub?"

"Range to Sierra Four, two thousand yards, speed twenty-one knots."

The captain pushed the button on a second digital stopwatch, starting the timer.

"Depth one hundred eighty feet. We're about to cross above the thermocline," the diving officer said. "It will be harder for them to hear us once we cross."

"Torpedo range, one hundred yards!" The sonar operator's voice cracked.

"Steady at one hundred fifty feet. We've crossed above the thermocline," the diving officer said.

The captain's concentration was unshakable and his eyes remained shut like a blind man.

"Sonar, conn. Is the torpedo following us by coming up through the thermocline?"

"No, Captain," the sonar operator said. "I, I can't hear it, sir. But it's definitely not punching through the thermal barrier."

"Chief?" Branson said. "What just happened? Are we safe?"

The chief of the boat looked at Branson the way a seasoned buyer might look at a slab of salmon before beginning to haggle with the vendor.

"Are we safe? I won't bother to justify that with an answer. At any rate, the torpedo is on its wire and being controlled by the Pakistani sub which can no longer hear us effectively since we're on different sides of the thermocline. So, they don't know where to guide the torpedo at the moment."

The USS *Colorado* maintained a depth of one hundred fifty

feet, hugging the edge of the thermocline, which was just thirty feet below them. Fear splashed across the face of the twenty-two-year-old communications officer, who looked like he'd just been pulled from a burning car.

The captain opened his eyes and exhaled, though no one would have noticed. He grabbed a clipboard, flipped the pages back, and began to write something. When he finished, he looked at LCDR Omansky.

"XO, if you were the Pakistani sub's skipper, and you were attacking us, what would you be doing right now?"

Without pausing, the executive officer blurted out in one breath, "I'd guide that torpedo up through the thermocline, pop the wire off, and have it actively ping for us."

"And what's the tactical advantage in doing that?"

The executive officer shrugged. "If I were the Pak skipper, I'd figure to have us nailed. The torpedo would be actively pinging for us above the thermal layer, and we couldn't duck below the thermal layer because he'd be sitting down there waiting for us."

"Leading the hounds to the hunters," the captain said, this time with a grin. "That answer is exactly why you'll get your own submarine command one day. You will make one hell of a skipper." With that, the captain turned the clipboard around to show the others what he had written a moment before.

1. Send torpedo up through thermal layer
2. Clip the wire, have the torpedo actively ping
3. We'd be trapped

The captain smiled and nodded his approval at the younger officer.

"Conn, sonar. Change in torpedo acoustics. The torpedo is punching up through the thermal layer. She's coming up after us, sir."

Branson's eyes locked on the captain. "Chief, why did the captain just start smiling? The torpedo is coming up after us?"

The chief said nothing. He was confused himself.

"Sonar, conn, aye," the captain said. "Estimated speed and distance to the Pakistani sub *Hamza*?"

"Conn, sonar, it's hard to tell, sir. She's still below the

thermocline so I'm having trouble hearing her. She's slowed. I'd say she's about six hundred yards out in front of us, heading toward us, but about a hundred feet below our depth." A few seconds elapsed. "Sir! The torpedo has come up through the thermocline and is actively pinging for us."

"She locked on us yet, son?"

"No, sir. The torpedo is headed away from us at the moment, moving at a decreased rate of speed. The torpedo is turning, she's turning. She hasn't locked on us yet. Hold a moment . . . she's turning in our direction. Conn, sonar! Torpedo has acquired! Four hundred yards and closing, increasing speed. She's at fifty one knots, sir."

Branson's breathing went shallow. The captain took a deep breath of his own, sat, reset the stop watches, then closed his eyes once again.

"All right people, time to earn your pay. Sonar, call out your best estimates on our range to the *Hamza*."

"Conn, sonar, aye," the sonar operator said, his voice beginning to shake. "The Pakistani sub *Hamza*, range, three hundred yards, depth, two hundred feet. She's now just fifty feet below us, sir. Heading right toward us."

The captain's body rocked in gentle succession as he counted under his breath.

"Conn, sonar. Torpedo range, one hundred twenty-five yards off the stern and closing! Pakistani sub, range two hundred yards off the bow."

The captain's nodding continued and his eyes remained closed.

"Conn, sonar! Torpedo seventy-five yards! *Hamza*, one hundred yards!"

The captain said, "Emergency deep! Sound collision."

A siren began wailing in all compartments of the boat, warning sailors of an impending impact.

"But sir," yelled the diving officer, "if we go deeper, we'll collide with the *Hamza*! She's right in our path below us! Captain, say again?"

The captain screamed out, threat threaded throughout his

voice, "Captain said emergency deep! Do it now!"

The submarine pitched downward straight through the thermocline and headed directly toward the PNS *Hamza*, which barreled forward, unaware the *Colorado* was in a violent dive and headed right into her path.

"Conn, sonar. Torpedo following us down, captain," Thomas said. "She might be faltering as we enter the colder waters." The sonar operator started to yank his headset off, fearing the torpedo impact was moments away, but stopped himself.

Everyone in the control room gripped tightly to avoid falling forward as the boat pitched, nose down.

"Conn, sonar! The torpedo is trying to reacquire! The *Hamza*, twenty yards! Collision imminent!"

"Everyone hang on!" the captain yelled. An alarm that sounded like a fire engine's horn pulsed throughout the interior.

The nose of the *Colorado* scraped the bow of the *Hamza* as the *Colorado* thrust downward. The impact was felt throughout the boat, and alarms sounded in forward compartments. The two ships scraped past one another just as the torpedo's pinging reacquired its target. A cacophonous explosion shuddered throughout the Colorado and many sailors looked back and forth in a frantic effort to find where the water would be rushing in. But when no water came, confusion permeated their faces.

A secondary percussion erupted and Branson grabbed the XO's arm. "Omansky! Are we sinking? What the hell just happened?"

But the XO's eyes were still locked on the captain. When he finally opened his mouth, a hiss that sounded like the opening of a freezer escaped. "Captain just saved your ass is what just happened."

"But, but the explosions? We've been hit!"

"No, we haven't. The captain dove the boat so close to the Hamza that when the torpedo reacquired, it honed in on the wrong sub."

In the control room, the captain opened his eyes and stood. He looked at his shell-shocked crew, many of whom still did not know they were out of danger, or what had just happened.

"Sonar? Conn. Is the *Hamza* breaking up?"

It took a few seconds for the response which came back in a

hushed, mumbled tone. "Conn, sonar. Yes, sir. I can hear the hull collapsing in multiple places. I can hear . . ."

"Hear what, sonar?"

"For a second, I could hear screaming, sir."

The captain turned to the executive officer. "XO, maintain current depth. Damage report. All compartments report in."

Members of the crew looked at one other and terror began to vacate their faces. It occurred first in the control room, then throughout the boat. Spontaneous, celebratory yelling was heard from neighboring compartments, and the sailors in the control room erupted in joyous unison.

The captain ripped the mic from the overhead and barked into it, "All hands, this is the captain! Knock that shit off! I said shut the hell up!" All aboard went quiet and the captain continued. "We might be alive, but forty-some submariners just died. They just started their eternal patrol. They were just like you—a bunch of young sailors eager to do their duty and sacrifice their lives for their flag if need be. And they did it. When submariners die, there's nothing to celebrate. Carry on."

Silence again became the mainstay throughout the boat.

"Dive control, make your depth one hundred feet. We need to tell Fleet what just happened." He then turned to the geologist. "Mr. Branson, has the computer finished chewing on the ultrasound images yet? We need to upload those to Fleet before somebody else takes a shot at us."

Branson's face was pale and he struggled to steady his shaking legs. "The images? Oh yeah, the images. I forgot about those. Must have fallen asleep there for a bit."

15

THE PENTAGON

The Pentagon, Washington, DC. Naval wing, third floor, A-ring, 2nd corridor, bay number 106. October 15, 5:17 p.m. EST.

The navy yeoman darted through the Pentagon hallway, dodging in between people as a single sheet of paper flapped without restraint in his hand.

"Make a hole!" he yelled as though still on board a ship, sidestepping in between one person, then another.

A marine guard standing post outside the office of Rear Admiral William Thornton saw the approaching melee, drew his weapon, and screamed, "Stand down! Halt or I'll shoot!"

The yeoman skidded across the slick floor in a wild attempt to arrest his forward momentum as both arms flailed in the air. As he stopped, he jerked forward his identity card and blurted between breaths, "I've got to see the admiral, right now!"

"Good Christ, man," the Marine said. "I almost shot you. He's in a conference and not to be disturbed."

"Not to be disturbed, my ass!" the yeoman yelled. "This is flash traffic! Level five. Open that goddamned door!"

"Oh shit."

The yeoman burst into the office, where the rear admiral sat with a phone to his ear. The yeoman held up the paper and said, "Sir! Level five!"

The admiral looked up with no change of expression.

"Let me call you back, General," he said into the phone. Turning to the yeoman, he said, "Level five? Oh bullshit. Don't tell me you got me off the phone with General Meers for another damned drill."

But as the admiral glanced at the paper, he stood and his face went ashen. He dismissed the yeoman, then read and reread the paper. His eyes struggled to focus on the words. The paper described, in the most terse verbiage, that the submarine USS *Colorado*, on maneuvers in the Persian Gulf, came upon a downed Russian nuclear sub, went to investigate, and had been fired upon by a third sub, this one belonging to the Pakistani navy. The Pakistani attack boat was destroyed, and now Pakistan was threatening US naval vessels in the region. It was a prelude to war.

"Mother of God." He pressed a red button on his desk phone.

"Yes, sir?" came a young voice on the other end.

"Assemble the Joint Chiefs immediately. This is level five."

16

THUNDERCLAP IN THE NIGHT AIR

On board the ferryboat Ammara. *Two nautical miles south-southwest of Karachi, Pakistan. Gulf of Oman. October 16, 3:11 a.m. local time (Oct. 15, 6:01 p.m. EST).*

In Pakistan's coastal region, a dilapidated ferryboat cut through the darkness, spurting coarse, black diesel filth from a low smokestack. The engines chuttered forward along the Karachi-Dubai ferry line about two miles offshore. Light waves smacked its starboard bow on exact, three-second intervals—the effect somewhat disconcerting in its perfection. The waning moonlight glowed against the otherwise-empty sea, illuminating a straight path behind them toward the west.

The American operative who had chartered the old vessel said nothing. He simply stared straight ahead. His head held rock-steady, but his eye movement was reminiscent of a Secret Service agent scanning a crowd. The grizzled beard itched against his throat, for he was unaccustomed to wearing one. But it wasn't the length of his facial hair that bothered him, it was the dense, unkempt nature of the beard that irritated his senses as the wiry mess fought the ocean breeze.

In his lifetime, he'd never grown his hair so long. *It's a look I'll be glad to shed when this damnable mission is over,* he thought. *This mission. Yeah, this mission. What the hell are they thinking? The president decides he needs to steal a nuke, so he invokes the Fifteenth Protocol.* He shook his head and lit a cigarette. *The Fifteenth Protocol: presidential authority to use nuclear force against a nuclear threat. Why in the world does a superpower like us need to steal a nuke? If he's got the authority to use nuclear power, why not just launch a missile and get it over with?*

He was entering his twelfth year as a CIA field operative and each assignment seemed to increase in intensity. Or perhaps it was the way his mind wouldn't focus like it used to, wouldn't focus at all, for that matter.

From the pocket of his tunic he withdrew a black plastic bag, and from within it, a small, cellophane-covered box that contained a new cell phone. He pulled out the only copy of his operational orders and studied the map coordinates. He then looked, for what seemed like the hundredth time, at the GPS to see how close the ferry was to the rendezvous point. The ferry was right on course and heading straight for the coordinates.

He tore the package open and deposited the trash at his feet without a second thought. The torn box swayed back and forth on the wooden deck, although one couldn't tell if the motion was caused by the wind or the waves. He pushed the power button on the phone and waited as the screen blinked to life and located its cellular signal. From memory, he dialed a number.

The operative jammed the phone against his ear and struggled to hear over the popping of the waves. He found closing his eyes helped him to concentrate on the faint sounds emanating from the phone's speaker.

On the other end of the line, the phone was answered, but the person spoke not a word.

The American began, his voice thick with grit, determination, and the solace known only to those in his profession. His words were a memorized script designed to ensure he was talking to the right person. "Every soul will taste of death," he said.

On the other end, the voice of a male in the closing days of his teenage years replied with the correct response. "And ye will be paid on the Day of Resurrection only that which ye have fairly earned." The accent, heavy of Pakistan's Pashtun region, was betrayed in its purity by a slight muddle of New York's Lower East Side.

The coded message complete, the American operative said,

"You have procured the vehicle?"

"It will be at your disposal at the prearranged time and place," the voice said, full of eagerness and mild vinegar. "All preparations have been made."

Both men remained careful not to disclose operational details of any kind. This was an unsecured phone line, and they would not betray their training.

"We are on schedule here. We expect to make contact soon. No mistakes, my friend." The American CIA agent stared into the moonlight, vacancy his solemn veil, and quoted his closing sequence. "When the wrongdoers reach the pangs of death, and the angels stretch their hands out, saying: Deliver up your souls." Without averting his eyes from the moon, he hung up the call, pressed his thumb against the battery, and flipped it off the back of the phone. The battery clattered across the deck and slid to a stop. He removed the SIM card, flicked it overboard, and chased it with the body of the phone. The phone parts disappeared into the dark, wet oblivion. "You make damn sure you're on the right tack," he said to the ferry captain.

"Yes, good sir," said the aging owner of the small boat. "We are right on top of the coordinates."

The ferryboat's captain was a simple man, and his voice cracked. He was not accustomed to being hired to sail in the late of night. His kameez tunic ruffled in the wind and slapped the back of his calves. The cloth was as worn and aged as his skin, yet showed signs of recent repair.

"Then where is he? I want to get off this floating coffin before I inhale the rest of the soot coming from that infernal engine."

"We will find him, good sir. We will find him. Allah will light the way."

The amount of time the CIA operative had spent in the Middle East ingrained itself into everything about his person; his gate, his mannerisms, his dress, and even his speech.

"If I find you've taken us to the wrong coordinates, I'll slice you like a pig and feed your entrails to the sharks."

"Yes, I am sure . . . we will find him. We will find him, Mr. Sir," stuttered the boat captain as he dabbed his forehead with an old rag.

After fifteen tense minutes of waves slapping into the bow in perfectly timed succession, the old captain cried out, "Yes! Yes! He is there! See him? The vessel is just off the port quarter." Relief vacated his voice like a clogged plumbing drain being cleared.

"Very well, then," said the American. "Bring us up alongside. And do it slowly." He glared at the old man. "I'd hate to ruin my shoes with your fresh blood if we were to bump."

The old man swallowed, hard.

There, fifty yards off the bow, sat a darkened silhouette, floating in the night water, light waves cracking against it in protest. The shape decried something akin to an upside-down boat, yet the closer the ferry puttered toward the silhouette, the more distinct the shape became. Instead of bouncing up and down, the tiny DSV mini-submarine lumbered in the chop, as though tethered to the bottom on a long, taut cable.

A single gunshot ruptured the night air like a thunderclap. The captain spun around with bulging eyes to find the American staring at him, motionless. The CIA operative collapsed to his knees, then flopped face forward onto the deck. He was dead. The captain's body entered paralysis as fear took its toll. He watched as thick, dark blood pooled on the decrepit wooden planks of the deck, then rocked in tandem with the waves. Then, along the starboard side of the deck, the lid of a storage compartment underneath a long, wooden bench seat opened and a shadowy figure emerged. The man's only distinguishing feature was a white patch in his hair. He stood as a tiny wisp of smoke eased from the barrel of a French-made 9 mm in his right hand.

"Pull alongside," said the voice of the new stowaway. The accent leaked telltale hints of a Pakistani heritage; pure Pashtun, scrubbed by years of Westernization.

The captain's bare knuckles grew white against the steering wheel, and his legs began to tremble.

The new man pointed his gun barrel. "Pay attention! If you want to be alive for Allah's sunrise tomorrow, you'll listen closely. Pull alongside the mini-submarine. Slowly! That's it, slowly . . . slowly. Now, reverse your engines. Quickly you fool, reverse your engines before you ram him."

The ferry retarded its forward motion and pulled alongside of the DSV. The old captain scrambled to throw rubber bumpers, tethered by fraying ropes, over the starboard side of his ferryboat—an effort to cushion it from bumping the tiny submarine.

Diesel smoke as thick as wire mesh wafted over the men just as the top hatch of the mini-sub opened. A bearded face emerged and the man threw a short length of rope to the ferry captain.

"Tenez la corde," said the man in the hatch with an accent thick with northern France. "Tenez la corde."

"In English, you fool," lashed the stowaway.

"*Hold the rope*," replied the man in the mini-sub's hatch. "Pull us tight against you. Yes, okay. Now, try to step over the railing and onto the top of the hull, but keep hold of the corde! The rope. Keep hold of the rope."

The mysterious Pakistani stowaway hopped off of the ferryboat and onto the sub's hull, regained his balance, then lumbered into the open hatch. He waved back to the ferry captain, signaling him to depart, and he and the other man disappeared into the bowels of the small craft.

The ferry captain watched as the hatch door on the tiny submarine closed and the locking mechanism spun three full revolutions. This had been the most stressful charter he had ever made. He looked back at the body of the dead American. What would he do with the body? He had been paid 2,400 rupees, roughly forty American dollars, for this charter. 2,400 rupees and a dead body. The money would please his wife, and go a long way in his fishing village. But at the moment, he felt lucky to be alive.

He eased the throttle forward and began a slow turn back toward the port at Nathia Gali Beach, around eight nautical miles to the west. He would be all too happy to leave the terrors of this night behind him. But the body. *What to do about the body?*

The wind alighted on his face and blew against his graying beard. He turned and looked behind him to see the green glow of the DSV mini-sub gurgle down just beneath the surface. Set against the sharp sparkling of moonlight on the water, it was a strangely beautiful sight. No one back home would believe his story, and he knew it. With the moonlight now to his back, he drew a deep breath and reached into the pocket of his long kameez shirt. From it he withdrew a crackled leather packet of tobacco, extracted a small draught, and placed it on a rolling paper. It was the first time in recent memory that he had seen his own hands shake.

His nerves were frayed, and a smoke on his journey home would calm him. The lit cigarette glowed orange against his face and cast shadows into the deep crevices of his leather-like skin. *The body. I must dump the body overboard. What else can I do?*

The captain turned to look at the corpse once more. "What's that smell?" he said. But then a singular thought struck him, and scared him to his core. *Petrol fuel*, he thought. The smell was petrol fuel. In the shimmering moonlight, the captain could see a small but steady torrent of gasoline streaming from a freshly cut fuel line.

Yet it wasn't his cigarette that triggered the explosion. It was a small detonator, tucked just behind the engine.

In the end, nothing was left of the old ferryboat that had bounced across these waters for the better part of forty years. This late at night, if anyone on shore saw the flames reflecting out in the bay, or even investigated the sinking of the vessel, they would conclude that a ruptured fuel line had caused the accident. But, for such a man as this, a poor ferryboat captain from Nathia Gali Beach, there would be no questions by authorities, no investigation into the cause, no answer to his wife's pleading as to what had happened to him, and most importantly, for Waseem Jarrah, the murderous stowaway and most wanted terrorist in the world, there would be no trail of witnesses.

17

WHERE I GO, YOU CANNOT FOLLOW

Inside the mini-submarine, DSV Nautile. *The Gulf of Oman. Heading north toward Karachi, Pakistan, away from the wreckage of the submarine* Simbirsk, *and from the rendezvous with the ferryboat. October 16, 3:22 a.m. local time (Oct. 15, 6:22 p.m. EST).*

After stepping off the ferryboat and climbing aboard the mini-sub, Waseem Jarrah surveyed the cramped inside of the vessel with its myriad of control panels, dials, and gages. He had never been inside such a craft. The interior LED lighting glowed forest green. The dim lighting was backdropped by the blackness of the night sea, visible through two small portholes, each with seven-inch-thick Lucite glass. He squinted in the dank space as his eyes adjusted to the green glow.

"It smells like a pig has been living in here," he said to the two sub operators. "You two are filthy. I detest filth."

The larger of the men looked at him with eyes glazed by exhaustion and stress. Without emotion, he said, "On est désolé, Monsieur Jarrah. I mean, we're sorry, Monsieur Jarrah." His sarcasm elicited no response. This time, the man's voice rose in volume. "We've been inside this tin can for eighteen hours! We're risking our lives here! You might be in charge of this mission, but that doesn't mean we have to take your shit." The three men sat, staring at each other. "The end is near," the larger man said. "We've almost completed our objective."

Jarrah's expression did not change. "It is odd to see you two, my French brothers in jihad. Do you not long to speak the tongue of our motherland? Has growing up in France polluted your blood?" Jarrah glared at the men, searching for their merits, but came up short. By way of distraction, he said, "Yes, I am too harsh with you. You have done amazing work, my friends. You have done something never before attempted. You have stolen a nuclear missile from a submarine sitting on the bottom of the ocean." He tucked a canvas bag behind himself. "Tell me about the mission. How long did it take you to find the submarine, the *Simbirsk*, after it had sunk to the bottom? Was it found where our partner Khalid said it was to be?"

"It was," replied the man. He had razor stubble on his face and his hair shone with sweat-induced grease. "It was within one thousand meters of his predicted location on the bottom. Khalid hadn't crossed the age of twenty when he died on board that sub. But he must have performed his role perfectly. I'll admit, I never trusted him. Les choses ne sont pas toujours comme elles semblent."

"Translation?"

"Things are not always as they seem. Anyway, after giving his life in jihad, the little prick is with Allah now, that's for sure."

Jarrah leaned forward and grabbed the neck of the sub operator's sweaty T-shirt and yanked.

"Well, you ungrateful little fuck. We get a man on the inside *of the Pakistani navy*. Do you have any idea what they would have done to him if they'd found out he was a saboteur? Khalid's actions were beyond brave. Allah was with him. That much is to be certain. He volunteered for this, and he is a hero. And here you sit, being critical of him. You lecherous pig."

"We all volunteered. Look at the two of us," he said as he placed a hand on the other sub driver. "We managed to convince the CIA, the beast itself, that we could be trusted with their mission to steal the nuclear weapon. Do you have any idea what that is like?"

"Don't hand me that shit," Jarrah cackled. "Being chosen by the CIA to pilot this mini-sub on their mission to steal the missile wasn't nearly as hard as you are stating. You were the most likely candidates right from the beginning, no? Don't deny it. The CIA tasks you two as contractors to pilot this DSV mini-submarine on a mission to steal a nuclear missile. The CIA needed a DSV mini-sub to pull off their little stunt, and *you* were its operators. Three months ago, the CIA hired you both, then purposely sabotaged the French research ship that the DSV was attached to. All of this in an effort to cover up their need to steal the DSV so they could use it to steal the warhead. After the French research ship sank in the Aegean Sea, everyone assumed the DSV was lost with it. The CIA got away with the crime and thus they now had the DSV they needed. Since you were already the DSV's operators, how hard was it for them to choose you for their ultimate mission? Hmm? Did you think they poured over a large pool of resumes and just happened to select the two of you? Bullshit. And another thing, did you ever consider what they were asking you to do in the first place?"

The two Frenchmen looked at him with blank faces.

Jarrah continued. "Let me enunciate this for you with crystal clarity, just so we don't have any miscommunications, what with the language barrier and all. What do you think they were planning to do with the missile they hired you to steal?"

"What was the CIA planning to do with the missile? I don't know . . . I, we, we didn't . . ."

"No shit, you didn't. They didn't tell you what they were planning to do with it, did they?"

The pair searched the floor for answers. "Well, no. They said it was none of our concern."

"I know *exactly* what they intended to do with it," Jarrah yelled. "But that is not the point."

"What is the point?"

"The point is this. After stealing a nuclear weapon from another country, did you think the CIA was going to just pay you and let you walk away?"

"You mean? They were going to . . . we aren't getting our payment? They were going to kill us?"

"I won't even justify that with an answer. Just consider yourselves lucky that I am one step ahead of them and have intercepted their plan."

"Monsieur Jarrah. I still don't understand. We have always

been loyal to Allah and to you. That is why we worked as double agents against the CIA. But, how did you know the CIA was going to attempt to steal a nuclear missile from another country?"

"That information is none of your concern," Jarrah yelled as he smiled through a toothy grin. "But since you two have been so brave and have fooled the CIA into thinking you were loyal to them, I will tell you this much. Let's just say that I had a man inside the CIA, and leave it at that."

"I am still confused. You had a man inside the CIA? Perhaps, as you say, it was easy for *us* to be hired as CIA contractors, but how did you get a man on the inside of the beast?"

"It took years. But some things are worth waiting for. This is not the result of short-term thinking. My plan of getting a man inside the CIA has been in the works for more years than you would believe."

"So your man on the inside found out about the CIA plot to steal a missile from another country, and you intercepted the plot? It is brilliant. Now you have a nuclear weapon. But what was the CIA's master plan? If they intended us to steal the weapon for their own use, what did they intend to do with it?"

Jarrah stared out into the bleak darkness, and his voice went monotone. "Remove a thorn from their side." His words matched the deadness in his eyes.

"Remove a thorn?" the sub driver said. "What thorn?"

"North Korea," Jarrah said. "And make it look like someone else did it."

"You mean they intended to detonate the weapon inside of North Korea? How did they get authorization to do such a thing?"

"You might be surprised to what lengths the United States will go to carry out its agenda."

The larger man did not realize he had been wringing his hands. "Je suis désolé . . . I mean, I'm sorry. Sorry for what I said about Khalid. He was a hero for giving his life to sabotage the submarine *Simbirsk* so we could steal this weapon."

"You are sorry now that he's dead?" Waseem Jarrah said. "Now that he gave his life for Allah? Is that what you mean? And what do you think of his loyalty now?"

The man stared out the porthole on the other side. "I guess I was wrong."

"Damn right you were wrong. But, don't get all misty-eyed about his demise just yet. He's not as dead as you might imagine."

"What are you talking about? He would *have* to be dead. He was on board the *Simbirsk* when it went down. He was the one that sabotaged it. He would have been killed in the explosion. And even if he wasn't killed in the actual explosion, the hull was compromised. We were just there. We saw the damage to it. Nobody on board that sub could have survived. . ." The words trailed off into the blackness outside the submerged craft. "Wait. He wasn't on the *Simbirsk* when it went down?"

"No."

"But how did he get off before—"

Jarrah interrupted. "He boarded yesterday morning, the morning of its deployment from Jinnah Naval base in Pakistan. His job in the Pakistani navy was that of a torpedoman's mate. Before the sub left port, he set plastic explosives just behind the transducer of one of the torpedoes in the storage racks, right on the underside of the warhead. After that, he set the timer and got the hell out of there."

The larger man's eyes darted back and forth—each termination of eye movement signaling another question.

Jarrah held up his hand. "He was prepared to give his life for Allah then, and he is still prepared now. But I have other work for him. I ordered him to get off of the sub before it sailed."

The larger man started to speak but was again cut off.

"I know what you're thinking," Jarrah said, "but we knew exactly what route that sub was going to take. They were scheduled to make another training run. They run the same pattern every time. We knew where the sub would be at exactly what time. We also knew Khalid had unrestricted access to the torpedo room, and that he would do an unbelievable job camouflaging the C-4 against the torpedo's underside. Other crew members would not have seen it. Khalid is a consummate professional, in case you hadn't noticed. Once the detonator was in place, it was inevitable. The explosive would detonate at just the right time. The torpedo it was attached to would then detonate, and that would cause a cascade of explosions from the other torpedoes. The vessel didn't stand a chance."

The larger man looked down.

"Khalid is alive? But if Khalid infiltrated the Pakistani navy, how, how did he get out of his duty on board the submarine right before it sailed?"

"We went old school," Jarrah said. "He found a bottle of syrup of ipecac in a local pharmacy in Karachi. They don't even make it anymore. But you drink that crap and it'll make you vomit in a 'projectile' sort of way. Khalid faked an appendicitis is what he did. They sent him to the base hospital before the sub threw off its ropes and left port. The doctors in the hospital later diagnosed him with gastroenteritis."

"So what changed your mind? You told us that Khalid would be a martyr. He would go down with the submarine *Simbirsk*. Why did you order him to get off? You're not getting sentimental on us, are you, Jarrah?"

"Sentimental?" Jarrah glared at the two sub operators much in the way a bull views a matador. "What is that supposed to mean?" he said as spit flew from his mouth. "Khalid is the only one with operational experience in the mountains of Pakistan, and I have a very important job for him later. Besides, I told you what I wanted to tell you! I told you what I wanted you to know!"

"Calm down. We're all under stress here, remember?" the Frenchman said. "We have a stolen nuclear weapon strapped right under our balls. It hangs from the bottom of this tiny vessel as we speak. Remember that? Just calm down. We'll get the job done, all right? This little DSV mini-sub may not have much power, but she'll have enough to get this cargo to port." An awkward silence cut the air. "I was wrong about Khalid. I trust him."

"All right," Jarrah said. "Now, tell me about what happened when you were stealing the missile. Once you found the submarine on the ocean bottom, was it difficult to extract the missile from the missile bay?"

"Was it difficult? In France we would say it was *baise-moi le côté*. It was 'fuck-me-sideways difficult.'" Sweat bubbled on the man's forehead and hung there, then rolled into his razor stubble.

Jarrah remained stoic. The attempt to lighten the mood had gone nowhere.

The man continued. "It took much longer than we expected to cut open the hatch of each missile tube on the submarine. The acetylene torch on this DSV is not as heavy as was needed. And, our intel was wrong about which silo the missile would be found. We had to cut into *four* tubes before we found the one weapon they had aboard."

Dismissing the problems as though they were skipped steps in a cake recipe, Jarrah's eyes gleamed. "And how much difficulty did you have lifting the missile out of the tube?" he said like a child waiting to open birthday presents.

Jarrah's rapid mood swings caused one word to pop into the larger man's mind, *schizophrenia*.

"How much difficulty? Well, let's see. We're in a miniature submarine that has a gross weight of forty-nine thousand kilograms, and we're trying to lift a seventeen-meter-tall missile that weighs seventy-one thousand kilograms. Hmm, difficulty? Merde. No shit! And yes, I'm rubbing your face in it. I told you the balloon apparatus you had devised wasn't going to be strong enough to lift the missile out of the tube."

Jarrah glared.

"But, just so you know, we didn't disobey your direct orders. We did attach the large deployable balloon to the missile anyway. As we inflated the balloon with pressurized air from our tanks, the balloon pulled toward the surface with great might against the weight of the missile. I'll grant you that. But, the combined efforts of the balloon and the mechanical arm on this DSV weren't enough to lift the weapon out of the missile bay."

Jarrah looked at the ground with pursed lips as though scolding a child who forgot their homework. "So you couldn't lift the missile up. You used the crane on board the deck of the Pakistani research ship *Padma*, to lift it out, didn't you? Didn't you?" he yelled.

The man backpedaled. "Well, it was either have the research vessel pull the weapon out, or leave it in the silo. How would that have sat with you? I bet you wouldn't have exactly greeted us with the love of Allah had we decided to leave the missile there, would you?"

Jarrah began to stand, but stopped just as quickly; the ceiling loomed just inches over his head.

"Don't be a smart-ass." It was a veiled threat. "So now you're telling me we've got a crew full of sailors on the *Padma* that know they just pulled a missile out of a nuclear submarine?"

"Monsieur Jarrah, no. Not even the captain of the *Padma* knows what he really did. Remember, his ship is floating on the surface and we are submerged, seventy-six meters below him. He had no idea what we were actually doing on the bottom. He believes that we were researching the tectonic plate that runs through the region, and that our DSV became stuck in the fissure and needed to be pulled free. The captain lowered the cable to us. He thinks he pulled our mini-sub free of the bottom. But, I also offered him a little cash bonus to stay quiet."

"What makes you think he will?"

"I told him we had another job for him, a very lucrative one. To stay in our good graces, he'll keep his mouth shut. And as far as his crew goes, they'll stay quiet as well. Most of them are too poor to risk losing a job like that. At any rate, we then spent the next hour using the acetylene torch to cut the missile in half so that it would be light enough for the DSV to carry."

"So," Jarrah said, "what is it you're *not* telling me?"

The man again glanced out the porthole, hoping to see a mermaid, or perhaps a giant squid—anything that might distract Jarrah from losing control over his volatile temper. "Even though it's been cut in half, the missile is very heavy against this tiny craft. We had used much of our air capacity trying to inflate the balloon mechanism. We had to recharge our air supply before it was exhausted, so we surfaced. It . . . it was daylight." The statement hung in space for a moment and the man braced for an explosion. "I'm sorry, but we've been very afraid the weight of the missile would pull us down to the bottom, and we'd run out of air."

Jarrah studied the man out the corner of his eye, the way a father might glare at a daughter who he'd caught necking with a boyfriend.

"You surfaced? During *daylight*?"

"We had no choice!" the man stammered. He looked back at Jarrah with the eyes of a servant. "We not only needed air to breathe, we needed to overcharge the ballast tanks to keep the DSV from sinking against all the weight of the missile." The man paused, waiting for Jarrah to respond. But when nothing came, he said, "There is one other thing."

Jarrah stared ahead as a vein on his right temple began twitching.

"We are concerned that the mechanical arm currently holding the missile beneath us is not strong enough. It was never intended to hold something this heavy. It may snap off, and the missile would sink to the bottom."

"Yes," Jarrah said, speaking almost though the slits of his eyes. "It may break. You know, it would be a shame if it broke and the missile sank, wouldn't it? I'd hate to see you two swim to the bottom to retrieve it. Just to get you down there, I understand we'd have to weigh you down quite a bit. Hmm, that would be a pity."

The two sub operators looked at each other. The smaller man swallowed and dabbed a cloth at his brow.

"How long before we reach the Pakistan Naval Academy jetty?" Jarrah said, his voice in sudden upbeat tempo.

"We're rounding into Karachi Harbor now. We're almost in the Baba Channel. As slowly as we are moving, it will be about two hours before we can make it to the jetty."

"Then speed up, you fools. The jetty at the Naval Academy is only two miles from the inlet of Baba. We've got to be there well before sunrise so the missile can be offloaded onto the truck under cover of night."

The larger man's cheek betrayed a slight tremble. "Monsieur Jarrah, we *are* at full speed. The tiny engine was not built to handle such a load. And, traveling submerged like this is slower. We would move faster on the surface."

"Then surface. It is dark outside. Our only concern now is

being seen and that is not likely in the dark. Just keep a watch on the radar for surface ships. I am not concerned about satellites spotting us at night. They can't see the missile beneath us and would never suspect a tiny craft such as this anyway."

The man's nerves frayed after having just witnessed another of Jarrah's sudden mood swings.

"Surface, surface," the larger man whispered. His voice sounded like the breath of a ghost.

The mini-sub surfaced, and crept its way north through warm night waters around the tip of Karachi harbor's breakwater, and penetrated the mouth of the narrow Baba Channel. The two protruding land masses that made up the peninsula formed a sort of thumb and forefinger that appeared to reach out into the Arabian Sea, lurching at vessels as if to gobble them up. If viewed from above, the peninsula looked like the mouth of a hidden dragon—open, welcoming, yet ominous.

Off the port side, the peninsula's coastline was lined with military buildings that outlined the Qasim Fort against the moonlit horizon. Qasim was surrounded by large gun emplacements designed to defend the harbor from any naval attack, and stood in stark contrast to the beauty of the shimmering waters. The beaches along the fort were skinned in heavy rocks, placed there to prevent erosion and to thwart enemy fast-attack boats from docking unencumbered. Light waves broke against the rocks, then bubbled into a froth before easing back into the bay.

"It is not far now, Monsieur Jarrah."

Jarrah arched his back against the cramped, claustrophobic space.

"Open the hatch, the air in here is stifling. Besides, we can't see anything from inside here. We'll miss the landing point."

The two operators glanced at each other. One nodded toward the GPS monitor that pinpointed their exact position and destination. Neither thought it prudent to inform Jarrah that they could easily navigate to the rally point using the sub's onboard technology.

Once the hatch was opened, Jarrah stood and stretched his

legs. Only his head was visible outside of the craft as it motored closer toward the rally point, an inlet carved into the land that was used for the docking and repairing large ships.

Jarrah scanned the coastline with binoculars, searching for the telltale outline of the only ship-to-shore crane that existed on this stretch of inlet. The crane was owned by the Pakistan Naval Academy. It stood forty meters in height, and would be easily distinguishable on a night as clear as this. About thirty minutes later, the crane came into view.

"I see it," Jarrah said. "About three hundred meters off the port quarter. Ease your way in. The water is getting shallow. We don't want to hit the bottom with this missile dangling beneath us."

"Are you sure no one will be guarding the dock?" questioned the larger man. "After all, it's owned by the Pakistan Naval Academy."

"We have monitored the pier for weeks," Jarrah said. "Nothing moves at this time of night. They will not even notice in the morning that their crane has been used."

The sub crawled forward and entered the wide mouth of the berthing channel at a speed low enough to not be heard.

On the shore, Jarrah saw a muted, red flashlight blink three times.

"There! That's the signal. I see him. Khalid is in place." He checked his watch. "Excellent, we have an hour of full darkness left. Come closer to the dock's edge, right next to the crane, then come to a stop. Now, check your sounding. What's the depth here?"

"Twelve meters."

Jarrah pulled the heavy port hatch down, then fought against its weight, closing the hatch tight, yet without a sound. He spun the locking mechanism to seal it.

"All right, we'll submerge here next to the dock and lower the missile to the floor below us. Do it very, very slowly. I don't want the missile so much as scratched when you set it on the bottom."

With painstaking stillness, the men descended to within five meters of the bottom. Then, the smaller man operated the remote control mechanical arm, and lowered the remaining half of the R-39 missile to the bottom with the softness of a mother laying her sleeping baby into its crib. Once the missile felt stable, he released the grip from the mechanical arm. The missile settled into a comfortable position, spewing silt in all directions.

"Now, surface against the dock. I'm getting off this submersible death trap. You two, are not."

"But," the man said, "the operational plan says we all get off here."

"Well if you jackasses had been able to get here an hour ago, as planned, we'd have time to load the DSV mini-sub onto the flatbed alongside the missile. As it is, we are out of time."

"So what are we supposed to do? Just drive this thing up the beach, and pull off at the Hooters in Karachi?"

The mini-sub breached the surface. As Jarrah opened the hatch, the driver maneuvered it against rubber truck tires that were strapped to the pier.

Jarrah stepped out and turned back to the sub crew. "Hooters? You Frenchmen hate Hooters, everyone knows this. Your next rally point is at the Kiamari main pier, just across the bay. There, you'll find your friends on the familiar Pakistani research vessel, the *Padma*, who apparently think they pulled you off the bottom of the ocean. Return the DSV to her split-stern docking bay. Oh, and when you get there, you'll find a nice little surprise waiting there for you. You have served Allah well. I think you'll like it. Now get out of here before I change my mind."

The two men smiled at one another.

"The *Padma* will have instructions for us? Wait, what about your bag? You've left it here under your seat."

"Oh no, my friends. The contents of the bag aren't for me. They are for you. Part of the gift I mentioned. But don't open it until you're aboard the *Padma*. It is but a small part of the perks. Stay submerged for your trip across the bay. It will be daylight soon. Don't be seen by anyone."

The port hatch closed, and the small craft turned to head out the mouth of the shipping bay and across the channel. Jarrah's eyes never left the vessel.

Just as it submerged, in his own cold way, he whispered, "Where I am going, you cannot follow."

With that, he turned to direct Khalid in retrieving the missile off the bottom and placing it on a flatbed truck. He glanced at the sky. "Time is short, we must hurry, Khalid."

18

WHAT WAS BEGUN

Mini-submarine DSV Nautile. *Karachi Harbor, the Baba Channel. October 16, 4:38 a.m. local time (October 15, 7:38 p.m. EST).*

"I don't care what you say," the smaller man said as they guided the DSV mini-sub across the harbor. "I'm scared. That son of a bitch scares the hell out of me. I'm telling you, *he's unstable.* I've told you that before. He's like a powder keg."

"You're being paranoid," the larger man said. "Once we get over to the *Padma*, you'll see. Jarrah may be dangerous, but you heard him. He said we had served Allah well. He is very generous with those loyal to him. He's probably organized a feast for us. My bet is, Jarrah's also sent a few of the ladies for us and the crew. Remember, the crew thinks they were instrumental in rescuing us from the bottom. The reward will make perfect sense to them. And don't forget, he also left that bag for us."

"I . . . I don't know," the smaller man said, again dabbing a cloth against his forehead. "Something is wrong."

"Quel est votre problème?"

"Doesn't it bother you what we've just done?" the man stuttered. "I don't know why I never thought this through. Look, I get the fact that we've been chosen by both the CIA and by Jarrah for this mission. And the fact that we volunteered for it.

Pulling off this mission should be very lucrative for us, but haven't you bothered to at least ask the question?"

The larger man shook his head. "All right, I'll bite. What question? And, make your depth sixty feet, we've got plenty of water below us in the middle of the channel here."

"This was originally supposed to be a CIA operation. We've stolen the weapon from them, and given it to Jarrah. What is *he* going to do with it? And once he does whatever that is, don't you think they're going to come looking for us?" The further the thought played forward in the man's head, the faster his voice became. "We'll be considered as associates with Waseem Jarrah, the most wanted terrorist in the world. We'll be blamed! We're going to have to run for the rest of our lives!"

"Calm down. You're becoming irrational. If you're going to ask questions like that, you're in the wrong business."

The smaller man began to breathe faster.

"Calm down," the larger man pleaded.

But the smaller man's chest heaved up and down.

"I . . . I can't breathe."

"Calm down. No one is ever going to know we were involved. Are you out of your mind? Who would tell them? As far as the CIA will know, we were intercepted by Jarrah. They wouldn't know we were working with him. Even if Jarrah were caught, he would never tell. It would be an act of madness on his part. Here, breathe into this paper bag. Close your eyes. That's it, that's it. There's nothing to be afraid of."

"Did you say *an act of madness* . . . like that of a crazy person? The CIA operative that Jarrah murdered on the ferryboat was probably crazy. And I told you, that son of a bitch Jarrah *is* crazy. He's fucking unstable! And you know he would *have* to want the weapon for a reason—to detonate it. And if Jarrah is going to detonate it, don't you think he'd want to erase his own tracks?"

The smaller man spun around behind him and lunged for the canvas bag left for them by Jarrah.

"What are you doing?" the larger man said. "Let it be. He wanted that to be a surprise for us upon our entry into the *Padma*."

The little man's wiry hands ripped into the pack. When his

eyes landed on the contents, they bulged. *"Surfacesurfacesurface!"* he screamed.

But it was too late. Enclosed in the pack was a perfect, four-by-four-inch square of waxlike plastic with a paper label that read "SEMTEX-H," all neatly affixed to a digital timer. The plastic explosive detonated in a cacophony that shredded the interior of the DSV, splaying metal, speckled with blood and flesh, in all directions. Both men were killed instantly, and the starboard porthole breached, unleashing a torrent of salt water that flooded in. The water choked and sputtered into the craft as air belched out. The sea water mixed into a salty, blood-laden stew. The nose of the tiny submarine pitched down and headed into the watery darkness below.

Jetty at the Pakistan Naval Academy. 4:50 a.m. local time.

"Hover the crane's arm over the missile," Waseem Jarrah said to his servant, Khalid. "Now, lower the magnet into the water. Slowly, slowly, Khalid! Do not activate the magnet until we have touched the surface of the missile. It is very fragile. We must be careful. Slowly, slowly . . ."

"I think we're on it!" the nineteen-year-old said. His voice was excited, like that of a small boy readying to open presents on the morning of Eid al-Fitr, the celebration ending the month of Ramadan fasting.

Midway across the bay, a large plume of air bubbles ruptured the surface of the water; its froth resembling the breathing of a red dragon just under the surface.

Khalid startled at the sound.

The plume of air and froth was gone as fast as it had appeared. There was no sound other than that of the air bubbles piercing the water; no boom, there was nothing.

"What . . . what was that?" Khalid exclaimed in a trance.

"It is done then," Jarrah said, paying the anomaly no further attention. "If you are sure you are on the missile, then activate the magnet."

"But . . . what was that?"

Jarrah barked, "Shut up!" but stopped himself, remembering that Khalid was a faithful servant whose purposes were critical to the rest of the mission. He leveled cold eyes at Khalid. "You knew it had to be done. What we are doing, it is like a gift from Allah. Our mission cannot fail. We can have no witnesses. You know this." Jarrah paused to let the nineteen-year-old absorb the fact that the DSV mini-sub, and those aboard, were gone. "What your older brother, Shakey, began in Kentucky, we must finish."

Khalid stared at the churning water.

"But, we, we . . . the Frenchmen have been training with us . . ."

Jarrah's eyes narrowed, and when Khalid saw the look of cold steel peering back at him, he recoiled. At last, he nodded in assent.

"Now, activate the magnet. We must get this missile off the bottom. The night's darkness will soon lose its battle with the light. No one can find us. Hurry."

As the enormous crane engine reversed, a chunking clank-sound rang out in the night as the missile's enormous weight locked the cable against the overhanging pulley. The crane's motor labored at first, then began a steady pull against the missile.

"My God," Khalid said. "The crane struggles. This missile is cut in half, yet the crane is at its maximum capacity."

"Yes." The last syllable stretched out like the hiss of a snake. "Without the rocket portion, the remaining upper half of the missile still weighs over forty thousand kilograms."

His eyes grew wide as he held both hands in the air.

"When it surfaces, you will see." His voice escalated in excitement. "It should still be close to twenty-five feet long." As it cleared the surface of the water, Jarrah beamed. "Look at it! It is magnificent. There! There you see the very *will* of Allah."

His eyes gleamed as if basking in the glow of discovered gold.

"Khalid, you and I have trained so hard for this. All eyes are upon us. We cannot fail."

The crane labored to swing the warhead onto the flatbed of the waiting tractor-trailer.

Jarrah knelt down, first on one knee, then on the other. The quiet sounds of his emotions welled forth, but were muffled as sea water poured from the missile onto the dock, unleashing a smell of salt, motor oil, dead mackerel, and burnt electrical wiring.

"I have waited so long for this," Jarrah whispered.

19

A SLURRY, BLACK AND THICK

Pakistan Naval Academy, coastal Pakistan. October 16, 5:21 a.m. local time (October 15, 8:21 p.m. EST).

Khalid's arms stretched wide to grip the steering wheel of the eighteen-wheel flatbed truck. His small frame looked almost childlike against the sheer width of the wheel. The moon had set, and light was just beginning to undulate against the horizon, causing the stars to lose their previous luster. The truck lurched forward, struggling as though tethered to the dock with steel cables. Finally, it pulled away and headed south toward the perimeter fence of the Pakistan Naval Academy. Khalid glanced out his window and saw the silhouette of a mosque just across the bay. It sat on the water, flanked on one side by an oil pier, and the other, a desolate span of undeveloped land.

Khalid disciplined himself to avoid distraction. He knew how much danger they were in. He also knew his critical moment in the service of Allah was not far off—he centered his thoughts.

He had committed to memory multiple escape routes from the military port region. He'd even rehearsed them on repeated occasions, always separating his training runs by several weeks to avoid suspicion. The primary escape route ran along the fence line of the military academy. The property was surrounded by twelve-foot cement walls topped with spun concertina wire. The wire's razor-sharpened edges gleamed against the headlights of the tractor-trailer as Khalid turned the huge wheel two full revolutions to the right and hugged the wall for a quarter mile, never shifting above third gear.

At Manora Drive, the truck ambled past the local public school, and headed toward the most dangerous part of the voyage—a thin strip of peninsula only two hundred yards wide that was their only escape route. It was a two-lane beach roadway. On one side stood small buildings that dotted the beach, on the other, a thick mangrove swamp that ran for miles.

From the passenger seat, Waseem Jarrah leaned back into a full recline, the elevation of his head just below that of the windshield. Draped across his lap was an AK-47 assault rifle. Khalid glanced at the weapon and noticed the safety catch flipped in the off position, and Jarrah's finger resting on the trigger guard.

"We must be cautious now," Jarrah said, speaking softly to avoid drawing attention. "Keep your speed low. We do not want to be stopped for excessive speed. If we're stopped on this godforsaken peninsula, there will be no escape. We are deep inside the Pakistani military stronghold. Getting past the military academy and the Himalaya Naval base is just the beginning. We can make no mistakes."

"Yes, Waseem," the apprentice said. He let his wavy, finger-long hair run free against the breeze of the truck's open window.

As the peninsula widened, the truck ambled past single-family homes lining the beach to the left. Most were blockish, and uninspired in design; framed in one ninety-degree angle after another. Some houses were surrounded by compound-style walls that made them look like tiny fortresses, while others sat unencumbered—open to the ravages of both man and nature.

"It is just ahead," Jarrah said. "Up there, as the road forks, stay to the right. We've got to get out of this area." He tightened his grip on the rifle.

The fork in the road was bordered by a small but densely populated fishing village known as Kakapir. Its people, a mix of Hindus and Sikhs, lived in tattered shanties, one leaning against the next. The fork in the peninsula roadway was the anchor for a community that was surrounded on all three sides by water. Ocean on one and mangrove on the others.

During times of heavy storms, the flimsy structures in the low-lying coastal area didn't stand a chance. However, the further one traveled up the Kakapir Road, the more solid the structures became. People living on this side were further away from the ocean, and buffered by mangroves and a tall berm known as Sandspit Beach. Even though the berm ran the length of the beach, fishermen could still access waterways that twisted their way through the mangroves to get out to sea.

"We still have to cross the bridge to Karachi, Waseem."

Waseem Jarrah squinted into the distance at the razor-thin bridge. If anyone had seen them at the pier loading the huge missile and had notified authorities, the bridge could be used as the ultimate choke point—they would be trapped.

"You have the RPG behind the seat?" Jarrah asked.

Khalid noticed tiny beads of sweat push their way through Jarrah's brow.

"Yes, Waseem. The rocket is behind you."

The pancake-flat bridge spanned a third of a mile, pushing straight across, twenty feet above the jostling mangrove waters. Reeds and cattails below swayed in the wind, which seemed to gust forth in sudden violence, then die down with no further voice.

Jarrah gazed to the far end of the bridge, scanning for any sign of trouble. But the harder he squinted, the more his mind's eye overtook his actual sight. He was at once propelled into the washy-gray visions of his own recurring nightmare. For the past several months, as the mission had drawn near, the nightmare had grated the deeper recesses of his brain, and he struggled against its magnetism.

The electric impulses rattling through his nerves were only exceeded by the focus of his one desire, to complete this mission and rain hellfire against the beast. His eyes squinted as he continued scanning the far distance of the bridge in an attempt to actively will his enemies into vapor.

He'd spent months planning each and every detail of the operation, and the fear of being caught on this bridge frightened him until it scratched his psyche and tore a path into his dreams. As the truck's front tires rumbled over the entrance to the long bridge, they entered the point at which pavement melds into cement—the gauntlet had been entered. There was nothing left to do; the truck was well past the point of no return.

Jarrah slipped deeper into his fog. The truck's wheels hummed. A salt-encrusted gust of sea air made a sudden and uninvited entrance through the open window, ruffling his thick black hair and parting his beard. The gust surged again, and leaned its shoulder into the truck the way a Sheltie dog herds cattle. Reeds in the mangrove bent horizontal, and mist, scraped from the surface of the marsh, sprayed across the tips of the grasses, buffeting the truck and taunting it. Jarrah's eyes grew wider and his chest heaved up and down. He continued his fixated stare at the furthest point of the bridge—a place where the horizontal lines of the road and bridge began at eye level, then flung themselves forward into eternity, converging until they melted into a single pinpoint.

Jarrah's eyes began bulging as the muscles in his face tightened. The wheels hummed louder, the gulls called out in ever-increasing volume, and the salt air pelted his face, mocking him. The speed of the truck seemed to increase, then increase again, and again. The pinpoint of the far edge of the bridge grew larger, and darker. And as they rolled closer, the darkness grew and seemed to form into the shape of a giant mouth. The humming of the wheels and screaming of the gulls grew louder and louder, until Jarrah raised his hands and crushed them against his ears. His grip on reality abated like rats fleeing a burning ship. The nightmare leapt from his subconscious mind and onto his conscious thought-stream.

He began screaming against the noise, all the time staring at the darkening mouth that grew larger and larger in his vision. Khalid reached for him, yelling something and pulling at him with one hand, while steering the truck with the other. Jarrah screamed against the vision before him. It was his worst nightmare—to get this close only to be captured.

The giant black mouth in his vision opened wider, beckoning his unavoidable entrance. The mouth blocked his only path, his path to absolution, and his chest struggled to vacuum up enough oxygen. To be in possession of this weapon, the very devil incarnate, only to be smitten by the enemy. That enemy, that awful enemy. Absolution had driven his life, and he would tear his soul in order to smite it.

Khalid yelled at Jarrah, trying to snap him from his fog. But it wasn't until Jarrah reached behind the seat and put his hands onto the rocket-propelled grenade, that Khalid slammed on the brakes. The truck swerved to the side and smoke poured from the tires.

"Waseem! Waseem!" he yelled, pulling against the man's arms. "Waseem!"

Finally, Jarrah peeled his eyes from the RPG and looked at Khalid, the lunatic inside barely recognizing his compatriot. Moments later his eyes retreated into a vassal-like state. It was like witnessing a rabid dog morph into a newborn fawn.

Khalid looked at Jarrah and tried to catch his own breath. After a few minutes of calming down, he shifted the truck into first gear, and let pressure off the clutch. The mission was still on track; they had not been discovered. Yet a chink in the armor of Waseem Jarrah's sanity cracked, and a slurry, as black and thick as the deepest depths of human depravity, leaked out.

The truck lurched forward, and for the first time, Khalid was frightened.

20

THE SCARRING OF METAL

NSA Headquarters. October 16, 8:21 a.m. EST.

Shock waves rattled the intelligence community as similar conversations about the incident with the submarine USS *Colorado* unfolded in two places. One, in the White House briefing room, where the president himself was said to be intensely concerned; the other in the Joint Operations Readiness Center located inside the headquarters of the National Security Agency in Maryland. There, top officials from the NSA, CIA, FBI, and military intelligence met early each morning to assemble daily briefings to be given to the president.

Today's meeting disturbed even Uncle Bill Tarleton, who under normal circumstances displayed little emotion. After the meeting broke, Bill walked into his command center and gathered his troops.

"All right, everyone, listen up. We're back into a level-five situation. So, I've got good news and I've got bad news."

Knuckles, Cade Williams, and the rest of Bill's team stood at their work stations. Cade was still considered the new guy, and had never seen what happens inside the NSA when things heat up.

He leaned to Knuckles. "Hey Knuckles, what's a level five?"

"You don't want to know," came the whispered reply. "The last time we had a level five, you ended up in the middle of a firefight inside the Thoughtstorm building, and Jana Baker ended up killing Shakey Kunde just before he could blow up a perfectly good bluegrass festival. I never thought anyone would make it out of that festival alive."

"I was afraid you were going to say something like that."

Uncle Bill continued. "Let's start with the bad news. Two days ago, at around 1 a.m. Indian Standard Time, one of our Virginia-class attack subs, the USS *Colorado*, on maneuvers in the Persian Gulf, stumbled across a downed ballistic-missile submarine. Now, there are several things that are downright screwed up about this situation. First of all, we don't yet know why the sub went down. But far more disturbing, the sub was a Russian-built boomer class."

"Sir?" Knuckles interrupted, "what's disturbing about the fact that it happened to be a Russian boomer? Don't those subs move in and around the Middle East?"

"Sure they do. But normally, a submarine stops its sea patrols after it's been scrapped."

"I'm not sure what you mean, sir," Knuckles said.

"The Russian-built sub that sank has been identified as a Delta IV, the *Simbirsk*. NATO records indicate that the *Simbursk* was decommissioned in 1996, and supposedly scrapped back in 2008. So, it sounds like the Russians told NATO they cut her into pieces, but instead turned around and sold her on the black market."

"Assholes," muttered Cade.

"Thank you, Cade," Bill said. "Anyway, it would appear that the *Simbirsk* was sold illegally to the Pakistani navy, who yesterday morning was none-too-excited to find that she'd been sunk."

"Yeah, I guess not," Cade said.

"At any rate, our submarine, the USS *Colorado*, came upon the downed Russian sub just after it went to the bottom. The propellers were still turning, except that the *Simbirsk* was on the ocean floor. While the Colorado moved in to see if they could detect the presence of survivors, a separate Pakistani fast-attack boat fired a torpedo at them, apparently thinking the *Colorado* had attacked the *Simbirsk* in the first place."

"Jesus Christ," Cade said.

"Yeah, that's what she said," jibbed Knuckles.

"Knock it off you two," Bill said. "The USS *Colorado* has a compliment of one hundred and thirty-four men, not to mention it's a multibillion-dollar piece of equipment. We nearly lost all of it. Fortunately, our sub driver outsmarted the Pakistanis. I won't get into the details, but he evaded the Pakistani torpedo in such a way that it ended up hitting the sub that fired it. But, in the process, the *Colorado* and the Pakistani sub bumped." Several analysts shook their heads as concern permeated the group of men and women. "I know, I know. Scary stuff. The *Colorado* was damaged. It wasn't good, but she can be repaired. At any rate, the Pakistani government is furious. From their point of view, the United States has deliberately sunk the *Simbirsk*, and their other attack sub. It's bullshit, of course, but they are livid. They're threatening all US vessels in the region, both military and civilian. It's as close to war as it gets." Uncle Bill paused for effect, then looked at his watch. "Four minutes ago, the President moved us to DEFCON three."

Several people in the room shifted positions, others covered their mouths.

"Sir?" Knuckles said.

"What is it, son?"

"You said there was good news?"

"Yeah, here's the good news. We get to stay in this room around the clock until we figure this thing out."

Knuckles replied, "Oh, you're right then. That is good news," as he slumped into his chair.

"I knew you'd like it. We've got some data coming in within the next ten minutes. Knuckles, teach Cade here what to do with it. The rest of you, I want to know everything going on in that region of the world, particularly at the mouth of the Persian Gulf. I want to see shipping traffic, military activity—that means anyone's military activity—civilian fishing vessels, cruise ships— if there's such a thing in the Middle East—mermaids, charter boats, the SS *Minnow*, Gilligan's Island stuff, whatever. If it's on the surface of the water or submerged, I want to know about it."

"Uncle Bill?" Knuckles said, "What's the data that we've got coming in?"

"The skipper on the *Colorado* was able to pull a long string of ultrasound images of the downed Russian-built sub right before he was fired upon. We also have sonar data from the USS *Colorado* coming in. It will show us anything happening up to and including the event. We'll want to use it to investigate any sonar contacts they were tracking in the area around the time of the incident."

Fifteen minutes later, the data started pouring in.

A man said from across the room, "All right, Knuckles, your data package is in. It's coming up now. Looks like a massive video file."

"That's affirmative. Cade, let's access this from over in the war room, we'll have a bigger screen to analyze the video with."

"So we're about to look at video footage taken of the downed Russian sub?" Cade said.

"Right, but remember, the sub may have been Russian-built, but it looks like they sold her to the Pakistanis."

"Got it."

Once the pair put the ultrasound video on the screen, the submarine disaster scene began to unfold. The video quality was highly detailed, albeit a bit greenish in hue.

"Hey, Knuckles, let's pull up some schematics on this sub so we'll have a better idea of what we're looking at. What's its name again?"

"The *Simbirsk*, a Delta IV class. Yeah, go ahead and see what we can access. Since she's an older boomer we should have a lot of data on her."

Cade tapped away on a laptop.

"Okay, here she is. The *Simbirsk*. A Soviet SSBN. Ah, Knuckles, that means ship submersible ballistic nuclear, or nuclear ballistic missile submarine. She's designed to carry nuclear warheads and launch them at us."

Knuckles looked over at Cade.

"No shit, nimbleweed. As if I don't already know what SSBN stands for. I bet you don't know what KGB stands for, do you? What else does it say?"

"They call it an Akula class, but we call it a Typhoon.

Personally I think our name for it is cooler."

"Well, the word akula means shark, so don't get cocky. That sounds pretty cool too."

"You speak Russki? Geez, you're full of . . . well, full of something. Let's see, it says she was built in the Sevmash shipyard in Severodvinsk. Where's that?"

Knuckles shook his head in disapproval. "You never studied. It's on the northwestern tip of Mother Russia, on the Barents Sea. It's a freezing-ass place. But, it's south of the ice pack for some of the year."

"Now how the hell do you know that?"

Knuckles continued staring at the video while Cade read further. "First entered service in 1984. It was part of the Northern Fleet . . . wow, look at this. It had a collision with the HMS *Splendid* in 1986. That must have sucked."

"HMS stands for Her Majesty's Ship, by the way," Knuckles said.

"Yeah, I knew that one. Your mother never gave you any toys when you were a child, did she? Okay, she was taken out of service in 1997 so her nuclear reactor could be recharged. Wow, that must have been a fun job. But looks like they never put her back in service. Hmm, in 2000 they put her up for demolition, but they don't record the demolition until seven years later. Huh, guess that whole recharging-the-reactor thing can be a pain. I guess they gave up and decided to scrap her."

"How about her size, number of crew, missiles she could hold?"

"Yeah, yeah," Cade said. "I've got your size right here. She can hold one hundred and fifty crew members. Jesus, that'd be a lot of food to haul around. Says her submerged displacement is forty-eight thousand tons. That sounds like a lot. Six torpedo tubes that fire type 53 torpedoes, whatever that is. Wow, this thing has multiple pressure hulls on it. I guess that's so if one hull is breached, there's still another hull underneath it to prevent flooding?"

"You catch on fast, my young Padawan."

"You're calling *me* young? Anyway, they can hold *twenty* R-39 ballistic missiles. Ouch, that doesn't sound good. Each with a maximum of ten MIRV nuclear warheads."

"R-39s? Well that's good news."

"Why is that? Are those friendly missiles or something?" Cade said.

"R-39s were closely tracked and dismantled according to NATO's Strategic Arms Reduction Treaty. So that tells us the *Simbirsk* didn't have any warheads on it when it sank. NATO inspectors would have made sure of that."

"Well that's good. Hey, so if the Russians never actually scrapped this sub, but they sold it secretly to the Pakistanis, why do you think the Paks would want a ballistic-missile sub in the first place? I mean, if it didn't have any nuclear warheads to launch from it, then what's the point?"

Knuckles thought about the question.

"I'm not sure. Pakistan already has nuclear launch rockets. But launching a nuke from a sub is a whole different thing. Anyway, maybe they wanted to use it as an attack sub. You know, to protect their coastline?"

"Yeah," Cade said, "I guess I can buy that."

"There's also another use for an old nuclear sub that I can think of," Knuckles said. "It's kind of harebrained, but sometimes what they do is take an older sub like this, remove the nukes, and convert the launch tubes into storage areas."

"Storage areas? Storage for what?"

"Typically it would be to move special-ops troops into a place undetected. Hell, you could put a hundred guys into those tubes, surface just off the coast of one of your enemies, and dump a bunch of the bad-ass operators onto the beach."

Cade looked up at the huge computer monitor where the ultrasound video continued to roll.

"So you mean to tell me that there could be one hundred and fifty guys, dead in that sub?"

"I can't imagine dying in a tin can like that," Knuckles said, reverence painting his words. "Okay, let's see if we can tell why this thing sank."

"This is amazing resolution. I've never seen any underwater video so detailed."

"All right, so this is the bow. Ah, the bow is the front of the boat, Cade."

"You're so proud of yourself, aren't you?"

"I don't see any damage here. All right, we're coming up on the sail," Knuckles said.

"The *sail*? You're making that up, right?"

"Cade, your dad was in the navy. The sail is the tower-looking structure that sticks up and contains the bridge. You know, whenever a sub surfaces, the people in the command center can go topside and look around. Okay, not seeing any damage there either."

But as the video image continued its roll down the length of the hull, both men went quiet.

"Oh shit," Cade said.

"That's a big hole. God almighty, what the hell caused that blast hole? Let me pause the video."

"Hey Knuckles, I don't know why I never considered this before, but, are we going to see dead guys floating around or something? I just . . . I never thought about it when I took this job. The sailors on this vessel are all dead. I've got kind of a sick feeling inside. Like I'm looking at something that is . . . hallowed."

"I don't know, Cade. This is our job though. We look at this stuff so no one else has to."

"Take a look at the blast hole. It's got to be, what, thirty feet across? And look at the bent metal around the edges. The metal on the hull is bent *upwards*, not inwards."

Knuckles replied, "So that means the blast came from inside the *Simbirsk*, not from outside. This was not a torpedo attack or a mine."

"Exactly."

Knuckles stood.

"We've got to tell Uncle Bill that the blast came from inside the sub itself and get this info to the Pakistani government. They've got to know that the US didn't attack their boat. I don't know what happened on board this sub, but whatever it was, the explosion originated from within the boat."

"Ho, wait a minute," Cade said as he pointed back to the

screen where the video continued rolling forward. "What the hell is going on there?"

On the monitor, the two studied the video images as though memorizing them. Further down the hull of the boat, four large portal doors on the top of the sub came into sharp focus. Each door stood open, their cavernous missile bays below, empty.

"Holy shit," Knuckles said, "those are the missile-tube doors. Why are they open?"

Cade looked off to the side. "Knuckles, you said this thing used to hold R-39 ballistic missiles, right? And all the R-39s were accounted for by NATO and destroyed, right?"

"Yeah. NATO doesn't play games with that stuff. There are strict rules on countries. Verification of the destruction of a missile like an R-39 is high. There's no way the Pakistanis had any R-39s on board this sub. Like I said earlier, the Paks have nuclear capability already, just not aboard subs."

"Okay, but I'm not sure if I feel better or not right now. Let's take a closer look at those open doors. I can see that there are no missiles inside the tubes, but why would the doors be open? And why just these four doors? Why aren't the doors open on any of the other missile bays?"

"That's a good question. There's no way an explosion that occurred inside the sub would cause the missile-tube doors to open. Wait, pause the video. What's that? Look around the outer edge of that one open door."

The two squinted at the monitor. Cade spoke first.

"It looks like, well, it kind of looks like burn marks you'd see left behind by a welding torch."

"It sure does," Knuckles said. "There's no way though. I mean, it's not as if there's some guy with a welding torch down here at three hundred and fifty feet of depth trying to cut open a bunch of missile bay doors. And even if there was, how would you expect to get a missile out of there, much less take it away with you? Not that the Paks had any missiles on this boat."

Cade looked over at Knuckles as a cold feeling permeated between them.

"Move the video forward, let's check the other missile-tube doors."

Their eyes locked on the screen. But what they saw next

caused Cade's jaw to drop. He peeled his gaze from the video and said, "I've got a really bad feeling about this. Get Uncle Bill in here, right now."

21

TWENTY-THREE FEET OF SIGNIFICANCE

NSA Headquarters. October 16, 9:21 a.m. EST.

Inside the NSA, the minutes turned to hours.

"Team two," Uncle Bill said, rubbing his neck, "you have the crew manifest from the *Simbirsk* yet? Come on guys, I know you're exhausted and this is a wild goose chase, but we've got to track down every angle, no matter how unlikely. I want that crew roster, and I want background information on all Pakistani naval personnel on board. If an explosion happened inside that boat, we've got to find out if there's any reason to believe it was intentional."

"I'm trying to access the roster now, sir," a female analyst with bloodshot eyes said.

Bill again rubbed the tightening ropes building in his neck.

"Sir?" Knuckles said. "Sorry to interrupt, but there's something you should see."

"Oh, there is? I bet I'm going to just love this. Hey," Bill yelled across the room, "who's got that sonar data? Where are we with finding out about any shipping traffic in the area? I want to see a list of every ship or sub on the sonar report from the USS *Colorado*, and I want to know where each of those vessels is at this very moment."

"We're on it, sir!" yelled an eager young man from team three.

"All right, boys, what is it?"

Cade and Knuckles showed Uncle Bill the ultrasound video of the downed sub. They finished by pausing the video as it focused on the last missile-tube door, frozen open like the mouth of a corpse.

Cade pointed at the marks around the missile-tube door. "See the way that these marks make a perfect circular outline around the first four missile-tube doors? None of the other, unopened doors have those. Then, there are these different marks on the hull's surface surrounding door number four. It looks like something metallic scrapped diagonally across the hull here. These diagonal gouge marks are the problem. We don't know what they are. I don't know, maybe they're nothing."

Bill studied the image as his fingers disappeared into the depths of his beard. "No son, those marks aren't nothing," he said as he stared at the image until his eyes lost focus. "I'm getting too old for this shit."

Bill walked back into the main room with Knuckles and Cade in tow. "But sir," Knuckles said, "do you know what those marks are?"

Bill yelled across the room, "Team three, anything yet?"

"Yes, sir," a man in khaki slacks and a wrinkled button-down shirt said. "I've got the list of all shipping traffic coming up on monitor six."

Bill studied the monitor.

"This is a list of all *surface* traffic. These are mostly trawlers. I see a fishing vessel . . . and an oil tanker. What about anything submerged?"

"Well, sir," the man said, "the only thing of significance that was submerged was the Pakistani attack sub that fired the torpedo at the USS *Colorado*."

With crossed arms, Bill stared at the man.

"The only thing of significance, huh? Well, let me ask you this. Were any deep-submergence vehicles, mini-subs, caught on sonar?"

The man's voice went dry. "Well, yes, sir," he stuttered. "How, how did you know that? A DSV mini-sub was caught on sonar, but, it's just a research sub. It's tiny, only about twenty-three feet long. It has no weaponry of any kind, just a mechanical arm and a bunch of underwater cameras and lighting for researching the ocean floor."

Cade and Knuckles looked at each other like two hungry cocker spaniels, unsure whether their bowls would be filled.

"The DSV *is* significant," Bill said. "It didn't cause the *Simbirsk* to sink. The *Simbirsk* was a victim of sabotage, probably from a member of the crew. That much is obvious by looking at the blast hole that tore through the hull. It's clear she was attacked from the inside, not the outside." He turned to Cade and Knuckles. "Boys, those circular markings around the four open missile-tube bay doors," he said, pointing to the video monitors, "could only have been made from a docking collar on a DSV mini-sub. The DSV didn't attack the *Simbirsk*, but once the *Simbirsk* sank, the DSV used its docking collar to attach itself to the first missile-tube door. It then used an acetylene torch to cut the door open and see what was inside. Then it moved to the second, third, and fourth doors, until it finally found what it was looking for in missile-bay number four."

Knuckles said, "So wait, you're saying that the docking collar from a DSV mini-sub is what made those symmetrical marks around the doors? But what do you mean it found what it was looking for in tube four? Found what? We know all the Russian R-39 nuclear warheads that used to occupy those missile bays were dismantled years ago. NATO confirmed it. So what was behind missile-tube door number four?"

Bill stared at Knuckles, waiting for him to follow his thoughts to their only logical conclusion.

"Son, what have I always taught you about Occam's razor?"

"In the absence of any other information, the most likely conclusion is the right one." The words rolled out as though read from the pulpit. "There *was* a missile in that tube," Knuckles said as he sat down.

"And when the DSV removed the missile," Cade said, "the missile dragged across the hull and caused those horizontal gouges, didn't it? Jesus Christ."

Bill spun around to face the room.

"All right people, we've got a broken arrow on our hands. The probability that the explosion inside the *Simbirsk* was intentional just increased by a factor of ten. This was no accident. Teams two and three, I want all of you to get the list of crew members of the *Simbirsk*. Split it up and start on the bios of each person. I don't care who they are. If they were on that boat when it went down, I want to know everything from their height and weight, to their shoe size, to their education and past jobs, to what kind of dowry was paid at the wedding." Heads nodded in unison but no one moved. "What is it?" Bill yelled. "You're tired? You want to go home? Get me that information!" He then turned to Cade and Knuckles. "You two, locate that little DSV. Find out where it is right now. If we can find that mini-sub, we can find the warhead. Start with the DSV's last known course and speed as recorded on the sonar data, then pull the satellite intel. Check all nearby ports, and don't assume anything. These research mini-subs typically are deployed by a larger surface ship, so check the waters for a research ship or anything that might be a match. If our satellites don't have anything, get on the horn with the Brits. At this point, we have no idea who stole that nuke, but it scares the hell out of me. Everybody in that part of the world hates Americans. I don't have to remind you what almost happened the last time those assholes got a nuclear device inside the borders of the continental United States—they almost fricasseed a perfectly good Kentucky bluegrass festival, and Jana Baker and Stephen Latent in the process."

"India and Pakistan hate each other, right?" Cade said. "Maybe it was the Indians who stole the R-39 missile from the Paks."

Bill shook his head. "I doubt it, son. India's been a nuclear power for years. I don't think they need one more nuke, and they certainly wouldn't go to all this trouble to get it. No, this is going to be someone who doesn't have one, and will stop at nothing to get it. And remember something. It's not the man that wants an arsenal of nukes that scares me. *It's the man that wants just one.*"

Bill walked into his office, where he stared at a red phone on the corner of his desk.

"Dammit, I've always hated this phone."

He picked up the receiver, pressed the only button, and closed his eyes. The call was answered on the first ring.

Bill said, "This is NSA priority-level fifteen. William Tarleton, clearance code, kilo alpha one one niner six zulu eight." He exhaled deeply. "Give me the national security advisor." Then, from under his breath, he muttered, "God help us all."

22

THE TOUCH OF COLD STEEL

FBI Headquarters, J. Edgar Hoover Building, Washington, DC. October 16, 3:45 p.m. EST.

Jana walked into the office of the director of the FBI, and stood in the doorway.

"You wanted to see me, sir?"

"Baker! Hell yes I wanted to see you. Finished your rehab and retraining I see. You look a hell of a lot better than that day in the ICU at Bethesda Medical Center. Damn, I was sure we'd lost you. How do you feel?"

"Like I could eat nails, sir."

Stephen Latent looked at her with the eyes of a father, but his shoulders slumped.

"Baker, I can hear it in your voice. Listen, nobody expects you to just bounce back as though nothing happened. You went through more hell than most of us can imagine. I hear your words, but . . . what's going on in that head of yours? Remember, I was in the field once too. I started in Vietnam, and I've seen people fight post-traumatic stress, myself included. Level with me."

Jana stared ahead as though looking at a locomotive's headlight. She hadn't realized her voice betrayed the inner tumult boiling inside her.

"No, sir . . . I'm . . . I'm fine. Better than ever. Looking forward to being back on active duty. You *are* putting me back on the active list, aren't you, sir?"

"Baker, being an FBI agent isn't all about being on the front lines, shooting it out with the enemy. We've got to be in top shape, not just physically, but mentally and emotionally as well." He looked at her with eyes that could see through steel.

"I'm ready, sir. I'm ready."

"All right, all right. I had to ask. As of this moment, you're back on the active list."

An agent leaned into the doorway, and interrupted.

"Director? You've got a call on line six. You're going to want to take it."

"Dammit. Take a message," Latent said. "Can't you see I'm with one of my team?"

"It's the Pentagon, sir."

Jana began to stand, but Latent held his hand out, waving her back down.

"What the hell does the Pentagon want?" He picked up the phone. "This is Director Latent. Yes, this is he, I said. Uh huh, I see, and . . . wait, can you repeat that?" He stood straight up. "NSA has tracked a *what*? All right, roger that." He hung up the phone and exhaled. "The whole world is going to hell."

Jana said, "Is everything okay, sir? Should I leave now? If this is above my pay grade, then I can—"

"No one's pay grade is as high as yours, Baker. You're a damned national treasure. I'm not going to brief you about that call right now, but that call is about to become your first new assignment. I want you on a plane to Ft. Meade. You're to be on the flight line in two hours. I'll call Uncle Bill and tell him to expect you. There'll be a jet on standby for you and the others on the team."

"NSA headquarters? The Box? Yes, sir. And thank you, sir. You won't regret assigning me. Oh, the team? What team?"

"Oh, it'll be made up of some of familiar faces."

With that, Jana smiled and walked out the door, knowing she'd just aced the interview.

FBI Academy

As soon as she was back at the training center at Quantico, Jana sprinted through the hallways and habitrails, as they were known, until she reached her dorm room, sliding to a halt in front of the door. Part of the adrenaline rush came from being placed back on active duty, part came from the excitement of being again assigned to do something important, whatever it might be, and part was the slight flutter of her heart in the hopes that being at NSA headquarters might put her in front of one Cade Williams. She felt alive again.

She yanked out her duffel bag, threw it on the bed, and began to empty the chest of drawers, followed by her tiny closet. Her jittery motions made her look like she was hyped on caffeine. It had been a long time since she'd felt this exhilarated and she found herself glancing at the clock on her nightstand every few minutes. When the phone beside her bed rang, she jumped.

"This is Baker," she answered. "Yes, sir. Yes, sir. I'll be downstairs in five minutes." A feeling of unannounced panic crept into her stomach as she glanced from one corner of the room to the next with a feeling that she had forgotten something. Then, her eyes locked on it. In the closet, bolted to the floor was the gun safe—her firearm—she'd nearly walked out of the room for the last time without her firearm. It would have been a mistake she'd never have recovered from.

For some reason, as Jana tapped out the four-digit PIN code and watched the safe door pop open, her breathing accelerated. The safe revealed its only contents, her .40 caliber SIG Sauer. All she could do was stare at the gun. As she reached her hand forward, it recoiled, as though the weapon were a rattlesnake that might strike at any instant. The hand trembled. Her mind struggled for a foothold as her eyes blurred and then returned to focus. Her breathing became erratic. Thoughts blasted from one part of her brain to another, then ricocheted into a third.

Staring at the gun elicited visions of the shooting. She could picture the terrorist, Shakey Kunde, a Glock in his hand, muzzle blasts coming from the weapon, the feeling of searing lead slamming into her chest, the smell of gunpowder, and the sight of the brilliant blue sky that she saw next . . .

Jana's eyes rolled into the top of their sockets, revealing only the whites, and she blacked out, collapsing on the closet floor in a heap. Several minutes later, she was stirred by a loud rapping on her dorm-room door. Her body sat straight up and she banged her head on the metal shelf above.

"Ow, son of a bitch," she said. "Coming, I'm coming. Geez, hold your horses, will you." Jana opened the door to find Kyle MacKerron smiling at her.

"Hey, numbnuts! What, did you fall asleep or something?" Kyle laughed. "We've got a priority assignment to get to."

"You're going on this thing too? No, no. I didn't fall asleep," she said as she pulled Kyle in and hugged him. "I'm fine. I'm almost ready."

"Hey, watch out for that hug. I don't want anyone getting the wrong idea. I mean, I've got a reputation to uphold around here, you know."

"Remind me to hit you later."

"Well, they were going to send just you on this assignment. You know, superagent and all? But, I convinced them to let me tag along, just so I could learn something from the pros."

"Oh, shut up," she said. "And what's all this? You're suited up in fatigues. What, do you have a raid to attend, or are you just happy to see me?"

"I'm trying out for HRT." Kyle grinned.

"Hostage Rescue Team? You? They're letting you try out? What, were they out of options or something? No one left to choose from? No one left who's dumb enough to apply? No one left who understands grits humor?"

Kyle held up both hands. "All right, all right. Give a guy a break, okay? I don't know. Maybe I'd be good at it."

"Man," Jana said, "I'm out of circulation for a couple of months, and I come back to find this. Delusions of grandeur. The bureau's starting to fall apart."

"Hey, we've got to get a move on before the director himself shitcans both of our asses. Let's get out to the tarmac. Need help with your gear?"

"Yeah, sure. Grab that duffel. Just have to grab my SIG." Jana walked back to the closet and refused to so much as flinch when she reached into the safe. But fear coursed through her veins as she placed her hand on the weapon, afraid she might be electrocuted by the touch of cold steel.

She choked down her fear and holstered the weapon. With Kyle at her side, Jana again felt exhilarated. The possibilities seemed endless as the two young agents headed out to a new assignment. The unknowns became Jana's new solace, her comforter, her supporter, her friend. The unknowns seemed to be the only familiar thing in her life. She now viewed unknowns as familiars, the way one might relish the sight of a favored knit blanket draped across the couch—trusted, warm, inviting.

What she and Kyle might be working on next, where they might go, and what they might see, provided a cheap kind of thrill, distracting her from the twisted demons pinging her psyche.

23

A PIECE OF THE PUZZLE

Marine Corps Air Base Quantico, Turner Field. October 16, 6:45 p.m. EST.

Agents Jana Baker and Kyle MacKerron traversed the four steps up into the Gulfstream V jet. The pilots were in a conversation with a man whose back was turned, and three men were already seated. Their conversation was low, but it was apparent they were arguing. One of them nodded toward open bench seats that hugged the left side of the cabin, signaling Kyle and Jana to sit. Jana whispered, "Who are those suits?"

"I recognize one. The others? I have no idea," Kyle said, his voice low enough to not be heard over the warming jet engines.

"And that one guy in the back, he's the only one *not* in a suit."

Kyle smiled. "I'm not in a suit. You're not in a suit. You got something against suits? You know, back home in Savannah, we don't discriminate against the suit-wearers. There's nothing wrong with them. They're just . . . casually challenged. As long as they eat grits, they're okay with us."

"Do all coastal Georgia boys talk like you? And do coastal Georgia women put up with it? It's a wonder any of you were ever born."

"Hey, in the land of Paula Deen's food, the way to a coastal girl's heart is through her stomach. And by stomach, I mean, you feed her grits and she's yours forever."

Jana shook her head. "Too much fresh air and salt water affecting their brains?"

"Welcome aboard, you two."

Jana turned to see FBI Director Stephen Latent towering above her.

"Director?" Jana rushed to stand, only to hit her head on the bulkhead above. "Ouch, shit."

Latent laughed. "Yes, yes. It's me again. It's damn good to see two of my best agents back from the grave." Latent turned over his right shoulder and yelled, "All right, pilot, let's get the hell out of here." The plane bumped into motion and rolled toward runway number three, at the west end of the airport.

Latent sat in a leather bench seat across from Kyle and Jana.

"Let me look at the two of you. Jesus, I thought for sure we'd lost you both." He looked down at his hands a long moment. "You know, they can teach you everything about being an agent, they can even teach you what to do as the director of the FBI, but they can't teach you what to say to a grieving mother or wife or husband when an agent is down and you're handing them a folded American flag. Folded American flags suck. I'm really glad that I didn't have to do that with either of you."

"Thank you, sir," Kyle said. But Jana was silent.

"No, I mean it. And there's something else I want to say to the two of you. You both took a bullet for me. Hell, you took a bullet for a lot of people. What you did on the Thoughtstorm case stopped a terrorist from detonating a nuclear device on US soil. You *secured a nation*. You both stared down your own personal dragons and kicked their asses." His mouth opened as if to say more, but he stopped. "All right, enough of this blubbery shit. Let's talk about more important things."

Both Jana and Kyle assumed Latent was about to get down to business. His next comments took Jana by surprise.

"Baker, so what about that young man, Cade Williams? You two have been apart a long time due to your training at Quantico. Are you glad that you're going to be around him again in an hour or so?"

Jana blushed and then glanced over the director's shoulder out the plane's oval window as the aircraft taxied up the runway.

"Oh, well, sir. Cade's going to be there working with us? But

Cade and I are just . . . no sir, it's nothing like that . . .' "

"Oh bullshit, Baker," Latent said. "I've seen the two of you. I'm not *that* old. Jana, there's a look in your eyes when you're around him."

Latent had a way of switching back and forth between personalities: one, the tactical commander barking out life-and-death orders, the other, a loving father figure.

Jana looked at him sheep-eyed, never having admitted her feelings for Cade to anyone, even herself.

"Do you mind if I give you some personal advice?" he said. "Don't make the mistake I made. I traded my wife away. No, it's true. Maybe not literally, but it's the same thing. She was everything to me. God, I really love . . . loved her." He glanced up, wondering if the pair had caught his faux pas. "And I traded her away, traded her for the FBI." Self-anger bubbled just beneath the surface. "But, we live and learn. My point is, don't let that old saying that 'experience is the best teacher' be what you live by. That's a load of crap. Experience is only the best teacher if it's somebody else's experience that you learned from. That way you have learned to avoid the mistake they already made. Jana, if there are feelings between you and Cade, and I know there are, then don't let your whole life go by without *you* in it. If there's anybody that should realize it, it's you two. We really don't have much time on this earth."

"Yeah," Kyle said. "I think that both of us are acutely aware."

"All right, time for introductions." He looked to the rear of the plane. "You other assholes, listen up. Not that you don't already know, but this is Special Agent Kyle MacKerron and Special Agent Jana Baker, probably the most famous agents in the bureau."

"Yes, we are very aware," a hulking man with perfect teeth said. "Philip Murphy, HRT."

"Yes, sir," Kyle said. "I'd like to work for you someday."

"Yes. I saw you on the course. Looked pretty good, actually. MacKerron, let me ask you a question. You like going on temporary duty to NSA dressed like you're about to invade Cuba?"

"Oh, the fatigues. No, sir," Kyle said smiling. "We just got the call. I didn't have time to change."

"Just giving you shit. Welcome aboard, son."

"Lt. Will Riggs, United States Army, 1st Special Forces Operational Detachment," another man said through a chiseled jaw.

"My pleasure," Kyle said, shaking hands with the wiry man.

"Ah, that means he's Army Delta Force," Latent said, as Jana and the lieutenant shook hands.

The third man, dressed only in jeans and an untucked button-down shirt, did not look up nor stand from his seat at the rear of the plane.

"Ahem," Latent said as everyone looked at the man. "Don't make me come back there and squash your nuts for you."

The man stood and extended a lackadaisical hand toward Kyle.

Jana couldn't help but notice each man on the plane had first extended their hands to Kyle, another male, before her. The boys' club lived on.

"Pete Buck," was all he said before sitting.

Latent's crossed arms and pursed lips spoke volumes. "Buck," he said, "you might as well get used to the fact that not only does everyone on board this craft know you're CIA, but that we're actually all on the same team. Just because the company had a couple of rogue agents that went out of control with the Thoughtstorm mess, doesn't mean we're going to hold it against the entire agency."

"I'll take that under advisement . . . *sir*," Buck said, as he stared at Latent.

Latent's eyes never flinched. It was an old-school staring match.

As the amount of testosterone on display rose to a toxic level, Jana rolled her eyes and thought she might vomit.

Pete Buck leaned his arm against the seat in front of him. Latent looked at Jana and the others and nodded his head toward the front of the plane. Jana, Kyle, and the two men took the hint and moved into seats further forward, just out of earshot. Whatever Latent was going to say to Pete Buck was not for public consumption.

Latent moved toward Buck like a father about to teach his cocky teenage son the lesson that "the tail doesn't wag the dog."

"Listen to me, you little shit. As the director of the FBI, I've got permission to grab your cocky little balls and pull downwards until my knuckles hit the ground." Latent slapped Buck's left arm off the seatback, causing Buck's torso to rock forward and his face to hit the top of the seat. The shocked man grabbed his nose, then stood up, squaring off in Latent's face. Latent stood like a granite statue in a light breeze. "And another thing, you are one hundred percent *on* this team, and you'll act accordingly. I own your ass. And if I find one shred of CIA information is withheld from anyone, I'll personally rip out your Adam's apple and hand it back to you."

Buck glared at Latent momentarily but seemed to realize he was getting in over his head. His eyes, once filled with self-centered avarice, took on a more glass-like pallor. He nodded his assent and sat down.

Latent walked back to the front of the plane.

"Don't worry about him. He'll be fine," he said. "Everybody in CIA is still licking their wounds. They felt just as betrayed as the rest of us when the whole Thoughtstorm terrorgate fiasco went down. We have to remember, it was just a few rogue senior CIA agents that went off the reservation. When Pete Buck stepped onto this plane, he was probably thinking we hated his guts just because of what happened. Not to mention the fact that Kyle here practically died as a result of CIA gunfire. And if it hadn't been for CIA funding, Jana never would have been involved in that firefight with Shakey Kunde and nearly have died herself."

The sound of Kunde's name rattled in Jana's mind. Her eyes drifted out the nearest window as she shuttered at the rhythmic ring, *Koon-dee*. It repeated in a deafening echo in her head, *Koon-dee, Koon-dee, Koon-dee*. She felt a wave of wet heat escape around her neck and across face. *Koon-dee, Koon-dee*. Dizziness pushed an unwelcome presence forward, but Jana mentally yanked against the sounds ringing in her mind until, at last, she broke free and looked at Latent and the others.

"You okay, Agent Baker?" Lt. Riggs said.

Jana snapped her head at him. "Okay? Of course I'm okay. Why would you ask that? Hell yes, I'm okay."

She had overreacted and she knew it.

The four men exchanged nervous glances.

"All right," Latent said, "let's do a debrief. Hey, Buck, get up here. It's time."

Pete Buck stood. He still carried a trace of his earlier swagger, but moved forward without hesitation.

Latent continued. "I don't think I have to remind you, what I'm about to tell you is highly classified. Here's the sitrep. We had a sub, the USS *Colorado*, a Virginia-class, patrolling the Persian Gulf. Believe it or not, it's typically a quiet area as far as submarine activity goes. Anyway, the *Colorado* came upon a downed Russian sub." Latent captured every ounce of their attention. "Now, our books show that this particular Russki sub was *dismantled* several years ago." He let that one hang in space a moment. "At any rate, it now appears that the Russians never scrapped her but instead must have sold her . . . to the Pakistanis."

Jana's mind swirled with questions.

"Sir?" Jana said. "How do we know they sold her to Pakistan?"

"You'll understand in a minute. Anyway, the *Colorado* went immediately to investigate the incident." Latent shook his head. "While they were on site surveying the wreckage, a second Pakistani sub fired a torpedo at them. Christ, it gives me the willies." Latent held up his hands. "No, they didn't get hit. The captain of the *Colorado* is brilliant. I know him. It took me a while to remember, but Uncle Bill reminded me that he was with us that first year at Georgetown. After freshman year, he transferred to the naval academy and restarted there as a freshman. Yeah, that's how dedicated he was. He's cool as a cucumber under fire, and was able to evade through a complex set of maneuvers and cause the torpedo to slam into the Pakistani that fired it. But, the two subs bumped in the process. They're still evaluating the damage."

"I'm sorry, maybe this is a dumb question, and not to make light of the event," Kyle said, "but this is a naval event. Why the FBI and CIA involvement?"

"Here's why," Latent said. "We may have a broken arrow."

All four men sat straight up in their seats and looked at one another. Jana looked at Latent as though he was speaking Yiddish, then said, "A broken arrow?"

"Lieutant Riggs?" Latent said. "You want to explain to Agent Baker what a broken arrow is."

The lieutenant caught his own reflection in the high-gloss polish of his shoes, then leveled his eyes.

"A broken arrow. It means a nuclear weapon is out in the open."

Latent continued. "Here's why we think that. The *Colorado*'s ultrasound scan of the first downed sub, the Russian-built *Simbirsk*, was uploaded to NSA. They analyzed the video, and it appears that the *Simbirsk* was sabotaged from the inside, causing her to sink. The sabotage was likely caused by one of the crew. We don't yet know how a crew member could have caused so much damage. But regardless, once it was on the bottom, a mini-sub, called a DSV, docked with the *Simbirsk* and used a welding torch to cut into the missile bay doors. NSA's analysis says it's highly likely something, something very heavy, was removed from one of the missile tubes. Right now, every intelligence service in the world that doesn't hate our guts is in panic mode, searching for that DSV and what it removed from that missile bay."

Lieutanant Riggs's mouth cracked open and his eyes rolled.

"Director, not to be the ultimate pessimist, but I've seen a DSV. Those vessels aren't more than twenty-five feet long."

"And?"

"If, and that's a big if, if there was a nuke on that sub, there's no way a DSV could get it out of the tube even if it wanted to."

"Why not?" Kyle said, leaning forward.

"We're talking about a Russian boomer, right? The nuclear weapons in those tubes are huge. We're talking something along the order of fifty feet tall. I've seen similar missiles on our boats. And weight? My God. I looked it up one time. A missile of this type would weigh in the neighborhood of one hundred and eighty-five *thousand* pounds." He spoke the words as if reading a countdown. "A DSV mini-sub wouldn't have a chance at lifting one out. It's impossible. The DSV itself doesn't weigh anywhere near that."

Latent tilted his head at Pete Buck.

"Buck? CIA have any info on this?"

Buck's crystal-blue eyes looked at each person in turn. "Well, the lieutenant is right and wrong all at the same time."

"How so?" the lieutenant said.

Buck drew in a deep breath and held it, as though about to retrieve a lost watch from the deep end of a pool.

"The DSV mini-sub is real; of that much we're sure. It's French built and owned. DSVs are typically deployed from large research ships. The original research vessel the French had it attached to was lost seven months ago in the Aegean Sea. That ship was the *Marion Dufresne*. Sabotaged. The DSV was assumed lost as well. It certainly wasn't something we were tracking." Buck looked around as if afraid someone was eavesdropping.

"Why not?" Jana said.

"Why weren't we tracking a DSV that might have been lost at sea? We had no reason to. Why would we?" Buck said with a touch of incredulity in his voice. He shook his head. "The *Marion Dufresne* was a scientific research vessel of about three hundred ninety-five feet in length. The ship and the DSV mini-sub are just used for research. You know, finding shipwrecks, mapping the ocean bottom, looking for marine life twenty thousand leagues under the sea, and all that crap? Why would we be tracking that? Not to mention the fact that this particular ship hasn't exactly had a stellar safety record in the past."

"Meaning?" Jana said.

"Meaning that the *Marion Dufresne* was first christened in 1995, and by 2005 it had already run aground once. Then in 2012, it played slalom with the Crozet Islands and tore a forty-foot hole in its hull. So," continued Buck, "when French research vessels that can't seem to stay afloat in the first place find themselves on the bottom of the ocean, the CIA generally doesn't get involved. At any rate, we've just asked the French government to do a more thorough investigation of the ship's sinking. They've never known why someone would sabotage a research vessel. But at this point, we have a working theory that states the boat was sabotaged in order for someone to steal the DSV."

"My, my. We are defensive, aren't we? Anything else?" Latent said.

Buck appeared lost in thought, then looked at Latent. "The broken arrow isn't just some theory either. It's real. We're positive we have a weapon out in the open."

"Now how the hell do you know that?" the lieutenant said.

"Because sitting on the ocean floor, about seventy-five meters from the wreckage of the *Simbirsk*, and wrapped in a length of steel cable, is the lower half of a Russian-made R-39 ballistic missile."

Latent's jaw pushed forward and the red flush in his face retreated.

"The *lower* half?"

"Yes, the rocket portion," Buck said. "The other half, the warheads, are missing."

Jana leaned back against her chair and stared through vacant eyes.

Stephen Latent stood, and leaned an arm against the bulkhead as he looked out the window. After a few moments, he said, "Lieutenant? How many warheads on a single R-39 ballistic missile?"

"The R-39 is a MIRV, sir. Ten. Ten warheads, each designed to act independently."

"What's the yield on each warhead?" Latent said, still staring out the window.

"Depending on the uranium, the yield is between one hundred and two hundred kilotons."

Latent turned his head to the lieutenant, afraid to hear the next word.

"Each," the lieutenant said.

Latent's shoulders slumped.

"We're on the ground in thirty-five minutes. We'll be at NSA working with Bill Tarleton and his team to help solve this mess. Right now they're trying to obtain a crew manifest for the *Simbirsk*. It might help us to find which one of the crew is most likely to have carried out the sabotage. If we can find that, it might lead us to known associates. NSA is also in a full sprint trying to find that DSV mini-sub. They're starting with the last known course and speed of the DSV, and poring through all the satellite data they can find."

"CIA is doing the same on our end," Buck said. "We've retasked a few birds to watch every port in the region."

Kyle leaned closer to Jana and said, "By birds he means satellites."

"Are you sure you want to be a night-club comedian?" she said.

The others laughed.

Lieutenant Riggs turned to Latent. "I see she can hold her own."

Jana said, "Sir, you say you know the captain of the USS *Colorado*?"

"Since the *Colorado* was damaged, she's in port at NSA Bahrain, under repairs. And, no, not the National Security Agency NSA. This NSA stands for Naval Support Activity. It's one of our naval bases. Yeah, I knew him. The sub's skipper is Burt Tyler. He was one of my second-string wide receivers at Georgetown."

"Figures," Jana said.

24

A PRESIDENT INFORMED

The White House. October 16, 7:49 p.m. EST.

"Well, Mr. President," the national security advisor said, "your bullshit plan is already unraveling. I can't believe you convinced me to do this."

"Foreman, I am growing weary of your insubordination. Now, what are you talking about?"

"One of our subs has been attacked."

"What? Why? Who the hell attacked us?"

"Shouldn't you instead be asking about the health and safety of the one hundred and thirty-four officers and crew?"

"Goddammit!" the president boomed. "Give me the information."

"The Pakistani navy. One of their fast-attack boats fired a torpedo at the submarine USS *Colorado*, which is on maneuvers in the Persian Gulf. The Pakistani navy believed one of their other nuclear submarines, *the one you authorized the CIA to sabotage*, had been attacked. They lost communication with it, and it was sitting on the bottom of the ocean. Our assumption is that the Pakistani attack sub believed the USS *Colorado* did it. At any rate, the Pakistani attack sub has now been sunk."

"Oh shit. What has been the Pakistani response? Have they escalated?"

"Not yet. And the sailors on the submarine *Colorado* are fine, in case you were wondering."

"I ought to fire your ass for speaking to me like that," the president said. "I am the president of the United States."

"You can't fire me and you know it. I know too much. I know that your hands are covered with this mess. And you need me."

The president's hands formed tight fists and the muscles on his jawline tightened.

"Did the mission succeed? Did our CIA operative offload the warhead before all this happened?"

"It would appear so, yes. But it's a little hard to tell. In this part of the mission, communication with our operative is at radio silence. We don't want a trail that might point back to you, sir."

"What's the plan?"

"We're monitoring the Pakistani situation closely. At this point, our sub has slipped away from the area and is en route to repair the damage she sustained. If the Pakistanis make a stink of it, I have no idea how we can possibly keep the incident out of the media, especially after the USS *Colorado* shows up at one of our bases in the Middle East with damage to her bow."

"Well keep it quiet then. Reach out to the Pakistanis immediately and make sure they know we didn't attack that first boat."

"Already done, sir. But as you might imagine, they're rather pissed off."

"You've talked to them?"

"Someone had to. They've just lost two of their subs."

"What did you tell them?"

"The truth," Foreman smirked. "Our version of the truth, anyway. I told them we had nothing whatsoever to do with the sinking of their first sub, and that our boat went there to investigate and lend assistance. I also spun it back on them, asking what right they had to fire on us without provocation."

"I bet they just loved that one."

25

THE MOST-LOGICAL CONCLUSIONS

NSA Headquarters, Operations Center. October 16, 8:48 p.m. EST.

"Well, well, well. Uncle Bill Tarleton," a smiling Stephen Latent said as he, Jana, Kyle, Pete Buck, Philip Murphy, and Lt. Riggs walked into the NSA command center.

Uncle Bill looked back with his signature blankness, shook his head at Latent, and walked over. He spoke to Jana first, however. She stood, looking at Bill the way a daughter looks at a father.

"It's this one I've been dying to see."

Jana leaned her head onto Bill's shoulder. "It's good to see you too, Uncle Bill."

He then turned back to Latent. "You've been taking care of my girl, I see?"

Latent looked at him shaking his head. "Same old Bill. You got that twenty bucks you owe me from Super Bowl sixteen?"

"Well, Stevie, since six months ago you thought I was dead, I figured you'd excuse me." The two men embraced.

From around the corner, Knuckles walked over, wearing a button-down shirt that covered his tiny frame like a poncho.

"Okay, okay, enough of this gooey stuff. We've got a broken arrow out there, remember?"

Bill laughed. "For those of you that don't know, this is Knuckles, one of my crew. He, ah, kind of has a problem with dividing attention to more than one thing at a time."

"Let me introduce the team," Latent said. "This is Lieutenant Dan Riggs, Army Delta Force. This is Special Agent Philip Murphy, commander of Hostage Rescue Team two. Special Agent Kyle MacKerron, bureau. You all know Special Agent Baker here, and this is . . ." Latent looked at Pete Buck with questioning eyebrows. "You want me to say it, or will you?"

Buck's face flushed but otherwise remained expressionless. "Pete Buck, Central Intelligence," he said, then waited for a backlash.

"Don't worry, Buck," Uncle Bill said. "We at NSA don't bite, but the food in the cafeteria's not that good. Welcome to the Box."

Buck nodded and shook hands with Bill. "Thank you."

"Now," Bill said, "you make yourself at home here, Buck. But for God's sake, whatever you do, don't sit in Knuckles's chair. He goes ballistic, and the results are not pretty."

Buck looked Knuckles up and down. "O-kay?" he said.

"All right, enough of the jocularity. Let's get you people set up so we can get to work finding out what the hell is going on here."

As the group walked over to a set of computer stations that awaited their arrival, Jana scanned the room, half-excited and half-nervous to see Cade. But when he was nowhere to be seen, the disappointment became evident in her expression. As she set her laptop down, Bill leaned against her desk.

"You know, I've always had a knack for reading people," he said in a low voice. "Don't worry, he's here."

"Who?"

"Uh huh." Bill looked at her a moment. "You know, I have a feeling that your grandfather had this kind of conversation with you when you were growing up on the farm. Am I right? I can see you, about sixteen years old, and there was some special boy, wasn't there? Your grandfather could see right through you too, couldn't he?"

Jana didn't answer and instead reached to Bill's thick beard and gently plucked free a small orange-colored crumb.

"More snack crackers, Uncle Bill? I don't know how your wife puts up with you."

"You and me both," he said.

Jana smiled, but when Bill looked over her shoulder, she spun around. There stood Cade, a sheepish little boy wrapped in a twenty-nine-year-old's body.

"I'll give you two a moment to get reacquainted. But, we do a sitrep in five, got it?"

Cade's mouth opened as if to say something, but only air escaped. He wanted to put his arms around her and pull her close, but feared his advances would not be accepted. After all, from his point of view, their previous time together had been partly a fabrication. He'd been in love with her from the moment he'd seen her. The shimmer in all that gorgeous blonde hair, the all-natural look of her eyes, and the trim athletic cut of her body. The only times they had actually kissed or even held hands were all part of an act—the act of working undercover just before they went into the Thoughtstorm building to steal the secret data. After that, he couldn't tell if she was interested in him but was afraid to let her guard down, or if it had all been just an act. Cade knew the wise thing was to suppress his feelings, even though suppressing them would be like walking into a florist's shop and trying to not inhale the fragrance.

But still, there was the slightest flicker in her eye when she wheeled around and saw him. For Jana, it was a struggle not to wrap her arms around his neck and kiss him as well. But, this was hardly the time or place for that. And she was still conflicted about her feelings. Were they genuine, or had they been a response to the intensity of the situation? Truthfully, she hadn't minded going undercover and acting like she and Cade were a couple on a date. And it had been her idea that, prior to entering the Thoughtstorm building, they should get used to each other, even to the point of kissing. They had to look natural in case the security cameras in the Thoughtstorm building were watching. Kissing Cade had evoked emotions she had so long tried to suppress. And now, with a nuclear weapon on the loose, she would have to focus. Any added distraction could jeopardize her ability to concentrate on the investigation.

For once, Cade fought off his shyness and took the initiative. But, "Hi," was all that escaped him.

Jana breathed out the jitters and said, "Hi, Cade," giving him one of her 1,000-watt smiles.

The silence eased upon them as if ushered in on a breeze. From across the room, Uncle Bill watched in disappointment.

"Well, that was uneventful. All right people," he said in sudden escalation of voice, "everyone gather around. Now that we've got new members on the team, let's sync on what we know. We're all well aware a nuclear sub was sabotaged, and it appears something very heavy was removed from one of the missile silos. Now, I've heard chatter from our other intelligence sources that say there was no warhead on board the *Simbirsk*. They say they want proof. Well, I think we have someone who can enlighten us on that. Let me introduce Pete Buck, with the CIA."

Buck stood and looked across the room into disdainful glares. After standing for a good twenty seconds, he said, "Well then, let's get this out on the table, shall we? I can see the looks in your eyes. Yes, I'm CIA, goddammit. Yes, several months back during the Thoughtstorm case, we had a couple of agents go about as far off the reservation as you can go. But you have to understand, the rest of us were just as disgusted as you are right now. We had nothing to do with the Thoughtstorm terrorgate scandal. At CIA, I led the internal witch hunt, and I even served a few of the arrest warrants myself. And believe me, it wasn't pretty. I investigated everyone. It ruffled feathers and people inside the agency were upset. I didn't exactly win any popularity contests. People inside the CIA look at me just like you're looking at me right now, like *I'm* a terrorist, *and it sucks.*" Buck stared around the room. "My brother. *My own brother* was a CIA security officer assigned guard duty at the Thoughtstorm building. I can assure you, he had no idea what was going on. He didn't have the security clearance for it." Buck tried to pull the lump out of his throat. "He's dead. He's dead, all right? He died in the firefight with," pointing to Lieutenant Riggs and HRT commander Philip Murphy, "FBI's Hostage Rescue Team and with Army Delta Force. He and the other officers thought the building was under attack. They didn't know. My brother laid his life on the altar of freedom. I consider him a patriot."

With that, the room descended into cavernous silence. A few of the NSA team members nodded in acknowledgment, ashamed at their stereotyping of the CIA in a post-Thoughtstorm terrorgate world.

Uncle Bill cleared his throat. "His name was *Philip* Buck."

Pete Buck cast a wide-eyed gaze at Bill.

Bill continued. "And if you enter CIA headquarters at Langley, you can see his name freshly imprinted on a bronze plaque. I've seen it. And I'd be honored if my name rested next to his someday." Bill spun around and looked at all the members of his extended team. "Anyone got a problem with that?"

Knuckles walked forward and held out his hand. In it, a black ball cap emblazoned with the letters *N-S-A*.

Buck stared at the cap.

"This was mine. I never wore it though—the chicks don't dig it." Buck accepted the gift but had no words. "Welcome to the team."

Buck finally cracked a grin. "The chicks don't dig it, huh?"

"It's not the hat that's the problem. It covers up the wild hair. Chicks can't run their fingers through it if I've got the hat on."

"Is that right?" Buck said, in a deep smile. "Maybe you could introduce me to a few. Ah, I'd leave the hat at home, of course."

"Good move." Knuckles extended a handshake.

The mood in the room lightened as people stirred and nodded to one another.

"All right," Bill said. "Mr. Buck, please enlighten the team as to this new info on the nuke. And please let us know how it was that our team of two crack NSA analysts missed seeing half of a nuclear weapon lying on the ocean floor just meters away from the *Simbirsk*."

All eyes rolled onto Cade and Knuckles. They looked at one another like two bakers who forgot to put the cake into the oven.

"Okay," Buck said, "let's take a look at screen four. What you're seeing in this video is the lower section of an R-39 missile lying on the bottom of the ocean. This section is approximately twenty-five feet long. It contains the three-stage, solid-fuel rocket booster. Just at the top of this section is the liquid-fueled post-boost unit. And along the top edge, just below where an acetylene torch cut the rocket in half, are the thrust ports that would have produced a gaseous wall around the missile, if it had ever been launched underwater. Those are there to reduce hydrodynamic resistance before it reaches the surface. Note that I don't use the term *warhead* in my description of what you're looking at because the warheads are missing."

Cade spoke first. "I don't understand. Knuckles and I have been looking at the same ultrasound images. We analyzed them thoroughly. I don't . . . we didn't see anything further than— what, Knuckles—twenty meters from the sub? We didn't see any of this."

"Don't worry about it, Mr. Williams," Buck said. "Yes, yes, I know who you are. And I can only assume that if I showed you a picture of my brother, you'd recognize him as well. You probably passed him in the hallways of the Thoughtstorm building a number of times when you worked there. Anyway, you guys didn't miss anything during your analysis. The video images you analyzed only showed the submarine and the span of ocean floor several meters from it. At CIA, we could see a bit more. We've been working with the manufacturer of this particular ultrasound mapping software for the last year and a half."

"What do you mean you've been *working* with them?" Knuckles said.

"What I mean is CIA wrote the software. Well, we didn't write the ultrasound mapping software initially. Instead, we . . ." Buck looked around the room, then over at Bill. "Bill, anyone in the room that doesn't have top-secret clearance or better?"

"Hell no."

"All right," Buck continued, "let's be honest. We hacked the source code from the software manufacturer, added some enhancements of our own, then uploaded it to their servers. Our code enhancements are obfuscated so that even if their software developers were to look, it's unlikely they'd ever see it. Anyway, our enhancements allow us to, well, let's just say that we can now download any ultrasound files that are recorded by that software anywhere in the world."

Cade was incredulous. "But that doesn't explain how you could see something sitting on the ocean floor seventy-five meters away from the center of the scan. The scan only recorded a zone that extended maybe twenty meters away from the sub."

"Right," continued Buck. "But the software code we added creates a much wider scan zone from the ultrasound recording device. And the only way you can see the wider parts of the video are by using our decryption algorithm. The ultrasound scanning *equipment* already had the capability to scan the wider area, but without the enhancements we made to the software, no one knows it."

"But, but," Cade stammered, "you're downloading someone else's ultrasound recording? And you're doing it without the owner knowing? That's like—that's like stealing their data."

Buck's eyebrows raised. "Stealing data? You mean kind of like the NSA recording millions of cell phone conversations from people all over the world? Storing them on servers, then scanning them, looking for keywords, so you can catch terrorists? Stealing data like that? Is that what you mean?"

Cade looked at Uncle Bill who nodded in assent. It was something the NSA had done for a decade or more.

Buck turned back toward the screen. "Okay, now that we've gone through that uncomfortable moment, here's the next bit of hilarity."

Cade and Knuckles stood speechless.

"Can you guys zoom that up a bit? Yes, over to the left. Okay, see this?" Buck used a laser pointer to draw attention to something that appeared to be wrapped around the body of the missile, just below the secondary planar fins. "This is steel cable. We estimate it to be twelve millimeters in diameter." He looked around the room. "This is what was used to pull the missile out of the missile tube."

"Wait," Knuckles said. "The DSV mini-sub used its mechanical arm to pull out the missile."

"Not possible," Buck said, as he tried to suppress his "I know more than you" swagger. "Has anyone taken a look at the specs of an R-39 missile? Like, say, how much it weighs? No? Well let me see if I can help. A fully fueled R-39 rocket weighs in at a hundred and eighty-five *thhhhousand* pounds."

Faint gasps reverberated across the otherwise-silent space.

"The entire DSV mini-sub doesn't weigh anywhere near that much. It couldn't possibly lift something that heavy."

Knuckles, who was normally three steps ahead in his thinking, said, "That means the cable wasn't attached to the DSV because the DSV wasn't strong enough to pull it out, right? The other end of the cable must have been attached to something a hell of a lot bigger. Hey, Cade, on the sonar reports from the USS *Colorado*, wasn't there a research ship heard floating on the surface? Like the kind a DSV mini-sub might dock with?"

Pete Buck smiled and nodded his approval as if actively willing Knuckles to puzzle out the next step.

Knuckles spun toward Bill with the look of a nine-year-old waking from a bad dream, "Uncle Bill . . . we're . . . we're looking for the wrong vessel!"

Even Bill with all his experience was two steps behind the boy.

Knuckles stammered, "It was the research ship all along! The research ship has to have a huge cable to raise and lower the DSV mini-sub. Don't you get it? First, the DSV uses its acetylene torch to cut into the missile bay of the downed sub, then the research ship lowers its cable to the ocean floor, and the DSV attaches it to the missile with its mechanical arm. The cable then is hoisted to pull out the missile, which apparently weighs more than my mother."

"Watch it," pointed Uncle Bill.

"Ah, sorry. But wait, wait. Pete, if the research vessel pulled the missile out of the missile bay, and all the way onto its decks, then why bother cutting it in half? Why not just steal the whole thing? It doesn't make any sense."

Bill stepped forward. "And what have I taught you about things that don't make any sense?"

Knuckles stared into his eyes.

"That the most logical conclusion is probably the right one," he said again. "The Occam's Razor thing. I always forget that." Knuckles began to pace the floor, then stopped as though he'd stepped on a thumb tack. "So if it doesn't make sense that the research ship would *need* to cut the missile in half, but the DSV *did* cut it in half . . . so if the research ship was going to carry the missile away, why did the DSV cut the missile in half? Why indeed? Wait a minute. The research ship wasn't going to carry the missile away, was it? The DSV cut the missile in half so that it would be light enough for *it* to carry the missile away? The research ship pulled the missile out, but DSV *did* carry off the warheads?"

"Hey!" blurted Cade. "Remember, what the captain of the *Colorado* said? He said his sonar operator noted that the DSV's propellers seemed to be running at a very high pitch, like its engines were in overdrive, yet it wasn't moving very fast."

Bill smiled at his boys. "The DSV was, in fact, carrying the missile. And the high pitch of the DSV's screw means it was towing a very heavy load." He wheeled back around to the rest of the team. "All right people, I know it seems like we're sure the DSV has the nukes, but I want full coverage. We've got two targets to acquire. Bring me that DSV mini-sub. But, I want that research vessel located as well, and I want it right now. And another thing, we don't even know who we're dealing with yet. Where the hell is my manifest of the *Simbirsk*'s crew?"

26

TENSIONS ESCALATES

October 18.

"WBS News at the top of the hour" a television anchor said. "We're taking you now to the United Nations where a developing story is emerging. Mike, what can you tell us?"

"This is Mike Slayden, reporting live. The tension over a missing Russian diplomat escalated today as the Russian delegation to the United Nations pushed for military action against North Korea. The envoy, who went missing on a diplomatic mission to North Korea several months ago, is the son of a senior Kremlin party official. And, WBS News has learned, the man is also a distant family relation to Russian Premier Dumanovsky. Premier Dumanovsky has threatened independent military action against North Korea if the United Nations refuses to act. As of yet, no word out of the North Korean capital city of Pyongyang. It appears that North Korea has declined all comment. At a press conference this morning, when President Palmer was asked about the escalating situation between the two countries, he said, 'Yes, the tension is high between the Russian federation and the North. It's quite concerning. In the past, Russia has shown strong support for North Korea and, against the wishes of the United States, has been a frequent seller of arms to the country. But Russia and the world cannot turn their back when envoys on missions of diplomacy disappear. It is unfortunate that Pyongyang will not cooperate, but continues in its posturing and efforts to not only become a nuclear power, but a nuclear power with long-range launch capability.' For now, keep watching WBS for the latest news, weather, and local traffic. Back to you Steve . . ."

27

REUNITED

Autumn Woods Apartments, Annapolis Junction, Maryland.

"Hey guys!" Cade said as he opened his door. "Well, well, well. The three of us together in my apartment again. The last time this happened . . . well, let's not dredge up that wound. Come on in!"

"I see you still have excellent taste in decorating," Jana said with a smirk.

"Hey," Kyle said, "he's a man, and men don't decorate. We don't decorate, don't do décor, don't know what feng shui is, don't do the dishes," Kyle glanced around the room, "don't . . . have wall hangings. Jesus man, she's right. Why don't you go down to Walmart and pick up something to hang on these walls?"

Jana hugged Cade and flicked a glance into his eyes. "*Walmart*, Kyle? You really know how to work the women, don't you?"

"Yeah, Cool Mac," Cade said, not wanting to relinquish his touch on Jana. "I agree with her. In fact, with as bad as men are, it's a wonder any of us are ever born. How *are* any of us ever born?"

"Alcohol," Kyle said. The three laughed. "Speaking of which," he said, holding out a brown paper bag crunched around a bottle.

"Oh, you brought me wine," Cade said. "It's a merlot, isn't it? Or maybe a Shiraz? Oh, you didn't. It's a Malbec!"

"Ah, no, nimbleweed. It's a man's drink, whiskey. Damn, I thought I taught you better than that in college."

"Hey, mister big-time FBI agent," Cade said, "it says *bourbon* on the bottle, not whiskey."

Kyle ambled over to Cade and put his arm around his shoulder, "Cadey, listen. There's one thing I never taught you about women." He looked at Jana. "With women, you've got to act like you know what's going on at all times. They've got to believe you know everything, can do anything, and all of this without you having to tell them. Bourbon and whiskey are the same thing, it's just that people from Tennessee and Kentucky like to argue that it's not. Got it? Besides, in old Western movies, John Wayne drank whiskey. This is important stuff, write that down somewhere."

Jana thumped Kyle on the shoulder and shook her head while laughing at the two of them.

Cade clapped both hands together and held them. "Okay, let's celebrate. For my two best friends. Can I get you a drink? A bourbon whiskey perhaps?"

"Yes," Jana said, "a shot of brown liquid for each of us. But, hey, let's not play quarters with the stuff, okay?"

"Yeah," Kyle said, "let's keep it to one shot apiece. Cade, the alcohol might get to her, and you don't want her to get too handsy with you."

"You know, I could probably whip you in a fight," she said to Kyle.

Jana had trouble looking Cade in the eye. But for Cade, the problem was deeper. He could see nothing else in the room. The intoxication of her perfume seemed to cause the whole room to spin. Yet a thin glass wall of awkwardness still existed between them.

Jana decided, at a minimum, that she would embrace the awkwardness instead of running from it.

"Well, now that we've established that it's been a long time since we've been together, I say we eat before we get down to business."

"Aw man," Cade said. "You guys aren't about to tell me we

have to raid another building or something, are you? I was kind of hoping one week of sheer terror with the whole Thoughtstorm debacle would suffice." He looked at Jana, wanting to say a lot more. "Not to say that everything in that week was bad." It was the best compliment he could come up with on short notice.

"Cade, pal, have I not taught you? Priorities, man, priorities. She said two things—eating and business. Eat, don't you get it? Food, man. Food first, then business."

"Men," Jana said, shaking her head.

An hour later, the three flopped down on the two couches—both of vintage Rooms to Go quality. Kyle broke the silence. "Hey, anybody else think that Lieutenant Riggs looks familiar?"

Cade and Jana, who sat at opposite ends of the same couch, both looked at him out of food-induced blankness.

"No?" Kyle said. "Well, I do. There's something so familiar about him. I just can't put my finger on it."

"Maybe you and he dated right after college."

"Very funny, Cade. Does Uncle Bill teach stand-up comedy classes here at NSA? It's just, there's something, some . . . presence about him. I don't know how to put it. It feels like I've known him for years. Like I could put my life in his hands."

"Well, maybe you two served together, back in Nam."

Kyle, who had been born twenty years after the Vietnam War, replied, "Yeah, that could be it. All right, maybe I'm imagining it."

Jana stood, walked to the tall countertop separating the den from the kitchen and leaned against it. The style of the Formica and matching white cabinets screamed 1990. "We seem to be having a lot of trouble on this case."

"Hey, hold on," Kyle said. "Should we be talking about this outside of the Box?"

"You just like calling it that, don't you? Don't worry about security. Uncle Bill sends Knuckles over here twice a week to sweep for bugs. Believe me, there's nothing listening in on us."

"The kid comes over here twice a week?"

"Yeah, has his own key and everything. I think he brings the chicks up here when I'm not home."

"A regular stream of girls in this apartment, Cade?" Jana teased. "Anyway," she continued, "it seems like we're having a lot of trouble getting satellite data so that we can find both the DSV mini-sub and the research ship. And how much help are we getting from CIA, anyway? I know we don't normally spend time poring over satellite data at FBI, but with everything available to NSA and CIA, I'm just surprised we don't have images close enough to see people on those two vessels and read what brand of cigarettes they're smoking. After all, this isn't Google Maps-image quality we're talking about here."

"Yeah," Kyle said, "and I'm a little surprised we don't have the crew manifest from the submarine *Simbirsk* yet, either. It seems to me that if NSA is having trouble hacking the list, CIA should be able to put somebody on the ground in Pakistan to try and do it."

"Hey, don't look at me," Cade laughed. "I'm not breaking into any more buildings to steal the secret files ever again. Especially not in Pakistan."

"No, nimrod. I don't mean you. But CIA must have operatives in Pakistan right now. We need to find out from Pete Buck what the holdup is. The way I see it, we've got a very short window of time to get ahead of this thing. A nuclear weapon out in the open? And there are ten MIRV warheads in the one missile? Shit, I'd hate to know what would happen if just one of them got into the United States. The only good news is that since they apparently cut the missile in half, at least we know they can't launch it at anyone."

"Tell me about MIRV again," Jana said.

Kyle wanted Cade to impress the girl, so he nodded for Cade to answer.

"MIRV means multiple independently targeted reentry vehicle. So, you launch one big rocket from a boomer submarine, and once the missile nears its intended target, the tip breaks into ten parts, each its own independent rocket. They all split off and go where they're programmed. It's a way to shower an enemy with multiple nukes at once."

"So, if the missile got into the wrong hands," Jana said, "which obviously it has, somebody could theoretically separate it into ten nuclear devices. All capable of what? Wiping out an entire city each, right?"

"Without a doubt," Cade said through a long exhale. "Last time, we just had one weapon to deal with. Hell, I thought chasing down that Shakey Kunde asshole was hard enough. But ten nukes? God help us."

Upon hearing the name, Jana felt another shooting pain rip through her spine. It started at her tailbone and terminated at the topmost vertebra. Her body shuddered and her face went pale.

"Jana?" Cade said. "You okay?"

"Ah, um, yeah. No, no, I'm fine. Why do you ask?" Jana cleared her throat in a veiled attempt to cover up her visceral reaction to the name of the terrorist that nearly took her life. "Anyway, if we don't find the missile quickly, these terrorists, whoever they are, might separate the warheads. Ten nuclear devices instead of one."

Cade nodded but didn't peel his eyes from her.

"Right, and we now know for sure that that is their plan."

"And how do we know that?" Kyle said, as his arms stretched across the top of the couch.

"Well, they'd have to," Cade said. "Like we said a minute ago, since the missile was cut in half, it's not as if they ever intended to launch it intact at somebody. The only thing it's good for now is to separate the warheads."

"Good point."

"Something else that's bothering me, although I guess I don't know why," Jana said. "It's the *Simbirsk*. I don't get the risk. I mean, it was originally a sub in their arsenal, right? And the Russians said they scrapped it, what, like ten years ago? Lying about it seems crazy. If they sold it, someday, somebody would have found out."

Kyle said, "Makes you wonder what else Russia is up to. If they're lying about having scrapped a boomer, and an R-39 warhead, damn, that's bad. I mean, I have to assume they lied about it so they could sell the sub to the Pakistani navy. It must have been one hell of a pile of money. But you're right, someday we would have found out."

"Now that I think about it," Jana said, "it makes me wonder if some other part of our government *did* know about the *Simbursk* already. It's hard to believe it just magically showed up in front of us now."

"Russia is definitely troublesome," Cade conceded. "And, they're not exactly a friend of the West, are they? I mean, they're always interested in selling oil and arms to terrorist nations. It's normally the Russians who block UN resolutions against countries like North Korea, Iran, and Syria. That's why it's been strange to listen to the news over the past few weeks about Russia and its threats *against* North Korea. The Russkies love the North. From their point of view, what's not to love? They get another dictator to sell arms to. What could be better?"

"Well, you're right about that, Cadey," Jana teased. "I'd hate to even know what happened to that missing Russian diplomat, though."

"Right," Kyle said. "One normally doesn't expect to go on a diplomatic mission to Pyongyang and simply get lost. He's either dead or worse. And did you catch the latest news? They reported the missing diplomat is a relative of the Russian premier."

"No wonder they're pissed," Jana said. "I don't mean to laugh, but if you're the leader of North Korea, you couldn't have screwed up worse than that."

The room got quiet. "It's another prelude to war," Cade said.

28

NARROW THE TRAIL

NSA Headquarters.

"Uncle Bill," Knuckles said with the timidity of a gerbil. "Well, we finally have the list of crew members of the *Simbirsk*. But the initial background checks don't flag anything special."

"Dammit! I was hoping we'd find somebody on board that sub that we could trace as having associations to a known terrorist organization or a government entity or . . . the Hitler Youth, or the Watergate scandal, something. You know, somebody whose ass we could go kick."

Knuckles looked at him, wishing he didn't have to disappoint.

"Yeah, I know. But, in better news, I was just talking to Cade here. Tell him, Cade.

"They've got a hit on the DSV," he said.

"Why didn't you tell me? Where is it?" Bill said.

"He's pulling it up on screen five. The Brits came up with a view from one of their satellites."

"Good old MI5," Bill said. "Cade, show me. Come on, son. We've got a broken arrow out there. This ain't no time to sleep."

Jana walked over and smiled at him. "Yeah, Cade, come on, show us the secret satellite photos."

"Jeez," Cade said, "working here is getting stressful. Okay, look, it's on screen five. You happy now? British intelligence sent these over about a minute and a half ago, okay? And in the last ninety seconds of my expert analysis, I've determined that, yes, this is our DSV mini-sub."

"These images suck," Jana said. "This looks like the same quality I'd get from Google Earth."

"Funny you should mention that. Google Earth it ain't, but this came from one of their commercial satellites, not a military one. So, we were lucky to catch this at all. As it turns out, no other birds were in the right orbit at the time of the attack on the *Simbirsk*."

"These terrorists," Kyle said, "they just have no sense of working with our schedules."

"And," Cade said, "the only reason we have this at all is because the nimrods were traveling on the surface during daylight."

"Real assholes," Bill said. "All right, looks like the DSV is headed north-northwest at the time these satellite images were taken. Get me a list of any port in the area of the Persian Gulf inlet. There will be several. But let's concentrate on that exact heading. What ports could they hit if they made no turns? That's the low-hanging fruit. We'll start with that."

"Way ahead of you," Knuckles said. "You're right, there are several, but if the DSV mini-sub continued its current path, there are only a few places that it makes sense to go, especially if they're not docking with the research ship. Let's see, that would put them right on top of Karachi, Pakistan. And, it looks like the Pakistanis have at least three ports near to that trajectory. There's a man-made jetty there called Sandspit, so . . . yes, look. If they push up into the Baba Channel, they'd have their choice of a few places to dock. Let's zoom up this view. There's a few docks there."

"What is that?" Jana said.

"The Pakistan Naval Academy," Knuckles replied.

"So," Uncle Bill was thinking out loud, "if they're moving at a slow speed as reported by the USS *Colorado*, what time of day would the DSV arrive if they went into the Baba Channel?"

Cade whipped out on an old-school HP calculator, a keepsake from his prior job at Thoughtstorm.

"That trip would take several hours and put them in the channel way past my bedtime. I'd put it at somewhere between two to three a.m., local time."

"They'd still be under cover of darkness. How very convenient. This is our hot spot," Bill said. "Team one, pull all the stops out. We need satellite data. I want to see where that DSV hit port, and I want to see it right now."

"Sir!" popped a voice from the other side of the room.

"What?"

"Flash traffic coming in on the blue line . . . hold on. The message says they've found our DSV. But . . ."

"Found it?" Uncle Bill said, rocketing toward the analyst's cubicle. "You mean found it as in live, in the flesh? Found it where?"

"The flash traffic originated from the USS *Colorado*, which is again patrolling the region."

"I thought the *Colorado* was at port undergoing repairs. Well son, *Jesus*, what does it say?"

"The commander reports that the DSV mini-sub is at the bottom of the Baba Channel. It doesn't look good, sir. She's sunk, sitting on her side. Let's see . . . the depth of the water is only about two hundred feet there. The *Colorado* sent a diver out to inspect. The report says the DSV's starboard porthole is blown out. Anyway, they say it's a total loss. There were two occupants inside, deceased."

"Holy shit," Cade said. "What about the missile?"

"No missile," the analyst said. "They're doing a sweep of the area to confirm."

Jana said, "Was there evidence that the porthole was blown out or in?"

"What's your point?" Bill said.

"If the porthole blew in, the fact that the DSV sunk is almost irrelevant. If, however, it's blown outward, that might indicate it too was sabotaged."

The analyst ran his finger across the computer screen the way one would read Braille. "Here, here it is. No, they can't tell. They actually looked for that. The porthole shows no signs of caving in either direction. The Lucite window is simply not there. Hold on. It says the condition of the two bodies is extremely bad. One of them, yeah, it looks like one of them is torn apart. The other, not so much. They can't even make out the nationality of the victims due to their condition."

"Doesn't that sound like an explosion?" Jana said.

Cade was always interested in supporting Jana. It was his juvenile way of hoping he'd get her to like him.

"Right. No matter how it sunk, it's not as though the two hundred feet of depth would cause any damage to the bodies when the ocean flooded in. It must have been an explosion inside the vessel."

Bill's eyes were closed, deep in thought.

"Halfway across the bay," he said in a low voice. "The mini-sub was halfway across the bay. And the missile isn't with the DSV? That might mean they offloaded the nuke at a dock in the immediate vicinity." He popped his head upright. "All right, people, listen up! New directive: team two, you work the north side of the bay. Team three, the south."

"What are we doing, sir?" peeped a young woman's voice.

"You're going to find every video surveillance camera in your territory and hack into it. I don't care if it's a camera mounted to a grocery store, a yacht-club parking lot, a bank ATM, anything. Start with the cameras closest to the docks, then fan outward. You're looking for any dock activity between the hours of two and six a.m."

"You know," Knuckles said, "if they did offload the nuke, that thing weighs a ton. They'd need a crane to get it out of the water. And just getting it out of the water wouldn't be enough. They'd need a truck or something to move it."

"You're going to have my job someday, son. And, you'll be welcome to it. This is going to kill me yet. Concentrate first on any dock with a large crane. And report any sightings of a truck large enough to handle a . . . what, a twenty-five-foot object that weighs more than . . . more than FBI Director Latent's ego."

Bill looked across the room at Stephen Latent, who was surrounded by several agents, deep in conversation. Latent grinned, extended a hand, and showed Uncle Bill a playful middle finger.

Bill turned back to his teams. "We've got to move on this, people. We're hours behind the eight ball here. In one hour, I want to be looking at surveillance video of a couple of assholes lifting a missile out of the—"

"Ah, sir?" Knuckles said.

"Dammit, son, I'm in the middle of a speech here."

Jana tried to obscure an obvious laugh, but the effort was a failure. "Oh, sorry Bill," she said.

"Anyway," Knuckles continued, "you might not have to wait that hour. Take a look at this." He pointed to screen two. "This is a camera view from a bank ATM close to the scene. In the background is one of only two docking cranes on the southern side of the inlet."

Cade leaned toward Knuckles, and whispered, "Teacher's pet."

"The crane is used as part of a ship-repair bay. Hold on, let's advance through these still images."

As Knuckles clicked, one image after another rattled across the screen. Everyone in the room was glued to the monitor, squinting.

"Wait, wait!" Bill said. "Go back. No, back. There! Look. Holy shit. This image is grainy as hell, but whatever is being lifted out of the water by that crane in the distance sure doesn't look like a ship. This is great work, son, but we're going to need a better angle."

Cade said, "And a better-quality image. Christ, the whole thing is so pixelated. You can't even make out what it is. That thing being pulled by the crane could be a missile, or these could be some fishermen hoisting a VW Beetle back onto shore after a night of drinking."

"But, I doubt drunk fishermen would have access to a crane like this at four a.m." Knuckles said.

"Who has another camera for me?" snapped Bill.

"Sir?" a man from the other side of the room said. "I've got something here, but . . ."

"But what?"

"It's going to take a little more effort to hack into this camera, sir. It looks like the Pakistan Naval Academy has several cameras mounted on the walls surrounding their property."

"Get on it. Knuckles, Cade, go camp out in that cube. The

three of you are going to hack into that camera now. And, no, I don't care that we don't have authorization to hack into a surveillance system owned by the Pakistani military. We don't have time for an ambassador to go down there and ask them politely, if you know what I mean."

29

BORDERS ON THE VERGE

Conference Row, Panmunjom, South Korea. Joint Security Area along the demilitarized zone between North and South Korea.

"We interrupt this broadcast with a special report. Please stand by for breaking news."

"I'm Mike Slayden, WBS News. Significant developments coming in to the newsroom now as tensions between Russia and North Korea have escalated once again. In what would appear to be an act of war, Russia has fired a missile into the heart of Pyongyang, the North Korean capital. We take you now to our Asia bureau chief correspondent, Tammy Cho, live from the South Korean side of the demilitarized zone. Tammy, what can you tell us?"

"That's right, Mike. Not since the 1950s and the Korean War have tensions escalated to this level. Although we cannot yet independently verify these reports, it does now appear that a Russian-built rocket has struck a building in downtown Pyongyang in the early hours of the morning. Unconfirmed reports state that the building, a type of control center for an electrical-power-generation station, was in total ruins. Widespread blackouts in the area seem to support the allegation. There have been no reports of casualties as yet, and so far, no official comment from the North Korean government or from Russian authorities."

"Tammy, there has been a buildup of tension between the two nations over that missing Russian diplomat. What are your sources telling you? Is this missile strike a retaliation from Russia?"

"That's right, Mike. Unnamed sources close to officials in the North tell WBS News that the Russians have grown tired of waiting for a response from North Korean leader, Jeong Suk-to, as to the whereabouts of their attaché. Russian Premier Dumanovsky has been very vocal of late, stating his impatience over the missing official. Mike, we're also monitoring reports from the neighboring city of Dongning, China. Dongning sits near the borders of both Russia and North Korea, and AP Newswire now confirms that Russian troops are massing in and around the port city of Kraskino, just across the border. Kraskino is less than ten kilometers from the northern-most tip of North Korea. That puts Russian troops in relatively close proximity to those from North Korea. At the same time, in the Russian port of Vladivostok, home of the fabled Red Banner Pacific Fleet, unnamed US officials are also hinting at heightened Russian naval activity there. Vladivostok is the closest Russian naval port to North Korea and sits less than one-hundred kilometers from the North Korean border. In the meantime, Mike, the government of South Korea is bristling at the thought of full-scale war erupting just across their borders. We'll be monitoring the situation closely and will break in with news as it warrants. For now, I'm Tammy Cho reporting live from the DMZ, South Korea. Back to you, Mike."

30

CONSPIRACY

The White House.

The president paced in front of his mahogany desk, the same desk used by John F. Kennedy as he faced an escalation of Russian troops into Cuba in 1961. He rubbed his neck. "The situation between Russia and North Korea is getting out of control. We underestimated Russia's response and it's going to screw our entire operation. Dammit, how could I have been so stupid?"

The national security advisor decided not to respond.

"Don't give me that snide look," the president said. "I know. You advised against this little operation."

"*Little* operation? Sir, you may be the president of the United States, but *you* invoked the Fifteenth Protocol. You authorized the stealing of a nuclear device from another nation so that you could detonate it inside North Korean territory and make it look like some other country did it. This is not a little operation. It's a covert act of war."

"Don't tell me my job!" the president boomed. "I'll not be talked to as though we're standing on the playground back in grade school. And let me remind you of something; you're in this as deep as I am. I may have invoked the Fifteenth Protocol, but you set the operation into motion. So stop sniveling. Now, let's get down to business. Where are we in the plan?"

"We know three things. One, the nuclear device has been successfully stolen from the Pakistanis. Two, so far, the Pakistanis have not been willing to publicly accuse us of anything. And, three, we don't know where the device is."

"What do you mean we don't know where the device is? It's a nuclear-fucking-weapon. We *have* to know where it is."

"Mr. President, I've told you before. On a mission like this, we have no contact with our CIA operative in the field. It's impossible. Once set in motion, all communication to field personnel is cut. The risks of the mission being compromised are too high."

"We have no communication with our operative? But don't you understand? The Russians are about to invade North Korea. Their invasion was never part of our plan. We have to abort the mission!"

"You never had to set this in motion in the first place."

"Oh hell yes I did!" the president said. "After that lunatic leader of North Korea threatened us by launching an ICBM at Hawaii, I knew he had to be stopped at all costs. He is inches away from putting a nuclear tip on another missile and nuking Hawaii for real. Our plan was to destroy the North Korean government. But now, if the Russians invade North Korea, and then a Russian-made nuclear device goes off inside the capital city, annihilating both the North Korean government and the occupying Russian troops at the same time," the thought played forward in his mind, "and UN inspectors later run tests and determine the detonated device belonged to Russia in the first place, it's going to look damned screwy, don't you think? Russia's not going to occupy Pyongyang and then blow up their own troops. UN inspectors will know it wasn't Russia who set off the device. The UN will find out it was us. We've got to get our CIA operative to abort!"

The national security advisor didn't flinch.

"The Fifteenth Protocol should not have been invoked. It should have never been conceived in the first place."

The president exploded. "Why can't we contact the operative?"

"The only thing we know about the status of the plan is that he was en route to rendezvous with the mini-sub the CIA stole a few months ago. The mini-sub was used to steal the nuclear weapon from the Pakistani submarine you had sabotaged. The operative rented an old ferryboat to go and make contact. His orders were to board the DSV mini-sub and take it to a port where both the nuclear device and the mini-sub would be offloaded. But, like I said earlier, any communication to an operative on a mission like this is operational suicide. It's never done, ever. We've attacked and destroyed two vessels of the Pakistani navy. Right now, we have no idea what is happening in the plan."

"Well, the Pakistani sub we stole the device from was a *rogue* vessel in the first place. What was it called? The *Simbirsk*? The Russians sold that sub to the Paks illegally, so I don't want to hear about that."

"Nevertheless, sir, between the *Simbirsk* and the other Pakistani sub that came to her defense, we've murdered two-hundred-some of their sailors. We've stolen a nuclear device. Communicating to anyone involved in the operation is too risky. Once an operation this big starts, it rolls through until completion, or failure." The national security advisor inhaled. "And, the situation is getting much, much worse."

"How can it get worse?" the president said.

"As you are well aware, the Fifteenth Protocol was invoked under utmost secrecy. Only a handful of CIA personnel are even aware of the operation's existence.

"Get to the point."

"Our own intelligence agencies, including both CIA and NSA, are now onto the fact that there's a broken arrow on the loose. And they're getting closer to tracking down where the stolen device is currently located."

"They are? How close are they to finding it? That might be perfect. If they find the device, they'll stop it before it gets to the North Korean border. I want them to find it."

"Are you sure you want them to find it, sir? I mean, if they find it, they're going to find it accompanied by one of our CIA operatives. Practically no one in the CIA knows what he's up to. So after they find him with it, then what? Do you think all of them are just going to throw up their hands and say, 'Oh, I see, this was all a big plot to blow up the North Korean government. Yeah, no problem.' Sir, the people in our intelligence agencies that are investigating this case might not know about the Fifteenth Protocol operation, but these are very significant elements of the CIA, NSA and," he paused for effect, "*the FBI*. They're all heavily involved in the investigation. I don't have to remind you that the current director of the FBI ousted the last president of the United States for a much smaller conspiracy."

"We're not conducting a conspiracy!"

The national security advisor rose. He was caught in between feeling out his oats and not wanting to chop his own head off. But, his anger got the best of him. "Look, my ass is on the line here, too, sir. So why don't you try telling that one to a Senate oversight subcommittee."

He stormed out of the Oval Office and let the door swing open behind him.

31

TENSIONS ALONG THE BORDER

Kraskino, Russia, on the Posyet Bay. About 15.1 miles east of the North Korean border.

". . . hold on folks. Yes, I've just gotten word that we're cutting live to Tammy Cho in the field near the North Korean border. Tammy, we understand there's a significant buildup of naval activity. Can you tell us what you're seeing?"

"This is Tammy Cho, WBS News, reporting live from Kraskino, Russia. Mike, we're just across the border from North Korea and China, and we've confirmed earlier reports that Russian troops are massing at this point, just across from us here. Kraskino is normally a very small hamlet on the shore of the quiet Posyet Bay, but the population of this sleepy Russian fishing village has swelled in recent weeks to somewhere over a hundred thousand as troops have moved into the area. The situation over the Russian envoy who went missing on a recent diplomatic mission to North Korea has escalated to an alarming level."

"It sounds like Russia is making good on threats to attack North Korea if their diplomat is not returned, safe and sound. Kraskino is a port, so what signs of Russian naval activity can you see in the bay from where you are, Tammy?"

"Mike, the Russian Navy is making no secret of their presence here. In fact, even though we are not being allowed to get any closer than we are right now, Russian press officials are with us on a daily basis and are providing information. Our reporting is not being restricted. In fact, it's being encouraged. From our vantage point, we can see several heavy Russian naval vessels anchored in the Posyet Bay. Apparently the Russians want the world to see them and to know that they take the issue of their missing diplomat seriously. Some of the vessels have been identified to us as follows: the RFS *Pyotr Veliky*, a Kirov-class cruiser, the *Soyuza Kuznetsov*, a Kuznetsov-class aircraft carrier, and the brand-new, never-before-seen ballistic-missile submarine, the K551 *Vladimir Monomakh*, of the Northern Red Banner Fleet. The sub is at surface here at the port."

"Tammy, what about on the North Korean side of the border? Are the North Koreans massing troops on that side?"

"With the aid of high-quality optics provided to us by our Russian media counterparts, we can just see the North Korean border in the distance, Mike. And yes, North Korean troops have dug in along the mountainous hillside. We can see heavy armor including tanks and troop carriers, and perhaps heavy artillery emplacements. With all the increase in—"

A cacophonous boom erupted into the microphone and the line clipped into sudden silence.

"Tammy? Tammy? Are you still there? Tammy? We seem to have lost you." He put his hand against his earpiece. "Tammy? Well folks, we seem to have lost communication with our colleague, Tammy Cho, who is reporting for us live on the borders of Russia, China, and North Korea. We'll try to reestablish communications with her and update you on the situation. For now, I'm Mike Slayden, WBS News. Now back to your regular programming."

Once they were off the air, Slayden barked into his microphone, "What happened? Did we lose the satellite feed? Where is she? What happened?"

32

EMBLAZONED

NSA Headquarters.

The images hacked from the surveillance camera that was mounted on the wall of the Pakistan Naval Academy were grainy at best.

"Ah, come on. Is that the best we can do?" Uncle Bill said.

"Sir, these images are from the Pakistan Naval Academy video monitors. The cameras aren't exactly state of the art."

"Knuckles, what about enhancing those pictures, son? Let's make it happen."

"Sir, the image quality you're seeing is *after* we enhanced it."

Bill's eyes shut.

"Son of a bitch. All right people, everyone turn your attention to monitor eleven and see what the best video-surveillance technology available when Ronald Reagan was in office can show us. We've got to see if we can identify the vehicle used to offload the missile, or identify a person. Something."

People from all over the office dropped what they were doing and moved to get a better view of the monitor.

As the video rolled, the image popped and flashed like it was a piece of World War II newsreel. It was black and white, and since the images were recorded in darkness, barely discernible. Regardless of the video quality and the lack of sleep shared by all, the teams watched with intent. Analysts from all over the room leaned in, some squinting through thick glasses, others craning their heads up or to the side in order to get a better view. There wasn't a person in the room who didn't want to be the one to discover the next crucial clue.

"Worse than my dad's old footage from Vietnam," Cade said. "And that was 8 mm tape. Good God, I can barely make out the fact that we're looking at a dock here."

"Are there any other video cameras mounted on the wall of the naval academy?" Jana said. "This is horrible. It looks like we're watching coverage of a blizzard."

Knuckles, who himself had become a bit smitten with Jana, blushed.

"Yes. Um, no. Well, yes, I mean yes, there are other cameras, but this one had the best angle of the crane and dock. And, well, the video quality was best on this one."

"You've got to be kidding me," she said with crossed arms.

"We might not be able to see any detail while they're loading the missile onto the flatbed, but there is a flash of an image from one camera as a truck drives right by it. It's another camera mounted on the wall about half a mile down the road, but the timestamp makes sense for when the flatbed should have been driving by there."

Bill showed uncharacteristic excitement. "Well hell, son, show me, show me."

"Charlie," Knuckles said, "bring that up on monitor four."

All heads turned to the new monitor and the room went deathly silent.

"Okay, good, now hold on. Give it just a second. There's a truck that blasts by this camera in just a . . ."

"That was it?" Cade said. "I couldn't even tell that flash across the screen was anything, much less a truck. Are you sure?"

"Sure I'm sure. What do I look like, a nimbleweed?" Knuckles said. But based on the nonplussed look from Uncle Bill, Knuckles tried again. "Charlie, replay it, but in slow motion. Reduce the speed by a factor of ten, okay?"

As the group watched monitor four, the blackened blur that had previously flashed across the screen went into slow motion and revealed a frame-by-frame lapse of the scene. The cab of the truck was now more clearly discernible, but the image blurred against the dark night.

"All right, freeze it!" Knuckles yelled.

The video froze in place, revealing the cab of the truck, the image jittering in accordance with the low quality of its resolution. Of the two passengers in the truck, only one face was visible. It was blurry, but the features were somewhat distinguishable.

"Damn, I bet we'll have trouble getting our facial-recognition software to come up with a match on that face," one man said. "The software might be able to make some educated guesses with it, but it's too blurry to make a definitive identification."

"But even if we have the computer extrapolate the missing pixels," another said, "it's just as likely to construct an image of the face of J. Edgar Hoover as anything else. This is worthless as far as facial-recognition software goes. It would take this guy's mother to identify him in that photo."

"Shit," Bill said. "Well that just about cracks the case. I guess we're back to square one."

Cade, however, was focused on Jana. There was something in her demeanor that he couldn't quite place. Maybe it was the way she squeezed her folded arms tighter against her chest, or the way her shoulders had rounded over. But whatever it was, it wasn't an expression he'd seen from her before, and Cade didn't like the look of it.

"Jana?" he whispered. There was no response.

Jana's body was frozen, her eyes locked on the monitor as she stared at the face.

Thoughts pinged from one side of her brain to the other. She couldn't control them. The resulting mental chaos would have looked like an old pinball machine with twenty steel balls bouncing randomly. Her mind went into vapor lock, a condition where thoughts become superheated and refuse to organize.

"Jana? You all right?"

It was when Cade placed a hand on Jana's shoulder that he noticed the shaking of her head and the deadness of her eyes. It started as just a tremor, but then the tight, side-to-side vibration increased in intensity until Cade realized something was dreadfully wrong. Cade nodded to Kyle and the two of them each grabbed her by an arm and whisked her out of the room. No one else had noticed; they were too focused on the video monitor.

"Jana?" Kyle said, but there was no response.

Now inside the adjoining war room, they held her by the arms to keep her upright. "Jana? Snap out of it. Jana, you're scaring me," pleaded Cade. "Kyle, what the hell is wrong with her? Jana!"

Kyle recognized the severity of what was happening, raised an open hand, and slapped Jana square across the face.

Cade lunged at his throat.

"What the hell is wrong with you?"

But Jana snapped out of it. Her faced flushed crimson and she began pulling and yanking against the grip of her two friends.

"No, no, no! Nooooo!" In the attempt to free herself, she dropped to the floor, then gripped either side of her button-down shirt and ripped it open, exposing herself down to the bra. Buttons flung in all directions as Jana grabbed at the scars on her torso—perfectly rounded scars left behind as terrifying calling cards from the shooting incident with Shakey Kunde.

Cade was so shocked he couldn't speak. Kyle, however, leapt into action and took Jana's face in his hands. He said in a calm Savannah drawl, "Jana? Jana, it's okay. It's okay. Look at me! It's going to be fine. You're safe now. You're safe. It's all over." The voice was soothing, like the feel of pure silk against smooth skin. Her eyes registered and she pulled her shirt back to cover the fully exposed bra and scars.

Those awful scars. They were there. They were ugly and they conspired together into what Jana perceived to be a plot to steal her sanity. She couldn't escape them. The scars had taken on a life of their own. It was a battle for her mind, and Jana was losing.

Cade was still stunned, but knelt down beside her. "Are you all right?"

"I don't know," came her bleak reply.

Kyle stood and helped Jana to her feet. "Jana, you've got to tell somebody. You can't hold this inside."

"Hold what inside?" Cade said.

Kyle continued. "Jana, you know what I'm talking about. I know what this is, and you do too."

"What *what* is? What's going on?"

Jana clutched at her shirt.

"Post-traumatic stress," Kyle said. "Jesus, it's bad. Worse than I thought. I thought I saw it earlier, but damn, this is bad."

Cade looked like a lost pup.

"Post-traumatic . . . oh shit. But, Kyle, how did you know? What do you mean you saw it earlier?"

"On the plane. Her behavior on the plane. It reminded me . . ."

"Reminded you of what?" Cade said.

Kyle stared at the two of them but didn't really see them.

"Reminded me of my dad." His thoughts drifted back to his childhood. "I was just a kid, probably about twelve years old. My dad . . . he was a firefighter, you know? That day he had lost a friend of his. He lost his best friend. Dad's fire chief later told me that some scaffolding at the fire scene had collapsed. Dad was up above and had hold of the guy but eventually lost his grip. He couldn't hold on any longer. His friend fell and died. Anyway, the aftereffects were unbelievable. Jana, you've got to get help. You need to take some time off. We can't be out in the field somewhere and have you freeze up. Someone could get hurt. You need help, and you need it now."

"Well it isn't very good timing, is it?" she lashed. "We're in the middle of another damned terrorism case, aren't we? And the frail little female can't hack it; is that it? I'm so sick of being looked at like I'm a little girl. I'm sick of it!" As she paced the room, she flung wild gestures into the air. Her blouse hung open once again. "I'm sick of being eye candy for a bunch of members of the boys club!"

The air in the room stagnated.

After a few moments of silence, Cade decided to break the tension.

"Then you might not want to walk around with your Victoria's Secret thing going on."

"What?" Jana glanced at her chest. "Oh shit."

All three laughed. She quickly covered herself again.

"I'm sorry. I didn't mean to flash you guys. And, I didn't mean to lash out at you like that. I know it's not either of you. It's just . . . it's so damn hard to prove yourself around here. What do I have to do to be viewed as an equal?"

"It's not that I don't hear you," Kyle said, "but being viewed as an equal in this boys' club is not your biggest problem. You need to get that stress in check."

"I will. I'll see somebody about it."

But Kyle knew better.

"Look, I hate to bring it up," Cade said, "but what happened out there just now? I mean, I know you had some kind of post-traumatic stress episode, but what set you off in the first place?"

At first, Jana didn't answer. But then she looked at him. "The face."

"What face?" Kyle said.

"The face on the monitor."

"What about it? Do you recognize it or something?"

"Yes, I recognized it. It's emblazoned on my damn brain." She could tell by the dullness in their expressions that neither of them knew what she meant. "It's Kunde. Shakey Kunde."

Kyle replied, "What do you mean it's Shakey Kunde? Jana, *he's dead*. You killed him at the bluegrass festival in Kentucky last year. Remember?"

Jana's eyes wandered off, and then found the floor. She rubbed the uppermost bullet scar on her sternum. "Yeah, I remember."

"Then what are you saying?" Cade said.

"I'm saying that face on the monitor, the one driving the truck. It's the spitting image of Shakey Kunde—a younger version of Shakey Kunde. It's not him, it's his younger brother. I'd bet my life on it."

33

THE RED PHONE

NSA Headquarters.

"Sir, we've got a bead on the flatbed truck out of coastal Pakistan!" Anne, an analyst with long brunette hair, yelled from across the room.

"What? Bring it up on screen two," Uncle Bill said. "Whose satellite imagery is this?"

"The Aussies', sir. The images are coming up now."

"God, I love those people. Okay, okay. How old are these images?"

"They were captured a couple of hours ago."

"Damn, well, we take what we can get. How sure are we that this is our truck?"

"Looks like our truck, sir," Knuckles said. "Let's zoom up a little closer on that. Cade, you got the controls there, pal? Yeah, look. Same make and model flatbed. And look at the bed. Looks just like what we'd expect. It's carrying something long and tubular, covered up by a huge canvas tarp. Now, Cade, on screen three, zoom way out. Let's see the surrounding area where the truck is driving. Look at the GPS coordinates. We're in the exact locale we'd expect the truck to have been. See? Back here is the Pakistan Naval Academy. And look. Sandspit beach, Manora Drive, the mangroves, the intersection with the hamlet of Kakapir. They hadn't gotten very far from the pier when this bird flew overhead. This has got to be our guy."

Cade flipped through the rest of the satellite images.

"It looks like the truck drove right along the beach on Manora Drive, then turned on Kakapir Road, heading north, but that's where the satellite goes out of range and we lose him."

"The Aussies have just sent over a bunch of other images from surveillance cameras in the Kakapir area," Anne said. "They may have lost him on satellite, but they say they have a bead on our truck on these other cameras. Looks like the truck stayed right there in the coastal Kakapir area. The last image was taken from the rear entrance of a store. That image is just thirty minutes old. The truck is parked out back. It's stationary, and the flatbed is still loaded. This looks like the same truck as the one in these satellite images. Maybe the terrorists are planning to offload the weapon onto a boat at one of the small piers in the area. The Aussies say the truck is still parked right here on the map."

Uncle Bill scratched his beard.

"People, I know it looks good. But before we can call the president to get authorization to send some SEAL team or other such force into the area, we better be damned sure. Keep in mind, we get to sit in this room and watch as they pull off a raid. We'd be watching it from one of our birds, or this surveillance camera. But it's not that simple. Everyone understand? We would be watching it on *TV*. But this is real, people. That truck might be carrying a nuclear device. Or it might be carrying a length of metal sewer pipe. Those soldiers we'd be sending in there are real men and women with real lives. They might die, or worse, they might accidentally kill some innocent restaurant owner who comes outside to ask the truck driver when his sewer line will be repaired. We've got to be sure."

Anne was a junior analyst but not afraid to speak.

"Sir, the satellite images may be a few hours old, and we may not be able to definitively tie the truck in the Aussie satellite images to the truck we're seeing on surveillance camera parked behind the store, but there's one thing I haven't told you."

"And what's that?"

"The satellite images don't come from a normal satellite. It's an experimental Aussie satellite that can detect radioisotope signatures. Whatever is underneath the tarp on that truck in the *satellite* images is no length of sewer pipe. It's throwing off enough gamma rays to light up their screens like a Bic lighter on a dark night."

"Why didn't you say so? Can we determine how many signatures?"

"Just the one, sir. And it's strong. Their people think the total gamma-ray flux is equivalent with what they'd expect from the full ten warheads. But it's impossible to tell if they've been separated or not."

"How the hell can their satellite see that?" Cade said.

Knuckles replied without looking up.

"The Optus D2 comsat satellite has an experimental system that can detect high-velocity spin-off particles from enriched uranium. Due to the small size and velocity of these particles, no amount of shielding can block them: not lead, not earth."

"It figures you would know that. So why don't we use this satellite to track the nukes wherever they go?"

"I wish it was that easy," Knuckles said. "Like most of these birds, the Optus D2 is orbiting at eighteen thousand miles per hour. It's not over the same spot on earth for very long, as you might imagine. And, it's the only one in the world with this experimental detection system."

"Can't we slow it down?"

"Cade, it's in low-earth orbit, not geosynchronous or high elliptical."

"What does that mean? It has no brakes?"

Knuckles shook his head. "Low-earth orbit means it's relatively close to the earth . . ."

"Believe it or not, that much I assumed."

Jana grinned at the two of them.

Knuckles continued. "Like us, the Aussies have satellites in each orbital pattern, but this one probably needs to be closer to earth so they have easier access to it. You know, for installing new instruments, fixing things that are broken, and upgrading their new detection system while they try to make it work."

"All right, all right. You done, professor?" Cade turned toward Uncle Bill. "Sir, given the time stamp on the satellite images, it would seem impossible the terrorists have had time to disassemble anything at this point. The weapon would have to be intact."

"I agree, but I damn sure wish we had a fresh satellite image of this truck that's sitting behind the store. I'd love confirmation that that is our guy. Given the circumstances, we need authorization for a strike team. I'll call the president, but we're talking about invading sovereign Pakistani territory. He's not going to like it. Shit, I hate using that red phone."

"Hold on, sir," Anne said, putting down a phone receiver at her desk. "You may not need to ask for authorization after all."

"I highly doubt that."

"It's the Aussies, sir. They aren't exactly asking for anyone's permission."

Bill looked over the tops of his glasses. "Asking for permission? Permission for what? What are you talking about?"

"You've assigned different members of the team here to work with other intelligence services around the world, right? I've been working with the Aussies. They're, ah," she stuttered, "they're hitting the truck, sir."

This time, even FBI Director Stephen Latent spun around in his chair.

"They're what?"

"Yes, sir. The Australians just informed me they're hitting the truck. They're launching a special ops team as we speak. They're not taking any chances with a broken arrow. They believe confidence is high. They say they're too close to let this thing slip away."

"Oh, hell," Uncle Bill said. "Do we have a bird coming overhead? We've got to put eyes on this before it gets ugly. We've got to see everything that's happening."

"Australia's carrier HMAS *Canberra* is in the Gulf of Oman and has a General Atomic Sea Avenger drone that they're also launching now, sir. We're asking if the Aussies will give us a live feed of the raid through the cameras on the drone."

Uncle Bill motioned Director Latent into his office. "Red-phone time."

"Wonderful," Latent replied.

As Uncle Bill and Stephen Latent left the room, Cade turned

to Knuckles.

"Professor, one word of advice."

"Yeah?"

Cade looked at Jana. "Chicks don't dig it when you talk about the nuances of geosynchronous, close earth, and elliptical orbits. Okay?"

Jana smiled.

"Okay, but what do they want us to talk about?"

Cade landed a hand on Knuckles's shoulder. "If that satellite can tell you the answer to that one, you let me know."

34

PARANOIA

The White House.

An aide made a hasty entrance into the Oval Office.

"Mr. President. Red line, sir."

"Thank you, son. Dismissed." He leveled foreboding eyes on the only other person in the room, then picked up the phone. "This is the President. In presence is National Security Advisor James Foreman."

"Mr. President, William Tarleton, National Security Agency, Directory Section Head. I've got FBI Director Stephen Latent with me, sir."

"State your code red, Tarleton."

"Sir, we have a possible location on that Homeland Security level fifteen. The weapon appears to be in coastal Pakistan. Kakapir, Pakistan, to be exact. A small hamlet approximately 5.6 miles from Karachi."

James Foreman hit the mute button on the red phone so he could talk privately with the president.

"Mr. President, may I remind you, if they find that nuclear weapon, they find our CIA operative, and your whole bullshit operation is blown sky high, not to mention your presidency."

The president bolted from his chair and launched himself at the man.

"I'll have no more of your insubordination, Foreman! I'll either have your undying loyalty or I'll offer you up as a sacrifice."

"You've always had my loyalty, sir. But this whole thing

sickens me—sickens me to the core!" He released the mute button and asked, "What's your confidence level, Tarleton?"

"Our confidence level on *identification* of the truck is about sixty percent. On the fact that a truck meeting that exact description is currently carrying a nuclear device, about ninety-five percent. But that's not what the code red is about, sir. It's about the Australians."

"The Australians? What about them?"

"Sir, there are two sets of surveillance images we're tracking related to the whereabouts of this nuclear weapon. One comes from an Aussie satellite, the other from—"

The president exploded. "Cut to the chase, dammit!"

"Yes, sir. Sir, the Aussies are launching a raid into Pakistan as we speak. The carrier HMAS *Canberra* is in the Gulf of Oman right now. A few minutes ago, an S-70A-12 Black Hawk helicopter with twelve Australian Army SAS operators aboard launched from her deck. We're tracking the gunship now. She's headed right toward our package."

"Right toward the truck? They're headed into Pakistani airspace? Who authorized this?" the president boomed. "Was it you? Did NSA tell the Australians to launch a strike? I want that team called back!"

At the same time James Foreman was again hitting the mute button on the red phone in the Oval Office, Uncle Bill lofted a bewildered look to Stephen Latent.

"Sir," Uncle Bill said, "NSA doesn't write US foreign policy, nor authorize any foreign government to conduct military raids into other countries,."

"Sir!" cried the national security advisor to the president. "Calm down. Do you want the whole world to know you're trying to hide something? You can't stop the raid now—it's too late." The phone was again unmuted.

"All right, all right, Tarleton. Keep me informed. I want to know what happens on that raid as soon as it unfolds. Got that?"

"Yes, sir."

Uncle Bill hung up the call.

"What the hell was that all about?" he said to Latent.

Stephen Latent paced the room, entranced in thoughts he wished were not there. "Where does he get off accusing you of ordering a raid into Pakistan? Is it me being paranoid again or does it sound like he's got something to hide?"

Bill shook his head. "The last time you got paranoid, I nearly had to bury you. I hate it when you get paranoid."

"There wouldn't have been a body to bury."

"I know that. And I also know if you'd have been vaporized in a nuclear explosion in Kentucky, I would have never collected on that bet you lost in Super Bowl sixteen. Got that twenty bucks you still owe me?"

35

OF SNAKES AND BLACK HAWKS

Australian S-70A-12 Black Hawk helicopter, call sign "Voodoo 12." The Arabian Sea, seventeen nautical miles south-southwest of Kakapir, Pakistan.

"Keep her on the deck, mate. I don't want to pop up on the Pak's radar, if you know what I mean."

"That's a rog, Lieutenant," the chopper pilot replied.

The lieutenant turned to the other eleven elite SAS operators huddled together in the cramped cabin, and spoke into the headset. "Listen up, mates. We're four minutes out. So I've got just one question for you ladies. If you're part of third squadron, Special Ops Command, based out of Garrison HQ, Campbell Barracks, Swanbourne, Australia, and flying in the dark of night at a hundred seventy miles an hour, fifty feet off the deck, and headed into harm's way, what do we call that?"

The team responded in unison. "A good day, sir."

"Who are we?"

"The snake eaters!" they replied in escalating volume.

"What do we say?"

"Who dares wins!"

"All right, we ditch at one mile from shore. When we jump from this helicopter into the blackness of night, I want a tight group. Nobody gets separated. The CRRC deployable boat will drop into the water first. Staff Sergeant Jones is on nav. He'll be the tour guide for our little ride on this rubber duck and will put us right up into the mangroves off Sandspit beach and into the back side of the hamlet of Kakapir. From there we'll beach it, then hump about half a click to here." He pointed to a map of Kakapir and the surrounding Karachi area. "Point Darwin, a lovely little place you ladies will find quite charming. A bit like the outback, you might say."

"Lieutanant, why are we calling it Point Darwin?"

"Because mate, if that nuclear weapon detonates, it will restart evolution."

The young soldier nodded. "Yes, sir."

"If we make a positive ID on the device, we hijack the truck—at all costs. I don't give a shit how many AK-47s are spitting hot lead at you, you hold your ground. We will take that truck. Am I clear?"

In unison, "Who dares wins. Yes, Lieutanant."

"Once we are in possession of the truck, we'll have two Chinook helicopters on standby hovering just off the coast. They've got the capacity to hoist that heavy son of a bitch away. And, we've got a squadron of badass helicopter gunships in support. With some luck, the terrorists will do a nice job bleeding, and the Pakistani military will have no time to react to our incursion."

"And if they do react, sir?" the young soldier said.

"Then God help them, mate."

"Lieutenant," the Black Hawk pilot said, "one minute."

"Roger that, mate. All right, snakes, lock and load."

All the operators tapped their palms against ammunition clips in the bottom of their weapons, then chambered a live round into the breech.

"And they all said?"

"Snakes, snakes. Who dares wins!" came the sequenced reply.

As the helicopter slowed over the black water below, the lieutenant flung open the sliding door. The thrash of helicopter rotors against the wind and waves produced a whirl of seawater-mist that rushed in and pelted everything in its path. At fourteen feet above the ocean waves, the deployable CRRC boat dropped and landed with a loud thump against the water.

"Go, go, go!" the lieutenant yelled.

Operators leapt from the helicopter and into the watery oblivion below. Once aboard the CRRC, the small boat pitched forward and propelled the heavily armed strike team toward the unsuspecting Pakistani coastline.

The boat rocketed across the waves from the drop-off point toward the coastline at high speed. Under cover of night, Staff Sergeant Jones used night-vision goggles to navigate his way into the shoreside entrance of the mangroves. The boat slowed to quiet its approach as it snaked further upriver through the reed grasses that began to surround them on all sides. Once underneath the second bridge spanning the river, they beached the boat and stowed it, then covered it with reeds. They began their jog toward Point Darwin which was half a mile away, and they were slowing for nothing.

36

THE JOINT CHIEFS

Ft. Meade, Maryland. Joint operations task force war room.

Members of the Joint Chiefs, flanked by National Security
Advisor James Foreman, began flooding into Fort Meade's joint
operations task force war room. With so much data pouring into
NSA, the war room had become the central hub of the
investigation. Bill Tarleton ushered them in with great haste.

On the main monitor, the men stared at a live infrared
satellite feed.

"These are the Australian operators we're watching? Where
are we getting this feed from?" Chief of Naval Operations,
Admiral Joseph Glass said.

"The Brits, sir. The images are coming in from one of their
military satellites. They've given us access. It's in orbit over the
Middle East at the moment."

The images clearly depicted a small watercraft weaving its
way in and out of a mangrove swamp. Distinctive heat
signatures of twelve men glowed iridescent green. The boat
grounded itself under a bridge and was partially obscured from
view.

"What in God's name possessed the Australians to do this?"
the national security advisor said. "Pulling a raid into Pakistan?
They must be out of their minds, especially with tensions so
high after the incident with the USS *Colorado*."

On the monitor, SAS operators departed the boat and broke
into a full sprint along the lower roadbed and headed straight

toward the sleeping village of Kakapir.

"Well, it's not as though we've never pulled a raid into Pakistan ourselves," Admiral Glass replied.

The generals exchanged stern looks at one another. None wanted to relive the tension-filled night of May 1, 2011 when Navy SEALs raided the compound of Osama bin Laden, deep within sovereign Pakistani territory.

"Well we sure as hell aren't about to send in any special-ops teams of our own. Tensions between the US and Pakistan are too high right now. They think we sunk two of their subs. What is the prime minister of Australia thinking?" National Security Advisor Foreman said.

Uncle Bill was shy by nature but never one to let his feelings fester too long. At this point he'd heard enough.

"Prime Minister Malcolm Turnbull is thinking he'd prefer to not have a loose nuclear device out on the open market for the highest bidder."

The comment elicited little reply.

"The Aussies have plenty of enemies in the Middle East, too," Bill continued.

"Still," General Wells said, "how much time do they have before daylight? They'll be sitting ducks."

For the first time, Chief of Staff of the Air Force General Mark Odierno spoke up. "And what happens if they find the nuke, but the terrorists detonate? What are the Pakistanis going to say then?" He leveled his eyes at Uncle Bill. "How long have you known the Australians were going to pull off this raid? Why are we just now finding out about it? Goddamned NSA!"

As the Australian SAS operators continued their sprint behind buildings and shanties in Kakapir in an all-out race toward their target, the room went deathly quiet—all eyes focused on Bill.

He looked at them with the pallor of a statue.

"General, I haven't slept in thirty-six hours. My team is made up of the best of the best." He launched from his chair and his volume escalated. "If it weren't for those people out there, and a bunch of others, every one of you would be dressed in hazmat suits right now, attempting to clean up fallout from a nuclear blast in Kentucky. Thanks to them, that never happened! The radiation would have spread east across six states by now. How long have I known about the Aussie raid, you ask?" He looked at his watch. "About thirty minutes. And by the way, during the Thoughtstorm raid, if I recall, it was a stolen *Air Force* Apache helicopter gunship that was used against the FBI's hostage rescue team. It nearly killed me, and it chewed my wife's Honda Odyssey minivan to bits. I should be dead right now. I've still got a piece of shrapnel in my ass from that attack. The Apache helicopter was stolen on your watch, not mine. I'm a patriot, sir, and I'd appreciate a little latitude here."

The national security advisor rose. "All right people, all right. We're all on the same team. Enough of this bickering."

"The Australian SAS operators are encircling their target," one of the other generals said. "It looks like that must be the truck."

"That would be it," Uncle Bill said. "God, I hope they haven't misidentified the truck."

"Misidentified it?" General Wells said. "I thought the Aussie satellite detected radioactive signatures from the truck."

"It did," Bill replied, "but that satellite went out of range. *This* truck was picked up on surveillance cameras in town, not from the satellite."

As the operators took up flanking positions, one darted between the truck and a building and slowly approached the cab of the vehicle.

"There's a heat signature inside the cab of that truck," Commandant of the Marine Corps Leland Phelps said. Each person in the room knew the statement's meaning—someone was inside the truck. If the individual called for help, or fired a weapon, or in any way signaled others, the entire operation could be blown right here. Not even a breath could be heard in the war room.

The Australian operator made a slow approach to the truck's cab, but as he closed to within five feet, the door of the cab swung open. The soldier attempted to hide by sliding underneath the truck near the gas tank.

"Dammit, why can't we hear what's going on? You know they're on the comm with each other," General Wells said. His glare was aimed at Bill.

"We're a little reticent to hack into the comm sets of our allies special-ops teams at the moment, General. But I'm sure if you give it time, the next administration will have a different set of morals."

As the man inside the truck stepped out, the soldier snatched his feet out from under him and body parts began to flail in all directions. It was difficult to see what happened next, but within moments, the truck driver's body lay motionless on the ground, and a pool of liquid escaped it. The heat signature of the blood was marked on the monitor by a dark, glowing shade of green.

"That's a kill," one General said.

Bill picked up a phone and dialed an inside extension. "Knuckles? Son, you picking up any chatter between the Australian carrier and the special ops team?" He put the phone on speaker.

"Yes, sir. They just supplied it. Sounds like they've got three gunships and two Chinook helicopters just offshore in support. Those helicopters are waiting for the go-code from the ground team before they move in to remove the nuke and extract the team."

The room went quiet again as SAS operators moved into positions on both sides of the truck and began untying what appeared to be a tarp over the flatbed.

"How much time do we have on this satellite before we're out of range, son?" Bill said.

"Nearly out of orbit now, sir. About sixty seconds."

"Shit!" the national security advisor said. "You mean we're going to be blind?"

The tarp was removed and two operators climbed onto the truck bed. They moved from the front of the truck to the back, and then repeated the process.

"What are they doing? What's that in their hands? Besides weapons, I mean," James Foreman said.

"Those are likely radiation sensors," one of the Generals said. "Geiger counters."

The soldiers hopped down and signaled one another. But just then, bright white flashes popped from the upper left of the screen. Soldiers wheeled around in that direction and the same white flashes erupted from the ends of their rifles.

"Firefight. Oh God," Foreman said, as he stood.

The room stirred into noisy chaos.

"Sir!" Knuckles said through the speaker phone. "The Australian Apache gunships are moving in to support! The team is under attack."

Soldiers spread out in all directions, returning fire and taking cover positions.

Bill yelled back, "But what about the nuke?"

"It's a negative, sir!"

"Say again?" Bill yelled.

"It's a negative, sir. It's not there! The nuke is not there. We picked up chatter from the aircraft carrier to the Apaches. The truck is carrying a pipe or something. They've recalled the Chinooks. It looks like the Pakistani military detected the intrusion into their airspace and are responding."

Bill looked back once more at the screen to see a flurry of weapons discharging, then saw one of the Australians go down. He couldn't bear to watch as the intensity of the firefight escalated. The video images on the screen began to distort and pixelate as the satellite's orbit took it out of range. Everyone knew the operators didn't stand a chance.

When the screen went dark the room again plunged into silence.

The commandant of the Marine Corps said in a reverent whisper, "*Semper fi.*"

Always faithful.

37

INTO THE MOUNTAINS

Goth Hussain, Pakistan. About forty-two miles north-northwest of Karachi. Driving along "the road to the north."

The flatbed of the tractor-trailer was skinned by a tarp that fully obscured its lethal cargo tucked neatly below. It stretched taught across the twenty-five-foot-long warhead, outlining only the topmost surface of its rounded exterior. To passersby, it may have appeared to be a length of pipe on its way to a job site. Sleeping underneath the protective blanket, the warhead itself was girded on either side by huge wooden posts running the length of the missile. The posts had been bolted into place, forming a cradle-like barrier, swaddling the missile to prevent it from rolling. As a final measure, the deadly weapon was lashed to the bed with four heavy chains that had been ratcheted into place.

As the truck lurched up the mountain hills, Khalid downshifted. The road was officially known as the Regional Cooperation for Development Highway, but Pakistanis in the area simply called it *the road to the north*, for it ran from southern Pakistan up into Afghanistan and toward the Himalayan mountains.

The truck lumbered forward in an all-out fight against the rise in altitude.

38

LIFE BOILS DOWN TO A FEW MOMENTS

Northern Pakistan.

The truck struggled to pull the 85,000 pounds pressing against the curvature of its flatbed. As Khalid downshifted, both he and Jarrah's torsos rocked forward, then back again. An odor reminiscent of an old gym locker permeated the cab, as stagnant breezes ebbed into the open windows.

After they left the flat coastline and pushed north into the hills, the two men in the truck had gone silent. From time to time, Khalid looked at his leader, hoping to read a sign in his expression, something, anything. Witnessing Jarrah's near meltdown while they crossed the Karachi Bridge had caused Khalid to wonder if Jarrah's mind had cracked.

Over the past several months of training together, preparing in complete secrecy for every eventuality of this mission, he'd noticed a wandering thought process that occasionally would emanate from Jarrah's speech and behavior. His words, if strung together on paper, would sometimes form more of an anagram than a sentence. Some words were out of place in his speech, and as such, his statements could be taken out of context. The effect was disconcerting. It was like listening to a madman. The more troubling thing to Khalid was that, in those days, there had been no one else to witness such ramblings. Khalid couldn't decide if he should purposely overlook Jarrah's instability, or if this apparent mental breakdown was necessary to the mission in the first place.

It wasn't a clearly outlined mission in the beginning, not to Khalid at least. Even though he had fed the information to Jarrah, and had then been hand-selected by Jarrah to carry out the final deed, he was still low man on the totem pole. Bits and pieces of information about the full mission were fed to him one nibble here, one nibble there. He was kept in a state of information starvation right up until training blissfully ended. At that point, he was given a briefing on what Jarrah described as "the full mission."

Jarrah outlined the scenario in which the US government planned to participate in the theft of a nuclear device from a Pakistani submarine. Jarrah intended to intercept that missile. What Jarrah would never speak of, and what Khalid would never ask, was a question that loomed in Khalid's mind—the question of *why*. It wasn't appropriate for him to ask such a question. To ask was to admit he had doubts, and doubts had no place at the table of the service of Allah.

Although Khalid did not know *why* Jarrah wanted to intercept and steal a nuclear weapon, he did know that life boils down to a few moments, and this one would etch his face into human history.

Even as children, he and his brothers had been groomed. None of them understood it at the time, but Waseem Jarrah's involvement in their childhood had a purpose. It wasn't until after the oldest brother, Shakey, had failed in his mission to detonate a nuclear weapon at the bluegrass festival in Kentucky that Khalid had learned of his death. Most of the rest of the story came together by watching the news coverage that followed. It took months to learn the more closely guarded details. But at least Khalid now knew—his brother and he had been groomed for just such a task, and the fact that his brother had failed in the final moments only heightened the pressure Khalid now felt pinching down upon his narrow shoulders. Mentally though, he was resolute. He would not fail to carry out his mission against the beast.

Khalid glanced again out of the corner of his eye. Jarrah looked as though he'd climbed out of the depths of depravity,

and could now see clearly. He turned his head toward Khalid
with the slowness of sand dripping from an hour glass. Khalid
looked back and forth between Jarrah's fresh face and the
curving roadway.

"We are not far now," Khalid said.

"Yes, 2.8 kilometers," Jarrah said. "Just 2.8 more kilometers."

"How do you know that?"

There was no answer, but there was a new, clear life in
Jarrah's eyes that had begun to take on a childlike exuberance.
Silence again ensued, and Khalid was left with only the sound of
the high-pitched, droning motor of the truck as it struggled up
and around the next bend.

The surrounding hillsides were craggled with sheets of sheer
rock, one stacked atop the other. Although they looked like they
might dislodge at any moment, in reality, they had sat in the
same position for thousands of years. But as they rounded the
last bend in the road, the tree line returned and the road
flattened, hugging the ridge lines.

The road thinned and Khalid thought back to Jarrah's reaction
at the bridge. If there was any time Jarrah might again feel
trapped, this was it. The mountain roads were desolate and
would not provide much cover if they came under attack. But
Jarrah's face had returned to stone, further cementing Khalid's
knowledge that his leader's thoughts and emotions were
unstable.

It wasn't until they rounded the bend and saw the old wood
mill that Khalid's heart rate begin to accelerate. Here they
would stop, and as such, would become vulnerable. To his
surprise, Jarrah snapped to life again and the color returned to
his cheeks. The volatility was worsening.

Khalid squinted to read the faded lettering across the front of
the building which had stood on this spot since its construction
in the early 1950s. The words read "Yasir Planking." In those
days, the forest was thicker, and the demand for wood strong.
But when wealthy industrialized logging companies invaded the
area, the tiny wood mill fell into disuse. It just couldn't compete.

As the truck stopped just short of the enormous sliding
wooden doors, Jarrah opened his door and bounced down onto
the compacted dirt, his energy that of a ten-year-old. A tuft of

chalky dust popped out from underneath the wide soles of his steel-toed boots and splashed against the cuffs of his blue jeans. He bounded straight for the doors and leaned his weight into one. It creaked, then gave up its brief struggle and began to yield to the kinetic forces pushing against it. The rusty door runners clanked to a jarring stop. After both doors had been opened, Khalid, still in shock at having witnessed Jarrah leap out of a droned slumber and into activity, was slow to put the truck into gear.

Inside, the wood mill had but a single overhead boom to lift logs into the air. The boom hung upside down, gripping the underside of a long steel beam that straddled the ceiling's topmost span. It looked like a mechanical bat in a cave, dangling from the ceiling.

Khalid's senses were heightened and his eyes darted from one side of the interior to the next, scanning for any movement. As he maneuvered the huge truck into the wood mill, his heartbeat quickened. He knew that to disassemble the weapon, they would need expert help, and introducing anyone new into their circle increased the danger tenfold. Khalid felt a clamminess flush against his face and wished all of this was over. Perhaps he too was becoming paranoid.

The worst part was the waiting. There was nothing to be done until the expert arrived. He was the only one with the kind of training required. Without his knowledge, it would be near suicide to attempt to disassemble the weapon and separate each of the ten MIRV nuclear tips.

Khalid rolled the vehicle into the center of the shed-like structure and looked around the dark interior for any signs of life. Jarrah noticed the wandering of his gaze, paused, but said nothing.

The interior of the narrow building was about twice the length of the semitruck. Overhead, streaks of bright sunlight pierced the aged roof and carved brilliant spots on the dirt floor. The radiance reminded Khalid of the eminent power of God and that he was about to embark on a mission of terrifying proportions. He prayed that he was right and that Allah's jubilance at his actions would bless him and carry him through until the final act.

Thus far, all had gone to plan. He had sabotaged the *Simbirsk*, and the warhead had been stolen and transported all the way here into the mountains. And although Khalid didn't know the exact details of his final objective, he knew that he was to carry out the assignment that his brother had attempted previously. Once the warheads were disassembled, he would carry one across the ocean and place it into the mouth of the beast.

As the truck engine shut down, it shuddered in one last act of defiance before uttering a quiet hiss. Jarrah was in full stride. He slung both massive doors closed and went to work pulling the steel-chain rigging into place above the flatbed.

The wood mill was so old, and the area so remote, electricity had never been brought here. The pulley system for lifting full-length trees from truck-level was hand operated and of a fairly common style. The ratchets and pulleys distributed weight so well that the act of lifting a massive tree from a logging truck was made relatively easy.

They began the process of securing the missile to the overhead pulley. Their operation was running right on schedule. But when Khalid saw something move on the hillside behind the building, he lunged for his rifle.

39

THE RAVEN'S CRY

Yasir Planking wood mill. Kakaheer, northern Pakistan.

The old man ambled out of the trees and walked down the hillside the way any nomad would. His skin was dark and made no effort to hide his years. He carried only a long walking pole, sauntering in the bright sunlight toward the rear of the wood mill. Khalid placed a nervous hand on an automatic rifle which lay against his side, but Waseem Jarrah only smiled.

"Right on time."

Jarrah walked toward the man and the two embraced.

"Salaam alaikum. Peace be with you," the old man said.

"Wa alaikum as Salaam And also unto you."

"It has been a long time, my young friend."

"Too long," Jarrah replied. "But nothing is too long in the service of Allah. Come, come inside, where we begin our final act of service together."

"We have been waiting, and now the time is here."

"Farooq, let me introduce you to Khalid Kunde."

"There is no introduction necessary. I know the boy," the old man said. "He will not remember me, but I was there at his birth and at his dedication." The elder's voice was raspy.

Khalid stared at the man, bewildered. "My dedication?" he said.

The elder placed an arthritic hand on Khalid's shoulder.

"Yes, my son. You and your brother, at the time of your births, were dedicated to the service to Allah. Now, your time has come. We have hours of work ahead of us. But first, we will eat and have tea. Come, come."

There was a giddiness to his demeanor and it reminded Khalid of an old storyteller that used to visit his home when he was a little boy.

"Your name is *Farooq*?" Khalid said. Before closing the sliding door, Khalid stared out into the bleak landscape, searching his mind for a face that would not surface. He turned toward the old man. "What is your full name, sir?"

"Ah, well. We will have time for that. We will have time for that later, my good boy."

Khalid whispered to Waseem, "This is the expert we were awaiting? Who is he? Why does he know me? He is to disassemble the weapon? Are you sure?"

Waseem shook his head. "So quick to doubt. So full of questions. Appearances can be deceiving."

Four hours later, after having separated the tertiary solid-fuel rocket booster, the remaining half of the missile body was uprighted and moved onto the dirt floor, using the crane and winch system. The old man spent another two hours separating the flattened nose-cone at the tip of the rocket to reveal what was underneath: ten deadly warheads. Each warhead was over four feet in height and independently encased inside its own sharply pointed cone, known as a dunce cap. The dunce caps strutted upward like sharpened fingers of retribution.

"You must have trained years for this very moment," Khalid said in revelry.

He looked to the elder but received no reply.

The man's wrinkled forehead furled, but his focus appeared unbreakable. After several long moments, the man looked at him with the eyes of a lion and said, "Not for *this* moment. Not for this one, my friend."

The work continued an additional four hours until all ten warheads had been separated from the main container, known as the bus.

The old man stood and stretched his lower back.

"We must remove the dunce caps from nine of them to separate their self-contained propulsion and guidance systems, and to remove the nuclear cores. We only need the nuclear components and triggers. Once separated, they will be easier to transport and conceal."

"Why only nine?" Khalid said. "What about the tenth one?"

It was Waseem Jarrah that answered.

"That one has a very special purpose. A *destiny*, you might say. One other, we will use. In fact, our entire mission only requires one of them. The other eight lethal brothers have a path all their own." He no longer carried any of the earlier burden of insanity, but his eyes glowed with avarice.

"Waseem," Khalid said, "you have not told me of our plans past this point. Will we drive the weapons from here in the truck?"

Jarrah glanced first at the old man, who continued in his work, then back at Khalid. It was a mild rebuke, as if to say "we discuss our plans in front of no one."

"Khalid, Farooq here is a good servant and wise enough to know that we had to tell him some of what we needed, which was to separate the warheads. The reason of *why* we need one of the ten to be left intact are unimportant to him. We needed the others to be separated from their propulsion systems to make them easier to transport. That is all he needs to know. Isn't that right, professor?"

"Yes, my good friend, yes. The professor knows all he needs to know. And he will go to his grave with just that information, as planned. Ah, it has been a good life in the service of Allah, has it not, Waseem? We have seen and done so many things."

"Indeed, it is true. We have. But your years far exceed mine, professor."

Khalid watched the two men and wondered what their conversation really meant. It occurred to him that the old man was almost saying good-bye. But Khalid was still haunted by the familiarity that he could not place.

"We are almost finished now, Waseem," the old man said as his eyes gleamed. "All ten devices have been prepared. Both of you now know what to do? I have shown you how to detonate the ones I have separated from their propulsion systems? And, you are sure you know how to set the other to detonate as we discussed? You know the sequences? They are complex, and you cannot deviate from what I have said. The consequences would be disastrous."

Waseem put both hands on the old man's shoulders and smiled.

"Over the years, you have been like a father to me. From the time I was but a little boy, you taught me all I know about the Koran, about our ways. And now, you show me the most loyalty I could ask any servant of Allah."

"I will miss you too, Waseem. You have been like a son to me."

Waseem's lower lip seemed to quiver, but only for a moment, then his eyes became steel.

The old man nodded in ascent.

"It will be all right, Waseem," the old man said. "It will be all right. This is the only way. We both know it. Come, it will be over quickly."

The old man took Jarrah by the arm and began a slow walk outside.

Waseem Jarrah looked at Khalid and said only, "Stay here."

"Wait," Khalid cried.

The old man turned to him.

Khalid's mouth hung open. "You used to read to me, didn't you? When I was a little boy? You read Koran stories to me. The Builder of the Kabah, the Ark of Nuh and the Animals. I was too little to say the name Farooq so I called you *the Faroo*."

The old man's smile warmed the bleak desolation of their surroundings, and he placed a crinkled hand on Khalid's face.

"Yes, when you were a little boy, I came many times. You used to call me the Faroo. My name is Farooq Mohmand. But now is not good-bye. Now is simply a time where our paths must move in different directions. We will see each other again, in the arms of Allah." The last word trailed off like a whisper.

Waseem and Farooq walked arm in arm into the stark sunlight toward an old well that sat just behind the building.

Khalid squinted against the bleakness, watching them.

At the well, both men turned toward the East and knelt.

Khalid could hear mumbled prayers. He watched as they went facedown, then back up several times. Moments later, they stood and embraced and a few silent words were exchanged.

Khalid knew what he was witnessing was something private, something solemn. But he could not bear to watch what he surmised would happen next and turned his back.

As he listened, the only sounds in the stark landscape was the hint of wind teasing the treetops, and a solitary, distant call of a raven—an ominous sign in any culture. Then, a loud crack shattered the serenity, followed by the hollow tinking sound of an empty brass shell casing as it bounced on the ground. The gunshot cut through the dusty air and echoed across the canyons then back again.

Khalid shuddered. He did not look back.

The footsteps of Waseem Jarrah carried with them the air of authority. There was work to be done and little time in which to do it.

40

PERSONNEL PARANOIA

NSA Headquarters.

In the aftermath surrounding the Australians' failed raid into Pakistan, Uncle Bill was made aware that Jana had identified the driver of the truck.

"I still can't get this out of my head," exclaimed the normally tranquil Uncle Bill. "A brother." Bill paced the floor and began to think out loud. "Jana said this looks like his brother. A younger brother. This lack of sleep is killing me. I can't think straight anymore. I'm missing something. Hmmm, I've got to think. Wait a second . . . oh crap. If Shakey Kunde has a younger brother then that would mean . . ." Bill stopped in his tracks, the fingers of one hand buried somewhere inside his cavernous salt-and-pepper beard.

Knuckles looked from Cade to Jana to Bill to Kyle, then back to Bill.

"Uncle Bill?"

But Bill heard nothing.

"I've got to think," he said to himself. "Shakey Kunde, the older brother. When we looked into his background, we found he had been planted into the United States young, very young. He was cultivated. Shakey Kunde is dead, and now we discover he has a younger brother." Bill was lost in thought. "From the time he was a kid, Shakey was cultivated." It was like listening to someone convince themselves of a wild theory. "He was raised for a purpose. And it was easily, what, twelve or fifteen years from the time he was first planted until he was activated? They put him into the university, had him study nuclear engineering so that he'd get a job inside a nuclear facility . . . so that one day he'd be useful. My God, if Shakey Kunde was planted in this country as a child, *and* he has a younger brother . . . that would mean . . . that would mean the younger brother might have been cultivated from an early age too! Planted here. Raised and trained for some purpose that would later become evident."

"Bill, wait, you're rambling. What are you saying?" Knuckles said.

Bill again began to pace; his face washed clear of all expression.

"Shakey Kunde had a kid brother!" He turned toward them. "Don't you see it?"

Knuckle's eyes darted across each person in rapid-fire succession. "No!"

"*He had a brother.* That means the most wanted terrorist in the world, Waseem Jarrah, the one who slipped right through our fingers last time, the one who pulled off dozens of terror attacks on US soil, who nearly fricasseed a perfectly good bluegrass festival in Kentucky, he mentored the younger brother as well. And the stolen nuclear missile we're tracking right now? It's Jarrah! Waseem Jarrah is behind it, somehow." Bill flung a finger into the air. "But that's not all!" He was starting to sound like a gameshow host. "No, no. It gets better! Want to go for double jeopardy where the scores can really change?" Exasperation oozed from his pores.

"I don't think so," Knuckles said.

Bill exhaled. "It means the younger brother could have been planted, too. Years ago, he could have been planted anywhere, anywhere in the US, including inside our government. Waseem Jarrah is number one on the FBI and Interpol's most-wanted lists. He's a patient man, and he doesn't make mistakes. He would have planted the younger brother somewhere vital."

"You've got to be kidding me," Knuckles said. "Oh, never mind. You don't kid. All right, so, I'm guessing you're about to do one of two things. Kill me or tell me we now need to do a bio on the younger brother that we didn't know existed until just a minute ago?"

"You don't think I'm not about to do both?"

Only Jana laughed.

Bill continued. "I want teams four and six working on the background of the younger brother. We've got to know everything. Hey, Buck, does CIA know anything about this?"

"Hell no."

"Well get on the horn with CIA and tell them to flush the personnel files. If the younger brother penetrated anywhere in there, God only knows what damage he could inflict."

"Well what about you?" Buck returned. "What about NSA? Don't you think you'd better make sure the son of a bitch wasn't working here either? Wouldn't want him snooping around and finding out you were eavesdropping on the Queen of England's cellphone calls."

"Touché, son, touché," Latent said as he laughed. "Don't let them give you any shit."

41

ONE NIGHT'S SLEEP

NSA Headquarters.

The next morning Bill called the NSA team meeting to order.
This was not business as usual. There were no jokesters around
the coffee machine. No young woman recapping her date from
the previous weekend, much less whether the young suitor was
likely to call today. No uproarious laughter and high fives
between the guys over how their alma mater's football team, the
Georgia Tech Yellow Jackets, had narrowly edged the virtually
unheard of Georgia Southern Eagles in the remaining three
seconds of play the previous day. No, no one on this team had
so much as left the building, nor would they. They would not
leave until the broken arrow was secured, or worse—a terrorist
had detonated the nuclear device.

Sleep was a rare commodity. "The Box," the square-shaped
monstrosity-of-a-building that headquartered the NSA in
Maryland, was well equipped to accommodate such situations.
Multiple rooms were available to house personnel who needed
to be on-site for days at a time. Shower facilities, cafeterias, and
even laundromats were available and employees used them as
required.

Uncle Bill's wife had become accustomed to his occasional
prolonged absences. She was a patient woman, but had once

carried out her threat to leave Bill behind and go on their three-week vacation across Europe, including a four-day cruise up the river Seine, without him. This extended absence from home was no exception.

But being a living legend within the agency had its perks. Bill was a softy at heart and had decided, after being stuck at the Box for fifteen days during the Thoughtstorm terrorism case, to take advantage of that status. He had asked an intern to drop by his house and pick up his little dog, Mr. Sprinkles, a miniature Chihuaha, and bring him to the office. He figured he had earned a few special privileges. When the intern returned to NSA headquarters, he was stopped at the security checkpoint.

The young man called Bill, not knowing what to do.

"They won't let me past. They say 'no dogs, no exceptions.' I told them that it was your dog, Mr. Tarleton. But they won't let me in with him. He's just as sweet as he can be, sir. But he's shaking like a leaf. I'm holding him in my arms, just like you said to do."

"Don't you worry, son. Just sit tight," Bill had said.

When Bill arrived at the security checkpoint, the shaking little pup hopped into his arms. But Bill was told the same thing, with the exception of service dogs, no dogs allowed. Bill then withdrew the contents of a manila envelope and dropped them on the security desk. The officer looked down.

"The first one is a photo taken on the street outside of the Thoughtstorm building the night of the raid. The white shards of metal all over the place are the remains of my wife's minivan, which I was driving. That's what was left after an Apache attack helicopter opened fire on it, trying to turn me into Swiss cheese. I'm fine, if you were asking, by the way. And the second item is a copy of the presidential citation I received. I'm taking my dog to work with me from now on. If you have a problem with that, I suggest you call the president."

Bill walked through the security gates without further ado. The only human being out of the over ten thousand employees in the Box to come to work with a two-pound dog in his arms each day.

"All right, people, listen up. New day, same assholes. Anybody get any sleep? Dang, I hope so; you're going to need it. And you people need a shower. It's starting to smell like the football locker rooms back at Georgetown around here. We need a fresh start. We need fresh thinking. We're behind the eight ball and it's beginning to piss me off. Okay, Knuckles here is going to go over the plan. Son, the floor is all yours."

"Thank you, sir. All right people, listen up."

"He already said that," Cade said.

"Oh, right. Anyway, we've got a lot to do. On screen one is what we know, and on screen two is what we're lacking. First, we've got a broken arrow out in the open. We've seen two or more individuals on surveillance cameras loading the forward half of a Russian-made ICBM onto a flatbed trailer and heading away from the vicinity of coastal Pakistan, right near the Pakistani military stronghold. One of the actors appears to be the younger brother of deceased terrorist, Shakey Kunde, who, when he was alive, wasn't exactly a lover of bluegrass music. If it *is* the younger brother, that puts him almost certainly in direct association with Interpol and FBI's most wanted man, Waseem Jarrah, mastermind of the entire string of terrorism attacks last year here in the United States, and behind the near annihilation of 16,000 people at the bluegrass festival in Kentucky. Next, we have fears that this younger brother may have been planted in the United States as a child by Waseem Jarrah. If that's true, Jarrah would not waste the opportunity. He would have planted him as a sleeper agent. For all we know, at this moment, the younger brother could be deep inside a sensitive place in our government. That's a wildcard, but a fairly plausible theory given Jarrah's past.

"Now let's focus on what we need and what we're doing. On screen two, you'll see the list. Once we saw the flatbed truck on surveillance cameras leaving the Pakistani coast, we began the process of examining our own satellites to see what coverage we have of the area, particularly during those times. We have full cooperation from Britain and Australia as well. We need to be able to see the entire region, right down to the level of being able to read the newspaper in some guy's hand. We've got to find that truck, and right now. That's priority one. If we do find it on satellite or by any other means, we've got our Navy SEAL and special-ops teams, and the teams of our allies all over the world on standby. We've got some secondary fears about this part, but we'll talk about that in a minute. Next, we need to start this morning by scanning the personnel files of CIA and NSA employees. We need to scan every photo to try to find a positive match against the younger brother of Shakey Kunde, if there even is a younger brother."

Jana coughed, interrupting.

"You have something to add, Agent Baker?" Knuckles said.

"When I said yesterday that it was Shakey Kunde's younger brother driving that truck, I wasn't identifying a matching set of dish towels. I said it's his younger brother, and it's his younger brother."

Knuckles swallowed.

"Yes, ma'am. We're going to have to do this manually, people. We can't use the computer to do a facial-recognition match."

Audible groans emanated from across the room.

"I know, I know. It's a pain in the arse, but the image from the truck is so grainy the facial recognition software doesn't stand a chance of being useful. It'll give us nothing but false positives. We're going to have to do this the old-fashioned way."

"But, you're talking about scanning every employee archive photo for CIA and NSA?" a woman said from the fourth cube to the right. "You're talking thousands and thousands of people. We'll never find him."

"Wait, wait," Cade said. "I've got an idea of how we can narrow it down. We start with the Pakistani records of naval personnel assigned to duty aboard the *Simbirsk*, remember? We were suspicious the terrorists had gotten someone on board to sabotage it, right? First, we scan those personnel records. Maybe we get lucky and find him there. If so, we'd then have a clear photo from which to work, and then we can use that photo with the facial-recognition software to scan CIA and NSA records automatically."

Bill grinned from behind crossed arms.

"I told you I was right when I hired you. You still want to work in the email-marketing-software world, son?" He turned to face

Jana, who was flanked by FBI Director Stephen Latent. "Jana, there's no one in the world who knows that face as well as you do. Would you do the honors?"

"Do I have a choice?" Jana laughed.

"Not really," FBI director Latent said.

"Okay," continued Knuckles, "now on to some of the other fun stuff, the secondary fears I mentioned a minute ago."

"You're so thorough," Cade said.

"Jealous," retorted Knuckles.

"It's like Abbot and Costello with you two," Jana said.

"Anyway, before I was so rudely interrupted, we have some other, rather unsettling concerns to discuss."

Not a sound could be heard over the quiet drone of humming laptops.

"At the moment we're tracking this as a broken arrow. What we're afraid of is that the actors might disassemble."

"Meaning?" a man said from the second cube from the left.

"And break the missile into its ten independent warheads."

The man slumped into his chair.

"My point exactly," Knuckles continued. "If it turns out that they have the know-how, the time, the opportunity, and the place . . . we could be tracking ten broken arrows, not one."

The room came alive as voices escalated and frustrations flared.

"Settle down, people, settle down," Uncle Bill said. "I know, I know. But don't shoot the messenger. We're all exhausted. I've got multiple teams coming in to relieve all of us. We're going to be working split shifts from now on. There's no way we can sustain this pace. We had a meeting with the Joint Chiefs this morning. We've been given new priority in terms of support for retasking of satellites, military support, more help from federal agencies—FBI, CIA, DEA, Customs, postal inspectors, Department of Agriculture inspectors, whoever the hell we want. After this shift, I want all of you the hell out of here and back at your homes. Get some sleep. But today, I need your full attention. Knuckles, continue, son."

"Look, this is just a theory of ours, okay?" Knuckles said. "This idea that they could break the warhead up into its ten independent parts. We doubt they have the technical know-how to make that happen. But since we have high confidence that we're dealing with number-one-asshole Waseem Jarrah, we've got to dig deeper into everyone in his network. Is there anyone in his known associates that could possibly have the type of knowledge needed to disassemble a weapon like that? Ever since Jarrah showed up on the radar screen last year, we've had multiple agencies doing bios on him and anyone he's ever known. All those poor professors he used to work with at Renneger Polytechnic Institute, where he was a professor and recruited students, probably had their lives turned upside down by our good friends here in the FBI. But they turned up nothing. Am I right?"

Latent, Kyle, and Jana nodded.

Knuckles continued. "So, we've had several of you doing further deep-dives over the last several days. Anybody turn up anything interesting?"

"Well, sir," a tall man named Carl said from the back of the room. He was rarely seen without his trademark bow tie, but he looked disheveled, his hair unkempt. "Lila found something. Well, a possible something, anyway. But I'm not so sure it's of any importance."

"It's okay," Uncle Bill said. "There are no stupid details in this room. Nothing is insignificant. Lila? Tell us what you found."

"Ah," Carl said, "she's asleep, sir. Please don't be mad. She's gone about forty-three hours without any sleep. You should see the bruises on her forehead from when she kept nodding off and banging her head on the desk."

"I understand. Why don't you tell us what she found."

"On the list of known associates, there's a man named Farooq Mohmand. He's from the same region of Pakistan as Waseem Jarrah and Shakey Kunde. Ah, sorry to mention the name, Miss Baker."

Jana shivered. "Why should you be? His corpse is in a pauper's grave. He won't be bothering me or anyone else anymore."

"Yes, ma'am. Farooq Mohmand was born in 1946. He appears to have come from some money, and to have traveled to the US to study."

"Where did he study?" Uncle Bill asked.

"Well, sir. That's where Lila's red flags started rising."

Everyone leaned in.

"He studied at Renneger Polytechnic Institute."

Bill nodded his head. "And I'll bet you'll give me three guesses as to what he majored in."

"No, sir. It will only take one guess," Carl replied.

"Nuclear engineering."

"Yes, sir."

"Shit."

"From there, he went back home to Pakistan."

"He didn't become a restaurateur in Pakistan, did he?"

"No sir, he went to work for the Ministry of Fuel, Power, and Natural Resources, under the direction of a man named Zulfiqar Ali Bhutto, who started their nuclear program back in 1972. It took a while, but by 1987 Pakistan had nuclear weapons capability. And over the years, both China and France have been involved in their program. It appears that this Farooq Mohmand has been working in the upper echelons of the program for a while."

Bill shook his head again.

"Sir, if Farooq Mohmand and Waseem Jarrah crossed paths at the university, then there's a distinct chance Waseem Jarrah has access to the technical know-how to disassemble the nuke into ten broken arrows."

Quiet again permeated the room.

42

TO IDENTIFY A SABOTEUR

NSA Headquarters.

With Cade's suggestion that they first do a manual review of the photos of all Pakistani naval personnel on board the *Simbirsk*, all eyes turned to Jana. If the younger brother of Shakey Kunde was listed as a crew member, they would know they were dealing with a Waseem Jarrah terror plot.

A cold shiver rode Jana's spine. *Just the thought of seeing that face again is enough to make me queasy*, thought Jana.

Cade slid a little closer to her, knowing how visceral her reaction had been the last time she'd seen the face of Shakey Kunde's brother. He noticed tight flexion of muscles in her temples and he whispered, "You're not going to go all Victoria's Secret on us again, are you?" He was rewarded with a smile.

"I *am* glad to be with you, you know," she replied.

He flushed a shade of crimson.

"Oh, don't be so surprised, Cade," the director laughed. "I'm no dummy. You think I don't know when one of my agents has her sights set? Can I give you some advice, son?"

Jana had not realized Latent was standing behind her. It was now her opportunity to turn a shade of crimson.

"Food," he said to Cade. "Food. It's as simple as that. Casey's Crab down on Fort Meade Road. Try the fried scallops. She'll love it, trust me. But for now, you two concentrate on the photos, okay?"

"Oh my God, I can't believe I'm being set up by the director of the FBI," Jana said. "Okay, okay. Photos of terror suspects first, fried scallops second. Wait a second, who the hell fries a scallop? Hey Knuckles, get over here. Where are the photos of the crew of the *Simbirsk*? I've got to eat fried scallops and I can't eat until I see those photos."

"Fried what? Dang I'm hungry. Uh, the photos? Yeah, we can pull those up on screen six. Just over there, ma'am."

"You don't have to call me ma'am. I'm barely old enough to be your big sister."

"Yes, ma'am. Oh, ma'am?"

"Well you certainly don't have to do it twice in one sentence."

"Why would anyone fry a scallop?"

"I'll tell you when you're older."

"Huh?"

"Never mind."

Cade's plan had worked. Jana was beginning to calm down. The earlier tension in her face vacated. His worst fear was that at some point Jana would have a meltdown right in front of the others. It wouldn't end her career, but it certainly would get her pulled from active duty, at least temporarily. He and Kyle would have to decide what to do about the situation. But Kyle was right. Something had to be done, and soon. If Jana blew apart during a field operation, lives could be endangered, including her own.

"Hey, Knuckles," Jana said. "I don't want the photos way up there on that big, stupid screen. Can I get them right here on this monitor? I want to sit down and look at them at this desk."

"Ah, sure, ma'am."

She glared.

"Oh, sorry, miss, ah, Agent, um . . ."

"Jana. Just call me Jana."

"Jana."

"Okay, good. I'll scroll through them one by one. How many personnel on board?"

"The *Simbursk* is a Typhoon-class sub, so she has a complement of one hundred and sixty sailors."

"One hundred and sixty, okay. That's not so bad. Let me take a look."

"But, that's just what she has living quarters for. When the *Simbursk* was in service, the Russians would have utilized all available compartments. The Pakistanis, however, saw no need to maximize the entire space since they operated so close to their own territorial waters. And, well, since they could easily resupply whenever necessary. Not to mention they had little need to man each of the two OK-650 pressurized-water nuclear reactors. They only needed to operate one of those—"

"Knuckles!"

"Oh, sorry. Based on the crew log for that morning. There were one hundred and forty-eight on board. All were signed on."

"All right, let me get to work here."

Jana began scanning from one crew member's photo to the next. Cade signaled Kyle and the two of them leaned over Jana's shoulder.

"How you doing there, little lady?" Kyle said in his pure Southern drawl.

She smiled at the two of them. "Just like old times with the three of us back together again, huh?"

"Nah, it's better this time," Kyle said.

"How so?" she said as she paged through the photos.

"It's the food. This time I get to go to the cafeteria at least."

Cade laughed. "And that's a good thing? I've been here a while. Give it time. Tell me what you think about it in a week."

"Are you kidding me?" Kyle replied. "Do you know that for breakfast they'll cook eggs to order for you?"

"No they won't," Cade said.

"Over easy."

"Now just how did you accomplish that?"

"It was simple. I asked the lady behind the counter if they ever served cheese grits. She glared at me a second, and then burst out laughing. I thought she was teasing me, but it turns out she's from Thunderbolt, Georgia, just outside my home of Savannah. She took me back in the kitchen and made me eggs."

"Just like undergrad," Cade laughed. "Always could get what he wanted where women were concerned."

Jana smiled, then turned back to the computer monitor, but as the next image painted itself across the screen, her face went pale and her grip on the computer mouse tightened as though she were trying to crush it. Both Kyle and Cade noticed immediately. She was face-to-face with Shakey Kunde's younger brother—the spitting image, and was again catapulted back in her mind's eye to the shooting in Kentucky.

"Jana? Jana?"

"Cade, let's get her up," rushed Kyle. "Jana, come on, we've got to get you out of here, now."

But Jana was frozen.

Director Latent was right behind them, and the sudden commotion startled him.

"What is it? What's the matter? Jana? Is she okay? What's wrong with her?"

Under the crush of Jana's grip, the computer mouse shattered and shards of plastic splayed in all directions. Jana's body went rigid and began to convulse. Cade and Kyle yanked her out of the chair and away from the monitor, the effect something akin to watching men move a mannequin. They lay her on the carpeted floor and rolled her on her side.

Latent yelled, "Someone call a medic! We need a medic in here now!"

43

THE ROAD TO DEATH

Yasir Planking wood mill.

"We continue our mission, my young apprentice," Waseem Jarrah said, while the barrel of the pistol still smoldered in his hand.

For the first time, Khalid saw a hint of remorse in Jarrah's eyes. Not weakness, but more like a touch of regret muddled in a pool of avarice.

"Where is the body?"

"Farooq leaned forward so that his body would fall into the well."

"Was it necessary? Killing him?"

The question was ignored.

"We are leaving this flatbed truck behind. It is too large for our purposes now. We have a second vehicle hidden in the storage shed around back. It's a pickup truck. Bring it around. We'll load the cargo." Jarrah checked his watch. "We are on schedule. Our next destination is not far, but we cannot be late. Our buyers are not men who number patience as one of their virtues."

Khalid started to question, but stopped himself.

"Yes, Waseem."

The white pickup was dingy and easily twelve years old, but looked much older. It was larger than a standard pickup, and the rear dual-wheeled axle would serve the vehicle well in carrying the payload of ten warheads. Now that the warheads had been separated from the main body of the missile, they were much lighter and easier to move. Yet they each weighed between eighty and one hundred and twenty pounds. The total cargo weight in the pickup bed was close to nine hundred pounds. They loaded each warhead into the bed and secured them in place.

"We will take this road into the low country," Jarrah said. "We'll be not far from the coast. Come, we must go now. There will be time for sleep later."

Khalid took one glance toward the well and saw a dark, wet stain on the stone rim. Somewhere in the watery darkness below was a corpse that no one would ever find.

The truck rambled up the dusty roadway until the terrain began to level off and, at last, descend into the flatlands below. From their vantage point, Khalid could see the coastline of the Gulf of Oman in the distance. During the descent, the truck's brakes squealed in protest.

Around forty-five minutes later, Waseem began looking for the next turn.

"Gadani Road. Also known as ship-breaking yard road. But the locals around here call it 'the road to death.' It will be on our left."

"It is where we will meet our contacts?"

"Yes, my young apprentice. The road leads all the way down to the water's edge. Gadani is a godforsaken village. A wasteland of the poor and forgotten. It's used as a boneyard for old ships. You will not be accustomed to such sights, Khalid. You left our glorious homeland when you were very young. You've been in the West too long. Sights such as those you are about to witness will shock you."

"What is here, Waseem?"

"They use the beach as a scrapyard. Giant ships are disassembled here."

"Why is it called 'the road to death'?"

"The workers. The workers die by the droves disassembling the ships. The work is dangerous. If a slab a steel doesn't crush you, a snapping cable might slice you in half. If neither of those, the toxins will do the job. This is a place of the forgotten. Memories come here to die."

"But the workers have no protections? The government does nothing?"

"You are thinking like a Westerner. You are in your homeland now, my friend. You are in Pakistan. It has been a long time for you. The government here does not care; there is too much money at stake. This place alone, this one port, if you want to call it that, is responsible for most of the steel needs of all of Pakistan. Not to mention all the small machinery that is salvaged."

"Where do the ships come from?"

"It is countries like Greece and Germany that send the most. Wealthy nations sell their dilapidated ships to the highest scrap bidder. And they don't care where the ships are taken or what happens to the workers who disassemble them."

The vehicle turned down the dirt road and began to rock across the gravel and potholes.

"How many die?"

"No one knows, and no one tells. These decrepit creatures work for around four dollars a day and most don't make it to the age of thirty. Not that many are killed outright. Most are sickened by the toxic substances and wastes that spill out all around them. Wait until you see; there will be old men there. The only problem is, they aren't really old. In truth they are no older than your brother was."

"What did you mean when you said it wasn't really a port? If they bring huge ships to dismantle, how could it not be a port?"

But when they drove past the low brush line and saw clear to the ocean, Khalid understood with startling clarity. Two massive ships, one a rusting oil tanker, the other a container ship that had once stretched the length of twelve city blocks, sat fully beached in the sand. Both were in various states of dismantlement. There was no dock, no port, no infrastructure. There were no buildings or facilities of any kind. The ships were simply run at full speed onto the sand until grounded. Then each ship was overrun with workers who would start the dismantling process. From a distance, the workers looked like little ants dotting a landscape, each dot moving about with its own purpose.

"I can't believe it. The ships are enormous. And just run aground like that?" Khalid held a hand to his forehead.

"Don't breathe too deeply, my young friend. You may inhale something toxic," Jarrah said as he laughed.

"But, what about all these people?" Khalid said. "They will see what we are doing."

Jarrah squinted into the stark light. His tone deepened.

"This beach makes the perfect place for our rendezvous. People here will ask no questions. They know that whatever we are doing, it is none of their concern." Jarrah tapped his AK-47 assault rifle. "We will not be disturbed."

44

BORDER ESCALATION

Along the North Korean border.

"WBS News, with news, traffic, and your local weather on the fives. I'm Mike Slayden. We're going live now to our correspondent, Tammy Cho, who is currently on the border with North Korea, Russia, and China. Tammy? We'd lost our signal with you earlier and were quite concerned. Can you tell us what happened?"

"That's right, Mike. Our signal was cut by authorities just as a Russian mortar salvo was fired over the border of North Korea. From our positions here, we can only see North Korea with the aid of high-powered cameras. But, we were able to record this footage earlier."

As Tammy spoke, video footage rolled, revealing a hazy and somewhat-shaky view of the rocky hillside that marked the border with North Korea. A distant explosion rocked the hill, sending debris in all directions.

"The Russians fired a single long-range mortar round at North Korean positions. They apparently did not want live streaming coverage if there was a response from the North, thus starting a full-scale conflict. They've reopened our satellite feed and that's how we're able to speak with you now. When asked for comment, we were told that this amounted to a warning shot. In naval terms, it's known as 'firing a shot across the bow.' But, Mike, military analysts agree, this could be just the beginning."

"And Tammy, what other military activity do you see on the

part of the Russians?"

"In the last thirty minutes, the submarine we reported on earlier, the K-551, *Vladimir Monomakh*, left port. We can no longer see her and we assume she has submerged. Fears are escalating here that the brand-new submarine may be headed into her first war. As for us, we've been given permission to move further west to a place called Khasan, Russia, which will put us on the Tuman River, about two thousand *feet* from the border with North Korea. Most of the North Korean troops have massed across from there, near the town of Tumanbon, North Korea, and tensions are expected to be high. For now, I'm Tammy Cho, reporting live from Kraskino, Russia."

"All right Tammy, that's a dangerous place to be. Safe travels. This is Mike Slayden. You've been watching WBS News."

45

THE HOSPITAL

Emergency Department, Acute Care Center, Laurel Regional Hospital, Laurel, Maryland. About twelve miles west of Ft. Meade.

"No, no. She'll be fine," reassured the physician as she reshouldered her stethoscope and glanced at Cade. "Her brain activity is normal. EKG, blood work, all look good."

"So what happened?"

"I'm glad you told me about the previous post-traumatic-stress-disorder episodes. But to be honest," the doctor continued, "after seeing these gunshot scars on her upper torso, PTSD would have been my first suspicion. The scars don't look that old. They're only in stage three of the healing process. The trauma she sustained must still be fresh in her mind. How long has it been since she was shot?"

"It was several months ago, in Kentucky. She was shot at the bluegrass festival."

"Oh, you mean this is . . . I didn't recognize her when she came in. We don't tend to focus on the face when we're in triage."

"No, I guess not," Cade said.

"So this is the agent that saved us all? Well I'm not surprised about the PTSD. Anyone who'd been through an ordeal like that would have to be superhuman to not be affected."

"So what now? When will she wake up?"

"We've given her a very mild dose of Versed. It won't keep her asleep, but it will help take the edge off when she wakes up and finds herself in a strange place. But I added a mild stimulant that will perk her up in just a bit here."

Cade shuddered. "She's awakened in a hospital like this before." He looked at Kyle. "In fact, you both have."

"Yeah. Can't say I liked it much," Kyle said.

"Anyway," the physician said, "she'll probably wake up shortly. If her PTSD is as severe as it sounds, these blackout events aren't completely unheard of. They're not *common* in PTSD, mind you, but it can happen." She looked at Kyle. "Did something traumatic happen to you as well? At the same time as Agent Baker?"

"Yes, ma'am."

"I'm not a ma'am. Call me Jill." She flipped a whisk of long brunette hair over her shoulder. "Kyle, is it? If this or anything similar has happened to you, you need to get help for it too."

"The bureau has seen to it, ma'am. I mean, Jill. I see a counselor."

"Good. Now what about Agent Baker here?"

"I don't think so," Kyle replied. "No, there's no way she was seeing a shrink. She'd never have done it."

"Why not?"

"She's had to fight her way through the bureau. I hate to say it, but it can be a male-dominated culture in there. And after her injuries, she had to rehab, then qualify to be on active duty again. She wouldn't have seen a shrink because she would have seen that as a sign of weakness."

Cade put his hands in his hair. "God, you're right. Why didn't I think of that? She'd never have sought out help, not while she was trying to get back on active duty. She'd have been afraid they wouldn't have reactivated her."

"Weakness, my ass," Doctor Jill said with a certain steeliness in her voice. "And, it's not her choice anymore. Men, I can tell you care for her very much, but I have a responsibility here. She's going to have a psychological evaluation before she can be discharged."

"You won't get any argument from us," Cade said.

"No, ma'am. I mean, Jill. We want her better, that's all. We're kind of a team, the three of us."

"Don't worry," Jill said, grinning at Kyle. "PTSD is something she can get a grip on. It's not going to take over her life, if she faces it head-on. But she's going to need your help."

Cade's eyes darted from Kyle's to Jill's and back to Kyle's.

Kyle said, "We'll be there for her. Of that you can be sure."

When Kyle said something, he meant it.

"There won't be any need to admit her to the hospital," Dr. Jill said. "She should wake up soon. But I'm not discharging her until she speaks with the staff psychologist."

Both watched as the doctor walked off.

"That is one attractive doctor," Kyle said.

"Is that what you got from the conversation?"

"Well, she said right from the start that Jana was going to be fine. After that, I figured a little harmless smile would be okay."

"Our best friend is unconscious and you're flirting with the doctor."

"I wasn't flirting."

"Were too."

"Was not."

"Honestly," Jana said, her eyes still closed. "You two are like a couple of old maids bickering with one another."

Cade startled.

"Jana? You okay? How do you feel?"

"Like everything is going to be just fine." Her tiny grin spoke volumes.

"That's the drugs talking," Kyle said as he laughed.

"But," she said as she sat up and glanced at her surroundings, "I must look awful. Another hospital? Drugs or no drugs, I don't like waking up in hospitals. Hey, Kyle, why did we take this job? I mean, maybe it would be safer if we all just moved down to Key West. You know, we could open up a little tiki stand on the beach and sell suntan lotion."

"She's actually starting to talk some sense now," Cade said.

"I'm hungry. Hey, what happened anyway? How did I end up here? I don't remember anything."

Cade started to answer but Kyle waved him off.

"I'm sure we can come up with some food."

"Great! Let's get out of here," Jana said.

"Hold on. It'll be a while before we can get you discharged. Kyle? Mind going downstairs and grabbing us three Chick-fil-A sandwiches?"

"No. You got ten bucks?"

"No."

"Well, I don't have any money," Kyle said.

"An FBI agent and a top-level NSA analyst," Jana said. "No money between the two of them. A couple of old maids, I tell you. Give me my purse. Where the hell is my purse? I had my purse. Who took my purse?"

"She's rambling," Cade said.

"I bet the drugs cause her to draw a positive on her next tox screen at work."

"I can hear you, you know?"

"Oh, right," Cade said. "Kyle, I think the bureau can spot us the ten bucks. Use the company credit card. Do something. Write it off, will you? Tell them you were on a stakeout."

"Three Chick-fil-A sandwiches coming up," he said. "Keep her company, okay, sport?"

"Who you calling *sport*?"

But before Kyle could retort, Jana pointed a sharp finger in the direction of the door. "You. Food. That-a-way."

Cade drew a long breath. "You sure you feel okay?"

"I'll be fine. I must look like hell though."

Cade paused, but before his shyness took hold again, he said, "You look great."

"You're so nice."

"No! No, I don't want to be nice. I hear that all the time. 'That Cade, he's so *nice*. He's such a nice young man.'"

"What's wrong with being nice?"

He stared at the floor. "Girls don't go for nice."

"Hey." She paused, waiting for him to make eye contact. "I like nice."

His feet shuffled back and forth. "You're just saying that to make me feel better."

"Cade, listen. Back in Atlanta. Back when we were working on the Thoughtstorm case. At first, I don't know. There were feelings. I wasn't sure if it was the fact that we had to spend so much time together. I mean, we had to do that undercover work and act like we were a couple in love. And I didn't know if the feelings were the tension, or what. But . . ."

"But what?"

"Maybe they were real."

"You mean, you had feelings for me too? Back then? You never said anything."

"I know. I guess I still don't know what is going on in my head."

"But girls always know their feelings."

"I don't. Growing up, I was kind of a tomboy. Raised by my grandfather, remember?"

"Yeah."

"Didn't exactly have a mom around. But look, I'll try, okay? I'll try to be better at this."

He smiled but shook his head from side to side. "That's the drugs talking."

"Well maybe I needed a few drugs in my system to slow me down just enough to listen to my own feelings."

"So, while you're still on drugs, you want to go out Friday night? I heard a rumor there is this great place to get fried scallops."

"Director Latent is really trying to set us up, isn't he?" She laughed.

"Is it working?"

"Yes." She leaned in and pecked him on the cheek.

"Hey, you two. Break it up," Kyle said as he walked back in. "You're not working an undercover case anymore."

"All right, all right. Leave her alone," Cade said.

"Hey, boys, I hate to be a downer, but I guess these drugs are starting to wear off. Was I dreaming or did I hear something about me having to see a shrink before I could get out of here?"

"Oh, that," Kyle said. "That's nothing, standard procedure. Hey, let's eat. I've got fried-chicken goodness in this bag."

"Stop changing the subject."

"Man, she's touchy," Kyle said.

"Watch it," Jana said with a playful grin. "Man, I really blacked out, didn't I?"

"Jana," Cade started, "after what you went through, there's nobody that could . . ."

Jana's anger began a slow rise.

"I can't believe it. Like a damned little fawn. Fainted dead away, at what? At the sight of some psycho who happens to look like a terrorist I once knew?"

"Jana, stop it."

She covered her mouth as though a thought struck her.

"Oh my God. Director Latent. He was right there. He was right there! I fainted in front of the director of the FBI. He must think I'm just another little girl."

"Dammit!" Cade yelled. "You're not just another *little girl*. No one thinks that, Jana. No one except you. Jesus! You start out a year ago as a brand-new agent. Right away you broke open the biggest terrorism case since 9/11. You stopped the actual bomber right before he could detonate a nuclear device on American soil . . . do I have to continue? No one thinks that of you. They think you've got more guts than anyone they know."

Kyle put his hand on her shoulder. "Jana, he's right. No one thinks of you as just some chick. You are one of the guys. In fact, there's more to it than that."

She looked at him, but said nothing.

"No one would have the guts to say it, but it's true."

"What?" she finally said.

"Most of the male agents wonder deep down inside if they'd have the guts to do half the stuff you did. When you were face to face with a hail of gunfire and didn't back down, that showed you had what it took to face your dragon and kick its ass."

The room went quiet.

Jana broke the tension. "You faced your dragon, Kyle. You kicked its ass, didn't you?"

"I guess so."

"That dragon's not so bad," she said.

"Not so bad?" Kyle replied. "Damn, girl. Mine had big frickin' teeth and breathed white-phosphorous hand grenades."

The three laughed.

"I'm not so sure why we're laughing," Cade said. "But it feels good."

"Laughter is an important part," a new voice said. When they all turned, an attractive woman in a wheelchair smiled at them. Her auburn hair was pulled back in a ponytail and the shape of her eyeglass frames gave off the distinctive flavor of young New York style. "I'm sorry to have overheard the last part of your conversation. Well, I'm not really sorry. It's a problem of mine. I eavesdrop. It's sick, I know." She was almost speed-talking. "But what I said is true, Miss Baker. If it is PTSD that brought you into the emergency room today, laughter is a big deal. You need people close to you to be a part of this. After the accident that put me in this chair, it was a big deal for me, I'll tell you that."

"I take it you're the psychologist?" Jana said.

"Kelly Everson."

"Kyle, I think we should step out," Cade said.

"No, no," Kelly said. "Don't. The support of friends is real, and if she wants you here with her now, you should stay. Besides, two good-looking guys like you? No, don't leave. You think I meet many good-looking guys while sitting in this damn thing?"

Jana said, "You're the strangest shri . . ." She caught herself just before saying the word *shrink*, "psychologist I've ever met." She fought back a grin. "But I don't need a psychologist."

"That means we are already on the same page. You think I'm strange, and you don't need a psychologist. Perfect! Now, I've got to ask you something. Kind of off-the-record, if you know what I mean. Which one of these guys did you kiss a minute ago? I don't want to get into trouble. I overheard that part too, you know."

"You aren't serious," Jana said, now losing her battle to keep a straight face. "I can't decide if I like you or want to shoot you. How long have you been listening?"

"For some reason, when I look at this guy," Kelly said, glancing up at Kyle, "I get the impression Doctor Jill, who treated you earlier, would have liked him. Hmm, yeah, he's her type, you know? Kind of thick across the shoulders, chiseled jaw. I can just see her flashing those new pearly whites at him. So I'm guessing you kissed this other guy. Am I right?" She leaned toward Jana and cupped a hand as if to convey something private. "Dr. Jill just got her teeth whitened. Such a big faker. She's my competition, you know."

Jana laughed. "What kind of hospital *is* this?"

"The best kind, apparently," Kyle answered.

Jana shook her head. "Men."

"Oh, we're harmless," Kelly said. Then she cleared her throat. "Well, Dr. Jill is harmless. Me? Not so much," she flashed pearly whites of her own at Kyle.

They all laughed and tension eased away as if floating on a breeze.

"Okay," Kelly continued, "so now that we've gotten that out of the way . . . hey, where the hell is that dog anyway?"

She looked behind herself.

"Dog?" Jana said. "Now there are dogs? In a hospital?"

Kelly whistled. "Here boy."

From around the corner appeared the face of a caramel-colored lab-Australian Shepherd mix. His tail wagged with enough force to rock his entire body all the way up to the head.

"This is Nut. Well, Nut for short. His real name is Coconut. He's pretty much crazy, but very sweet." The caramel-brown color in Coconut's coat carried all the way through to the nose, mouth, and eyes. As if out of instinct, Coconut walked straight to Jana and leaned his body into her legs—the wagging continued.

"Oh, he's cute," Jana said as she began petting him. "Oh, look at his toes. You must have stepped in white paint, didn't you, boy?"

"Smart as hell too. But there's more to him than that. Nut isn't just some random rescue dog we let walk around our sterile hospital facility."

"I guess not," Jana said as she leaned down to let him lick her cheek.

"He walked straight to you."

"Yeah?"

For once, Kelly slowed down.

"He can sense it, Jana. He can almost smell it."

"Smell what?"

"He's one-of-a-kind. At least in my book, he is. Let me ask you something. Have you ever seen how dogs or other animals start to act strangely before an earthquake? Or seen one of those service dogs that can sense when their owner is about to have an epileptic seizure before any signs are present? Well, meet Coconut. He can smell it, Jana. He can sense the chaos in you that you aren't even aware of. The hospital doesn't need me around here to diagnose post-traumatic stress disorder. I can just bring in Nut for that."

"Wait," Cade said, "you're telling me that dog can tell someone has PTSD?"

"I didn't believe it either, at first. But it kept happening. So, I tested the little sucker. A few weeks ago, I took him down to the VA hospital with me. There were about fifty people in the waiting room who were just there to be with loved ones—you know, they're not there for treatment of anything. And then I asked one patient who I needed to diagnose for suspected PTSD to go and mingle amongst them. Now, Coconut here is a complete nutcase of a dog. But I tell you, without fail, he wove his way from one person to the next and, within about a minute, he leaned against the PTSD patient."

Coconut licked Jana's hands. "Oh, you are smart, aren't you? And need some attention, I see. A PTSD dog?" She grabbed the extra skin around his jowls. "How do you do that, Coconut? Did somebody train you to do that? What else can he smell?"

"Hot dogs. This doe-eyed little sucker ate a hot dog right off my plate last night before I could even blink."

Nut cocked his head to the side.

"But he's trained all right. Well-trained. Although he did piddle on the tile floor in my condo." Nut groaned at her. "Not his fault though. I should have gotten up earlier in the morning to let him out. Don't tell the Paws people, okay? They'd be so mad."

"Paws?"

"Paws for Veterans. It's an organization down in Melbourne. Florida, not Australia. Anyway, it's a lot sunnier down there than here. They take dogs out of shelters and train them to help veterans deal with symptoms of PTSD. The dogs help with a lot of things like anxiety and panic. Ahem, that's something we might want to discuss in your case, Miss Jana. And they can do a lot of other things such as help with sleep issues, like nightmares, by waking you up if you're having one, and then they help calm you down. They're pretty amazing little guys."

"I don't need a shrink," Jana said. "I don't have any of those symptoms."

"Jana!" Cade said. "Look, we're your friends. And sometimes . . . sometimes a friend has to step in and say what needs to be said. Something is wrong and you need help dealing with it."

Kyle squared himself in front of Jana. But she averted her eyes.

"You're the toughest damn agent I know. You are. But if you want back in, this is what it takes. You took one look at that terrorist's face and had a full-blown panic attack, and then another one where you blacked out, and ended up here. It's not a game anymore, Jana. This is real. You want to be on active duty again? You want to track down these . . ." He looked at Kelly not wanting to disclose too much information. "These terrorists? Well, you're going to have to face this. Come on, Jana. Think of it as just another part of training. We went through all kinds of training to get here. This is just another piece of it."

Jana looked down at Coconut. He plopped his head on her lap, then let out a low gurgling sound, something akin to a growl, but much more comforting.

"Well, you agree with them, boy?" After a long exhale, she said, "All right. PTSD, huh? I've got to see a shrink for PTSD. You guys suck, you know that?"

"That's why you love us so much," Cade said.

"She's in! High fives everybody," Kelly said as she raised her hand to each of them in turn. "Well, from down here, low fives, anyway." She glanced at her watch. "Hey! My shift is ending. I'm starved. We really should get to know each other. Let's go eat. I know this great little place for fried scallops. It's called Casey's Crab, down on Fort Meade Road. You'll love it. Trust me."

"Casey's Crab again," Cade said. "That's the second time we've been told to go eat fried scallops. Well, we might as well find out what that's all about."

Kelly spun her wheelchair around and led the three friends,

flanked by a wagging Coconut, out the front doors of the hospital. Cade walked behind the group and held his hand to shade the brilliant sunlight. As he looked at the others, he felt the distinct presence of a new, positive direction. Things were on their way to getting better—with Jana, at least.

46

LEAVE NO TRAIL

Gadani Beach, coastal Pakistan.

Khalid stared at the great expanse of beach. "We are to meet them in broad daylight? On the beach like this?"

"Money is a beautiful thing, my friend," Jarrah said. "Just a little goes a long way here. No one will say a thing."

"What will happen?"

"So many questions. We will meet several boats here. It is all arranged. We have a very valuable product to sell, and our buyers are greatly interested in taking delivery. With all the ship workers moving about, it will not be difficult to blend in."

"And this is it? This is where I go on alone?"

"In an hour, you'll be on your way. Now, keep driving on this dirt road. It will dead-end into the sand. Our contacts will have their small boats beached already. They will be here, you will see."

Khalid drove until the road melted into deep sand. A group of small boats were anchored about two hundred yards down. As he wove between what seemed like hundreds of laborers, he stared out at them.

"Their eyes, they are like the walking dead."

"Still alive, but not many who come here leave here. Keep going, and move closer to the water. The sand is more compact there."

"Why do they live like this? Four dollars a day?"

"What else is there for them to do? They are the forgotten."

The truck lumbered across the beach under its heavy payload. The pickup stopped in front of a group of eight small watercraft, each anchored in the surf.

"Khalid, all these people we transact our business with today are brothers in jihad. All except one, that is. See that boat on the far left, off in the distance? That is him."

"Who?"

"He is the only one who is not our brother. He is a contractor. You recall the one warhead in which we left the guidance system intact?"

"Yes. It weighs a ton. That one is for him?"

"Yes," Jarrah, said, staring at the distant boat. "But he is not to be trusted. His job is simple. He is to prepare that warhead for shipment—shipment to its new home." Jarrah laughed.

"Where does it go?"

"North Korea. To the capital city, Pyongyang. There is much you do not know, my apprentice. But at this point in our mission, it is important to make the Americans believe that their CIA mission is on track. Before Farooq died, he enabled the guidance system on that warhead. The weapon knows its intended GPS detonation point. It will detonate automatically once it reaches the heart of Pyongyang."

"So you are really going to destroy that city?"

Jarrah foamed, "*I am not going to destroy anything in that city!* The Americans are. Those foolish pigs believe this little package is the answer to their political problems with the North."

"But why bother?" young Khalid asked. "Why wouldn't you just take the device and sell it to the highest bidder, like the other eight? Why bother sending it to North Korea?"

"It is important to make the Americans think their mission to destroy the North Korean government is still on track." Jarrah began to laugh hysterically and the sudden swing of emotion curdled Khalid's stomach. "After all," he said, "if the beast thinks the mission is on track, there's no need for them to pursue us. Understand? Stay in the truck and keep an eye on that far boat. If anything looks out of place, if anything happens, don't hesitate. Use the rocket launcher if need be, and don't worry about witnesses."

Khalid swallowed. "Yes, Waseem." *The sooner I'm apart from him, the better. He's losing his mind.*

While Jarrah spoke to the other boat runners, he glared at the boat on the far left—its sole occupant still on board. After a few moments, each boat runner in turn gave Jarrah a memorized series of numbers, a code. Jarrah withdrew his smartphone and tapped the screen, inputting the numbers.

What the hell are they doing? Khalid thought. Then Jarrah and one man walked back toward the truck.

"We are complete," Jarrah said. A glass pallor had overtaken his face once again. One at a time, each boat runner came to the truck, walked to the rear, and picked up a single eighty-pound parcel, then walked back to his boat. Each boat departed in turn. Only two parcels remained in the truck bed—the remaining eighty-pound weapon, which sat tucked inside a sturdy rucksack—the other, the full warhead guidance-system combination.

"But what happened, Waseem? I thought you were to sell those weapons. Where is the money?"

"Geneva, the Cayman Islands, and everywhere in between. Banks in Munich, Luxembourg, Staad, Marseille, Stockholm . . . the money is all there, my young apprentice. Don't look so surprised." Jarrah glared into the bright reflection on the rippling waves. "The global banking system is not as secure as you might think. You need only concern yourself with one task." Jarrah squinted at the distant boat. "Drive toward him, slowly."

"I am to depart with this one? The one who will make delivery to North Korea?"

Jarrah said nothing. The only movement detectable was a tension stringing across his temples. After a few tense moments, he said, "Khalid, before you start your journey to the land of the beast, you have two tasks. First, make sure the delivery of the package to North Korea is set. Make sure he arranges it correctly. And then . . ."

"And then?"

Jarrah looked at him. The deadness in his eyes reminded

Khalid of the way he looked right after he'd killed the old man at the sawmill.

"Your role in this mission must not be compromised. You must make it all the way to your intended destination. But we can leave no trail of witnesses. Do I need to spell it out for you?"

Khalid swallowed. "No, Waseem."

He was to kill the boat runner.

47

FRIED GOODNESS

Casey's Crab, Laurel, Maryland.

"Well this place sure fits the hole-in-the-wall description," Cade said as the four went inside with Coconut trotting just behind.

"Hey," Kyle said, walking back to their table. "Just got off the phone with Director Latent. He's relieved as hell that you're all right, Jana." Kyle removed one of the chairs and slid it away so Kelly had room to pull her wheelchair into place.

"She'll be fine," Kelly said. "She's a trooper. Or a federal agent, or something." The others laughed. "And who's this Latent character? He sounds like a big fingerprint."

"The boss," Kyle said. "Anyway, he definitely wants us all to take a break. He doesn't want to see Jana in the situation room again until she's damn good and ready. Sorry, Jana. His words, not mine. And, he doesn't want us to leave her side until she's feeling up to it."

"You know, your dimples move when you talk," Kelly giggled.

Kyle secretly wanted to get closer to the fragrance of her auburn hair, but he didn't react. It was as if he didn't know how. "You, ah, you aren't exactly shy, are you?"

"Shy? What for? Life's too short for that. It's too much for you?"

"No," Kyle said, as he leaned an elbow on the table and looked at the depth of her brown eyes. "I, uh, just never met anyone like you before."

"That's because you're from the South. Your girls are usually more reserved? That accent of yours is telltale coastal Georgia. Am I right?"

"Savannah."

Cade leaned to Jana and whispered, "I've never seen him like this."

"What was that?" Kyle asked.

"Oh, nothing," Cade said. "I was just telling Jana that this place is supposed to have the best fried scallops."

"Uh huh," Kyle said, never taking his eyes off of Kelly. "You mean the *only* fried scallops."

Jana too sensed the apparent crush Kyle had on Kelly, but changed the subject.

"I'm surprised the restaurant let us in here with Nut."

His ears perked up, yet his head did not rise from its resting place on Jana's foot.

"Service dog," Kelly said. "We have a lot of veterans around here. Some have service dogs like him, so the restaurants and businesses are used to it. He's going to stay with you, you know?"

"Coconut?" Jana said. "I get to keep him?"

"He's yours now. I'll miss him, but this is what he's trained for. Just look at him. He doesn't want to leave you for a second."

"It's really that bad, isn't it?" Jana said. "My PTSD, I mean."

"You have no idea how great it is to hear you *own* it. It can take people a long time to come to grips with the fact that they have PTSD. Owning it is the first step."

"And the second?" Cade said as he placed a hand on top of Jana's. When Jana didn't remove it, Cade silently congratulated himself for having the guts.

"Lots of talking about it," Kelly said. "Recognizing the stress, what triggers it, and how to minimize that. And Coconut will be there to help. He goes with you everywhere."

"Everywhere? Kelly, he's a dog. My job isn't exactly like that. One minute I'm in the office and the next we're going on a raid somewhere and kicking down a door."

"Everywhere. And that's final," Kelly said.

She turned her attention to Kyle.

"Now, Kyle, tell me about you. I want to hear everything."

Kyle stared. When he finally spoke, it came out in fits and starts. "Oh, me? There's not much to tell. There's the FBI and we're on this big case and everything . . ."

This time, Jana whispered to Cade, "My God, he's so nervous. He's never been in love before, has he?"

"No."

"After all the women he's been with? Not one?" It was too much to contain. Jana felt as though she was watching a fifth-grader ask a girl to dance for the first time.

Cade and Jana continued their muted conversation. "Jana? Have you ever been in love?"

"No. You?"

"Yeah, once. Her name was Courtney."

"Really!" Jana said. "Whatever happened to her?"

"Well, her family moved away right after first grade. So that was the end of that."

Jana gave him a playful smack on the arm. "Oh, stop it."

"No, it was a big deal. We dated in first grade for like three weeks. I'm still heartbroken over it."

"And what are you going to do to get past this gaping hole in your heart?"

"I guess I'm going to have to fill it somehow." Cade looked in her eyes and wondered if he should kiss her right there, but chickened out.

"Well, maybe this will help." She leaned forward and kissed him briefly, but deeply. "I've been wanting to do that for a while now."

"My, my," Kyle said from across the table. "I'm starting to blush. Stephen Latent was right. Apparently the way to a girl's heart *is* through fried scallops."

48

TO INFILTRATE AND DESTROY

NSA Headquarters.

"All right, so the younger brother of Shakey Kunde was actually on the *Simbirsk*?" Bill said, "You're sure?"

"Well, sir, about as sure as we can get at this point," Knuckles replied.

FBI Director Stephen Latent leaned into the conversation.

"Yeah," Cade said, "I'd say Jana's, I mean Agent Baker's, assessment is going to turn out to be spot-on."

Knuckles looked at him. "Assessment? When she was reviewing photos of the crew of the *Simbursk*, she passed out."

"That's my point," Cade said. "She knows her stuff. In fact, there's no one else in the world more qualified to make that identification than her. Do you agree, Director Latent?"

"Stake my reputation on it."

"Something is wrong here," Uncle Bill said. He looked at Latent. "Stevie, I don't like it. Just think about what we're saying here. This younger brother of Shakey Kunde is most likely a full-time recruit of Waseem Jarrah. The chances that we're going to find him having been planted inside the United States when he was a kid are huge. *That's Jarrah.* That's what he does. He makes multiyear investments in planting someone into a place of vital importance to his jihad. Years later, he activates that person, and all hell breaks loose. But now we're saying the younger brother is also the guy who infiltrated the Pakistani navy, got on board one of their submarines, set up some kind of timed explosion that would sink the vessel, and then got off before she left port?"

"Maybe he's a versatile guy," Knuckles said, looking for a laugh that never came.

"Versatility isn't what scares me. Versatility is good . . ." Bill stopped, but his mind railed forward. He began to pace the floor again, lost in thought. The words poured out as if he was talking only to himself. "Jarrah plants the little brother as a child into the United States so he can get embedded in the culture, embedded into American society. He'd have all the right papers, citizenship, birth certificate and all that, so nobody would think to question his background. He grows up here, finds his way into our government somewhere, or at least into someplace vital. After all," he said, his arms flailing in the air, "that would be the point, right? I mean why send him over here if it wasn't to get him into the perfect position so that someday he could . . ."

Latent said, "Bill, what are you getting at?"

"Knuckles," Bill said, "now that we have a photo of the face of the younger brother, where do we stand on running the facial-recognition software against all photos of NSA and CIA employees?"

"Wait a second," Latent interrupted. "Bill, are you thinking what I think you're thinking? But, that would mean . . ."

"It would mean this is much, much worse than any of us thought." Uncle Bill paced again, transfixed on his idea—an idea that he hoped couldn't be true. "Step back from all this for a moment. We've been too 'down in the weeds' on this thing. We're not thinking big picture."

"Big picture?" Knuckles said, but Latent quieted him.

"Let him work, son. Let him work."

"We've been too focused on the fact that they have a nuclear device, and where that device is, and how we're going to intercept it. We never sat back and thought about how in the hell they set this up in the first place. I mean, think about it. They are well financed, they somehow have a DSV mini-submarine, and the talent to operate it? Who the hell has that?

Nobody but either an immensely well-funded research corporation, or a government would have any idea how to obtain and then operate a DSV. And it can't be a coincidence that the younger brother magically finds his way onto the exact Pakistani sub that just so happens to have a nuclear missile on board. Not to mention the fact that this was a sub that the Pakistanis weren't supposed to have in the first place. It had to be the best-kept secret in Pakistani naval history. Nobody, and I mean nobody, outside of a government intelligence service, could have found out that the Pakistanis had illegally purchased a Russian sub with a nuclear missile. Jarrah *couldn't* have known all that information. It's just too big. He would have had to have inside information. And then, he would have had to have known how to sabotage the *Simbirsk*, and where it would be at that exact time so the tiny DSV could intercept and steal the missile. A missile, by the way, that they had to have the help of a research vessel on the surface to extract."

Latent slumped into a swivel chair and glared at the floor.

"It is all too big for anyone other than a government to pull off. Shit, I never thought of it like that."

"Wait," Cade said. "I'm still not following."

Latent and Bill looked at each other. It was Latent who broke the silence.

"An infiltration. An infiltration followed by black ops."

"It's the only explanation," Uncle Bill replied.

"An infiltration? An infiltration of what?" Cade said.

"And black ops?" Knuckles said. "Black ops to accomplish what? And by who? What are you talking about?"

Bill turned to them and rubbed his eyes.

"Somewhere, we're going to uncover that this whole thing started out as a government-sponsored black operation. This has all the hallmarks of one of our intelligence services trying to pull off something big. Something . . . I don't even know what to call it."

"But at some point," Latent said, "something went wrong and the government operation, with the help of insider information, was intercepted by Jarrah."

"Not just intercepted, Stevie, hijacked. Jarrah knew from the *inside* that some big government operation was about to happen, and his guy, the younger brother, was his source. It's the younger brother. He worked somewhere vital."

"And that means we're not just looking for a random government employee. He'd have to be embedded deep inside one of our intelligence services, or perhaps one of the services of our allies. He's not just a low-level employee."

"No," Bill said. "He's got to be somebody with access." He and Latent turned toward Pete Buck. "Pete, the CIA is the only American agency that could put operatives into the field to try and conduct a mission this big. We need a level-fifteen clearance into the personnel files, and we need it right-the-hell-right-now."

Buck's mouth hung open.

"You can't be serious. Director Latent, are you buying this crap? You think the CIA or some other agency of ours was trying to steal a nuclear device from the Pakistanis? Are you two out of your minds? What the hell would we do with a stolen nuclear device in the first place? We have a thousand of them at our disposal. And you think the CIA would actually be involved? I've heard just about enough of this shit!"

Bill walked to him and put a fatherly hand on his shoulder.

"Pete, it's the only explanation. And what about that French research vessel? The one that originally had the DSV mini-sub attached to it. How did it sink? What was the vessel's name?"

"The *Marion Dufresne*," Knuckles said.

"It was one of just a few research vessels in the world that had a DSV mini-sub on board," Uncle Bill said, "and it sank under strange circumstances just three months before any of this happened—sabotaged. There is no other explanation. The CIA could have pulled that off. The CIA has the funding and intel. They must have learned that the Pakistanis had purchased a rogue submarine from the Russians. If that's true, and they did find out about the illegal submarine purchase, very few people in the CIA, NSA, or any other part of our government would have been told. That kind of information would flow straight to the president, it's just too sensitive to let be widely known. And let's think further. The CIA has the *capacity* to infiltrate the

Pakistani navy. The CIA has the *capacity* to coordinate the sinking of the *Simbirsk*. The CIA would have assets who could operate the DSV mini-sub to help extract the warhead. What is the CIA going to do with a stolen nuclear missile? Hell if I know, but I intend to find out."

Latent found a chair behind him and flopped into it. "Oh shit."

All eyes went to Latent.

"Stevie?" Uncle Bill said. "You don't look so good. The last time I saw that look on your face, we were undergrads at Georgetown and I had to hold your head over the toilet."

"Bill, something just occurred to me. I think we better talk." With that, the two men headed for Bill's office.

49

PRESIDENTIAL ACTS OF WAR

NSA Headquarters.

"Stevie, what is it?"

"Bill, what you said back there. What you said about it being the CIA that is behind the whole thing."

"Yeah. Load of shit, right?" Bill said as he laughed. Latent, however, wasn't laughing.

"I think I better sit down again."

"Christ, Steve, what's wrong? Talk to me."

Latent buried his face in his hands.

"It's happening again. The protocols. They're happening again. It's just like last year during the Thoughtstorm case; after we found those fingerprints that belonged to a CIA employee. The National Crime Information Center computer told us it had identified the prints, but they were classified. C12 stuff, remember? I'll never forget staring at that piece of paper that the fingerprint technician handed me. It was a printout of how the computer had classified the prints we found. It was a code sequence, 14.6 E.O., written at the top of that paper. E.O., an executive order. And 14.6 corresponded to the Fourteenth Protocol—the president's authorization for the CIA to conduct terror investigations on American soil, without oversight."

Bill slumped into his desk chair, a worn, black-leather model that looked like it would fit perfectly onto the set of a 1960s movie.

"What are you getting at? It's another executive protocol?"

"Fifteen. It's the Fifteenth Protocol."

"I don't think I want to hear the rest of this," Bill said.

"15.8 E.O. is the official nomenclature. The fifteenth in a series of executive powers granted to the president after 9/11, all with no oversight."

"What powers does the Fifteenth Protocol give him?"

Latent paused, almost collecting his thoughts. "Nuclear," was all he uttered.

"What?"

"Nuclear, Bill. The authorization to use nuclear force against a nuclear threat."

Bill's eyes widened as he peered over his glasses. "*Nuclear* force? What the hell are you talking about? He's got authority to use a nuclear weapon, *without oversight?*"

"Bill, this is classified stuff. I know you've got a clearance as high as mine, but hardly anyone knows about the protocols. Even after the Thoughtstorm case, that part of the investigation was something we couldn't release to the general public."

Uncle Bill bolted from his chair.

"Well why the hell not? These protocols, these damned executive orders are pissing me off. They're bullshit! How in the hell can we grant the president, a single man, that kind of authority?"

"Don't shoot the messenger, Bill. You know I hate this crap as much as you do. You and I are on the same page. And, we're on the same team."

Uncle Bill let out a long exhale.

"I know Stevie, I know." He looked around the room. "So what kind of nuclear force? Is it as simple as that? The president can just nuke somebody that is perceived as a nuclear threat?"

"My knowledge of the Fifteenth Protocol is limited. He'd only be able to use that level of force under extreme circumstances. But yes, that's basically it."

"If the president has authorization to use nuclear force at his own discretion, without Congress or anyone else being involved, then what is it that's going on in this case? Are we actually saying *the president* authorized the theft of a nuclear device from another nation? For what purpose? What's he trying to do? And why doesn't he just use one of the million nuclear weapons that we keep stockpiling?"

Latent stood and looked through the glass wall and into the situation room.

"We're missing something, you and I. We're missing a piece of the puzzle. If any of what we're saying is true, then we're missing the exact thing you just said. We don't know what he's getting at, why he wouldn't just use one of our existing weapons, or why he'd need to use nuclear force in the first place."

"And against who," Bill returned.

"Whom."

"Whatever. Steve, we have to know his plans, and I mean all of them. We have to know the president's intended target with this nuclear device."

"I wasn't thinking about that. I was thinking only about where the damned device is heading right now. Whatever the president's original plans were, those plans are screwed now. The terrorists have stolen the device."

"Yeah, I know, but once we find the terrorists and fry their asses, we've got to go after the president. I don't care whether he had authorization or not. What I care about is that he's committing acts of war against Pakistan in the process."

"Acts of war without Congress knowing about it. All right, so while we're looking for where the terrorists are taking the nuke, I'll start digging into what the president's intended target was. There's got to be a way to find out, but it won't be easy. President Palmer may be an asshole, but he's not stupid. He wouldn't invoke the Fifteenth Protocol without a damn good reason. Not that there's any justification for it, mind you."

"Right, he would. He would have to be targeting a country that is threatening nuclear action against us. He can't invoke the Fifteenth Protocol to protect one of our allies, right?"

"Right," Latent said. "The protocols were established right after 9/11 with the sole intent to protect the sovereignty of the United States."

"Well," Bill said, "if he feels we're being threatened by another country, the list of nations threatening us is short as hell. I mean, think about it. What countries threaten us frequently?"

"I can think of two. Iran and North Korea."

Once the words *North Korea* rolled off Latent's tongue, both men stopped.

"North Korea. Damn, Steve, I think you've hit the nail on the head. They're always spouting off one of their tirades at us. But it's not like they launched a nuclear missile at us or anything. Our intel doesn't even believe they have long-range launch capability, much less a missile with a nuclear tip. And I don't think they've even mastered missile navigation in the first place. Even if they had a long-range missile, it's doubtful they could hit us with it. I'm not so sure they're the threat."

"Well, something sure lit a fire under President Palmer's backside. Hell, I know the man. I deliver the daily threat assessment to him personally most mornings."

"I know," Bill said, "but like we said a minute ago, we're missing some part of the puzzle. What if the situation between the US and North Korea is far worse than either of us knows? After all, it's not as though you and I are given every single bit of intel that our country uncovers."

"Bill, I thought you knew everything. Don't you listen in on the cell phone calls of all the world's leaders?"

"Oh, shut up. But come to think of it, you haven't called your mom in a while. Might want to get on that."

"You aren't!" Latent said.

"No, Stevie, no. I'm not listening in on your cell phone calls. I could though," Bill smiled. "Uh oh. Here comes Knuckles. He doesn't look happy."

Knuckles, flanked by Cade, was waved in by Uncle Bill.

"What is it, kid?"

"Sir, you're not going to like it," the peach-fuzz-laden young man said.

"Spit it out."

Knuckles voice shook when he spoke. "It's worse than any of us thought. We found him. We found him."

50

BORDERS ON FIRE

Khasan, Russia, on the Tuman River. Directly across from the city of Tumanbon, North Korea. About 0.2 miles from the North Korean border.

"Why can't we get a satellite feed? This thing is starting!" reporter Tammy Cho yelled to her cameraman over the sound of heavy gunfire.

"The satellite signal isn't there! I've got nothing, shit. Tammy, stay down! Come on, we've got to get out of the way of those tanks."

Mortar shells landed not far from their position, and Russian tanks returned fire. Explosions were visible just across the river in North Korea. Tammy looked up and saw dozens of rockets fired from a multiple-rocket launcher streak toward North Korean positions.

"Charlie! I don't give a shit about the live feed. Start recording. Get this on tape!"

"Way ahead of you, but we can't stay here! The Russian tanks are moving forward. We're right in their path!"

"Screw them. Put the camera on me and make sure you're getting those explosions in the background. Cut to me in three, two . . ."

Tammy stayed crouched behind a rock bed and held a microphone as the camera began to roll.

"This is Tammy Cho, WBS News, reporting from Khasan, Russia. Just across my shoulder is North Korea, separated only by a thin strip of the Tuman River. The Russian military has just opened fire on the city of Tumanbon, North Korea, just in the distance ahead of us."

A North Korean mortar shell exploded nearby, raining earth and shards of rock all around them.

Both Tammy and the cameraman flattened onto the ground and the camera view went sideways.

"Keep filming! The North is returning fire and we're caught in the middle. The Russians are moving their tanks directly toward us and we assume they are about to cross the Tuman River and push into North Korean territory. This is the beginning of an invasion and we're on ground zero. Charlie, move!"

Tammy leapt forward and yanked the cameraman out of the path of a fast-moving Russian T-90 tank.

"That was close," Tammy said. "As you can see, we've just been passed by several dozen Russian tanks. They're apparently the first wave of a ground offensive."

A single rocket streaked from the North Korean hillside and slammed into one of the tanks, which slowed but did not stop.

"A Russian tank was just hit but it doesn't appear to be crippled. Wait, there's something coming . . . look up!" Dozens of white streaks zipped across the sky, crossed into North Korean airspace, then arced downwards. Explosions ripped apart the hillside and tore into several buildings in the distance.

"The salvos of Russia's military are in full swing . . . I can see in the distance behind us a group of what appear to be fighter jets streaking this way."

Mortar fire from the North Korean side rained down with increasing ferocity. The reporters were again pelted with dirt and debris.

"Tammy! We can't stay here," Charlie yelled as a full squadron of Russian Sukhoi Su-34 fighter-bombers flew overhead, each firing multiple missiles at North Korean targets.

Despite the panic in her cameraman's eyes, Tammy continued.

"We've just been overflown by what are apparently Russian fighter jets, who have unleashed a barrage of ordinance at North

Korean positions. Charlie, we've got to move closer."

"Closer?"

"Come on. Get behind this Russian troop transport."

Charlie lowered the camera. "Tammy, we can't. People are dying up there!"

"Get your shit in check!" she yelled. "This is the chance of a lifetime! Reporters dream of moments like this! Pick up that camera and don't stop filming, no matter what happens. Let's go!"

Tammy ran behind the forward movement of a group of several dozen troop carriers.

"On me in three, two . . ." Tammy again raised her mic. "We've fallen in behind a Russian troop carrier. This is the BMP-1 amphibious infantry fighting vehicle." Tammy yelled over the roar of the vehicle's diesel engines. "It can hold up to eight additional troops inside, but as you can see, Russian foot soldiers are all over the top of these transports as well. Unlike the first salvo fired by the Russians from Krashinko, this is not a bluff. This is a full-scale invasion. Charlie, turn the camera around so people can see the mass of ground troops moving this way."

The camera's eye caught sight of a wave of thousands of Russian foot soldiers.

"These soldiers are believed to be part of the Russian 155th Marine Brigade, a division of the Russian Naval Infantry that is often used as a first line of attack."

Metallic sounds slammed into the surface of the troop carrier as 7.62x54R-caliber rounds fired from North Korean weapons struck several of the Russian soldiers. One soldier rolled off the top of the troop carrier and landed on top of Tammy. She crumpled under the weight. The man's head was torn apart and brain matter splashed across Tammy's face and torso. She rolled him off and sat in stunned silence.

"Tammy! You okay?" Charlie said as he grabbed at Tammy. "Come on. We're sitting ducks. That troop carrier is our only cover. We've got to keep up with it." He wiped his shirt against her face to remove the bits of gray matter and bone fragments.

Tammy ran with him as she regained her composure. "No, don't wipe it away. Get the camera on me while we run . . ."

Charlie pressed his headphones against his head. "Tammy! I'm picking up a signal. I think the satellite feed is back online. Yeah, the station is cutting to us live!"

In his headset, he heard ". . . Mike Slayden with news, weather, and traffic on the fives. We're about to go live to the borders of Russia and North Korea to our correspondent, Tammy Cho. Tammy, do we have you now?"

"Yes, Mike," she yelled. "We're embedded with Russian troops and taking fire from North Korean positions just ahead of us. Full-scale war has broken out as Russian troops are now invading the North."

As the troop carrier motored forward, screams were audible from soldiers riding on its top as they again came under fire.

"Tammy, you're covered in blood. Are you all right?"

"Yes, Mike. This is not my blood. Some of the Russian soldiers we're embedded with have been hit and I got a little too close. As they make this first push into the city of Tumanbon, North Korea, more casualties are expected."

A North Korean MiG-29 Fulcrum fighter jet streaked across the sky and unleashed a single missile that headed directly toward them.

"Tammy, get down!" Charlie yelled.

The missile screamed past and slammed into a Russian tank about fifty yards to their rear. The sound was so loud Tammy could hear nothing but a constant ring in her ears.

"Tammy? Tammy?" anchor Mike Slayden interrupted. "Folks we may have lost contact with our reporter, Tammy Cho."

"I'm here, Mike," she yelled. "That was a missile fired from a North Korean fighter jet. It's taken out a Russian tank. Mike, we're going to have to hightail it out of here. I can see North Korean troops coming over the hillside toward us to thwart the Russian advance. Reporting live from the front lines, this is Tammy Cho, WBS News." Once the feed was cut, Tammy grabbed Charlie. "We're getting the hell out of here! Run!"

51

BOATS OF DESTRUCTION

NSA Headquarters.

"Found who?" Latent said.

Cade cut in. "His full name is Khalid Safeer Kunde. Yes, his last name is *Kunde*. Jana was right. He's the younger brother of Shakey Kunde. And you were right too, Uncle Bill, about him having penetrated somewhere vital."

Knuckles stepped in front of Cade, hoping to assert his expertise.

"He's deep. He's not only *in* the CIA, he's as deep as one can get."

"You've got to be kidding me," Bill said. "Like how deep?"

Neither Knuckles nor Cade wanted to be the one to deliver the worst of the news, but Knuckles spoke anyway. "He's an operative."

Bill's glasses slid off his nose and landed on his desk.

"An *operative*? I get the fact that we were right, that he was either in the CIA or NSA, but an operative? Are you sure?"

"Get Pete Buck in here!" Latent said as he stood up.

"He's not out there, sir," Cade said, almost backing away. "Once the facial-recognition software pegged Kunde's face in the classified CIA employee files, he ran out."

"Ran out? Where to?" A vein on Latent's forehead pursed.

"The head," Knuckles mumbled. "He ran to the toilet. I think he hurled. He's awfully sensitive about his agency getting caught up in another scandal."

"I know he is," Latent said. "Dammit. Sorry, I didn't mean to yell at you both."

"Want us to go bring him in here?" Cade said.

"No, let him handle it in his own way for a bit. He'll come around."

Bill punched a button on his desk phone. "Yes, sir?" returned a voice through the speaker.

"Lara, get me Lawrence Brennan on the line."

"Lawrence Brennan? You mean . . ."

"Yes, Lara. The director of the CIA. And when they tell you he can't be disturbed, tell them it's priority-level fifteen." He hung up. "We're going to get to the bottom of this. We've got to know what *Khalid* Kunde was working on and what his assignments were."

"The damage could be unbelievable," Latent said. "This is espionage at an unprecedented level."

"Tell them," Knuckles whispered to Cade.

"I'm not telling them. You tell them."

"What now?" Latent said. "Come on. Out with it."

Knuckles cleared his throat. "Yes, sir. Ah, sir, there's more news. The Aussie satellite? You know, the one that can detect the radioisotope signature given off by a nuclear device?"

"Yes. What about it?" Uncle Bill said.

"Well, it overflew the region again about ten minutes ago."

"And?"

"It was in orbit over the target area just long enough to catch this."

He placed several satellite image printouts onto Bill's desk, laying them down one by one.

"This first one is of a pickup truck. In the bed, you can see a large radioisotope signature. If our calculations are correct, this nuclear signature is equivalent to ten warheads."

"Well that's good, right?" Latent said.

Knuckles looked down. "Not exactly, sir. The satellite detects gamma-ray flux from enriched uranium. But the particles are more dispersed now."

"More dispersed?" Bill said. "Uranium leakage?"

"Not likely, sir. They're all there, and the amount of gamma-ray flux is exactly what it should be for ten warheads. I don't see any leakage here. If I had to guess, I'd say they've separated the warheads."

"They separated the warheads," Latent groaned. "Son of a bitch. It's nearly impossible to track just one. What if they move the warheads to different places? How the hell will we ever find ten warheads?"

"I'm afraid they have moved them, sir. This one, the last image taken before the satellite lost orbit and fell out of range. Take a look at the pickup truck now."

Uncle Bill and Stephen Latent stared at the image. It showed a pickup truck on the beach, but the nuclear signature emanating from the back of the truck bed was weaker.

"We calculate at the time this image was taken that two of the warheads were no longer in the back of the truck. And see these tiny boats just off the beach? Look at this one and this one." He pointed to the small crafts. "They both show telltale signs of gamma-ray flux. Each of these two boats now has a warhead aboard."

Bill again slumped into his chair, which squeaked as he sat. "They're moving the warheads. This is the last photo? We can't see if they moved the rest of them?"

"That was the last photo. We can't see, no," Cade said. "But look at the other small boats spaced out in the surf right in front of the pickup truck. From these photos, I'd say they're offloading the nukes into each of these different boats."

Bill counted the boats, "One, two, three . . . seven? *Seven* boats?" He gave a panicked look to Latent. "Stevie, we'll never be able to track seven separate vehicles."

What they could not see was the presence of the eighth boat. It was just out of range of the satellite photo. And, moments after the satellite had lost visibility over the area, Khalid Kunde and two nuclear warheads had boarded the eighth boat and headed into the unknown.

52

TRAIL STOPS HERE

The White House.

"Why are you looking at me like that? Spit it out," the president said.

The national security advisor scowled at him.

"You arrogant son of a bitch. Well, it's out now. The NSA and CIA have confirmed it."

"Confirmed what?"

"One of the CIA operatives working your little pet project has been seen on camera, *and identified*."

"Wait. Seen on camera doing what?"

"Seen on camera leaving the scene where a nuclear device was pulled from the water in coastal Pakistan and loaded onto a flatbed truck. He's the driver. He was caught on a security camera."

The president took a seat and buried his face in wrinkling hands.

"Yeah," continued the national security advisor. "Exactly. Now do you see? Our own agencies have found his personnel file in the CIA database. They know he's a CIA operative, and they now know he must have been tasked on a mission to steal a nuclear device from another nation. But it gets worse."

"I don't think I want to hear this."

"Well, you're going to hear it. First you'll hear it from me, then you'll hear it in a barrage of questions from WBS News, then Fox, BBC, then NBC. Shall I continue?"

"Spit it out, dammit!"

"It's about the operative seen on camera in Pakistan taking *the device*," the words spat off his tongue as if coated in dirt. "He's off the reservation."

"*What?*"

"He's gone rogue. It means he's departed from the operational plan."

"I know what it means!"

"Look, we sent two CIA operatives plus two CIA contractors to Pakistan to steal the nuclear device so that you could blow the North Korean government back to the stone ages, and make it look like someone else did it. One operative was to sabotage the Pakistani-Russian sub, the *Simbirsk*. The other was to rendezvous with the mini-sub and carry the warhead to port, where he would offload it and transport it to North Korea. The first operative *did* sabotage the *Simbirsk*. But that was supposed to be the end of his assignment. He should have disappeared into nowhere by now."

"So what about him? Why are you telling me this?"

"He hasn't disappeared into nowhere! He is the one that was seen on camera at the port where the nuclear device was offloaded onto a flatbed truck."

"What the hell is he doing there? Where's the CIA operative that was *supposed* to transport the device?"

"We have no idea. Radio silence, remember? We have no way of communicating with our operatives during this phase of the operation. But where is the operative that is supposed to be offloading the nuclear device you ask? I'd say he's dead."

"How the hell could you know that?"

"One, because he wasn't the one caught on camera offloading the device. And two, the device was being offloaded at the *wrong port*. According to operational plans, they should have offloaded at a port much farther west. The device is not even in the right location."

"It's what?"

"Christ. Do you need me to spell it out for you? Originally, the plan was for the device to be transported via a mini-submarine, and it was. The mini-sub was supposed to rendezvous at night with a ferryboat where our operative would board it, then the mini-sub would be taken to a location about thirty miles west of where we found it on camera. It's in the wrong place! The entire mission is screwed!" the national security advisor was nearly yelling.

"But," the president retorted, "that doesn't mean this guy went off the reservation. Maybe the operational plan changed."

The national security advisor glared at him.

"This operative seen on camera driving the flatbed truck loaded down with a missile? He's supposed to be dead right now. And before you question what *dead* means, dead means dead. He was to be neutralized right after he set the explosives on the Pakistani sub. We had a third man on board that sub with those instructions. He was to assassinate our operative. We weren't going to take any chances in case something went wrong. Trail stops here, right? No loose ends, right?"

He stopped long enough to allow the president to catch his breath, but when no words emerged, he continued.

"What it means is that the entire mission has been compromised. Our first operative, who was in charge of the whole operation, is likely dead. Our second operative, who is supposed to be dead, is apparently quite alive and well, and driving away with a nuclear device with ten warheads in its tip. We have a broken arrow! The device is out in the open, you jackass!"

"Mother of God."

"No shit! And do you think that this operative did all of this by himself?" the sarcasm stabbed the president in the gut. "Hell no. He had to have had help. In fact, he probably had a lot more than help. Our operative had to be a double agent. He's working for someone else."

"Our CIA operatives are vetted. They're polygraphed, they're screened. There's no way he was working as a double agent."

"Oh, of course not!" boomed the national security advisor. "Like we've never had a double agent inside the CIA! Are you insane?"

A vein on the side of the president's head throbbed.

"And which foreign government do you think this double

agent is working for?" the president said.

"He doesn't have to be working for a foreign government, does he? He could be working for a terror organization. Am I right? Maybe you'd care to venture a guess which internationally wanted terrorist is most likely behind this?"

The president's eyes scanned the floor for an answer that was not there. When the idea hit him, his eyes widened. "Don't say his name."

"Waseem Jarrah. Waseem Jarrah is his name, and he's not only the most likely suspect, it looks like the NSA has confirmed that the second operative is actually the brother of the terrorist who was stopped trying to detonate a nuclear device at the bluegrass festival in Kentucky last year! Certainly you remember that little incident."

The president straightened himself and decided the tongue-lashing would end.

"Just shut your mouth. I don't want to hear any more of your disrespecting of this office. I am the president of the United States and I will not be talked to in this manner!"

"Sir, my loyalties lie with the president. But if word of this gets out, you may not be the president much longer."

As the national security advisor began a hasty departure from the Oval Office, the president stopped him. "Jarrah? Waseem Jarrah. What are his plans? Where is the device headed?"

"The device? *The* device? It's no longer just a single device, Mr. President. Jarrah has separated the warheads. The Australians just detected that little fact by using an advanced satellite of theirs. There are now ten individual warheads, all headed in different directions into the Gulf of Oman. And, we no longer have eyes on them."

53

A CIA PENETRATION

NSA Headquarters.

The next morning, Pete Buck walked into Bill's office to find him head down on his desk, snoring.

Buck knocked on the open door, but there was no response.

"Sir? Mr. Tarleton?"

Bill's head rocketed upright. "No, no! I'm coming, Mom. I'll be right there. I can't find my books . . ."

"Sir? Mr. Tarleton, you all right?"

Bill rubbed his eyes. "Oh shit. I was dreaming I was late for school and couldn't find my books. Jesus, after all these years chasing terrorists you'd think dreams of being late for a final exam would be replaced with bombs going off or something. What is it, Buck? Hey, you don't look so good."

"You're right about that."

"You're three shades of green, son. Have a seat. Well, have a seat if you're not about to hurl, that is."

"Hurl, sir? I haven't heard that word in years."

"Kind of sticks to us old-timers. What's on your mind? You ready to give up this CIA crap and come to work at NSA?"

"Never crossed my mind," Buck said. "Sorry, it's just . . . I have some information. I think you're going to want to hear it."

Bill stood and arched his back.

"Sir, I think you're going to want to sit down for this one."

"I don't think I can take much more of this," Bill said. "Do I need to hear this one alone? You know, for my ears only, or do some other people need to hear this with me?"

"Might as well get the others in here. This is going to be ugly, so might as well get it all out on the table at once."

"You *are* about to hurl, aren't you?" Bill pressed a button on his phone. "Knuckles?" he yelled. "Knuckles? You there? Wake up, son." He heard a mumbled reply. "Get Director Latent, and bring Cade, Jana, and Kyle in here. They might as well hear this." He looked through his office window out into the situation room. "What the hell is that? Does Jana have a dog with her? Never mind, I don't want to know. Just bring them in here."

Once the troops had assembled around the walls of the tight office, Pete Buck stood, but everyone was distracted at the sight of Coconut.

"I suppose," Bill said, "that just because I get to have my dog running around here that you thought you'd bring yours?" Bill was grinning, although it was hard to tell underneath the beard.

"Service dog, Uncle Bill. You don't mind, right? Everyone, this is Coconut. Don't worry, he's friendly. And so far, he hasn't even piddled on anyone's shoes." She grinned at Bill. "It's better than having me flip out every time we talk about the Kunde brothers, right?"

"Anything is better than that. All right, Buck here has something rather unsettling to tell us. Buck? You have the floor."

Pete Buck wasted no time.

"It's everything you thought it was." He addressed Latent and Bill directly. "And I mean everything."

"Which part?" Latent said.

"All of it. Your theory that CIA is involved. It's all true. I've got a source close enough to pinpoint it all. The director of the CIA, however, is going to either deny it, or he himself actually has no operational knowledge, which, wouldn't surprise me."

Buck laid out everything he knew. Khalid Kunde was, in fact, a CIA employee. Had been employed there for three years. Stellar background and credentials. He was an operative. His most recent mission deployed him to Pakistan to infiltrate the Pakistani navy and carry out the destruction of a submarine. His operational exposure afforded him other knowledge as well. He was told the reason the sub needed to be destroyed. He knew the United States was attempting the theft of a nuclear device from the submarine. But, his handlers told him the reason the weapon had to be stolen was because Pakistan had illegally purchased the submarine from the Russians and that they were threatening to launch against India, their sworn enemy. The Pakistanis, Buck explained, had made no such threat, but that was the justification Khalid was given for such an aggressive act. By the time Buck had finished, Bill's office hung in stunned silence.

Jana was the first to speak. "The more I know, the less I want to know."

Latent piped in. "There will be time for that later. Right now, we've got to buckle down and find out where in the United States Waseem Jarrah is going to target with a nuclear blast, not to mention where the other nuclear warheads are headed."

"We all know he's headed here, somewhere," Jana said. "Waseem Jarrah isn't going to hold a nuke in his hands for long. The thing will itch a hole in his pocket until he gets it to detonate on US soil."

"What we're also suspicious of," Latent said, "is what the actual reason was that the CIA carried out this mission in the first place. It's the real reason they wanted to steal a nuclear device from another nation."

"And what was that?" Jana said.

"We have one idea," Bill replied. "But, Buck? How about you. Did your source in CIA shed any light?"

"No, sir. He hasn't gotten that far."

Bill stared at his desk. "We have one working theory. It's a load of crap, but it's all we have at the moment. Stevie? You want to do the honors?"

Latent stood. "Like Bill said, this is just a theory. It's thin at best. But what occurs to us is that the US has been getting a lot of threats from North Korea lately."

"North Korea? What do they have to do with Waseem Jarrah?" Jana said. Coconut looked at her, then plopped his head on her foot.

"Nothing," Latent continued. "But if the US actually stole a

Russian-made nuclear device, it wouldn't have been done without a purpose in mind. The theory is that the device could be detonated inside North Korea. The US would be able to take out the North Korean government, who has been threatening the US constantly, in one swift blow. And, anytime there's a nuclear accident like this, NATO would send in inspectors. They'd be able to tell that it was a Soviet-made device that had detonated. It would look like the Russians were responsible."

For the first time, Knuckles spoke. "Serves the North Koreans right." Everyone looked at him. "Not that I condone that sort of thing. But after that last news flash, the theory makes sense."

"What are you talking about?" Cade said.

"The North Korean missile thing. Didn't you see it?"

"See what, son?" Bill said.

"It's on the secure channel. You're kidding, right? You haven't seen it? CIA personnel on the ground confirmed it about two hours ago. The remains of a North Korean missile were recovered on a hillside on an uninhabited island off Hawaii. Why are you looking at me like that? I didn't launch the thing. But apparently, the North Korean military did."

"Stevie," Bill said. "Holy shit. If the North launched a missile on us, and *hit* us, that would mean . . ."

"That would mean that they do have long-range launch capability. That would mean it's not just a blustering tirade coming from their leader, but that they actually launched on us. It means the president would be justified to use nuclear force against a nuclear threat. He authorized the Fifteenth Protocol."

"What type of missile was it?"

For once, Knuckles spoke with authority. "A Taepodong-2 ICBM, sir. No nuclear tip, obviously. In fact, no explosive tip at all. But a long-range missile large enough to carry one. I don't understand it. Why launch an ICBM at us with no intent of destroying anything?"

Uncle Bill and Stephen Latent knew why. The North was provoking the United States. It was an unveiled threat.

"This just keeps getting worse," Bill said.

54

IT'S ALL ABOUT CONTROL

Miani Hor Inlet. Thirty-three miles north of Gaddani, coastal Pakistan.

All Khalid knew was that the boat runner was not a brother in jihad.

Why did Jarrah not tell me more? he wondered.

The boat bounced across the waves as Khalid and the only other occupant sped northwest along the Pakistani coastline. The man said nothing, and Khalid watched his every move. Wind and salty mist pelted them as the fast boat and its deadly cargo made the forty-five minute journey to a coastal inlet known as Miani Hor. The horseshoe-shaped harbor of Miani Hor was desolate with the exception of a tiny fishing hamlet on the far-eastern side. The boat, however, kept a large distance between itself and the village. Khalid surmised the driver did not want any additional prying eyes to note their presence.

The waters inside the inlet were much calmer than those on the open ocean. The driver turned west and headed into the river of a protected mangrove swamp, never decreasing speed. The smooth waters narrowed and the driver's boating skills became more apparent as he weaved the boat back and forth through the narrowing channel. About ten minutes later, he approached a beach and throttled down on the engine.

Khalid's heartbeat began a slow increase in tempo. *Either we're switching vehicles, or he's going to kill me. For his sake,* thought Khalid, *he better keep his hands where I can see them.*

Khalid let his right hand slide onto the hardened composite handle of the Glock 19 tucked in his waistline.

As the boat slowed, Khalid saw something he had not expected—a small, twin-engine turboprop airplane parked on hard-packed sand that had apparently been used as a makeshift landing strip. The door was ajar and a single man leaned against the fuselage. When Khalid glanced at the boat driver, he found the man staring at him, his eyes cold.

There was no choice other than to proceed. Trust was not an option.

The man beached the boat and spoke for the first time, his accent, telltale northern Spain.

"I can see it in your eyes," he said. "The distrust. Believe me, friend, if I wanted to kill you, you would not be sitting here right now. And why not? Why wouldn't I just kill you and take these two magnificent prizes for myself? These nuclear devices are worth a fortune on the open market."

He smiled, yet Khalid only tightened the grip on his Glock.

"But that is not my way. There is a reason I was hired for this above all others—I always deliver what I promise. These two warheads? These are not the most valuable cargo I have ever transported. And yet, they will get to their intended destination, just as you will."

Khalid didn't speak as his eyes scanned the horizon for the presence of any other threat.

"Come. We must load the warheads onto the plane. Time is short. It is possible, however unlikely, that a fisherman could wander up these waters. We don't want to be seen."

Khalid stood and watched as the pilot walked toward them.

"Relax. My name is Rafael," the boat driver said. "You look surprised. Is it so strange to find someone sympathetic to your cause from Spain? It shouldn't be. But don't be too fooled about my loyalties to Waseem Jarrah. My association with him puts me in harm's way. No, my loyalties lie with the highest bidder. In other words, my loyalties are for sale. But lucky for you, Jarrah pays well."

The pilot climbed aboard the boat and looked at the two

warheads, packed in canvas.

He said, "They are smaller than I expected. Like two small mummies. Help me get them into the plane. Let us load the larger one first. One hundred and twenty pounds, correct?"

The moment Khalid glanced at Rafael, the airplane pilot exploded forward and tackled him, pinning his arms to prevent Khalid from drawing the gun. Rafael pounced like a cat and wrestled the handgun from Khalid as the two men forced Khalid's hands behind his back. In a matter of four seconds Khalid found himself handcuffed. His chest heaved as he fought a futile battle against the restraints.

The pilot ran his hands across Khalid searching for any other weapons.

"He is clean," the man said.

Khalid stared at Rafael. "Jarrah is ruthless. He will find you, and you know it!" His tone far more defiant and angry than frightened. "Get off of me! Take off these handcuffs!"

"Relax," Rafael said. "And you are correct about him being ruthless. But you mislabel our friend Waseem Jarrah. He is not simply ruthless, he is also psychotic. Yes, he will find me. But that is only if I fail him."

"And what do you call this?" Khalid erupted.

"Control," replied Rafael. "The reason I am still alive today is *control*. My partner and I trust no one. We certainly do not trust you. Let me ask you something. What were your instructions? You expected us to deliver you and two nuclear weapons, and then you'd just shake our hands and say good-bye? No, no, my friend. You can't have any witnesses to something this big, correct? You would have killed us as though our lives were worth nothing more than those of a couple of young pigs. And why not? Why would you leave us alive after we'd been a part of this? Leave no trail," Rafael laughed. "Don't look so surprised. I do not know how you acquired these nuclear weapons and I do not care. Nor do I care what their intended purpose is, or why. That is not my part. My part is to deliver what I say I will deliver. The fewer questions I ask, the more my employers trust me. And, the more they pay."

"What are you saying? That you are not about to kill me and dump my body in the swamp?" Khalid's eyes spoke vinegar.

"No, killing you is not an act of loyalty to my employer. Both you and your cargo will be delivered as ordered. You, however, will have no chance to kill us. We are not fools." He scowled at Khalid, then looked at the pilot. "Hurry! We must get him into the plane and start the engines. I will bring the smaller package. Then you and I will together load the larger one. I do not like standing on this beach so exposed."

An instant later, Rafael struck Khalid across the back of the head with the Glock, and everything went black.

55

THERE IS ANOTHER

City of Chekka, coastal Lebanon. Warehouse of the Holcim Liban cement factory.

"No one knows about you," Waseem Jarrah said to a man standing in the shadows. "And I've worked very hard to keep it that way."

Jarrah paced the dusty, gravel-covered floor.

"I know you have, Waseem," the man replied. His voice was coarse as if parched by rock salt. "I will not fail you. I can be trusted."

"Can you? Can you be trusted? This is not a game we play. The role I task of you is crucial to this mission. Unless it is executed flawlessly, our plans will fail."

"When have I ever gone against your teachings?" the young man said. "I have done nothing but show my loyalty. And besides, I am the only person that could pull off this assignment. You said it yourself. What could be more perfect? The beast will never suspect a thing. They don't even know I exist. Putting this part of your plan into motion increases the chances of success by tenfold."

"You are right about that. They don't know about you. Recite for me again the details of your exact assignment, and leave out nothing."

The man wiped a bead of sweat from his brow and cleared his throat; he knew he was being tested. If Jarrah approved, he would enter the jihad and play a pivotal role. As Waseem continued to pace the dusty warehouse floor, the man outlined from memory every detail of the mission with which he was tasked.

When he was done, Jarrah stopped. "I am impressed. And you understand there is no returning from this jihad?"

"Yes, Waseem. I am prepared for the beginning, the middle, and the end."

"No matter what happens during your mission, you will either be killed or sickened beyond any hope. If the latter, you will die a horrible death. Your sacrifice will not go unnoticed by Allah." Waseem handed the man a set of car keys. "The package is in the trunk. Before you board the vessel for your long voyage, remove the device from the trunk and carry it with you, then destroy the car. Leave no trace."

"My whole life has been one of leaving no traces, Waseem. I will not fail you."

"Your voyage will put you into the American port just before he gets there. The timing of your arrival is critical."

Jarrah walked into the brilliant sunlight and disappeared around the side of the building. The man stared after him. When he was gone, the man went to the vehicle outside and opened the trunk. Inside was a package he would carry with him until his death.

56

THE BRIGHTNESS OF OMAN

Sohar Airport, Al Batinah North Governorate. Along the northernmost coast of the Sultanate of Oman.

An hour and twelve minutes later, the plane's tires barked on the runway at Sohar Airport. The landing startled Khalid out of unconsciousness. He was disoriented, and his head throbbed.

"Where are we?" he demanded.

"Oh, awake, I see," Rafael said, as he squinted into the brilliant sunlight. "How is your head? I hated to do it, you know."

"Bullshit," Khalid said. "You didn't hate it one bit."

Rafael let out a long exhale. "So young. So much—what is the word?—ambition. You are exactly where you are supposed to be, in Oman. You and your cargo, just as promised." He glanced back at Khalid. "You are angry with me, yes? But you are alive. And more importantly, so am I."

"What happens now?" Khalid said as he strained against the handcuffs.

"Just as you planned. Your freighter awaits. The airport here is only six miles from the coastline. Your ship departs in one hour. Both you and your package will be on board."

"But what of Jarrah's *other* package? The one you are to arrange delivery for?"

"You needn't concern yourself with that. The larger package will be delivered to its final destination as instructed, you can be assured of that. It will arrive there in ten days' time."

"Good, because I'd hate to see Jarrah hunt you down."

"No you wouldn't. But, there will be no need. You are young. You do not yet see the value of loyalty." He peered out the windshield of the plane as it taxied to a halt in front of a black van parked on the tarmac. "In my world, loyalty is all I have."

Khalid stared at the van. "My transportation?"

"Once you are away, they have instructions to release you from the handcuffs and return your pistol. You will find it, unloaded and disassembled, in your bag. And remember something. The couriers driving this van have no idea who you are or what your cargo is. I can't stop you from trying to kill them, but, in my book, killing them would only bring more attention to you than leaving them be."

"Aren't *you* the humanitarian?" It was a rebuke. *How much does he know about the mission?* Khalid thought. "And once the other package reaches its destination in ten days' time, then what?"

"I have no idea," Rafael replied. "But a package like this has but one purpose, and you and I know what that is."

Khalid's eyes flared.

"Ah," Rafael said, "you are still disappointed that I know what the package contains. I had to know. Otherwise I would not have known how to ship it. A package of this type must be well concealed if it is to arrive at the appropriate destination, in the heart of Pyongyang, North Korea. I always know what the packages I deliver contain. That way, I won't end up hand-delivering it all the way to its destination, only to be vaporized because it was a nuclear device."

Khalid's eyes widened. "You were instructed to hand-deliver the package, weren't you?"

"Yes, but even though I am not hand-delivering the package, my contract will still be fulfilled. It's just that Jarrah will not have tied off another of his perceived *loose ends.*"

"But he will find you."

"I am not a loose end. Once the package arrives and presumably detonates in Pyongyang, he will not bother looking for me because he will assume I am dead. And you? You will probably be dead by then anyway. I do not know your mission, but I imagine you to be another sad jihadist. A martyr. No, you will not be alive to tell Jarrah to come after me, and both of us know it."

Khalid yanked against the handcuffs, but the effort was futile.

The van backed up close to the plane. As the pilot switched off the twin engines, Rafael opened the door. Outside, both doors on the back of the van popped open, and Khalid stared into the black interior that awaited him.

57

THE RUSSIAN ADVANCE

North Hwanghae province, Kangnam, North Korea. Taedong River inlet. About ten miles south of Pyongyang.

"Reporting now, I'm Mike Slayden, WBS News. As the now two-week-old Russian advance into North Korea continues, WBS News has learned that heavy armor has advanced all the way to the capital city of Pyongyang. The merciless Russian air assault on the city has not relented since fighting broke out. With the Russians poised to take over the city, questions are swirling about what they intend to do next. Now, we go live to our correspondent in the field, Tammy Cho. Tammy, where are you now, and what can you tell us about the Russian advance?"

"Mike, we're embedded with the Russian 155th Marine Brigade, just a few miles from the heart of Pyongyang, the North Korean capital. The town we're in is called Kangnam, and the fighting here has been intense. The area is normally tranquil. Lots of smaller cooperative farms and some light industrial complexes. But today, the city is engulfed in a last-ditch attempt to stop the Russian advance before it enters the capital. The troops we're embedded with face constant sniper fire from the myriad of buildings ahead of us, and the barrage of artillery attacks is ongoing. But Mike, one thing is now certain. Russian forces are in control of the skies over Kangnam. We've not seen a single North Korean Mig fighter jet in over ten days. In fact, if we pan our camera to the east, off in the distance can be seen a squadron of Russian fighter jets headed north to pound Pyongyang. The other sight that's become familiar to this region over the last two weeks is the occasional missile streaking across the sky overhead. The scene is reminiscent of the Gulf War where US missiles flew above us with regularity, heading to destinations unknown. These appear to be the same type of low-flying, guided missiles that are likely targeted at military or government facilities in the capital city. It's an eerie sight, Mike."

"Tammy, any indication where the missiles are coming from?"

"Mike, we're too far away from the bay to tell, but in all likelihood, the missiles are coming from one or more Russian submarines now patrolling the Yellow Sea. Perhaps the K-551, the *Vladimir Monomakh*, Russia's newest ballistic-missile submarine, last seen in the waters near Kraskino, has entered the war. For now, this is Tammy Cho, WBS News."

58

NORTH KOREA MAKES A PURCHASE

Port of Sohar, along the northern tip of coastal Oman.

Rafael and another man sat in a van near a dock platform. A container ship dwarfed the surrounding buildings and blotted out the scorching morning sun.

"We are here to deliver the heavier package? How will the package make it all the way into North Korea?" Rafael's partner said.

"It will be escorted."

"Escorted? Escorted by who? Another martyr? These people are as stupid as any group I've ever seen. Giving your life for some ridiculous cause."

"No," Rafael said, "not a martyr. Waseem Jarrah has but a limited supply of those. And my guess is that he's earmarked his best martyrs for other destinies. No, the package will be personally escorted by representatives of the North Korean government." A grin painted his face. "They'll take it right into the capital city themselves."

"Oh, bullshit. Why would they do that?"

Rafael laughed. "They're buying the thing."

"What?"

"North Korea has been combing the international black market, looking to buy a warhead and guidance system so they could complete their missile system. They seem to have long-range strike capability already, but they need to pair it with a nuclear tip. Well, here you go. Here's your nuclear tip."

"But . . ."

"What they don't know is that the warhead is already armed; preprogrammed to detonate upon arrival."

The partner spun around and looked at the crate behind him, then blurted, "It's *armed*?"

Rafael only smiled. "Relax. These devices don't detonate until they reach their preprogrammed destination. It works the same way when they're launched at a target. Typically, a missile like this arms itself in midflight as it nears its intended destination. But this one is already armed. The GPS guidance system, however, won't enable the detonation until it is precisely on its coordinates."

"You mean the North Korean government is going to buy an armed nuclear device, carry it into the heart of their own capital city, and it will detonate?"

He stared through the windshield into the sunlit glow cascading across the topmost edges of the massive ship in front of them.

"A pretty good way to get the package there, don't you think? And look over there. Our contact has arrived." Rafael laughed through the words. "Bombs away."

59

NOTHING TO GO ON

Autumn Woods Apartments. Three weeks later.

As the weeks tumbled by, the intensity of the search for loose nuclear warheads increased. And as higher priority was assigned to the case, more resources were assigned as well. The three friends regularly found themselves in Cade's apartment in the evenings, decompressing and talking about the day's events. The one wildcard was the presence of Dr. Kelly. She and Kyle had become quite the couple, and her frequent presence was a good thing for Jana, whose battle with post-traumatic stress continued. Daily counseling sessions with Kelly helped air the demons—demons whose roots dug deep. But Kelly was the only one of the group that was not privy to the details of the case— details that required the highest levels of top-secret clearance. Kyle, Jana, and Cade had to filter their conversations when they were around her, which was constant.

The greatest problem Jana faced was that her demons were still present in her day-to-day life. In most PTSD cases, the traumatic events responsible for causing the episodes were things that had happened in the past. But for Jana, the situation was different. She was actively tracking the same terrorist who had originally orchestrated her demons in the first place, Waseem Jarrah. And to Jana, it felt as if he was a puppeteer, pulling against strings deep within her brain. Her concentration suffered, and her once nonexistent temper began to flare.

Jana and Cade, though, were hitting it off. But although Jana found Cade's shyness cute, she was the one leading the relationship, and that bothered her.

"Cade," Jana said, "this apartment is exactly like your barren apartment on Lenox Road in Atlanta."

In the background, the evening news played on the television.

Kyle interrupted, "You mean it doesn't have any pictures, house plants, nicknacks strewn about, little bowls filled with potpourri?"

"Well, I just think we need to spruce it up a bit. You know, this place needs a woman's touch." Coconut, always at Jana's side, pushed his muzzle into her open hand. "That's it, boy. You agree, right? Yes, of course you do." Nut wagged until the back half of his body rocked back and forth.

"I'll second that motion," Kelly said as she lifted herself from the edge of the couch and onto her wheelchair. "Hey, Jana, let's go down to Target and fill up a cart with all kinds of sappy, girly decorations. You have a key to this place, right? We'll just sneak in and get it done while he's at the office doing whatever he does all day at the NSA."

"You guys," Cade said as he laughed. "Honestly, I try, okay? I mean, look over there. There's a wall hanging right there."

"Wait a second," Kyle said. "She has a key? Dude, you didn't tell me that. Man, I didn't know you two were getting married." He raised a high five to Cade, but Cade shook it off.

"The velvet Elvis tapestry, Cade? You're going to call that a wall hanging?" she said as she giggled. "And what's that yellow-brown stain on Elvis's shirt? Mustard?"

"All right, all right," Cade said. "I get it. Women don't consider Elvis to be *decor*. But, yeah, I think you're right. That beautiful piece of artwork came out of a Dairy Queen, so it probably is mustard."

Kelly laughed. "Cade, we'll have to spend some time in therapy analyzing the velvet Elvis tapestry." She looked around at the others. "Okay, well, I know when it's time for you guys to talk shop, so I'm going to go. It was a great dinner, Cade."

"You don't have to go," Kyle said. "I thought we would go together." He gave her a grin.

"Well, you have a key to my place, don't you?" she said.

"Dude," Cade said. "You giving me grief about Jana having my key? You've got a key to Kelly's?" After there was no response, he continued. "It wasn't a great dinner though. The spaghetti was terrible."

"Maybe we can advance our cooking technology just a bit past popping open a can of spaghetti sauce," Jana said.

"Laugh it up," Cade said. "So we all know. If the way to a woman's heart is through her stomach, my cooking isn't going to cut it."

"Well if she has her own key," Kyle said, "something must be working."

After Kelly left, the three flopped down on the two couches. Kyle was the first to speak. "I still can't believe what Latent told us. I mean, I knew North Korea was threatening us, I just had no idea they'd go so far as to actually launch a missile at us. And nobody knows about it. Not the media, the public, nobody but a few people in our line of work."

"From what Uncle Bill said, it's likely they launched at us just as a threat, a statement," Cade said.

"Wake the sleeping giant?" Jana said.

"What do you mean?"

"It's stupid of them," she continued. "Right after the attack on Pearl Harbor, the commanding admiral of the Japanese Navy said he thought the only thing they'd succeeded in doing was to *waken the sleeping giant.* And he was right. What does the North Korean government think we're going to do? Sit down and take it?"

"Wait," Kyle said, "you aren't condoning the CIA plan, are you? The plan to detonate a nuclear device inside North Korea?"

Jana wasn't backing down that easily.

"Kyle, what did you expect us to do? Wait until that dictator puts together the technology to launch a missile that far, hit exactly what it's aiming at, all while carrying a nuclear tip?"

Kyle shook his head at her. "Jana, the United States is not a nuclear *threat.* We are a nuclear *deterrent.* There's a difference."

"*They're* the nuclear threat. North Korea doesn't seem to care that we're a nuclear deterrent. If we have to use force to stop them, then so be it."

"Can you hear yourself?" Kyle said, his anger escalating. "Innocent people would be killed. You think it's okay to kill all the civilians in North Korea?"

Cade jumped to his feet. "Whoa, whoa. Let's all just take a minute here. We never argue like this."

"That's because Miss Nuclear Threat over there has changed. Jana, since when did you get so hard?"

Her fingers wandered across one of the bullet scars near her sternum.

"Since my chest got filled with lead. I don't have patience anymore. I don't have patience for anything anymore."

"Jana," Cade said, "are you all right? Have you talked with Kelly about this?"

"Yes, I've talked to Kelly about this. It's just that, I get, I get so angry."

Kyle moved a hand over the spot on his own ribs where a bullet scar from the raid on the Thoughtstorm building remained. "You think I don't get angry about being shot?"

Jana drew a breath. "I know, Kyle. It's not just me. You got shot too. We were so sure you were dead in that stairwell. I'm sorry. I don't mean to be so needy. It's just that I don't know where all this anger is supposed to go."

"Jana, you can talk to me too," Cade said. "I'm here for you. I'm always here for you. You know that, right?"

She placed a tender hand on his face. "Yes, I know."

"You two don't get all sappy on me now. Well if you're talking to Kelly about it, I won't press the issue any further. But talk to us anytime you need to. I get angry too, but it's you we're worried about."

"Maybe I'm still mad at you," Jana said, almost whispering.

"Mad at *me*?" Kyle replied. "What did I do? It's not Kelly, is it? I thought you guys liked her. Is that what this is about? You don't like me dating her?"

"No, no," Jana said. "I love Kelly."

"That makes two of us," Cade said.

"It's not her. But I am mad at you." She swallowed hard. "Do you have any idea what it was like to leave you in that stairwell?

To think you were dead?" Tears welled in her eyes. "I left you in that stairwell in the Thoughtstorm building, and it turns out you were alive." She looked down. "Once you got shot, you were *my* responsibility, and I left you there."

"Both of you look at me. You thought I was dead. I made that happen. I had to make you think I was dead. If I hadn't, you would have never left me. You never would have been able to carry me out of there without getting killed yourselves. I did what I did because I thought I was dead anyway. I was bleeding out, and no one could do anything about it. I needed you two to get out of there to save yourselves and to get the stolen data out of the building so that it could be analyzed to stop the next morning's terrorist attack. I didn't know what else to do."

"Well you scared the shit out of me."

Cade slid over and pulled her close.

"I'm sorry," Kyle said. "I apologize to you both. It won't happen again."

"Happen again?" Cade said. "Hell, it better not happen again. You getting all shot to pieces? And me, in a firefight? Me? Good God, I barely knew which direction to point that gun. You won't find me up to my eyeballs in flying bullets ever again."

The tension began to ease from the room.

"Let's hope not," Jana said, as she wiped a tear from her face. "All right, I think I've said my piece. But I'm still mad at you."

"If you're still mad at me, then what's that little grin?"

"I know something you don't know."

"Are we back in third grade?" Kyle said. "Okay, I'll bite. What do you know that I don't know?"

"No, I think I want to see you squirm for a bit."

"Oh, will you just tell me already?"

After a few moments, Jana said, "Riggs."

"Riggs? You mean Lieutanant Riggs? What about him?"

"Remember what you said about him? About how there was something familiar about him that you couldn't place?"

"Yeah?"

"I know why you recognize him."

"Jana," Cade said, "you're killing the man. Out with it."

"He was there that night. That night in the stairwell." Jana's smile retreated and her eyes found the floor. "In the Thoughtstorm building. Kyle, when you were hit, and we left you, Riggs and the other operators on his Delta Force team carried you out. They're the ones that evaced you off the rooftop."

Kyle slumped back on the couch. His mouth opened but no words escaped. After a few moments, he said, "Oh my God. I remember almost nothing. Nothing but his face."

"Anyway," Jana said, "when I found out, I thanked him."

"I'll thank him myself," Kyle said. "In fact, I might kiss him on the lips."

"That's a lovely picture," Cade said.

"Now," Kyle said, "can we get back to what we were saying a minute ago. Jana, you can't support this CIA plan."

"I know. I don't want to see the people of North Korea get melted down like those poor people in Hiroshima. I don't. But what are we supposed to do? We can't wait for them to take another missile shot at us."

"I know," Cade said, "but between NSA and FBI, we're now supposed to find not only the nukes heading to US soil, but the one headed to North Korea. The question is, how?"

Kyle thought about that for a moment. "Uncle Bill says finding the one headed to North Korea is darned-near impossible. The only thing we can do is pray the Australian satellite finds it first."

"Needle in a haystack," Cade said. "The device could be anywhere. Could be headed that way on a plane, a container ship, anywhere."

"Container ships," Kyle said. "Man, there's no way to cover all the shipping containers that come in on one of those things. Does North Korea even get container ships sent to them? Do they import anything?"

"I don't think so," Cade replied. "Well, maybe. I don't know. But even if they didn't, they'd still buy some stuff from other countries. It would get there one way or another. After all, before the Russians decided to invade the place, they were selling arms to them. Not to mention large-scale centrifuges used in the manufacture of nuclear material. Believe me. If a shipment needs to get there, it will."

"Guys," Jana said, "we need to focus on any nukes headed to US soil."

"I know," Cade said. "But we've got nothing to go on. Not even a lead. At least last year Uncle Bill was able to find a clue about the bomb headed to the bluegrass festival before it was too late."

"Cade," Jana said, "he found that clue four minutes before the device was to detonate. We just happened to be there. It was pure luck."

The room went quiet for a minute.

Kyle said, "I've got a sick feeling inside. Like we're going to have no idea where to look. And then it will be too late."

"I've got the same feeling," Jana said. "We've got to concentrate on finding Kunde's younger brother. He's our only chance."

"What about finding Waseem Jarrah?" Kyle said. "We find him, we stop the whole thing."

Jana looked at the blank space on the wall. "He's a ghost. We're not going to find him. Especially if he's not even coming to the US."

"How do you know he's not coming here himself?"

"It's not his style," she said. "Just like last time. When the big one was set to detonate, he was on a tanker ship heading back to the Middle East. And we'll never find him over there."

"You're full of positivity," Kyle said.

"Cade," Jana said, "you're going to get rid of that velvet Elvis tapestry, right?"

60

A BROADCAST CUT SHORT

Pyongyang, North Korea.

"Mike Slayden, WBS News. We're again taking you live to Tammy Cho in the North Korean capital. Tammy, from your position, is it clear that the Russian military has taken full control of Pyongyang?"

"Without a doubt, Mike. The celebrations taking place behind me in downtown Pyongyang are a clear indication. Our understanding is that Russian Premier Vladimir Dumanovsky will be making the announcement within the hour. What isn't clear is what happens next. Now that the North Korean government is no longer in control, what does the Russian government intend to do? The motivation behind this invasion has always been the lack of cooperation from North Korea with regard to Russia's missing diplomat. If foul play was involved with the disappearance, one would have to believe the Russians will get to the bottom of it.

"The battle into the capital city has been costly for the Russian military, Mike. But as the streets are clearing, small celebrations are breaking out, like the one behind me. The words being sung by the Russian soldiers can be translated as, 'This Victory Day, air saturated with gunpowder, it's a holiday with temples already gray, it's joy with tears upon our eyes. Victory Day!' Those lyrics come from a song composed some thirty years after the Russian victory over Nazi Germany in World War II. They are sung each year on May 9 in celebration of that day of victory."

"And what of the whereabouts of North Korea's leader, Jeong Suk-to? Has he been seen in public since this invasion began?"

"No, Mike, he hasn't. Speculation is swirling at this hour as to his location and status. One unconfirmed report says that Jeong Suk-to has been assassinated in bed at his private residence, but many here have doubts. It wouldn't be the first time that the young leader's early demise has been incorrectly reported. There are many unanswered questions and—" A loud cracking sound interrupted the broadcast and the signal went dead.

"Tammy? Tammy, can you still hear me?" Mike Slayden said. "Tammy, are you there? Well folks, it appears we've again been cut off from our reporter Tammy Cho inside the North Korean capital of Pyongyang, where Russian troops have just declared victory over North Korea. We'll take a station break. For now, this is Mike Slayden, WBS News."

Once the television camera signal was clear, Slayden called out to his station manager. "Chuck, why'd we lose the signal again? I'm getting sick of being cut off in the middle of a broadcast!"

"No shit. I don't know. Hold on, Mike." Chuck pressed his headset harder against his ears and began speaking to someone in the control room through his mic. "Dave? Yeah, I'm here. What happened? I thought we fixed this. Where's my goddamned signal?"

"Chuck, the ping is gone," replied the man across the headset.

"What do you mean the ping is gone? Listen, I can understand how we could lose the signal from the portable broadcast unit at Tammy's location, but the ping is coming from our satellite truck, which is parked well outside the city. What is it, a mile away from her location? Not to mention that we set up a redundant broadcast feed from her location so this wouldn't happen again."

"All I know is Tammy's portable broadcast signal is gone, the signal from the satellite truck is gone, and the redundant signal is gone as well."

"What do you mean the redundant signal is gone? You're

telling me all three feeds went offline at the same moment? That's impossible."

61

TREMORS

Hawaiian Volcano Observatory, Volcanoes National Park, Big Island of Hawaii.

"Ouch. Shit, what was that?" Karl Vargman, a second-year intern at the US Geological Survey monitoring station said.

"What do you have, Karl?" Makelo Kama, his supervisor, replied. Makelo's tone was one part droll and one part unadulterated exhaustion.

Karl removed the headphones from his ears. "Christ, we just had a spike! It's only a 3.6 magnitude, but we might have some seismic activity starting. It could be a precursor to something larger, like volcanic activity."

"It's too early in the morning," Makelo said as he rubbed his eyes. "Dang interns. You guys get so excited. One little spike pops across the seismograph monitors and you get all giddy on us. Are you sure?"

"I'm an intern, not an idiot."

"Well, based on the coffee you made this morning, that topic is up for debate. Let me see what you have, rookie. Is it just a spike, or is it sustained?" Makelo leaned over the workstation. "See, it's just a spike. Notice how there's no continuation in the amplitude? And, see here," he said, pointing to the wavy line on the monitor, "the amplitude is flat. We in the seismic community call that *attenuation*. A reduction in amplitude of a wave over time."

"Asshole."

"Thank you. Just because I have a hangover doesn't mean I don't have it in me to be demeaning to an intern. But, wait a minute." Makelo studied the monitor further. "Where the hell is this coming from? I can't . . ."

"What's the matter, boss?"

"Distance from us to the epicenter of the tremor is 4,485 *miles*? But that would mean . . ."

"Boss, what is it? And how does the computer know how far away the event was?"

Makelo spun a rolling desk chair into place and sat at the monitor, then began banging away on the keyboard.

"We're tied in with seismology stations all over the world. This signal was picked up everywhere. Jesus, look at all the places it's registering. We're part of the International Monitoring System. We get feeds from the Berkeley Digital Seismic Network, which lit up like a Christmas tree. And look how it registered at all these monitoring stations from Asia and Australia. Marble Bar, Western Australia, Port Moresby, New Guinea, Qiongzhong, Hainan Province. But, it can't be. It just can't be."

"It can't be what?" stammered the exasperated intern.

"Okay, rookie, look at this. See how the P-waves dominate the seismogram? Think about how different the waveform looks compared to the typically dominant S-waves of an earthquake or a volcanic eruption."

Karl scowled. "Yeah, I see that, now that you point it out. But we didn't study any waveforms that look like this. What is it?"

Makelo shook his head. "I just can't believe it. There's only one thing that creates P-waves like this, and the triangulation says it's coming from Pyongyang, North Korea."

"So what is it?"

"It's a nuclear detonation."

62

RUNNING OUT OF TIME

NSA Headquarters.

"Sir? I've got a priority flash alert coming in," a woman said, pressing her hand against her headset.

"Oh shit," Uncle Bill said, "what is it?"

Cade, Jana, and Kyle looked over. It wasn't until they saw the woman cover her mouth with her hand that alarm bells inside each of them began to blare.

The words came out in a reverent, choked tone. "Bright boy, sir."

Stephen Latent moved toward the woman's workstation. "Where?"

"Satellite indicates a nuclear detonation detection. Latitude, 39.1 degrees north, longitude, 125.45 degrees east. It's coming up on screen six now."

"Where is that?" Latent said.

It was Knuckles who confirmed. "Pyongyang, North Korea, sir."

Bill and Latent looked at each other. "Please, God, don't tell me we were right," Bill said.

"We were right."

"What's the yield?" Bill said, speaking of the device's blast capability. "Can you calculate it based on the blast radius? And didn't we get a launch detection?"

"No launch detected, sir," Knuckles said, stammering to answer the questions fast enough. "Looks like this one didn't travel through detectable air space. Yield, yield, ah, looks like an initial blast radius of just over 1.1 miles. That would put this device at about 100 kilotons."

"1.1 *miles*?" Latent said. "But that would cover the bulk of the downtown area of Pyongyang, right?"

"Yes, sir," Knuckles replied. "Looks like the blast was centered right in the middle of it."

"Stevie," Uncle Bill, said "you know what this means?"

Latent didn't answer.

Cade spoke next. "It means the United States may have just vaporized 3.2 million people."

Jana looked at him.

"They wouldn't have all been hit with this blast," Knuckles said in a tone devoid of emotion. "But, the North Korean government, including much of its military, is certainly gone. And one thing's for sure, this weapon was not homemade."

"How do you know that?" Jana said.

"The yield, 100 kilotons, is massive. It's a far larger weapon than anyone other than a government could build. For comparison, the homemade weapon that they tried to detonate in Kentucky was half a kiloton."

"That's even more reason to believe we were right. It's an act of war," Stephen Latent said. "And I'm pretty sure this one tracks all the way to the Oval Office."

Bill said, "We don't know that. It's just a theory. No one outside this room knows about it."

"If I can prove it, everyone in the world will know about it."

"Steve," Bill said, "think about what you're saying. The United States, another conspiracy that leads all the way to the top? If it's true, and word ever got out, the entire world would come at us. Even our allies would become our enemies. We couldn't be trusted." He walked over to Latent. "This could change the landscape of the United States on the world's stage, forever."

"Then so be it," Jana said. "If we have to defend ourselves against our enemies, so be it."

"Jana?" Cade said. "I can't believe you just said that. Those are innocent people."

"I know," she replied, though her eyes were despondent. "I can't believe it actually happened. I didn't think it really would happen. This means a lot more than the fact that the North Korean military machine has been neutralized." All of them looked at her. "It means Waseem Jarrah's plan is in full swing. It means that that son of a bitch is out there, somewhere. And he's laughing at us."

"Jana? You all right?" Kyle said. "Hey, Jana?"

But her body had gone rigid. Coconut, who was always at her side, looked up at her and cocked his head. He began to whimper and paw at her, then pushed his head into her leg. Finally, she snapped out of her stupor and looked at the dog.

"What? Hey, boy. No, I'm fine."

Cade and Kyle exchanged nervous glances.

Jana continued. "What are we going to do now? Sir," she said to Latent, "that detonation was a single device. There are nine others still out there. You know one or more of them are headed this way. We can't just sit here. We have to do something before one of those goes off in Washington or New York or Atlanta."

"We have no leads, Agent Baker," he said. "We've got a country three thousand miles wide and no leads with which to narrow our search. But, we do have facial-recognition systems running at every airport, scanning every face, looking for a match to the younger brother of Shakey Kunde. Let's just hope that we find Kunde before it's too late."

"Jana," Knuckles said. "We're doing everything we can. Don't forget, we've also got a network of radiation-detection devices deployed all over the place. It's not just the one Aussie satellite that can detect the presence of nuclear material. We've got detectors on the ground. And they're a lot better at detecting the presence of a device than that satellite."

"But how many places could a man walk into this country carrying a weapon in a backpack undetected? Remember, we're talking about an eighty-pound device. It's not that hard to imagine it being carried in a rucksack or other large backpack." She looked at Uncle Bill. "Where do we have detection devices stationed?"

"They've been in place for years. Knuckles? You want to pull it up on one of the monitors for Agent Baker?"

"Yes, sir. On monitor three. See? We've got them positioned at every major airport and at every shipping port. We've also got them stationed around Washington, DC and the Maryland area, New York, Chicago, Hollywood . . ."

"Hollywood?" Jana said.

"Yes, Hollywood."

"Who the hell cares if they—"

"Watch it, Jana," Kyle said.

"Yes," Uncle Bill said. "Jana, Hollywood is a major symbol of America. And these radicalized people really hate our movie industry."

"Okay, okay," she said. "So, all those green dots on the monitor indicate a detection device? How sensitive are they?"

"Very sensitive," Knuckles said. "There's a high probability that a device the size we're looking for would be detected, even if it's housed inside a shipping container coming off a cargo ship."

"Sir?" a woman about three cubes over and to the right said. "We do have one blind spot in the detection network." She pointed at the monitor.

"Just one blind spot? Look at the map. What about the entire border with Mexico? What about the million places a person could slip across the border with Canada? What about just showing up in a little boat off the east coast and walking onto shore?"

Coconut gurgled at her. It wasn't a growl per se, but Jana got the point. She petted his head. "Sorry, boy. I'll try to keep my temper under control." He licked her hand.

"What blind spot are you referring to?" Latent said.

"Brunswick, Georgia, sir," the woman said. "At the shipping port there. Yesterday morning. It just went down. The detection station, I mean. Its status on monitor three indicates its offline. It looks like there's a work order in place to get it fixed though."

Jana couldn't help but interrupt. "It's offline? How does a nuclear-material detector go offline?"

"Could be anything," Knuckles said. "It's a piece of digital equipment. They break sometimes. What's the big deal?"

"What's the big deal? The big deal is that some terrorist nutjob is trying to waltz a hundred kiloton device into our backyard, and apparently, the door is unlocked."

"Yes, ma'am," Knuckles said. "I didn't mean it to sound like I was taking this lightly. It's just that I didn't see any reason to be suspicious just because one detector in a network of hundreds happens to go offline for a while."

Kyle stepped forward. "It went offline yesterday? Sir, we better get a list of ships that arrived during the time it was down."

Latent said, "We better get a team down there. Bill, if we get a crew down there, and a device had been smuggled in with the detector offline, would there be any residual radioactivity that could be picked up after the fact?"

"Possibly," Bill said. "You're thinking Kunde's younger brother might have slipped in, and it just so happens that our nuclear-monitoring station at that one port was offline at the exact time? Seems like quite a coincidence."

"No, it doesn't seem like a coincidence at all," Jana said. Latent looked over at the woman who originally reported the monitor being offline. "We need an immediate assessment of that monitoring station. There's a repair crew scheduled to go over there? Call them right now." He turned to Jana and Kyle. "You two. I want you on a jet in thirty minutes. Get on the horn with the FBI field office in Savannah, Georgia. That's the closest one. We'll need everything they've got."

"Cade?" Uncle Bill said. "You go with them. You've got a good head for the field. They might need your help."

"The field?" Cade said.

"Come on, Cade," Jana said through a smile. "We'll try not to get you killed or anything."

"Comforting. Very comforting."

63

BOUND FOR THE BEAST

Port of Sohar, Oman.

As the van came to a halt, Khalid could hear a seagull in the distance. The handcuffs dug into his slight wrists, and the black canvas sack that had been placed over his head allowed no light to penetrate. But the smell of salt water and stale fish was a dead giveaway—they were at the port where Khalid would board a cargo ship. The lack of the slightest vestige of light made him feel like he was in an abyss—a place with no beginning and no end. Without the sounds and smells, Khalid might as well have been on the surface of the moon.

The rear door of the van slung open and two men jumped in. The doors slammed closed behind them.

"Do you know who I am?" Khalid said, though his voice was muffled underneath the shroud. At once, the shroud was removed and he squinted against the sliver of light.

"Not a word from you," a voice said. The accent was Middle Eastern, Jordanian perhaps. The two black-hooded figures were silhouetted against the faint light. "You are at your destination. What do we want, you ask? Our skins. We have fulfilled our duty to take you here. But we are not fools. Whatever it is you go to do, whatever instructions you have for hiding your trail, you will not be given the opportunity to silence us. After this moment, if we see your face again, we'll slit your throat as if you were a pig for slaughter."

Khalid squinted at the men. Both of their faces were hooded

and completely obscured. "Then let me be on my way."

The other man moved behind Khalid and drew a handgun in the process. He jammed it into Khalid's back.

"When these handcuffs are removed, you will slowly exit the van." His voice was angry, and he spoke in clipped English. "Any false moves and I'll put one slug in each kidney, and watch you bleed out."

As Khalid stepped out of the van, he looked back. The driver had already started the engine. His companion, still aiming the gun through the open door, pushed Khalid's heavy backpack out and onto the ground. The van pulled away as Khalid rubbed the soreness in his wrists and looked at the enormity of the cargo ship in front of him.

An hour later, Khalid was aboard and the vessel departed en route to the shipping port of Brunswick, Georgia, on the southeastern coast of the United States. Khalid was on his way into the mouth of the beast. He was, however, unaware that his backpack was not the only one containing enriched uranium and heading in the same direction.

64

SLIPPED THROUGH THE CRACKS

Malcolm McKinnon Airport, St. Simons Island, Georgia. May 1, 9:07 a.m. EST.

The FBI's Gulfstream 5 touched down with a light tire screech on runway 22, a 910-foot strip of tarmac on the southern tip of Saint Simons Island.

"Who's that coming to pick us up?" Jana said, looking out one of the Gulfstream's telltale oval-shaped windows.

"Treasury," Kyle said. "Homeland Security has one of their Federal Law Enforcement Training Centers here. They've sent out a few agents to assist."

"Don't you federal agent people train at the same place?" Cade said.

"No, nimbleweed," Kyle said. "The bureau and others like the DEA train at Quantico. Secret Service, ATF, and Customs train at Federal Law Enforcement Training Centers. They call it FLET-C, for short. There's other locations in New Mexico and South Carolina."

"But you're all Homeland Security now."

"Old habits die hard, I guess," Kyle said. "But don't worry, killer. I grew up not far from here. There are great restaurants. You'll be fine."

Cade looked at him. "Is that what you think I'm worried about? The food?"

"No. Just thought you'd be wanting to find another place with fried scallops. But sorry, not down here. This is more of a shrimp-and-oyster place. In fact, there's a place up the road near here in Darien, Georgia, called B & J's. Best fried shrimp you'll ever put in your mouth. Even got written up by the Boston Globe."

Jana playfully smacked Kyle. "He doesn't have to find the best restaurant around to impress me." Coconut stood and licked her hand. "It's okay, boy. I'm fine. And don't worry about Kyle. He's not normal."

Coconut plopped his head onto Kyle's lap. "Good boy. See? He likes me. I told you."

"And besides, Kyle," Jana said, "you're the one we're worried about. So far from home and without your girlfriend."

"Kelly Everson is sweet on me, that's all."

"I have no idea what that woman sees in you," Jana said as she laughed. "And she's so smart and cute. I just don't get it."

"Give him hell, Jana," Cade said.

"Okay, Romeo. And what are you getting all 'up' about? You're the one all ooey-gooey in love and everything."

"Oh, like you're not! Come on, Kyle. Admit it. Kelly's got you wrapped around her little finger. For the first time in your life, you've fallen for somebody."

"All right, boys. Enough of the history lesson. It's go-time."

"Yes, ma'am," they both said in unison.

As the plane slowed to a halt on the tarmac, the FLET-C vehicle came to a stop alongside.

"Come on, Coconut. Let's go catch bad guys," Jana said.

A few minutes later they were in a vehicle hurtling across the causeway bridge that spanned the intercoastal waterway.

"What do we know about the radioactivity detector so far?" Jana said, trying to speak above the sound of the siren and gunning engine.

The Secret Service agent in the front passenger seat spun around. "We've got it covered. Jesus, as if we need some hotshot to fly down here to tell us what to do. A team is on-site at the port of Brunswick, at the site of the radiation-detection surveillance equipment. We'll be there in a few minutes. Just keep your pants on."

Jana pressed. "What's the status of the equipment? Do we know why it's offline? Does it look compromised in any way?"

"Well," the man said from behind Ray-Bans with lenses so dark she couldn't see his eyes, "there's a problem with the unit."

"What's the problem?"

"It's not there."

"What do you mean, it's not there? Where is it?"

"That's just it, Baker. It's not there. It's gone. It's just an empty metal casing."

"Presumed stolen?" Jana said.

"No, idiot," the agent replied. "We build these things with legs and it just went down to the beach for a quick dip in the surf."

"Hey," Cade said, "she's just asking you a question."

Jana gripped Cade's forearm. "I can take care of myself."

"Well this guy's got no right to be an asshole."

The agent spun around one more time. "I get a year-long reassignment from priority protective duty to come down and become an instructor at the training center, which is a bullshit assignment to begin with, then I get pulled off a training exercise to come out here and babysit you people. I don't have time for this."

"A training exercise?" Cade said. "A training exercise? Do you have any idea why we're here? Do you know who Agent Baker is?"

"I don't care why you're here," the man barked. "All I know is I get pulled off the course to be your taxi driver. And of course I know who she is. She saved the day at the bluegrass festival in Kentucky, right? You think I give a shit? You think she's the only one that's thrown herself in front of a bullet in the line of duty? My father was Tim McCarthy. Do you recognize that name? He threw himself in front of a stream of bullets that had taken a liking to Ronald Reagan. Took one in the gut. Got awarded for valor, all that shit, so I don't want to hear it. Now let's just get this over with. We're about two minutes out. The port is just off to our south. It's on the other side of that bridge in the distance."

Kyle shook his head. "How big of a port is it?"

"Second largest on the eastern seaboard," the agent said.

"Good God," Jana said as she stared into a sea of brand-new

NATHAN GOODMAN ▫ 281

cars parked bumper to bumper in the massive parking area below.

"Yeah, we get lots of cars shipped in from overseas. They're driven off the ships and they park them until they are loaded onto eighteen-wheeler car-hauler trucks and shipped all over the country."

Jana leaned closer to Cade and Kyle. "Would make for a pretty good way to escape the area, wouldn't it?"

"What do you mean?" Kyle said.

"Think like a terrorist. You stow away on one of these container ships that's loaded down with new cars being shipped from overseas. You have somebody on-site here disable the nuclear-detection sensor, right? Then, after some cars are loaded onto a car-hauler truck, you sneak into one of the cars. It would be a quick way to make an escape into the interior of the country."

"Dammit," Cade said, "you're full of good news. That's a lot of cars. But let's not get ahead of ourselves, okay? There's no reason to go all paranoid until we find out if any trace radioactive material can be found nearby. Other than the fact that we seem to have a radioactivity sensor that's gone to the beach for a while, this whole thing is a goose chase and we all know it."

The Secret Service agent pressed against his earpiece and listened.

"Time to get paranoid," he said. "Our guys scanning the only container ship that arrived in the last twenty-four hours just had a Geiger counter go apeshit. They say it's picking up traces of uranium."

"Dammit, I hate it when she's right," Cade said.

The Ford Excursion barreled down the highway at 95 miles per hour, sirens blaring. As it wound its way into the entrance to the Georgia Ports Authority and came to a stop, Jana said, "Come on, Cade. Time to earn your pay."

"Radioactive material coming into the United States?" the agent said. "Doesn't sound good. Look, I'm sorry about being an asshole earlier. Whatever you're doing, I'm sure it's important. I shouldn't have snapped at you. I just get sick of having a top-secret security clearance, and all I do all day is train greenies."

Jana put her hand on his shoulder. "Forget it. And listen, don't think that just because you're training people, you aren't doing something important. What you're doing is just as important as what your dad did for the country back in Reagan's day."

The Secret Service agent added, "Thanks. It's not easy to live in the shadow of someone else. Good luck."

65

A DEVICE'S ORIGIN

"Mike Slayden, WBS News, reporting live from the Pentagon with a special report. Pentagon officials have just revealed that a major explosion has occurred in the heart of North Korea's capital city of Pyongyang. It was only yesterday that Russian troops, currently at war with North Korea, took control of Pyongyang and declared victory. The pentagon will not confirm or deny multiple reports coming in from the region. Those reports indicate the sighting of a massive mushroom cloud above the city. If confirmed, that would mean a nuclear device has been detonated. It's not clear at this time what could have triggered such a blast. North Korea has long had nuclear devices in its arsenal, but the idea that they would detonate one of them on their own soil seems unlikely. The fact that Russia just took control of the city, thereby effectively taking control of the entire North Korean government, makes this an even more confusing situation. For comment, we turn now to Doctor Harris Stovall, professor of nuclear sciences at the California Institute of Technology. Dr. Stovall, if this was a nuclear blast, what effects can we expect to see?"

"Well Mike, we'll first be interested in the size of the blast zone. That will give us estimates of the approximate loss of life we can expect. From there we'll be able to predict the amount of radioactive fallout. It will also give us an indication of the size and type of device used."

"And what can we learn by knowing the size and type of device?"

"Most large nuclear weapons are manufactured by governments, Mike. If this one is small, it might instead indicate a homemade device. But if it was anything upwards of ten kilotons, then the likelihood is that it was manufactured by a government. From there we'll want to collect radiation samples from the area. We'll be able to tell the gamma-ray variant used, and from that we'll know exactly who produced this device. With tens of thousands of Russian troops massed inside Pyongyang, I can't imagine the device to be of Russian origin. Perhaps we'll instead find it was, in fact, a device produced by North Korea itself."

"Dr. Stovall, thank you for your comments. We'll have more on this breaking story . . ."

66

THE PORT

Port of Brunswick, Colonel's Island Terminal, Oglethorpe Bay.
About seventy-eight miles south of Savannah, Georgia.

The second largest "roll on, roll off" port in the country, the port of Brunswick, Georgia sprawled before their eyes. A parking lot with thousands of newly imported cars, each covered in white, stick-down plastic, engulfed a mass of acreage. As the SUV screeched to a stop at a control facility near the dock, two men ran toward the vehicle, one holding FBI credentials.

"Agent Baker?"

"Yes."

"Special Agent Lyons, bureau, Savannah field office."

"Hey," Kyle said to Cade, "how come everyone down here assumes she's in charge? What am I, chopped liver?"

"Well, did you save the free world from a nuclear holocaust?"

"Oh, shut up."

Agent Lyons said, "What's with the dog? This way." The group ran toward the dock where an enormous container ship stood anchored. Coconut was not more than two feet from Jana at any time. "You're going to want to see what we've found on board this cargo ship."

"What is that lovely odor?" Cade said to Kyle as they ran.

"Pure Golden Isles seagull crap. Nothing else like it."

"Would you two knock it off? What have you got, Agent

Lyons?" Jana said as they ran toward the monstrous vessel docked at the port.

"We don't normally have equipment like this just laying around the field office. But Secret Service uses Geiger counters and other sensors in their training out at FLET-C. And, they've got a state-of-the-art lab over there."

"We were already told there was a discovery of radioactive material," she said, as the group headed up a wide gangway to board the ship.

"Right," Lyons said, "and a minute ago, they were able to identify trace elements of the material which help us know where the nuclear material was manufactured. From what the lab says, these elements cannot be completely removed during the processing of the uranium. They can detect the fissile material before a device explodes, or after. We'll be able to tell the processing methods used, and the region of the world where the uranium was originally mined."

"What were the results?" Cade said.

"It's uranium 235. Highly enriched," Lyons replied. "The lab say they can trace the source back to Siberia, east of a place called Lake Baikal. That means we're talking about the Russians. But it's weird."

"What is?" Cade said.

"The lab has every known source and type of nuclear material in the world in their database. They're saying this particular nuclear material shows trace elements that were in common use in the 1980s and 90s, but not since."

As they ran, Cade looked at Kyle.

"The missile stolen from the *Simbursk* would have been manufactured around that time. Sounds like a match."

"It's definitely our guy," Kyle said.

They ran onto the ship and followed Agent Lyons into the bowels of its cavernous interior. The hallway was moderately lit but one fluorescent bulb flickered at the end.

"How much radioactive material have they discovered?" Jana said. "Is it dangerous?"

"The pathways through the ship only show trace amounts. Not much more dangerous than getting a couple of x-rays. But the berthing room where this device must have been stored is covered. We've got it triple-walled with plastic sheeting until the hazmat crew arrives from Quantico. Our detection equipment is sensitive, from what they tell me. In this particular berthing cabin, it's blowing the needle off the Geiger counter. Okay, here we are. It looks like the material spent the duration of its voyage right in there, underneath that bunk. This is normally a crew cabin. Luxurious, huh?"

"Just lovely," Jana said. "I particularly like the gray walls and distinct lack of a window."

"Porthole," Kyle said.

"Whatever. Agent Lyons, how was this discovered? I mean, this ship is enormous. Yet in a matter of hours you guys found the berth where the device was stored?"

"It took longer than you think. We spent several hours in the beginning just looking for anything at all. To be honest, none of us thought we'd detect anything. But then, we had a hit at the service entrance where all the food supplies are loaded onto the ship for the crew. After that, we knew we would find a trail. And, there's a limited amount of crew berths. The ship is huge, but there's only a crew manifest of thirty-six. And like I said, when we swept this cabin, the Geiger counter went apeshit."

"Have you interviewed the crew? Any suspects we should be aware of?" Jana said.

"The entire crew of this vessel is Korean. So not your typical Middle Eastern terrorists. We've been working mostly through a translator to question them."

"How did you know we were looking for someone of Middle Eastern descent?" Kyle said.

Agent Lyons scowled. "I may not have temporary duty at NSA like you do, working alongside the director of the FBI, but I didn't just fall off the turnip truck. This ship's last port was Oman."

Jana leaned toward Agent Lyons. "No one really likes him."

"I heard that," Kyle said. "But, of the crew, who else bunked in this cabin? Obviously if the material was stored under that bunk, the other bunkmates would be able to describe the person who slept here for two weeks on the trip from Oman."

"Again, no turnips here. We've got the other crew members in containment. They've been exposed to a lot of radiation. They all three describe a man of Middle Eastern descent with a strong accent. We're trying to get a police sketch done of him now. But we had a hard time finding a sketch artist. There are none in the region. Not at our field office, not at FLET-C, the local sheriff's department, local cops, nothing. But follow me. The artist we *did* locate is topside, on the bridge, trying to come up with a rendering of your suspect now."

"I thought you said you couldn't find a police sketch artist."

"Yeah, we had to improvise."

As the group wove their way through a myriad of passageways to the port side of the ship. They went up three levels until they were finally topside. Coconut trailed behind, trying to nudge his way past the others to get closer to Jana. When they walked onto the bridge of the ship, Jana paused in the porthole. Inside the bridge, seated behind an artist's easel, was a teenage girl. She was listening to an interpreter who was translating for a Korean-speaking crew member. As the crew member described facial features of the suspect to the girl, she made wide, confident strokes with her charcoal pencil across an oversized artist's sketch pad.

"Well," Jana said. "You *did* have to improvise. How old is she?"

"Fourteen," Agent Lyons said as the girl looked up at him. "How's it coming along, Pete?"

"Great. Be done in just a minute," the girl said as she swept a long waft of straight brown hair from her eyes.

Jana grinned at Lyons.

"Where did you find her? And wait a minute. Pete? You found a teenage girl named Pete to draw a police sketch?"

"Like I said, it was short notice, I improvised. When her mom finds out I pulled her out of fourth-period algebra, she's going to be pissed. And that's nothing compared to how pissed my other daughter, Jenna, is going to be when she finds out Pete got to be involved on a case with me. Agent Baker, meet my oldest daughter, Meg. But don't look at her sketch yet. She gets a little bent out of shape if you look at her artwork before it's done."

"Your daughter? But you just called her Pete."

"Yeah," the girl said, "I liked Peter Rabbit when I was a kid, so

Pops always called me Pete."

"Very nice to meet you, Pete, or Meg. Have you ever done this before?"

"No, but I've done a ton of portraits. It's just that I've always had the person sitting in front of me to look at while I draw. But I think this is coming along fine. Hold on, almost done."

"Hey, Pete," Lyons said, "any chance this can be our little secret?"

"Well," the girl replied, "that depends on whether or not you're taking me to Bruster's for a dirt sundae afterward. Hot fudge and extra gummy worms."

Lyons looked at Jana. "She drives a hard bargain."

The girl turned the sketch pad toward the crew member for him to take a look. The man stood and in a mix of broken English and Korean, he said, "I geuleul Ahmed. He say he name Ahmed."

"Wow," Jana said. "He seems to think you've created a good likeness. Can we have a look?"

"Sure," Meg said. But no sooner had she begun to spin the pad toward them did Cade reach forward and grab it. The teenager scowled at him.

"Jana, is this a good idea?" Cade glanced down at the drawing. "Holy shit. It's him. It's definitely the younger brother, Khalid Kunde. Jana, the last time you saw a picture of him, the results weren't so pretty. Maybe you should sit this one out."

She crossed her arms and was about to refute Cade's assertion, but stopped short.

"You're right. But look, I've got to be able to look at him. I mean, if I can't even look at a picture of him, what's going to happen when I see him in person?"

Coconut crushed his head against her side and whimpered.

"Shhh, it's okay, boy. You'll help, right?" His whimpering escalated as he sensed the tension beginning to grip Jana's lungs. "Turn the sketch around, Cade."

Cade looked at Kyle, who nodded. "She's right. She has to deal with it."

Cade rotated the canvas and Jana stared eye to eye with an

incredible likeness of Khalid Kunde, the younger brother of Shakey Kunde. Her focus locked onto the deep, black eyes, and the color in her face began a slow retreat. Jana's breathing escalated, but Coconut nudged his nose into her hand. The softness of his muzzle was disarming, and helped Jana fight the vapor lock building in her mind. Coconut provided the crucial bridge she needed to distract and relax her, and after a moment Jana turned away. It was a minor victory, but an important one.

Meg said, "I don't understand. You don't like it? It looks like him, right?"

Jana turned and looked at the drawing once more. Her voice quieted. "It looks just like him. You did a great job, Pete. But, the left side of his face? He has a scar there?"

Meg's confidence went unabated. "I drew it exactly as it was described to me. I can't imagine it's wrong. He's been on this boat for a couple of weeks, right? I'd bet that his bunkmate here would know about his having a scar."

"Okay." Jana's voice was shaky.

"Hey, you okay?" Cade said.

"Yeah. Yeah, I'm fine. I just . . ."

"What is it?" Kyle said.

"Well, I don't recall Kunde's younger brother having a facial scar. Remember the close-up we had of him driving the truck out of that port in Pakistan? That view was of the left side of his face. I don't recall a scar."

"But it's definitely him, right?" Cade said. "I mean, scar or no scar, this is Khalid Kunde, right?"

Jana shivered. "Oh hell yes it's him. Meg's drawing is the spitting image. Let's get an APB out. Use the drawing as the photo for the APB. He's here. I can't believe he's really here."

Kyle placed a call to the Chatham County Sheriff's office to enter the all-points bulletin and get it distributed to every law enforcement agency in the Southeastern United States.

Jana pulled Kyle, Cade, and Agent Lyons closer. "And Kyle," she continued, "tell them armed and dangerous, but we can't mention his cargo. It might cause an all-out panic."

"I didn't think about that," Cade said. "But you're right. Not to mention the fact that we'd be tipping our hand that we know he's in the country with a nuclear device. If word of that slipped out, he'd know we were on to him and he'd just find a nice spot to detonate."

Jana said, "Kyle, tell them the subject has just been escalated to number one on the FBI's most-wanted terror watch list. That should communicate the sense of urgency without tipping our hand too far."

"Got it," he said.

"Agent Lyons," Jana said, "was the cargo of this ship mainly new cars?"

"Yes, all of the cargo was cars. They've been offloading them all morning. The process usually takes a couple of days. Why?"

"When we came in, we saw the parking lot. There must be five thousand new cars out there. We're concerned the suspect might have slipped inside one of them after it was loaded onto an eighteen-wheeler transport truck. We'll need to add that to the APB. Every car-hauler truck within a two-state radius needs to be stopped by the state patrol and searched. We also need to find out how many trucks have departed this port since the ship docked, and where each tractor-trailer is headed."

Cade shook his head. "The possibilities are endless."

67

INTO THE INTERIOR

About two miles east of Metter, Georgia. On board an eighteen-wheel car-carrier tractor-trailer, heading west on Georgia Interstate 16.

He knew better than to remain hidden inside the brand-new Kia Sorento on the bed of the auto-transport truck for too long. The risks he had already undergone on board the container ship as it crawled across the Atlantic were enough. Now, barreling northwest on Georgia Interstate 16, he peered out to look at his surroundings. Pine trees lined both sides of the rural freeway and seemed to stretch for miles. The question was how to exit the moving tractor-trailer without being seen and without getting killed or injured. He glanced at his backpack as it lay upon the SUV's floorboard.

A highway sign flew past. In a blur, he read the words:

Exit 104
Metter - Reidsville
23 121
Exit two miles

Two miles. Two miles, he thought. *How can I get the truck driver to pull off at that exit?* But before he had a chance to reason through the different possibilities, the sound of a police siren screamed from behind. His heart leapt against his sternum until it felt like a balloon that might pop. He jammed his hand into the side pocket of the old military-style rucksack and withdrew his Glock. *Not now. Not now. I can't get this far and get caught.* With limited options at his disposal, his mind raced.

The siren continued its droning wail, and the tractor-trailer began to slow and pull to the median. The rutting sounds of the tires against the pavement's rumble strips thudded through the interior of the cramped Kia. The truck came to a stop and he looked out the back windshield, but it was no use. His view behind the truck was obscured by another Kia chained to the flatbed. *What if I'm caught?* He could not be captured, at any cost. Even if it meant an all-out firefight with police. That was better than giving up. To give up was to be swallowed by the beast, and he had no intention of being swallowed.

His hand tore into the main compartment of the rucksack and he pulled back the sack's reinforced Denier Cordura material to reveal a bulletproof vest. As he donned the vest, his chest heaved. *Allah, I am coming.* His breathing became erratic, yet his hearing became more sensitive, almost to an unnatural level. He felt as though he could hear the footsteps of the state patrol officer walking up the right side of the truck toward the cab. When the footsteps neared his hiding position, they stopped. Khalid froze—one hand on the Glock, the other on the Kevlar vest that he was still struggling to secure into place.

They cannot find me. They cannot discover my mission.

He pointed the pistol at the window that sat just inches from his face, and applied tension to the trigger.

He stole a furtive glance to see only the top of a stiffened drill-instructor-style hat belonging to a Georgia State Patrol officer move past. He ducked before being seen. Sweat from his right hand needled itself in between his skin and the knurled surface of the Glock. His grip tightened. What was happening now was inevitable, and, in fact, necessary. But this was neither the time nor the place of his choosing. To have a firefight out here on a rural freeway was the farthest thing from ideal. The overall mission of Waseem Jarrah's jihad required more time. If he were drawn into a gunfight, he'd have little chance of success.

He had dreamt of one thing over the past many years—to

fulfill his final destiny. He had pictured it in his mind's eye thousands of times. It had even crept its way into his dreams, which he could picture now. The surroundings, the sounds, the smells—it was all so vivid and he rededicated himself to do anything in his power to bring his objective to fruition. His older brother, Shakey, had reached his final destination, the bluegrass festival in Kentucky, a year prior before he had been struck down by the beast. It had been a noble cause; to strike at the heart of the beast in a place so unexpected, so unprotected. To vaporize sixteen thousand Americans. Just the thought of it gave him hope, but anger welled against his current situation.

His brother Shakey's death was something he could never get out of his mind. He remembered that night at his Uncle's home in Pakistan vividly. He had known that the time of his brother's jihad was close, but no one would tell him what mission Allah had chosen for Shakey. And not even his close association to organizer, Waseem Jarrah had been enough to garner him the information. Jarrah would not divulge his secrets. But the one thing that Jarrah *had* told him was to watch the television news broadcasts on May 1. And there he sat in front of the television, watching all day and into the night. But no news broadcast of an attack on the United States came. Later he learned the beast had stopped his brother in the moments before detonation. May 1 was the anniversary of the assassination of Osama bin Laden, and it had gone unavenged. The beast had won.

His older brother had come so close. But in the end, the only thing his brother had accomplished was to bring the beast into a more heightened state of alert. The United States had descended into panic in the weeks and months following the failed jihad. Borders tightened, and CIA activity increased in countries like Pakistan, Jordan, Oman, Iran, Iraq, and Syria. It had been maddening. Congressional leaders in America called for more funding for the war on terror. And there had been no opposition in Congress, nor amongst the normally divided American people. The funding had come, and, with it, increased covert operations overseas.

Around his hometown, everywhere he turned, more and more of his brothers in jihad had begun disappearing. A few sensed the noose tightening around them and vanished of their own accord. But the rest were swallowed by the beast. Swallowed by the Central Intelligence Agency.

CIA operatives would come in the night. Sometimes their target would be just the individual jihadist. But other times, the man's entire family would disappear as well. Where had they been taken? No one knew for sure. But all suspected them to be languishing in an underground chamber somewhere, enduring questioning under the CIA's torturous methods. Once information was extracted, more jihadists disappeared, and the cycle continued.

He refocused his thoughts to the present situation. Now it was his turn. He would carry out a mission of utmost importance, one of vengeance and avarice. It would be his moment, his triumph; a triumph of the jihadist's way of life. One day his brothers in arms would walk on the roof of the White House, and the thought made him laugh.

He heard a muffled conversation taking place between the truck driver and the state patrol officer, but he could understand nothing. Footsteps then moved back toward his hiding place and he again pointed the weapon at the window.

This was how they got Shakey, he thought. *Not me. You will not take me. Not without tasting the demon, that is.*

The officer's footsteps came closer and became heavy and solid against the pavement.

68

HE COULD BE HEADED ANYWHERE

Port of Brunswick.

"All right," Cade said, "what's our move? If we assume he's boarded a car-carrier tractor-trailer, where do we go? How do we know which way he's headed?"

Kyle's hands went into the air. "All we have at the moment is that a handful of car haulers have been pulled over by local law enforcement in various parts of the state and searched. That's not much to go on."

"That's nothing to go on," Jana said. "There must be a hundred trucks that have left this port over the last twelve hours. We've got to think like a terrorist. If you were a terrorist with a nuclear device you're just itching to let loose, what direction would you head? You've got the whole United States at your fingertips. Where would you go?"

"Jana, wait a second," Kyle said. "We know he's had a lot of help to get this far, but I'm not so sure that if he did stow away in a car carrier, he'd even know where that particular truck was headed. I wouldn't doubt if he just boarded the first one at the front of the line and was satisfied just to get the hell out of here."

"No," Jana said. "He had help. Someone on the ground here removed that piece of radiation-detection equipment. Someone is helping him. He would know which vehicle to board. He's got a specific target in mind where he wants to detonate. He has to. Waseem Jarrah would have seen to that."

"Hold on," Cade said. "Even if he did have help on the ground here, we're out of time. We should leave these other agents to lock down the port and investigate everyone that had access to that radiation detector, but we don't have time to wait around for an answer. We have to roll the dice and pick a direction. We're way behind the eight ball on this one."

"Cade," she said, "I'm with Kyle. He could have gone in *any* direction. Just look at the map for God's sake. There's the I-95 corridor. It would take him north or south. He could be headed up this state highway here, Interstate 16, and headed west. There's a myriad of rural routes he could have taken. It's impossible to know."

"That's my point. We have no idea where he's headed, and we have no way to find out right now. We've got to just make an educated guess and take a chance. Like you said, think like a terrorist. If I were a terrorist with a nuclear device, I'd head north, up I-95 toward my most favorite place in all the world, the White House."

"Come on, Cade," Kyle said. "I see where you're coming from, but if he knows we've got radiation detectors at our major ports, he knows we've got them surrounding Washington, DC. The terrorists can't disable all of them. He'd never get in there without the device being detected."

"One square mile," Cade said.

Jana squinted her eyes at him. "What?"

"Just like the bomb in North Korea, the blast radius of the device is one square mile across. Remember, those detection devices were put there to protect against a homemade device from being walked up the White House lawn. But this is no homemade device. It's military-grade. He might be detected on the way into Washington, but the blast radius is so large that by the time he's detected, he'd already be in range to destroy much of the city. Even if he's not quite within range of the White House itself, he could take out a huge swath of our government."

Jana and Kyle stood with crossed arms, looking at one other.

"He's right," Kyle said. "This asshole could be headed to DC.

When he gets to the outskirts, he could climb on something as small as a Vespa motor scooter and drive right up Pennsylvania Avenue. Or hell, he could take any of the alphabet streets on his way to the White House and be well within the one-mile radius."

"Alphabet streets?" Cade said.

"Yeah," Jana replied, "you know, D Street, E Street, F, G, H. They're all over DC. Kyle's right. He could get plenty close enough even with a detection alarm blaring."

"So, are we going?" Cade said.

Jana didn't look up. "Agent Lyons? We're going to need your bureau car."

69

NOT TO BE TAKEN ALIVE

On board the car carrier.

The car carrier's engine restarted and the truck lurched forward. Khalid loosened his grip on the Glock and allowed himself to breathe. But as the truck rolled down the highway, its speed did not increase much. He glanced over the rim of the window to see the approaching highway exit. The next road sign repeated:

Exit 104
Metter - Reidsville
23 121
Exit 1/4 mile

He's exiting, he thought.

The state patrol officer apparently had instructed the truck driver to pull the vehicle off the exit.

The police somehow know I'm here! They must have figured out my plan to board a car hauler to escape the port area where I entered the country.Perhaps car haulers all over the Southeastern United States are being stopped and searched at this very moment. His mind scrambled as thoughts of what to do next bounced from one side of his mind to the other. Time was short and his heartbeat exploded. He had to come up with a plan and execute it right now. Beads of sweat pursed through his brow.

He watched as the car hauler exited the highway, turned right, and pulled into the first business. The sign read, *Clifton's,* a Shell gas station and convenience store. The man's thoughts became frantic.

Not here. I can't get caught now. It's too early. It will ruin my overall mission.

He rose from his crouched position in the back of the little Kia and struggled to see the state patrol car. When he spotted it, his stomach soured. It was behind the truck and its blue lights were rolling. As the truck slowed to a stop in front of the convenience store, the officer pulled the police cruiser behind and to the right of the truck.

If I'm going to be stopped here, I'm not going without a fight.

His hand again found its way to the trigger of the Glock. Then he saw something so foreign to him that it caused his mind to go blank. The officer walking toward the car hauler was a female. He couldn't believe it. He could feel his heart pounding in anger against the inside of his chest wall.

A woman. A woman! I can't believe these pigs put women in any position of authority. She's just like the woman who murdered my brother before his jihad. I will not be stopped by a woman.

But before he could rise up and fire his weapon, he heard sirens approaching in the distance. Two more police vehicles were speeding to the sight. The stakes had just escalated, and now he would be faced with three or more officers.

From the state patrol officer's point of view, there was no indication yet that there was a terrorist on board the car hauler. However, her orders were clear—all car transport trucks were to be pulled over and felony stop procedures executed. Those included calling for backup, blocking the truck from being able to flee, and approaching with extreme caution, weapon drawn. A thorough search was to be conducted on each car on the flatbed. Only at that point could the truck be cleared and released.

The truck driver climbed down from the cab and moved quickly to get out of the way of the police activity. His faded John Deere ball cap fell to the ground as he fled.

The female officer approached with her weapon pointed toward the cars. Her eyes scanned from one car window to the next. But it was nearly impossible to see past the reflections on the glass. The two other police cars turned into the gas station and screeched to a halt on the opposite side of the truck from the first officer.

The man now realized his chances of escape were zero. He closed his eyes and said in a whisper, "Allah, I am coming into your arms." He reared up, aimed, but just before he pulled the trigger, an idea flashed in front of him. There was time to try one last thing.

70

A FRANTIC ESCAPE

Parking lot of Clifton's convenience store. Metter, Georgia.

"Attention in the vehicle," the female State Patrol officer yelled, still having no idea anyone was actually stowed away inside one of the brand-new cars. "This is the Georgia State Patrol. Put your hands in the air and slowly exit the vehicle." The other two officers moved behind her then toward the cab of the eighteen-wheeler.

The man in the Kia fiddled inside his rucksack until his hand landed upon the objects he needed. He withdrew an Atlanta Braves baseball cap and pulled it low over his brow to help obscure his face. He then pulled out two other small packages and ripped into them. One contained a single flashbang grenade, a device designed to disorient any foe; the other, a packet of firecrackers strung together into one long, floppy cord. He slung the heavy rucksack over his shoulders and prepared for an all-out battle.

With the speed of a cat, he raised up and fired three rounds in quick succession through the glass of the passenger door, striking the female officer in the chest. He then flung the flashbang grenade out onto the pavement where it detonated with a cacophonous boom. The female officer went down and the other two officers fired wildly in the direction of the truck, crouching as they flailed to find cover.

The man withdrew a cigarette lighter and lit the fuse on the firecrackers, dropped them on the floor of the Kia, and lurched out the passenger door on the other side. The fireworks erupted and created a sound similar to automatic gunfire. One of the police officers fired round after round into the cars as he ran for cover in front of the truck's cab. The other officer ran straight into the fray, grabbed the female officer off the ground, and hauled her out of the line of fire. He dumped her into the arms of the convenience-store owner who had come outside. The female officer had been hit twice in the chest, and the male officer ripped at her bulletproof vest to see if the bullets had penetrated. It was then that he saw her police cruiser fly past the building with a man in the driver's seat.

The man gunned the engine of the cruiser and turned toward the main road, drove up the small embankment, and launched the police vehicle into the air in a frantic attempt to escape. The vehicle crashed to the pavement and sparks flew from the undercarriage as other drivers slammed on their brakes to avoid a head-on collision. His own tires screeched as he raced in the direction of the small town. It would be his only chance to disappear into the citizenry and evade capture.

Fireworks in the backseat of the Kia continued to erupt in a spitfire torrent while the other male state patrol officer reloaded his 9 mm handgun and fired more rounds into the cars on the flatbed.

The main street into the town was divided by a grass median with centuries-old oaks overhanging the road from both sides. The trees shaded the entire vista and he accelerated past 1920s homes with white columns and wide porches. The scene looked bizarrely idyllic for a person in such a state of panic. He turned left, then right, then left again, and skirted the edges of Metter's downtown square and sprawling courthouse building. As his patrol car careened through stop signs, other motorists screeched their tires in an effort to avoid collision. Only one thing was on his mind—escape.

The cruiser burst onto Route 46 and headed away from town, accelerating to 80 miles per hour before slowing and turning at a street marked Hiawatha Road. Here, the road curved back and forth providing him much needed cover. He saw a farmhouse in the distance and began to reduce his speed. A pickup truck sat parked at the barn adjacent to the little house. Across the field, a combine tractor stirred dust as it harvested what appeared to be soybeans.

The cruiser rolled onto the long dirt driveway of the little home and drove around the back of the barn—it was now out of sight.

Within minutes, he hot-wired the pickup truck and began to drive away, keeping his speed low to avoid attracting attention.

But out in the open soybean field, a farmer named Wes Clayton looked over his shoulder and saw his new Ford F150 four-door pull onto the paved road and disappear.

71

SWARM

Interstate 95, just south of Savannah, Georgia.

The team left Brunswick and raced up interstate 95, heading north; the direction of Washington, DC. Jana gunned the engine but even with the siren blaring on the black Ford Excursion, she had a difficult time maintaining a high rate of speed due to the number of cars on the freeway. As another car failed to yield, she again applied her brakes. "Move dammit!" she yelled.

"Jana," Cade said from the backseat, "calm down. We don't even know if we're headed in the right direction, much less what we're looking for."

"Any car-transport truck." Then she uttered, "Not on my watch."

"What?"

"I said *not on my watch*. This will not happen on my watch. I'm going to stop this son of a bitch just like I stopped his asshole brother."

The engine roared but the sound was swallowed by a combination of the siren and car horn Jana was applying.

Jana's mind began to drift and images of the muzzle of the Glock that Shakey Kunde had fired at her a year earlier flooded her mind. The gun barrel had erupted in white-hot bursts as he squeezed the trigger repeatedly. The pain of the impacting bullets popped across her torso, and Jana gripped the steering wheel harder.

Perhaps it was the tone of her voice, or perhaps it was the way her body went rigid, that caused Coconut to stand up from the third row of the SUV and begin groaning.

"What is it, boy?" Kyle said from the front passenger seat. But then, he looked at Jana. "Jana? Jana? You still with us? Hey." He shook her, but received no response. She was beginning to spiral down into that place where thoughts become overpowered by the magnetism of past events.

Coconut yelped over and over.

"Jana!" Kyle yelled as he grabbed the steering wheel in case she blacked out again.

But no sooner had he gripped the wheel did she slap his hands.

"I'm all right. Good God. Get your hands off the wheel."

"Are you sure? You locked up there for a second."

"I know. I just get so mad, and my mind goes back. You know, back there to when it happened?"

"Look, pull over up there. Let's switch drivers," Kyle said.

"Kyle, I'm fine. Don't you get it? I'm starting to recognize that I'm slipping away. I'm starting to see it as it happens. And Coconut is helping. He's catching me before I go too far too fast."

Cade started to interject something, but his phone vibrated. "Cade Williams," he said.

"Cade, this is Uncle Bill. We've got a hit! There's just been a firefight in a place called Metter, Georgia. Looks like it's about sixty miles from your location."

"A firefight? Are we sure it's related?"

"I've seen the video from the security cameras at the convenience store. It's him all right. Not to mention the fact that he was stowed away in a car-hauler tractor-trailer the state patrol had just pulled over. It's our guy."

"Jana," Cade blurted, "change of plan. We're not going north toward Washington. We're going west to Metter, Georgia. Uncle Bill?" he said into the phone. "Got any more details? The firefight, how bad was it?"

"One officer down. She's going to be okay. Looks like she took two in the chest but the vest saved her. They're searching the interior of the car he was stowed away in now. Looks like he used firecrackers to distract the officers into thinking it was automatic-weapons fire. I've got an FBI team from Savannah and one agent from Statesboro en route. They'll handle the on-scene investigation. You guys stay on the trail. We've got to stop him."

"He made a clean getaway? Any hints where he headed?"

"He stole a state patrol cruiser and blasted his way out of there. He headed into the town. We had him on a bank surveillance camera as he drove by, but that's where we lost him. There's probably a hundred state patrol officers converging from all directions. Everyone is looking for that stolen cruiser. And, Cade, when I say that we've got to stop him, that means at all costs. Am I clear?"

Cade gulped. "Yes, sir. I'll tell the agents here."

"One more thing. Bureau has a team of hazmat specialists on board a Gulfstream 5 headed to the port at Brunswick right now. They'll be there before you know it. But even though we're still analyzing the radioactive material from the boat and the dock, this is real. The analysis thus far points to the same type of radioactive material that would be found in the stolen Russian warheads. This isn't just a broken arrow, it's a broken arrow inside our borders."

"Sir, anything you can do to help us find him?"

"We're picking up nothing from the Aussie satellite. We've retasked the thing to scan the new area. But it won't be in range for another two hours. Now that we know where to send it, we might have a chance at picking up the radiation trail."

"Well we're going to need to catch a break, sir. I mean, he could be anywhere. And I know the police will swarm the area and search everywhere, but I doubt he's still in that town."

"I agree," Bill said. "He's got an objective and he's not just going to hide out until he gets caught. He's going to move until he gets to where he's going."

"Sir, where *is* he going? I mean, last time, at least there was an indication of the intended target. This time, we've got nothing. They're way ahead of us."

"I know, Cade. Knuckles and I have been scouring the Southeastern United States looking for potential targets. And we've lost the element of surprise. Khalid Kunde obviously knows we're onto him now. The only thing we are sure of is that he's headed on a westerly path. It might be just a ploy, but it seems like he's going to stick to the back roads in order to get to his target. I'm scared he'll make it all the way to the closest major city, Atlanta, then detonate in the downtown area."

"What's the population of Atlanta?"

"About six million. A detonation in the downtown area would take out at least a million. Not to mention the radioactive drift. Cade, I know you're not field personnel, but I sent you into the field for a reason. I need your mind cranking. You've seen how these people work. We can't allow this to happen."

"I know you did, sir. I'm going to do whatever it takes. That much I can promise you."

The call ended. Cade sat in the backseat and stared out the window. He began to understand that the three of them were the most likely people of anyone to find Khalid Kunde. Uncle Bill was right, they had to do anything in order to stop him.

With uncharacteristic confidence, he looked up. "Kyle, I'm going to need a weapon."

72

A HAZMAT DISCOVERY

Port of Brunswick.

FBI Special Agents Larry Fry and Dan Keller arrived at the port in Brunswick and began an immediate sweep of the container ship. Both were hazardous-material trained and a year prior had discovered integral clues that helped lead to the discovery of Waseem Jarrah's first plot to detonate a nuclear device on US soil. Both ambled through the passageways of the giant ship dressed in DuPont Tyvek level-A hazmat suits. Researching the entire ship for trace radioactive material had proved to be daunting. The search had taken several hours and both men were exhausted. After completing a sweep of the interior of the vessel, they were now walking the pier, searching for any other signs of radiation.

Agent Keller broke the monotony and spoke through his respirator.

"Larry? Remind me why we're sweeping this entire pier for radiation? I mean, we already found the smoking gun. That container ship is hot. We didn't just nail it down to which cabin the device was stored in, we isolated the type of radiation all the way to its gamma-ray variant. And hell, man, it's hot in this suit. The humidity must be one hundred percent down here. Did I mention that I hate these Michelin Man suits?"

"Keller, every time you and I put these things on, you remind me."

"So why search the pier? We've got to be two hundred yards down from the container ship right now."

"We're just being thorough, numbnuts. I don't see why we'd find anything way over here either, but I'm not going to go home wondering. Besides, lots of container ships are in and out of this port each week. You never know."

"You're just mad because your Final Four bracket sucks," Keller said.

"It doesn't suck. I'm telling you, it's golden. If you don't put Georgetown in the top of the bracket, you're giving up the ultimate chance to brownnose the director."

"You even think Director Latent looks at the Final Four board? And even if he did, he isn't going to promote you to GS-16 just because you chose his alma mater to win it all."

"He might," Fry said. "He'll promote me before he promotes your sorry ass."

"Hey, wait a second. Holy shit. Take a look at this."

Both men squinted at the small monitor on the handheld RAE Systems Neutron II radiation detector in Keller's hand. The device's cesium and lithium iodide scintillators were hundreds of times more sensitive than the Geiger counters used earlier by the first agents on the scene. The device was registering a trace amount of uranium.

"But, that's impossible," Fry said. "That's weapons-grade uranium. Why the hell would there be any of it out here? Look at the levels. It's barely registering. It's nothing compared to the levels we were picking up on board the ship. That ship is covered in radiation."

The two men looked at each other. "Larry, I don't like this."

"Me neither. You and I both know this can't be a fluke. I realize this is just a trace amount, but there's no way this material got here by accident. And it didn't just drift over here on a breeze. Another ship would have been docked here."

"But wait a minute," Keller said. "Another ship? Now you're telling me we've got two ships, both with traces of nuclear material? Weapons grade? You can't be serious. What are the odds?"

"We're not talking about the Final Four here. It's the only

explanation."

Then Agent Fry spun around, looking back at the original container ship.

"How could I have been so stupid? Dammit!" He yanked his walkie-talkie from his belt. "Six, six, this is Fry! Patch me through to the director."

The reply crackled back. "Oh, come on, Fry. What do you have?"

"Give me the director, and give him to me right now!"

73

OF TRAILS AND DECEPTION

Port of Brunswick.

In the situation room at the Box, an agent walked over to Director Latent. "It's Special Agent Fry. They're on-site at the port in Brunswick and calling for you, sir."

"This is Latent," he said into the radio.

"Sir," Fry screamed, "I'm on scene in Brunswick and we're doing a sweep of the area for any other traces of radioactive material. It's a setup!"

"What?" Latent rocketed out of his chair.

"The container ship. It's a setup! I'm telling you, it's a staged crime scene."

"What do you mean it's a staged crime scene?"

"Sir, I can't believe I didn't see it earlier. The container ship we just searched, the radiation levels are *too* high. It didn't make any sense to me at first, but this uranium was exactly what we were looking for because it's the same type used in Russian R-39 ballistic missiles, so I dismissed it. But why would the levels be so high? The amount of radiation we found on the ship is off the charts."

"What are you saying?"

"Sir, we just found a trace amount of the same type of material *about two hundred yards down the dock*. The only way this material could have gotten here would have been if there was a second container ship docked here. But these amounts of radiation are much more consistent with what I'd expect to find if a terrorist transported a weapon." Fry was speed-talking. "I didn't realize it until we found the second site. When I saw the trace amounts we were detecting, it hit me. *This* is the proper level of radiation I'd expect to find, not the massive levels we're finding on the first ship. The first ship is staged. I'm telling you, it's a decoy. The terrorists want to throw us off the real trail!"

"A decoy?" the director yelled. "You mean we're tracking two terrorists, not one? And one of them is a decoy?"

"That's exactly what I'm telling you. The decoy terrorist is laying down a trail of radiation that any idiot with a Geiger counter could follow. That's why the first agents on the scene were able to pick it up with basic equipment. It's unlikely they'd have even detected the trace amounts we're seeing at the second site. We're being duped. We're on the wrong trail!"

74

THE TELLTALE SCAR

Interstate 16 westbound.

Kyle hung up a phone call and turned to Jana who was still driving the SUV. "Jana, a farmer on the outskirts of the town of Metter just reported his pickup truck being stolen."

"Is it our boy?"

"There was a police cruiser left where the pickup had been parked. So it's definitely our guy. The truck was last seen headed west on Hiawatha Road. Shit, Uncle Bill may be right, he may be headed for Atlanta."

Jana accelerated. "Well, let's stop him and kick his ass before he gets there."

Kyle turned up the volume on the FBI vehicle's police radio. A report was being relayed that a pickup truck matching the description of the one stolen was just seen driving on the main road in front of the same convenience store where the shootout had occurred. The driver was described as a man of Middle Eastern decent, wearing a baseball cap.

"Holy shit," Jana said.

Kyle replied, "He's trying to double-back and throw us off his trail. But by now, he's probably just gotten back onto Interstate 16. My bet is he's heading west, toward Atlanta."

Cade leaned forward. "We're only a couple of miles from the Metter, Georgia exit, right? He'd be just ahead of us, headed west; same direction as us."

"Get out of my way!" Jana screamed at a silver Honda Odyssey in front of her. Her pulse exploded.

"Jana," Kyle said, "kill the siren and lights. We don't want to tip our position." He unzipped his duffel and withdrew an MP5 submachine gun. Both he and Cade donned navy-blue flak jackets emblazoned with the letters F-B-I.

Cade said, "Jana, you need to get your Kevlar on," but everyone knew there was no time. The SUV wove in between cars, passing the off-ramp of the Metter exit.

About four minutes passed as Jana wove in and out of traffic. Coconut began a slow, steady whimper. Without looking behind himself, Cade reached back and petted the dog. "It's okay, boy. She's okay. She's just a little intense at the moment."

"Hey," Kyle said, looking through a set of Steiner binoculars, "I think I . . . yeah, that pickup up there meets the description of the stolen one. Get clear of this jackass driving the Acura so I can see the license plate. Oh shit, that's him all right." Kyle picked up the radio mic and relayed the sighting. "We're not waiting for backup. We're going to do a felony stop on him right now. We've got to catch him off guard so he doesn't have a chance to detonate. Pull up alongside and smash into him to force him off into the median. Cade, whatever you do, keep that handgun pointed in a safe direction. Don't shoot one of us when we bump. As soon as we stop him, it's your job to make sure the device is in the truck. You're looking for a backpack."

"Got it," Cade yelled.

Jana did not hesitate. She gunned the engine until she was alongside the pickup. Without so much as looking at the driver, she jerked her SUV to the right. The two vehicles collided with a metallic thud. The pickup bounced off, swerved, then lost control, and skidded into the wide grass embankment. Dirt and debris flew everywhere as the truck spun sideways, then rolled onto its roof.

Jana slammed on the brakes as she pulled onto the median. All three jumped out, weapons drawn, and ran toward the pickup. Coconut wasted no time and ran beside Jana.

The driver had been thrown clear of the vehicle and lay in a crumpled heap. "He's over there!" Cade yelled, pointing onto the grass.

The man's mouth gaped open as he gasped for air, having just had the wind knocked out of him. Kyle was on top of him in an instant and yanked the man onto his stomach. He jammed his knee into the top of the man's neck and handcuffed him. Jana hovered over the man, pointing her SIG Sauer at his skull. While Cade ran toward the truck, the other two paused a moment to catch their breath.

Jana gritted through clenched teeth. "Roll him over."

Kyle looked at her. "Are you sure?"

"Do it!" she screamed.

When his face came into full view, Jana saw the incredible likeness. Coconut jammed his caramel-colored muzzle against her leg. She took two deep breaths. Her eyes darted between the coal black of the man's eyes and the scar on his left cheek.

"Khalid Kunde. FBI agents. Where is it?" Jana said. "Where's the bomb?"

Cade yelled from the pickup truck. "It's here. The backpack is here. But inside of it . . . I don't know what it is."

"What do you mean?" Kyle said.

Cade ran toward them. "The backpack is there, and there's something inside it, but it's not a nuclear weapon."

"What the hell is it?" Jana said.

"It's a silver-looking metallic sphere. About the size of a grapefruit. Must be heavy as hell because the backpack weighs a ton. I don't understand."

It took a few moments, but the man's eyes registered something against Jana's. Even in the Middle East, FBI Special Agent Jana Baker had become known as the one who had stopped Shakey Kunde. He had memorized that face; a face that one day he had hoped he could extract vengeance against. He reared up to spit at her, but Kyle crunched a steely grip onto his throat.

The man gagged.

"Let go, Kyle," Cade said. "Khalid, what is that in the backpack? Where is the bomb?"

The man laughed, then his eyes became milky. "What time is it?" he said.

"We're asking the questions!" Jana screamed as she jammed

her boot into his side.

He coughed, then said, "Do with me as you will. It will not change the inevitable. You tell me the time, I'll tell you what you want to know."

"We don't have time for games!"

But Cade interrupted. "Jana, wait. Khalid, why do you want to know what time it is?"

Cade glared at his own watch. It read 2:13 p.m. His mind scrambled. *2:13 p.m. 2:13 p.m. What's the big deal with 2:13 p.m.?*

"It's two thirteen," he said. "Why?"

The man laughed again. "Two thirteen. Three minutes to go! You are too late. We will strike in three minutes, and one day my brothers in jihad will spit on the roof of your White House."

"You'll burn in hell!" screamed Jana, as she kicked the man in the gut once more.

"Jana! Stop it," Cade said. "We have to know what he's talking about."

The man's jaw slid back and forth as if he had been chewing gum and the gum had become dislodged. Cade thought the behavior odd, but continued.

"Khalid, we told you what time it is. Now what's that in the backpack? Is that not the real bomb?"

The man laughed. "You don't even know who I am. You are so far behind in the game. You don't even know about me! But I will tell you. The object in the backpack is a container of uranium. Threw you off the scent, didn't it?" he laughed.

"That's bullshit," Jana said.

"Is it? Even you must know that it takes more than uranium to construct a nuclear device. Where is the triggering mechanism? How do you think I would detonate it? That is not the real device. Our plans worked perfectly. And like I said, you don't even know who I am."

"You are Khalid Kunde," Jana said. "The younger brother of Shakey Kunde."

Jana's body began to shake and Coconut's whimpering escalated. The dog pushed his head again and again into Jana's side, but she was slipping away. She shook her head in a violent manner and stared down at the dog. That was all it took. Jana was pushing through. She was breaking her own curse, but the man laughed once more.

"Why are you laughing?" A vein on Jana's forehead pulsed. "Your brother didn't laugh, you little shit. He squealed like a pig when I killed him!"

The man reared up at her only to be pummeled down by Kyle.

"You know nothing!" the man roared. "My name is *not* Khalid Kunde. Surely by now you have ascertained that your CIA has been penetrated by Khalid Kunde. If you know that, then you know exactly what Khalid Kunde looks like. And does Khalid Kunde have a scar on the left side of his face? No! Take a look at my face. Not only is there a scar, but it is obviously a very old scar. Are you starting to get the picture now? I am not Khalid Kunde, my name is Khunays Kunde. And since your time is at an end, and you have no idea who I really am, I'll tell you. To Muslims, the name Khunays means *hidden*. Do you need me to spell it out for you, you arrogant pigs?"

"Hidden? Hidden?" Kyle said. "Who the hell cares what your name means." But Cade put his hand on Kyle's forearm.

"Hold on. *Hidden*. You mean you've been hidden this whole time?"

"Very good. Khalid Kunde and I are twins, identical twins. Our older brother, Shakey, was nearly successful at melting sixteen thousand of you filthy pigs. But today, his name is avenged! Today, my twin brother, Khalid, will rain hellfire."

"Twins? You and Khalid are twins? Then that means . . ." Cade ripped a 9 mm SIG Sauer from his belt and jammed it into the man's neck. "Three minutes? What happens in three minutes? What happens at 2:16 p.m.? Tell me!" But then Cade froze, entranced in a thought. "Kyle?" his voice shook. "What's today's date?"

"The first, why?"

"The first of May? May first? 2:16 p.m.?" His voice choked to a whisper. "Oh, God." Then Cade launched at the man's throat. "Where? Where? Where is Khalid going to detonate?"

The man's laughter infuriated the trio. Cade raised the pistol to strike the man with it and Khunays closed his eyes against the impending blow.

When the blow did not come, Khunays said, "Yes. May first. 2:16 p.m. Adjusted for your local time, it's the precise date and time of day that the beast murdered Osama bin Laden. My brother Khalid will strike at the mouth of the beast itself, the heart of the CIA. And my job of throwing you off his trail is at an end."

75

THE TAMING OF THE BEAST

Parking lot of Immanuel Presbyterian Church, Savile Lane, McLean, Virginia. 2:15 p.m. EST.

The backpack lay on the floor beside him like a giant serpent coiling in preparation to strike. Khalid had parked the van in the parking lot of the Immanuel Presbyterian Church, the grounds of which sat just half a mile from CIA headquarters. With a blast radius of one mile, the entire facility would be wiped from the face of the earth.

As far as Khalid could tell, Waseem Jarrah's plans had been executed flawlessly. He and his twin brother, Khunays, would meet Allah together today. Their jihad was at an end. The CIA, FBI, and NSA had taken the bait. The false trail created by Khunays had led them to believe that he was the bomber and that the intended detonation site was downtown Atlanta, not CIA headquarters in Virginia.

Khalid intended to rip a mile-wide crater in the land, and into the very fabric of the beast that sought to swallow his people whole.

Khalid knew how his older brother Shakey had died and he was determined that he would not suffer the same fate. He wore a Kevlar vest and held a Glock .40-caliber handgun at the ready. He would not be taken alive.

His instructions for detonating the device were simple. One turn of the primary arming switch to arm the device, then a full revolution on the secondary switch on the side of the R-39 warhead to set it into motion. The device would then lock itself into a thirty-second countdown from which there was no turning back.

He looked at his watch. It indicated the time was now 2:15 p.m. As the watch's second hand swung past the six, he did not hesitate. The device entered its 30-second countdown and Khalid was about to realize his jihad. He bowed as if in prayer, ready to greet Allah.

76

A DETAIL OVERLOOKED

The grassy median along Interstate 16.

Cade yelled into the phone. "Uncle Bill! It's a bright-boy alert! It's imminent. Today's date! We missed the date. Today is May first. At 2:16 p.m.! He's going to detonate at the exact date and time of the Osama bin Laden assassination. This is payback that they failed to carry out last time!"

"Where?" Bill stammered.

"He said it will occur at the mouth of the beast! Langley! It's Langley, Bill. Khalid Kunde is going to take out the CIA at exactly 2:16 p.m. We've only got a minute to stop him."

In the situation room at NSA, Bill wheeled around. Stephen Latent saw him from across the room and would later say he'd never seen Bill's face so pale and defeated.

All Uncle Bill could do was stare at the map of the United States on the nuclear-detonation monitor, which was on permanent display on video screen eight. His hand gripped the phone with force strong enough to almost crush it. A moment later, a large red blip illuminated on the screen over Virginia.

An alarm blared overhead and the monitoring system autozoomed the map and centered it on the site of the detected blast. The epicenter was just west of the city of McLean, Virginia, at the edge of the Potomac River. It wasn't Atlanta or Washington, DC that had been the intended target, it was CIA headquarters. The blast at CIA occurred at a distance of fifty-eight miles from the headquarters of the NSA, but it only took moments for the shockwave to ripple under Uncle Bill's feet. Several people looked up at the monitors, registered what was happening, and screamed.

"Uncle Bill? Uncle Bill?" Cade said from the roadside in south Georgia. Then he looked at Jana and Kyle. "He's not talking to me anymore."

But in the background, Cade could hear people inside the situation room at NSA react to what must have been the detected nuclear detonation. The epicenter, Langley, Virginia. Cade's brow furled as he looked at Khunays who lay handcuffed on the grass.

Khunays's jaw again began to slide back and forth.

Khunays spoke with a grin. "Do you think because hellfire has come to your putrid country that this is over?" He laughed a sinister laugh. "My new friends, it has just begun."

"Hey! Grab his mouth!" Cade yelled as he lunged at the man. "Don't let him . . ."

But it was too late. Khunays bit into a cyanide capsule concealed in his gumline and was gone.

Kyle pried open his jaw and swept the capsule clear only to find the inside of the mouth covered in white foam.

Cars on the rural highway continued to roar past as the trio of friends slumped into the grass next to the dead man. Coconut lay half his body onto Jana's lap. A look of unadulterated defeat painted itself across her face.

None of the highway travelers passing by knew that the first nuclear attack against the United States had just been executed with flawless perfection. None knew that several hundred thousand Americans had just lost their lives.

The three friends sat and stared at the grass as it waved in the breeze created by the passing cars. No one moved, no one spoke, but instead all tried to comprehend the enormity of their failure. They had been pawns in a perfectly played chess game— a game of deadly proportions—and they had lost.

77

NEWSFLASH

"Breaking news, this is Mike Slayden, WBS News. Reports are pouring in now from the greater Arlington, Virginia area. It appears that a nuclear bomb has detonated just north of the city. We're seeing helicopter footage from the devastated area now. An hour ago, the landscape before you was a thriving metropolis. Fears are mounting that few within the blast zone, which appears to measure about one mile in width, are left alive. Several hundred thousand people are feared dead. The blast zone appears to be centered on what was the headquarters of America's premier spy agency, the Central Intelligence Agency. The Emergency Broadcast System has been activated in the surrounding areas, and people are being told to evacuate as quickly as possible. If it is confirmed that this was, in fact, a nuclear blast, radioactive fallout will permeate the downwind landscape. Washington, DC, about six miles to the east, is being evacuated as we speak. The White House press office issued a communique which indicated that the president is now on board Marine One and is being moved to an undisclosed location . . ."

Section Three

The Aftermath

78

UNEXPLODED ORDINANCE

In the days and weeks that followed, Kyle MacKerron, Cade Williams, and Jana Baker returned home. To everyone's surprise, Jana seemed to handle the catastrophic failure better than anyone. Perhaps it was the assistance she received from Coconut as he jammed his muzzle against her side whenever he detected excess stress. Perhaps it was her utter resolve to never give up the fight against Waseem Jarrah. Or perhaps it was the knowledge that she had given everything she had to the pursuit of saving lives. But in any case, somewhere amid the chaos, Jana had made a conscious decision that she would not live a defeated life.

Jana and Cade's romantic involvement with one other escalated. In the face of so much death around them, it seemed pointless to allow shyness to impact their feelings for one another. Kyle too was swept up in his relationship with Kelly. In the weeks that followed, Kelly would help them all. For Kyle, it was the first time he'd ever been in love, and he barely knew what to do with himself.

The country slowly came to grips with the enormity of the disaster. The extraordinary loss of life created a level of pain whose full impact would not be understood for years to come. Nuclear fallout descended upon downwind areas east and north of ground zero. Most of those areas became uninhabitable, but the few people that remained monitored the compass direction of prevailing winds in a way they never had previously. If winds were predicted to blow into their area, all fled.

Thousands fell victim to radiation poisoning. No single hospital system could handle the load, and as such, hospitals as far away as Chicago became overwhelmed with the influx of radiation victims. Countries all over the world pledged billions of dollars to aid the US in its darkest hour. The attack was eventually seen for what it was—an attack on humanity itself. Whatever the cause, whatever the reasons, whatever the motivations, and whoever was to blame, the end result signaled to many that mankind might just destroy itself yet.

It would be years before anyone could ever again inhabit the devastated areas. And the CIA, an organization that could trace its roots back to the 1940s, was in utter ruins. Only the Special Activities Division, the tactical operational wing of the agency, survived. Most key personnel assigned to duty at CIA headquarters at Langley had perished in the bombing. The few people that were left reorganized and tried to piece together what remaining assets they had and to deploy them effectively. Congress called for a higher level of intelligence funding than at any time in history. Yet with so few functioning intelligence assets available, much of the money went unspent.

The global war on terror rose to a fever pitch. Countries that previously had seemed more interested in funding terrorists than fighting them took a new position. Their governments realized that to be aligned with terror was to be an enemy of the globe. Terrorist organizations in all corners of the world went into hiding for fear of annihilation.

But the terrorists themselves were not dissuaded. They counted their losses, licked their wounds, and continued their vigil, waiting for their next opportunity to strike.

When the news hit that the specific gamma-ray variant used in the nuclear devices that had detonated in both North Korea and Virginia were also traceable to 1990s-era, Russian-built warheads, the world reacted viscerally. Russia, in particular, bore much of the blame due to their failure to destroy all missiles aboard the *Simbirsk* in the first place. The horror was compounded as Russian citizens realized that thousands of their own soldiers, all either fathers, brothers, or sons, had been killed in Pyongyang, North Korea, with a weapon built by their homeland.

Of the original ten warheads separated from the single Russian-built R-39 ballistic missile, only two were detonated in terror attacks. Australian SAS special operations commandos recovered two others in daring nighttime raids carried out at great cost. Two others were believed destroyed when Russian air forces unleashed dozens of KAB-1500L "bunker buster" bombs into terrorist strongholds in the Hindu Kush Mountains of the Afghan central highlands.

There are three theories as to the whereabouts of the remaining four warheads. One says that they are hidden on board separate cargo ships that continue their global travels to this day. Another says the devices are buried somewhere in the sands of the Middle East, waiting to be unearthed at the right moment. And yet a third theory, perpetuated by a group of hard-core conspiracy theorists, believes that the devices are being held in storage, deep below ground. The location? Ground zero—at the site of the former headquarters of the CIA.

As for the involvement of the president of the United States . . .

79

OF PRESIDENTS AND CHOICES

A secure bunker, location unknown. Three weeks after the detonation.

"The director of the FBI to see you now, sir," the president's personal assistant said.

"Thank you. Send him in."

Stephen Latent walked into the temporary Oval Office, wearing his finest navy pinstripe. He held his head high into the air as one who believes strongly in what he is doing. He stopped in front of the desk.

"Latent. Have a seat. What's on your mind?"

"I'll not be sitting, sir."

"What's with the attitude? Sit down. I'm busy here," President Palmer said.

"Mr. President. I'll get right to the point. As director of the Federal Bureau of Investigation, under article III, Section 3 of the United States Constitution, I charge you with conspiracy and treason against the United States of America. You have the right to remain silent. Anything you say can and will be used against you—"

The president remained motionless, then exploded out of his chair.

"You'll not talk to me like that! I am the president of the United States!"

In uncharacteristic calmness, Latent replied, "And you are directly responsible for the detonation of two nuclear weapons, one on US soil."

"Bullshit. What the hell are you talking about? I never— "

But before the president could complete his sentence, Latent removed a sealed manila envelope from his jacket pocket and floated it into the air. It slid onto the desk and came to a halt at the president's fingertips.

"What's this?" Palmer said.

"Open it."

"I don't have time for this."

Latent's voice almost growled. "Open it."

When the president complied, he found a single sheet of paper inside. On the paper, just below the presidential seal it read,

Classified: 15.8. E.O.
Access level C12 eyes only.

His mouth dropped. It was the original written authorization he had given to National Security Advisor James Foreman to carry out the Fifteenth Protocol operation.

"That's your signature, isn't it?" Latent said, although he knew the answer.

The president simply stared at the paper, his mouth dangling.

"You knew!" Latent said. "You not only knew, you authorized it. A sitting president whose bullshit agenda cost the lives of millions of innocent people. You are under arrest."

"Latent," the man stammered, "you have to understand the responsibility of this desk. North Korea had launched a missile at us. They had to be stopped. It's my responsibility to keep the country safe."

"And it's my responsibility to keep this country safe from people like you."

"You can't possibly arrest me," fumbled the president. "You can't go to the media with this! The repercussions . . . would be catastrophic—catastrophic to the United States. World leaders, even our allies, would turn against us. It would be open season against the United States! What do you intend to do?"

Latent's pause was painful for the president to endure. "I intend to give you a choice."

"A choice? What choice?"

"It will be up to you."

"Up to me to do what exactly?"

"You can choose to walk out of this office right now and tell the media yourself. *In handcuffs*," Latent stabbed. "You'll tell every news organization in the world what you've done. You'll tell them you authorized a secret operation to steal a nuclear device from Pakistan, which you then planned to use to attack North Korea, and blame the Russians for it."

"I'll do no such thing. Latent, the scandal would be unprecedented. I'd be disgraced, thrown out of office."

Latent walked over to the man and towered over him until the president fell into his chair. He then said through gritted teeth, "And stand trial."

The president stammered but could not get any words to come out.

"Or," Latent said, as he reached inside his other jacket pocket and withdrew a much thicker, heavier manila envelope. He dropped it on the president's desk with a metallic thud.

"Or what? What's this?"

Latent turned and walked to the door.

"That, Mr. President, is your choice." Latent glanced at his watch. "You have exactly two minutes to decide."

"Wait!" the president yelled. But Latent closed the door behind him.

The president ripped into the heavy envelope and gazed wide-eyed at the contents. Inside lay a stainless-steel Walther PPK .380-caliber handgun.

With the feel of cold steel in his hand, he slumped into his chair and stared into oblivion.

~~~~~~

Get a free copy of Book 1 in this series, *The Fourteenth Protocol*, by visiting

NathanAGoodman.com/fourteen/

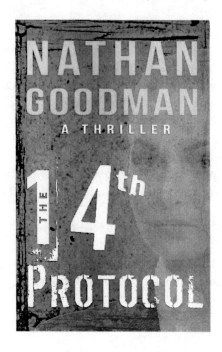

~~~~~~

Interested in more from the author? Sign up for notifications of upcoming works at

NathanAGoodman.com/email

Please provide a rating for this novel on the retailer's website.

Nathan A. Goodman is a husband and father of two daughters and lives in the United States. The first novel in this series, *The Fourteenth Protocol*, was an immediate bestselling international terrorist thriller` . It was written with one very specific goal—the author wanted to show his daughters a strong female character. He wanted them to see a woman in difficult circumstances who had the strength to prevail. And he wanted them to know that if they have the guts, they can succeed even in places that are perceived to be "a man's world."

CPSIA information can be obtained at www.ICGtesting.com
Printed in the USA
LVOW10s2304201016

509668LV00007B/149/P